It's Only Love

A Green Mountain Romance

Ella wanted to kiss him—badly—but more than that she wanted to know his thoughts. "What're you thinking right now?"

"About how much I want to kiss you. I'm asking myself if this is real, if I really get to kiss Ella Abbott any time I want to. I'm wondering how I got lucky enough to have someone like you care so much about someone like me."

She curled her hands around his wrists and felt his pulse hammering under her fingers. "What does that mean? Someone like you? What's wrong with you?"

"Everything," Gavin said softly. "Every freaking thing is wrong with me, but for the first time in a long-ass time, I want to make what's wrong about me right. For you."

"Marie Force has become one of my favorite go-to authors and [the Green Mountain] series is one of my very favorites."
—Fresh Fiction

"Marie truly just has a way of telling a story that draws you in, and never lets you go." —Guilty Pleasures Book Reviews

It's Only Love

Marie Force

BERKLEY BOOKS, NEW YORK

BERKLEY

An imprint of Penguin Random House LLC
375 Hudson Street, New York, New York 10014

IT'S ONLY LOVE

A Berkley Book / published by arrangement with the author

ISBN: 978-0-425-27550-4

PUBLISHING HISTORY
Berkley mass-market edition / November 2015

PRINTED IN THE UNITED STATES OF AMERICA

10 9 8 7 6 5 4 3 2 1

Penguin
Random
House

CHAPTER 1

◆◂◆◆▸◆

Grief is the price we pay for love.

—Queen Elizabeth II

Resigned to another Saturday night at home, Ella Abbott settled into her sofa with her two best friends—Ben and Jerry. She'd been spending a lot of nights with these guys lately, which she would regret the next time she stepped onto a scale. But who cared about scales or exercise or anything else for that matter when your heart was broken?

It was all she could do to get up, take a shower, dry her hair, eat something that tasted like nothing, go to work and barely function once she got there. She went through the motions day after day, one foot in front of the other with a stiff upper lip that quivered an awful lot when she was alone. No one needed to know that.

She dug her spoon into yet another new pint of Cherry Garcia, which was the only thing that made her feel better. So she overindulged. Whatever. She'd happily pay the piper as soon as she stopped feeling like utter crap.

In the last couple of weeks, she'd had no choice but to accept that nothing was ever going to come of her fierce love for Gavin Guthrie.

"And how's that going for you?" she asked the ice cream.

"Are we at the acceptance stage yet?" She took another bite and then one more. "Nope, still stuck firmly in denial."

If only he hadn't kissed her. If only she could take back that one perfect moment of utter bliss on the beach in Burlington during her sister Hannah's wedding last summer. Not knowing what it was like to kiss him would make this whole acceptance thing a hell of a lot easier.

And it wasn't just a kiss. That would be oversimplifying what'd happened between her and Gavin while everyone else was listening to Nolan serenade his bride. She'd dared to put her arms around Gavin, wanting only to offer comfort as his late brother's widow got remarried. But then he'd kissed her—and not the way she'd dreamed for all the years she'd been thinking about him.

No, this kiss had been rough and untamed and powerful, the single most incendiary kiss she'd ever received from anyone.

Thinking about it now, she rubbed her finger absently back and forth over her lips, which had tingled for hours afterward. And during those hours she'd had to act like everything was fine, like her entire world hadn't been redesigned in the course of five unforgettable minutes.

She'd relived it a thousand times since then. The way he'd swooped in like a man who'd been drowning until she came to rescue him. The way his tongue had swept into her mouth and his lips had pressed so tightly against hers they'd felt bruised later, not that she minded. Bruised lips had been a reminder, for days afterward, that it had really happened. It hadn't been a figment of her overactive imagination.

Gavin Guthrie had really kissed her. And then he'd walked away like it hadn't changed everything between them. He'd pulled away so abruptly he'd left her reeling. Worst of all, he'd actually *apologized* for kissing her. She shuddered, recalling what he'd said.

"Christ, Ella. I'm sorry. I don't know what I'm doing. I'm so fucked up today. I'm sorry. I shouldn't have done that."

But that wasn't all he'd said. No, he'd had to take her breath away with a sweet caress to her face and even sweeter words. *"You're beautiful, Ella. Inside and out. If I were going to let something like this happen with anyone, you'd be the first one I'd call. But I've got nothing to give you, and it wouldn't be fair. It just wouldn't be fair."*

Even though he'd walked away from her after that, his words and that kiss—that incredible, unforgettable kiss—had filled her with foolish, giddy hope, which had been snuffed during two less memorable encounters with him since then. Both times, he'd reminded her once again that he had nothing to give her and refused to suck her into the disaster his life had become.

The first time she saw him after "The Kiss," he'd told her he'd been spiraling since the wedding, locked in the kind of grief he'd experienced when his brother Caleb first died after stepping on a land mine in Iraq. As happy as he was for Hannah and Nolan, both of whom were close friends of Gavin's, seeing his brother's widow remarry had rekindled his grief. And knowing that, knowing he was alone and suffering so badly, was killing Ella one spoonful of Ben and Jerry's at a time.

Her phone rang, which was a welcome interruption from the direction her thoughts were taking. He had already rebuffed her multiple times. She wouldn't try to reason with him again, but damn, she wanted to. Good thing she'd turned to ice cream rather than booze. With some liquid courage in her belly, she'd probably get in her car and drive to his house to plead her case yet again.

She went to the kitchen to grab the phone. "Hello?" In the background she could hear loud music and louder voices. Suspecting a wrong number, she nearly hung up.

"Yeah, I got a guy here who has you in his phone as his ICE."

"His what?"

"His 'in case of emergency.'"

She immediately thought of her brother, Wade, who would list her ahead of any of their siblings, except he didn't have a cell phone as far as she knew. "Who is it?"

He ignored her question and continued his tirade. "You'd better come and get him the hell outta here before I call the cops."

With the phone tucked in the crook of her shoulder, she stashed the leftover ice cream in the freezer and went to find some shoes. "Where are you?"

"Red's Bar out on 114. Come quick. I'm giving it half an hour, and I want him out of here. Guy's nothing but trouble. I knew it the second he walked in here with a chip on his shoulder the size of Texas."

"I'll be right there. Don't do anything until I get there."

"Thirty minutes." He hung up on her.

Ella was out the door a minute later and heading out of Butler shortly after that. As she navigated the one-lane covered bridge by her parents' house on Hells Peak Road, it occurred to her that no one knew where she was or where she was going. Not that she felt the need to check in every time she left her house, but heading to a roadside bar late on a Saturday night—alone—was definitely out of character for her.

In the back of her mind was the nagging suspicion that it might be Gavin at the bar. But why would he have her listed as his ICE, a term that was completely new to her as someone who didn't have a cell phone. What was the point? There was no reception whatsoever in their town, and almost everyone she knew lived in Butler. If no one could call her and she couldn't call anyone, why get a cell phone? Where would Gavin have gotten her number and why would he list her, of all people, as his ICE?

She dismissed that idea almost as soon as she had it. His parents would be his points of contact anyway.

She refused to let her foolish hopeful heart lead her on a wild-goose chase through the dark Vermont night on a mission to rescue one of the men in her life. Maybe it was Lucas or Landon. Both of her younger brothers had been known to party and get into trouble on occasion. Not bad trouble, more the mischievous kind. Though they drove her crazy most of the time, both knew they could call her if they were ever truly in trouble.

As did Max, the youngest of the ten Abbotts. But with his girlfriend Chloe's baby due at any minute, he was probably in Burlington with her, waiting for something to happen. And wouldn't Chloe be his ICE?

Ella was still trying to figure out who would have listed her as his emergency contact when she pulled up to Red's, which was, apparently, a biker bar. Row after row of neatly parked bikes lined the lot, their chrome fixtures illuminated by the lights.

"That's a lot of bikers." Ella swallowed hard at the thought of walking in there alone. She should've called Charley or Wade to come with her, except the pissed-off guy on the phone had given her thirty minutes to get there, which hadn't been enough time to round up reinforcements.

"Get moving, chickenshit." Ella took another minute to find the courage to walk into a bar where she wouldn't know a soul except for the man who'd made her his emergency contact—without her knowledge. Whoever he was would get an earful about doing that without telling her.

The gravel parking lot crunched under her feet as she made her way to the front door. Inside, voices and music competed to create a deafening roar. How did anyone stand it in here for more than a few minutes? It was also dark. She could barely see a foot in front of her with all the lights focused on a band on a stage on the far side of the huge space.

"Help you, sugar?" a deep voice asked.

"I'm looking for the manager or the person who would've called about a patron who needs a ride home." She ventured a glance up at him and then kept going until she finally found his eyes, gasping at his sheer size. The man was at least six foot six or seven, a wall of solid muscle. Ella wasn't sure if she wanted to run from him or beg him to keep her safe in this unfamiliar place.

"Right this way." He took her by the arm and led her through a mass of sweating, dancing bodies.

More than one hand copped a feel of her as they pushed through the crowd with Ella holding on to her escort for dear life. She swatted at the roving hands and stayed with the giant, who took her to an office in a deep, dark corner.

Ella was shown to a room where Gavin Guthrie was in the middle of a fierce argument with another man with bright red hair, presumably the Red in Red's Bar.

"I didn't do anything!" Gavin said, his voice slurring. "I had a few drinks! So what?"

"I know what you did to the bar down the road. You're not welcome in my place."

"I paid my cover like everyone else. You can't just kick me out." He took a lunging step toward the other man, staggering.

"Gavin," Ella said.

Freezing in place, Gavin did a double take when he saw her standing next to the giant of a man who had stayed, probably to watch the show. "What're you doing here?" he asked in a much softer tone than he'd used on the bar owner.

"They called me to come get you."

"Why you?"

"My question exactly."

"Will you get him out of here, please?" the frazzled bar owner said to Ella. "We don't want any trouble."

"Let's go, Gavin." Despite the fact he was obviously drunk, disheveled and disorderly, he was still gorgeous. And furious, too. With one last filthy look for Red, he crossed the room to where Ella stood next to the giant.

The giant looked down at Gavin and handed over his cell phone. "I realized who you are, and I just want to say, I'm sorry."

The big man's gently spoken words nearly reduced Ella to tears. She could only imagine what they did to Gavin.

The kind gesture seemed to defuse Gavin's fury. He sagged, visibly, as if he'd been reminded of why he'd gotten drunk in the first place. "Thanks." With his hand on Ella's back, he opened the door and guided her through it. The giant came with them, helping them through the crowd to the main door.

Outside, Gavin headed for his truck.

Ella looked to the giant for help.

He went after Gavin, grabbing his shirt and spinning him around. "Dude, you're in no condition to drive. Let your lady drive you home."

"Leave me alone." Gavin tried unsuccessfully to shake off the giant. "No one told you to call her."

"If I had a girl like her at home, I wouldn't be hanging out here."

"She's not my girl."

Ella wanted to turn and walk away so she wouldn't have to hear anything else that would further lacerate her already wounded heart. She wanted to leave him there to deal with whatever was going on by himself. But she couldn't seem to get the message from her brain to her feet, so she stood riveted in place while the giant tried to talk some sense into Gavin.

"Just go with her and make this easy on everyone, will you?"

"What business is it of yours what I do?"

"Making sure everyone who leaves here does so safely is my business. If you don't want me in your business, get in her car and *go*. Then we won't have anything further to talk about."

"Fine. I'm going." Gavin stalked over to where Ella stood, arms crossed, watching him swerve as he crossed the parking lot. She pulled out her keys and pushed a button on the key fob to unlock her white Honda CR-V.

Gavin got into the passenger side and slammed the door.

"Thanks so much for your help," Ella said to the giant.

"No problem. He's a decent guy who's heading down a bad road. I hope he can figure out his shit before trouble finds him."

"I hope so, too."

"You have a good night now."

Ella got into her car and nearly dropped her keys in the dark, which was when she realized her hands were shaking.

"You don't have to do this," Gavin said. "I can call a cab."

"I don't mind."

Ella started the car and pulled out of the parking lot, heading for Butler. Gavin never said a word as they got closer to the town line, where she took a left toward his house, rather than a right toward hers in town.

The closer they got to his home on the grounds of the logging company he owned, the harder it became for Ella to refrain from asking him how she ended up in his phone as his ICE. She kept telling herself she was better off not knowing. What good would it do? He'd sent her away twice before, so what would make this time any different? Just give him a ride and leave it at that.

Except . . . How was she supposed to drop him off, go back to her life and forget about the fact that out of all the people he knew, *she* was the one he wanted called in an emergency? Why her? Did this count as an emergency? Ella knew herself, and she'd never get a minute's peace if she didn't ask him why.

She pulled up to his log cabin on the far side of the logging property and turned off the car. Being here reminded her of the time she'd come a couple of months ago, after hearing he'd been arrested in a fight at another bar. He'd sent her away then, and he probably would again.

"Thanks for the ride. Sorry about all this."

"It's okay."

He reached for the door handle. Was he really going to get out and that would be that?

She forced herself to speak before she missed the opportunity. "Gavin?"

"Yeah?"

"Why am I in your phone as the one to call in an emergency?"

CHAPTER 2

*Hope is being able to see that there is
light despite all of the darkness.*

—Desmond Tutu

H e stared at her, long enough to be unnerving, before
he spoke. "Can you come in for a minute?"

"Oh, well . . ."

"I'm sorry. You were probably doing something and had
to leave to come rescue me from myself."

"I was actually on a date." He didn't need to know the date
was with a sofa and two guys named Ben and Jerry.

"Oh God, El. I'm so sorry. I hope you've met someone really
nice who treats you the way you deserve to be treated."

"Do you? Do you really?"

"Of course I do! You know I care about you, and I want
you to be happy."

"If that's the case, then . . ." *No, I won't say it. I will not
give him the satisfaction of knowing that no other man could
ever make me happier than he does, even when he's pushing
me away. Again.*

"Then what?"

"Nothing. Never mind."

"Come in. We need to talk."

As her heart did a happy dance for the ages, Ella shook her

head. "If you just want to tell me—again—all the reasons this will never happen, I'm good. I got the message the first half-dozen times you explained it to me."

"That's not why I want you to come in."

Go, go, GO, her heart cried. *For the love of God and all that's holy, get out of the car and go into that cozy log cabin where the man of your dreams lives.* Ella had always been one to follow her heart, but this time her heart was in deep conflict with the brain that was telling her to *run, run, RUN* before he could hurt her again.

"Please, Ella?"

Her brain didn't stand a chance against her heart when he said *please* in that soft, urgent tone. She reached for the door handle.

They met at the front of her car, him still a little less than steady on his feet, and her certain she was making yet another in a string of huge mistakes where he was concerned. Then he put his hand on the small of her back to guide her up the stairs, and that was her undoing.

Why did he have to be so perfectly imperfect? Why did he have to be everything she'd ever wanted, wrapped up in one devilishly sexy, deeply wounded package? Her feelings for him ran the gamut from unbearable to undeniable to untenable and back again, an endless circle of frustration.

Her heart simply couldn't take another self-inflicted wound—self-inflicted because she kept going back for more even though he'd repeatedly told her there was no hope for anything between them. She didn't blame him. At least he'd always been straight with her. She blamed herself for being unwilling to take no for an answer.

So as she climbed the stairs to his front door, she attempted to manage her expectations. Nothing would happen. They would talk. She would stay until she was certain he was okay, and then she'd go home alone the way she always did, this time without a lacerating wound to nurse for the foreseeable future.

From behind her, he reached around to open the door, which wasn't locked. The brush of his arm against her shoulder sent a tingle of awareness to parts of her that only seemed to stand up and take notice of *this* man. Only he had the power to activate all her systems with just the slightest contact of his body against hers. It made her wonder what it would be like—

No. Not going there. Under no circumstances are you going there. Well . . . No!

While she should be listening to her better judgment and distancing herself, instead she wanted to purr with the simple pleasure that came from being close to him for however long the moment lasted. She'd never claimed this situation was anything other than pathetic. At least she was remaining true to form in her "relationship," such as it wasn't, with Gavin.

She stepped into his home ahead of him. The door closed behind them with a resounding thud, and suddenly this felt like a bad idea. A very bad idea, indeed. The last time she'd been here, after hearing he'd been arrested for fighting in a bar, she'd left work to come check on him and had ended up crying all the way home after he sent her away.

"I, um . . . I should go."

"I was going to make some coffee. Can I entice you to stay for that long?"

If she drank coffee at this hour, she'd be up all night, but she'd be up all night anyway, analyzing every second of this bizarre evening. "Sure. I guess."

Gavin got busy making the coffee. The only sign of his slight intoxication was the mess he made pouring the water into the back of the coffeemaker. Aim, shoot, miss. Those three little words were like a metaphor for this entire situation, and the thought nearly made her laugh out loud. Except . . . There was nothing at all funny about unrequited love. It sucked every bit as badly as the songs, books and movies claimed it did.

"Have a seat." He pointed to the stools at the counter. "I'll be right back." He disappeared into the hallway that presumably led to his bedroom and the bathroom.

The urge to follow him, to force a confrontation, to jump his bones—something, *anything*—was so strong that instead of giving in she got busy in the kitchen, poking through cabinets in search of mugs, taking a carton of half-and-half from the fridge and giving it a sniff to make sure it was still good, and locating spoons. Gavin took his coffee with just a touch of cream and a teaspoon of sugar. How she knew that she didn't even know. She'd been paying close attention to her late brother-in-law's sexy younger brother for as long as she'd known him, which was starting to measure in decades, rather than mere years.

Pathetic.

In all that time, she'd dated other guys. Even had the misfortune of sleeping with some of them. But she had never once felt anything even close to what happened every time Gavin Guthrie walked into a room. Take now, for instance. He'd changed into a T-shirt and old sweats, washed his face and, judging by the minty fresh scent that came with him, apparently brushed his teeth, too. Drops of water clung to the ends of his longish dark hair, and the scruff that covered his well-defined jaw made her want to rub against him in the most shameless way possible.

Then the coffeemaker beeped, and her brain took over once again, shoving her rapidly beating heart aside to remind her that she was having a cup of coffee that would keep her up all night and then getting the hell out of there.

Gavin had no idea what he'd been thinking when he all but begged Ella to come inside with him. Hell, he barely recalled putting her name in his phone in case of an emergency at a time when his entire life seemed to be one endless emergency after another.

He still had no business dragging Ella into his crap, but at the same time he couldn't bear to let her drive away not knowing when or if he might see her again. She was like a breath of the freshest, coolest mountain air, infusing him with a warm ray of sunshine in the bleak landscape inside his mind.

Things were bad and getting worse. Pushing her away, repeatedly, hadn't made anything better. In fact, during a wide-awake moment the night before, Gavin had undergone an epiphany, during which he realized that pushing Ella away was part of what had made everything worse. Thus his invitation for coffee, which had been reluctantly accepted. Not that he could blame her. Ella was a lot of things, but a fool had never been one of them. And she'd be a total, unmitigated fool to shackle herself to him.

He poured the coffee into the mugs she'd placed on the counter, stirring cream and half a packet of sweetener into hers. How did he know how she took her coffee? He didn't recall *not* knowing that. He barely recalled a time before he knew Ella and the entire Abbott family. He and his brother Caleb had been friends with Ella's brothers Hunter and Will since they'd moved to Butler when the Guthries were in fifth and sixth grades. Caleb had started dating Hannah when they were all in high school, and the two families had been close ever since, never more so than in the difficult years that followed Caleb's death.

Gavin pushed his thoughts away from that sorrowful topic. He was getting sick and tired of the relentless grief that refused to give him an ounce of slack lately, especially since Caleb's dog died and Hannah got remarried. Life went on, even when you thought it couldn't possibly. Maybe it was time to allow his life to move forward, too.

He couldn't seem to picture that life without Ella as part of it in some way, but he had amends to make where she was concerned, and there was no time quite like the present.

Gavin put the mug on the counter in front of her and brought his with him to sit on the stool next to hers. "Listen, El . . . I wanted to tell you—"

She held up her hand to stop him. "Please, don't. I just can't rehash it all again."

"How do you know what I was going to say?"

"Because," she said with resignation that tugged at his heart, "you've said it all before, and there's only so much rejection a girl can take before she begins to get a complex."

"Eleanor, look at me." His use of her full name clearly startled her as she looked up at him with those wide, liquid brown eyes that could hide nothing, her lips parting with surprise. Yeah, he'd thought about that kiss on the beach in Burlington a few thousand times since, and hearing she'd been out with another guy made him feel panicky in addition to all the other unpleasant emotions he'd been contending with lately. "I never meant to reject you. It had nothing *at all* to do with you. I need you to know that."

"So you say."

"I mean it. Every time we've . . . talked . . . in the last few months, I've walked away from you because I *had* to, not because I wanted to." She was very focused now on her mug of coffee rather than him, not that he could blame her.

"What happened tonight?"

"Tonight," he said with a sigh, "I discovered my reputation is beginning to precede me. I had a couple of beers with some guys from work, and decided to hit Red's on the way home for a nightcap. I was minding my own business at the bar when Red came in, saw me there and turned it into a federal case because of what happened down the road. I tried to tell him I don't want any trouble, but he wasn't hearing it. Somehow that big dude got ahold of my phone, and . . . And, well, you know the rest."

"What was your plan for getting home?"

"I'm not an idiot, Ella, despite how it might seem lately. I was going to call a cab."

She jumped up, those same soft eyes now flashing with anger. "If the bouncer hadn't stopped you, you would've driven home. For God's sake, Gavin, don't make everything worse by lying to my face."

"I never would've driven home. I would've walked before I drove—I've done it before." When she eyed him skeptically, he ran his hands through his hair. "I know how it looked, but that guy was pissing me off getting up in my grill the way he was."

"*Someone* needs to get up in your grill to make this crazy shit stop!"

In all the years he'd known her, he'd never once heard sweet, lovely Ella Abbott yell at anyone—or swear—and since she was one of ten siblings, that was saying something.

Her raised voice did the same thing to him a slap to the face would have. It woke him up once and for all. He closed the small distance between them, hooked an arm around her waist and tugged her in close to him.

If she'd been surprised before, she was flat-out stunned now.

"The only person I want up in my grill, Ella, is you." And then he kissed her the way he'd been dying to since that day at the beach, since the day he'd gotten his first taste of her and developed a hunger for her that had kept him awake on many a night after he pushed her out of his life.

Just as she could only take so much rejection, he could only take so much temptation. Eventually, someone was going to snap.

Her hands, which had been lying flat against his chest, were now pushing hard—hard enough for the signal to reach his kiss-addled brain. She tore her lips free, and that was when he realized only one of them had been enjoying that kiss. "Stop it." She rubbed her forearm over her lips, seeming to wipe him off, which actually hurt him more than it should have. As if he had any right. "What're you doing?"

"I thought that was rather obvious." Since her mouth was apparently unavailable, he directed his attention to the long, elegant neck that had occupied far too many of his Ella-related fantasies.

But she was having none of that either. "Knock it off, Gavin. Whatever game you're playing, I'm not interested." The tears that gathered in her eyes said otherwise, but she turned away from him and headed for the door.

He chased after her, placing his hand flat against the door to keep her from opening it. "Stay, Ella. Please, don't go." Lowering his voice again, he said, "Please."

Her shoulders slumped and her forehead landed against the door.

Gavin put his arms around her from behind. "Come here."

She turned into his embrace, and he gathered her in close, the top of her head fitting perfectly beneath his chin. And just that simply, everything felt better than it had in years.

"If you're screwing with me, Guthrie, I'll kill you with

my own hands, and I'm more than capable of that after growing up with seven brothers."

The low rumble of laughter caught him off guard. He couldn't remember the last time he'd had cause to laugh. "Duly noted." Tightening his hold on her, which seemed to be in direct relation to the fragile hold he had on his sanity, Gavin ran his lips over her smooth dark hair, which always had a shine to it. That was something he found endlessly fascinating. "I'm not screwing with you, Ella."

"Then what is this?" she asked tentatively. He could hardly blame her for that. He'd given her more than enough reason to be tentative where he was concerned.

"This is me admitting that I need you, that I'm tired of fighting whatever this is that's been happening between us for years now, that—"

She drew back to look up at him. "Gavin?"

"What?"

"Shut up and kiss me."

CHAPTER 3

***

Grief is in two parts. The first is loss.
The second is the remaking of life.

—Anne Roiphe

G avin did exactly as he was told, capturing her mouth in a deep passionate kiss that had her clinging to him, trying to get closer, until he abruptly pulled away. "What about the guy you're seeing?"

Ella had to think about that for a second, and then she began to laugh. "The *guys* I'm *seeing* are named Ben and Jerry."

"There're *two* of them?"

"How much did you drink tonight? Hello? *Ben* and *Jerry*? Ringing any bells?"

"Ice cream," he said on a deep sigh of relief.

"Thank God. I thought you'd finally managed to pickle your brain with all the beer you've been drinking."

"You said you were on a date . . ."

"With my sofa and a pint of Cherry Garcia. It's become somewhat of a Saturday night routine lately."

"I thought you were seeing someone else."

"Is that why everything suddenly changed for you?" she asked, trying to break free of his hold.

"No. God, no. I was jealous as hell, but this is about you and me and no one else."

"You were jealous? Really?"

"Insanely."

They stared at each other for a long, charged moment.

"Just because I've pushed you away doesn't mean I haven't wanted to pull you closer, El."

"If you're messing with me, I swear . . ."

"I'm not messing with you. I'm exhausted, Ella." He took her by the hand and led her to the sofa, where he sat next to her, turning to face her. "I'm . . . I can't do this anymore."

"Do what?" she asked hesitantly. Part of her didn't want to know what it was he couldn't do anymore. It couldn't be her. He hadn't exactly . . . done . . . her. *Stop it, Ella. Let the man talk.*

Raising his free hand to his head, he ran his fingers through his hair repeatedly while he seemed to be looking for the words he needed. *"This,"* he finally said after a long period of silence. "Half a life spent living mostly in the past, only sort of in the present, devoid of hope and drowning in grief. I can't *bear* it another minute. None of it is going to bring Caleb back."

Blinking back tears, Ella reached for him.

He leaned toward her, dropped his head and, for the first time, allowed her to shoulder some of his burden.

Ella ran her fingers through his hair, hoping to offer whatever comfort she could. Selfishly, she'd wanted to run her fingers through that hair for years and wasn't about to miss the opportunity. If only she could think of something she could say that would help him. But the only words that came to mind were self-serving. And then it occurred to her . . . Maybe by serving herself, she could serve him, too. "You're not alone, Gavin. You don't have to do this alone."

"I worry about taking you down with me."

"I'm a lot stronger than you think."

"I know that. I've always known that."

"So what now?"

"I guess we take it a day at a time and see what happens."

"I don't know if I can do that." As the words left her mouth, Ella wanted to take them back. Here he was offering what she'd always wanted, and she was about to tell him it wasn't enough? Was she *insane*?

"What do you mean?"

She took a deep breath, determined to fight for what she really wanted from him. "I can't go day by day and see what happens. I can't take that kind of risk. Not with you."

"I don't have much more than that to offer."

"Yes, you do, Gavin! You have so much more inside you, and it's trying to get out. You just said half a life isn't working anymore. So either you go all in or you don't. But I'm not willing to settle for half of you—one foot in, one foot out. *That* doesn't work for me."

With his elbows on his knees, he stared off at a point over her shoulder, seeming to think about what she'd said.

"The last time," she said tentatively, "after you were in the fight and I came here to check on you . . ."

"What about it?"

"It was *weeks* before I could take a deep breath that didn't hurt."

"Ella . . ."

"I didn't tell you that to make you feel bad. I told you so you'd understand why I can't do this halfway. I just can't take that chance."

"I'm afraid I'll let you down in some way."

"You're a *man*," she said teasingly. "Of course you will."

He offered a small smile. "You know what I mean."

"Maybe this isn't the right time." A ripple of pain attacked her entire body as she said those words, but she couldn't afford to be stupid or too hopeful where he was concerned. Despite the steps forward they'd taken earlier, he was still waffling.

"May I say something that might be extremely unfair in light of the mixed signals I've sent you for far too long?" he asked.

"Um, okay. I guess." While part of her wanted to put her hands over her ears so she couldn't hear something that couldn't be unheard, she was far too curious to do that.

"I told you that since Homer died and Hannah got remarried, I've been spiraling back in time to when Caleb first died.

I've felt almost as bad as I did then, except for the rare occasions when you're close by. That's the only time the spinning stops."

Ella had no idea how to reply to that. It was, perhaps, the most important thing he'd ever said to her. She swallowed hard as she acknowledged what it had taken him to admit such a thing to her.

"I *need* you, Ella. I'm no longer capable of pushing you away, not when I feel so much better when you're here. I feel like a selfish bastard for dragging you into my nightmare, but I can't fight it anymore."

Maybe she was insane or at least downright crazy, but there was no way she could walk away from him after hearing him say those words in that pleading tone.

"If you're asking me to commit to a genuine relationship," he continued, "I'll do it if it means I get to have you in my life. I'll take you any way I can get you."

Even though alarm bells were ringing loudly in her mind, Ella pretended not to hear them. How could she possibly pay any attention to them when the man of her dreams had just said what she'd waited *years* to hear? He felt *better* when she was around. He *needed* her. He'd take her *any way he could get her.* She could work with that, couldn't she? She could damned well try.

"I-I should probably go," she said, though that was the last thing she wanted to do. "It's getting late."

"Stay."

Never had one word packed a bigger wallop. Ella was on the verge of hyperventilation. Spend a whole night with Gavin Guthrie? She needed oxygen. She needed a reality check. She needed a toothbrush.

"Ella? Are you okay?"

"Yes, of course I am. I was just thinking about what I need to do tomorrow. I have . . . Dinner. With my family." *For God's sake, Ella, he's not asking you to move in. What the hell does dinner have to do with anything? You've waited forever for an opportunity to be close to him, and you're bungling it!* "That's later in the day."

"So nothing in the morning?"

He didn't need to know that Sunday morning was her usual errand time. Gavin Guthrie was asking her to sleep over. Groceries could wait. "No, nothing in the morning."

"Great, then you can stay?"

"I . . . um . . . Sure. Okay." The last word came out as a squeak that she covered by coughing. She was acting like a virgin on the threshold of the big event, when she was a long way from that. But having the man she'd adored from afar for her entire adult life ask her to spend the night with him wasn't something that happened every day.

Suddenly, she was far more nervous than she'd been the night she'd lost her virginity. This felt like a much bigger deal in every possible way.

"You're freaking out, aren't you?" he asked.

"What? No, I'm not freaking out."

He smiled, as if he didn't believe her, and got up from the sofa to offer his hand. "Come on. Let's find you something to sleep in."

Following him and holding his hand as he turned off lights and led the way to his bedroom, Ella wanted to wave her free hand in front of her face to cool herself off. She was on the verge of seriously overheating—and blowing this up into the most important event of her entire life. But wasn't it? Wasn't it quite possibly the single most important thing she'd ever done?

She began to feel a bit nauseated, which was definitely not the mood she was going for. *Stop overthinking it. You're not going to have sex with him. You're only going to sleep with him. But what if he thinks I agreed to sex? Did I agree to sex? Am I hyperventilating? How will I know? I've never hyperventilated before.*

The flannel shirt he'd worn earlier was lying across the foot of his bed. "This is fine," she said as she released his hand and reached for the shirt.

"Bathroom is right in there. There should be extra toothbrushes in the cabinet. Let me know if you can't find one."

"Okay, thanks." Ella ducked into the bathroom, thankful

for the moment alone to collect herself. If he could act like this was no big deal, she could, too. Or she could at least *try* to act like it was no big deal when it was the biggest of big deals.

Moving quickly, she removed her boots, jeans and sweater. After a brief debate, she took off her bra, too, because she'd never be able to sleep with it on. She pulled on the flannel shirt that fell to her thighs. The shirt smelled like him. Unashamed, Ella took a full minute to breathe in the rich, appealing scent of him coming from the shirt.

Yeah, she had it bad, and it was going to get worse before this night was over. Of that she had no doubt. Her fingers trembled ever so slightly as she fumbled with the buttons, managing to button the shirt wrong the first time.

In the cabinet, she looked for a toothbrush and encountered an economy-sized box of condoms. And yes, she checked to see if it was opened—it wasn't. As she put it back on the shelf, she noticed the size: extra large. She took a moment to day-dream about Gavin Guthrie's extra-large—

Oh, for God's sake! Did she really need to know what size condoms he bought? It wasn't *bad* information to have. But why the big box? Who was he planning to get busy with?

"Toothbrush, Ella," she muttered, aggravated with herself and now him, too, because she couldn't very well go out there and ask him who he'd bought all those condoms for. She found an unopened toothbrush and used his Colgate-with-whitening toothpaste. No wonder his smile was so perfect, and yes, she was being ridiculous glomming on to these little details the way a stalker would.

And then she spotted a bottle of cologne on the counter, and being only human, she had to take a good long sniff and then sigh with the pleasure. Gucci Black. Sigh . . . Here was the essence of Gavin in a bottle. *Put it down, walk away, brush your teeth and stop acting like a freak!*

Ella hated when common sense interrupted her day-dreaming. She brushed her teeth and used his brush on her hair, trying not to think about her hair intermingling with his on the brush because that would be weird.

Then she took a long look in the mirror, summoning the calm control she needed to get through this night with him. Wouldn't it be something if she'd waited all this time for a chance with him only to blow it by acting like a lovesick freak? What if he caught her sniffing his cologne? Or worse, his shirt?

Stop! Just stop it and be normal. Except she had no idea how to "be normal" when Gavin Guthrie was in the room, let alone next to her in a bed. She was never going to survive sleeping with him.

She emerged from the bathroom to discover a whole new challenge. Gavin had removed his T-shirt and sweats and was sitting on the bed wearing only a pair of boxer shorts. Holy hell. And she was supposed to act *normal* in the face of his insane hotness?

"Make yourself comfortable," he said, brushing by her. "I'll be right out."

If he looked in the cabinet, he would know she'd seen the huge box of condoms that were in front of the toothbrushes. What did it matter if she'd seen them? It wasn't like they were going to need them. Or were they? What did he think was going to happen here tonight? What if he came out of the bathroom with the box in hand, prepared to get down and dirty?

Before she could do something ridiculous like pass out on the floor of his bedroom by failing to breathe, she got into bed and pulled the covers up to her chin. She couldn't be lying there like a mummy when he came out, so she turned on her side and confronted that yummy scent all over again on his pillow. Wait! Was this his side of the bed? Should she be on the other side?

"Oh my God, Ella, calm the hell down before you have a stroke." *Wouldn't that be something? Imagine the story I could tell . . . On my first night with Gavin, after years of lusting after him, I stroked out from the thought of sharing a bed with him, so he had to take me to the emergency room where we spent a very romantic evening with me attached to IV poles.*

The soft flannel of his shirt abraded her nipples, which

were apparently standing at full alert, aware that something monumental was about to happen. By the time Gavin emerged from the bathroom, shut off the light and slid into bed next to her, Ella was on the verge of a full-on thermonuclear meltdown.

She'd told herself she could do this. She could get closer to him, knowing she might be setting herself up for disaster if he happened to change his mind at some point along the way. But after this, after sharing a bed with him, after sleeping next to him and God knows what else might happen during the night? Yeah, she'd never get over it if he decided to walk away after that.

Ella was thinking she should get out of there while she still could, but then his arm came around her waist to draw her closer to him, and she was lost, absolutely, positively *lost*.

She wasn't going anywhere.

CHAPTER 4

❖

Hope is the thing with feathers that perches
in the soul—and sings the tunes without
the words—and never stops at all.

—Emily Dickinson

E lla wasn't sure where to put her hands. Or her legs. Or the rest of her, for that matter. He was going to think she'd never been in a bed with a man before, when she had. Not that he needed to know that. She'd never been in bed with a man who mattered as much as this one did.

"Relax, El. It's just me, your old buddy Gavin."

That made her laugh. "Right. That's all you are. My old buddy Gavin."

"I'm sorry for what I've put you through."

"Gavin . . ."

"Hear me out. You have to know it wasn't easy for me to walk away from you. It wasn't easy that day on the beach or when you came here to check on me after I got arrested. At Will's wedding, all I wanted was to dance with you, to hold you, to touch you. God, you looked so beautiful that day in the gold dress. I couldn't take my eyes off you."

"I'm sorry I said no to you."

"I wasn't surprised. I haven't given you much reason to say

yes." He ran his hand over her back and Ella began to relax ever so slightly. "You know you're taking on a real fixer-upper here, right?"

Ella laughed at his terminology. "With a little work, I think that fixer-upper could be a real gem."

"You think so, huh?"

"I know so. But I have conditions."

"I'm listening."

"No more bars. No more fighting. A lot less drinking."

"What else?"

"If you're spinning, you come to me. You talk to me. You don't try to drown it out by drinking or fighting or anything else that might be deemed self-destructive."

"You don't want me around when I'm in one of the dark moods."

"Yes, I do. That's what I'm telling you."

"Ella . . . You don't know what you're signing on for."

"After all this time you can honestly say that? I know exactly what I'm signing on for, and all your warnings haven't pushed me away yet. Why do you think that's going to work now?"

"You deserve better."

"Probably."

His grunt of laughter made her smile in the dark.

"But for some strange reason, you're the one I want."

"That makes me feel pretty damned lucky."

"Don't screw it up."

"I'm apt to. It's been a long time since I had an actual girlfriend."

"Oh, I remember, what's-her-name. *Dalia*. Ugh, what kind of name is *Dalia*?"

His hand slid down her arm to take hold of her hand. "Put away those claws, tiger."

"Whatever became of her anyway?"

"She couldn't cope with me after Caleb died. She tried, but eventually she stopped trying, and I didn't care enough to notice she'd gone."

Ella couldn't help feeling a tiny bit sorry for the other

woman, not that she hadn't been glad to see her go. She'd noticed—probably before Gavin did. "There hasn't been anyone since then?"

"Here and there, but nothing serious. I haven't had the capacity for serious. I've been focused on the business and my parents and just getting through every day."

"That's no way to live, Gav. You know that, don't you?"

"It's all I've been capable of."

"I won't ever pretend to understand what you've been through since you lost Caleb. I can't imagine losing any of my siblings, let alone my only sibling. For what it's worth, the day we lost him was the worst day of my life."

Gavin squeezed her hand.

"All these years later, there's still a dull ache in my heart with his name on it. He was one of the most amazing people I've ever known."

"Thanks for that, El," he said gruffly. "Helps to know he's remembered so fondly by everyone."

"We loved him very much. But . . ."

"Ah, I knew there had to be a *but* coming . . ."

"He would hate, absolutely *hate*, if his death ruined your life. I didn't know him anywhere near as well as you did, but I know that much for certain."

His deep sigh served as his only reply.

Ella forced herself to continue, to get this out so they could move on from here. "No one will ever take his place for you, and there'll be a hole in your life where he should be for as long as you live. Living half a life doesn't honor your brother's memory, Gavin. It would make him mad as hell that you aren't taking full advantage of the years you got that he didn't to live for both of you."

"Sounds to me like you've been thinking about this for a lot longer than tonight."

"I have. You know when something happens and you think of the perfect retort after the fact?"

"Yeah."

"That always happens to me after I see you. I think of what I wanted to say the next day or the next week."

He released her hand and cupped her face.

Ella waited breathlessly to see what he would do next. She didn't have to wait long.

His lips came down on hers, soft and sweet and persuasive. "Everything you said is absolutely true." Another kiss. "He would be mad as hell at me and wouldn't hesitate to say so. And he'd tell me to get my fucking hands off you and go sleep on the sofa."

"He would not."

"Yes, he would. I had a little thing for you way back when."

A blast of anger took her by surprise. "Don't say that. Don't start rewriting history." She tried to pull away from him, but he wouldn't let her.

"I'm not rewriting anything. When we were in college and Caleb was hot and heavy with Hannah, I wanted to ask you out. But you were still in high school, and Caleb told me to leave you alone. He said you were far too young and sweet for the likes of me, and he was right about that."

"No, he wasn't." It was infuriating, all these years later, to realize that he'd had feelings for her, too.

"If I had to bet, he was concerned that if I screwed things up with you it would screw things up for him with Hannah. He threatened me with bodily harm if I so much as looked at you."

"I can't hear this. I . . . I just . . . I should go." Before she could make a move to leave the bed, he had her secured to the mattress with the weight of his big body on top of hers, his erection pressed into her belly.

"Don't go. Please don't go."

"All this time, Gavin." Ella was on the verge of tears that she held back by closing her eyes tightly. "I can't bear to think of what might've been."

"We're together now. We have right now and tomorrow and the next day and a fresh new opportunity that I'll do my best not to royally screw up." He kissed her again, more intently this time.

Ella wrapped her arms around his neck and opened her mouth to his tongue. Her emotions were all over the place, but when he kissed her so passionately, she couldn't think of anything but right here and right now with the man she'd craved for so long. His kisses set her on fire. She curled her legs around his hips, seeking relief for the ache that grew with every sweep of his tongue.

Seeming to sense what she needed, he rocked against her. Then his hand was between them, unbuttoning the shirt of his that she wore.

She should stop this before it went any further. Neither of them was in any way prepared for this to happen, but she couldn't bring herself to stop it. Not when she'd wanted him so badly.

Without missing a beat in the kiss, Gavin pushed the two sides of the shirt aside and brought his chest down on hers, making Ella moan from the bliss of his chest hair brushing against her tight nipples. This was insanity. She wanted him more than she'd ever wanted anything in her life.

He broke the kiss, gasping for air. "God, Ella . . ." Burying his face in her neck, he took a series of deep breaths.

She caressed his back in small circles, working her way down, learning each hill and valley of his muscular frame and making him tremble under her hands. Reaching the waistband of his boxers, she faced a dilemma. Keep going like she wanted to or stop like she knew she should?

After years and years of checking out the way that sexy ass looked in denim, she found she couldn't resist the temptation to smooth her hands over the tight globes that grew tighter as she explored him.

"Fuck," he whispered on a long exhale. "Ella . . ."

She squirmed under him, his erection pressing against her.

"I want to touch you, too," he said.

"Please . . . Yes." Maybe it was shameless to all but beg him, but when a girl's dreams were coming true, she hardly had time to be concerned about shame.

He used his arms to lift himself off her, going up to his knees. Pushing her legs apart, he bent over her to kiss her left breast. The scrape of his late-day whiskers against her skin made her feel feverish. Then he closed his lips around her nipple, tugging and sucking as he continued to press his erection between her legs. The combination was too much and just right all at the same time. "Gavin . . ."

"It's okay, baby. Let it happen. You're so sweet and sexy."

His words triggered her orgasm, which ripped through her body like an out-of-control freight train.

She came down from the incredible high to discover she had fistfuls of his hair and was about to give him two very big bald spots.

"That was so hot," he whispered against her lips. "I can't wait to be inside you when that happens."

"Mmm." The thought of that was more than she could process with her body still humming from the most powerful orgasm of her life. If he could do that while barely touching her, she was almost afraid of what else he was capable of. But she also couldn't wait to find out.

"You okay?"

"Mmm-hmmm."

He moved to his side, taking her with him.

She cuddled up to him, her legs intertwining with his like they'd been sleeping together forever. All the earlier awkwardness was gone and in its place was a growing sense of familiarity that she'd yearned for with him.

The press of his hard cock against her belly was a reminder that only one of them had found this encounter to be particularly fulfilling. She flattened her hand against his stomach and dragged it down to cover the hard column of flesh, discovering that he most definitely needed those extra-large condoms. Holy moly!

He drew in a sharp deep breath and covered her hand with his own, stopping her from moving.

"Let me," she whispered.

"I can't. I'm right there."

"That's okay." She pushed his hand aside and began to stroke him through the thin cotton of his underwear.

"Ella . . ." His voice sounded strangled.

"It's okay."

He got harder and longer. His grip on her arm tightened and his breathing became labored.

Ella leaned in closer to kiss him, dragging her tongue over his lips before delving inside his mouth.

Groaning, he thrust into her hand and came.

She stayed with him all the way through it until he relaxed against her.

His hand slid inside her shirt and curved around her back. "I feel incredibly lucky that you'll even speak to me let alone do that."

"We're both lucky to have this opportunity to be together this way. Promise you won't hurt me, Gavin."

"That's the last thing in the world I want to do."

It wasn't exactly a promise, but she'd take what she could get where he was concerned.

CHAPTER 5

*Grief can take care of itself, but to get
the full value of a joy you must have
somebody to divide it with.*

—Mark Twain

Waking with Ella tucked up against him, Gavin replayed the night before, picking over every detail and every minute they'd spent together. What she'd said to him about Caleb and how he was left to live for both of them had struck home. It was true and something he'd been aware of for quite some time, while he tried to find a way through the relentless grief to get back to living.

He could barely remember what his life had been like before the day that shattered all their lives. In the ensuing years, he'd put himself back together as best he could, but none of the pieces fit quite the way they used to. He was like the old ceramic vase his mother had treasured until he and Caleb had knocked it over while wrestling one day and then attempted to cover up their crime by gluing the fragments back together.

The vase had never been the same, and neither had he after his brother died. He'd coped, of course. He'd had no choice but to carry on. He had parents who needed him, a business that had been new to him at the time of Caleb's death, and with everything he had sunk into it, letting it founder wasn't an option. In many ways, the business had saved him by giving him something to focus on.

Last night Ella had shown him in only a few hours that there was a huge difference between existing and living. He felt more alive and aware and alert with her in his arms than he had in years. The constant, relentless pain that held him in its tight grip had lessened at some point, and he had her to thank for that.

She was taking a huge gamble with him. He hadn't been joking when he called himself a fixer-upper. *Disaster area* might be a better term. But he was determined to be worthy of her, even if his better judgment was still telling him he ought to leave her alone.

After what happened last night, however, leaving her alone was the last thing he wanted. Though he'd gotten up and changed into clean underwear and flannel pajama pants, his hand had once again ventured inside the open front of the shirt of his that she wore. Her skin was so soft and her hair smelled so good. Like fresh air and sunshine and happiness. Ella was the most joyful person he knew—always smiling and happy and laughing.

It would kill him if any of that changed because of him. *I can't let that happen.* She'd already nearly killed him once when she asked him to promise that he wouldn't hurt her. It would ruin him if he ever hurt her, so he made a silent vow to be careful with her, to treat her like the most fragile, important, priceless thing in his life. Because she was. The way she'd come riding to his rescue more than once and kept coming back even after he'd sent her away was evidence of her commitment to him.

She stirred, mumbled something he couldn't hear and then opened her eyes.

He got to watch her initial surprise at seeing him and then felt her relax when she remembered why she was there with him.

"Morning." He kissed her forehead and ran his fingers through her hair.

"Morning."

"Did you sleep okay?"

"Uh-huh."

So she wasn't particularly chatty in the morning, or perhaps she was rethinking her decision to spend the night with him. He couldn't say he blamed her, but he really hoped that wasn't the case.

"I . . . um, I should get going." Clutching both sides of the unbuttoned shirt, Ella turned over, dislodging the hand he had on her ribs. She got up from the bed and went into the bathroom, closing the door behind her.

Suddenly, Gavin was panic stricken at the possibility that she had regrets about what had happened last night. He couldn't let her leave without making sure she was okay. Moving quickly, he got up, found a T-shirt and went straight to the kitchen to put on coffee and mix pancake batter. By the time she emerged from the bedroom fully dressed, he had pancakes cooking on the griddle and coffee ready.

He poured her a cup and pushed it across the counter to her along with the cream and sweetener she preferred.

"You didn't have to do all this." She focused on the coffee rather than him as she spoke.

"Seemed the least I could do for you after you came to my rescue last night." Gavin put the first two pancakes off the grill onto her plate along with two sausage links. He slid it across the counter to her along with a knife, a fork, a tub of butter and a jug of her brother Colton's syrup.

He could almost see her internal debate. Stay and eat or get the hell out of there. Until she decided, he poured more batter on the griddle and bit his tongue so he wouldn't try to talk her into staying if she really wanted to go.

When she finally took a seat at the bar and began to spread butter on her pancakes, Gavin breathed a sigh of relief. He took his own plate and coffee to join her. They ate in silence for a few minutes before he couldn't take the quiet any longer.

"What's wrong?"

She looked up at him, seeming surprised. "What? Nothing is wrong."

"Something is different this morning. Are you sorry you stayed? Sorry we did what we did in bed? Sorry you ever took that call last night?"

"No, none of that," she said, but her face flushed with a rosy color that only added to her natural beauty.

"Then what? You're having morning-after regrets of some sort."

"I'm not."

Gavin knew something was afoot, but he couldn't very well drag it out of her. He ate his breakfast and drank his coffee and tried to figure her out.

"It's terrifying," she said after a long period of awkward silence.

"What is?"

"This, you, all of it."

"Terrifying?"

She nodded and seemed to force herself to look at him. "The little taste I had of what it might be like . . . If you change your mind—"

"I'm not going to change my mind." Turning his body so he faced her, he reached for her and when she leaned into him, he wrapped his arms around her. "I have no idea what's going to happen with us, Ella. Maybe after all these years of wondering, we'll find out we're better as friends than we are as lovers. Maybe we'll give it our very best effort but it just won't work out for one reason or another. Maybe it'll be the best thing to ever happen to both of us, the forever kind of love people dream about. I don't know how it'll unfold. But I promise you this—you'll get my very best effort. I'm in this with you. I have been for a while now, and I'm not going to change my mind, especially not after having the exquisite pleasure of sleeping with you in my arms. I can't wait to do it again."

"I slept better last night than I have since before Hannah's wedding."

"So did I." Brushing her hair aside, he kissed her face, her neck, and nibbled on her ear. "You know what that means, don't you?"

"What?" she asked, sounding sort of breathless, which made him smile.

"We ought to do it again tonight. Maybe tomorrow night, too."

"You think so?"

"I do. I definitely do. We've got a lot of sleep to catch up on after months of sleepless nights." He drew back so he could see her face and the lovely eyes that gazed at him with such adoration, even when he didn't deserve it. "Don't be terrified. Not of me. I couldn't stand to make you feel that way."

"I'll try not to be. You're filling me with giddy hope, something that's been in short supply where you're concerned."

"You're filling me with hope, too, which has been sadly lacking in my life for far too long." Because he couldn't resist the sweet temptation of her lips for another second, he kissed her, hoping he'd earned the right to with his reassurances.

She relaxed into his embrace, her arms encircling his neck as she fell into the kiss, her tongue stroking against his. God, she was so sweet and so sexy.

"You taste like maple syrup," he said, his lips still touching hers.

"So do you, but that's what we're supposed to taste like. We're from Vermont. It's in our DNA."

He smiled down at her. "What're you doing today?"

"I need to hit the grocery store before dinner at my parents' house at three."

"Dinner is at three?"

"Every week. Why?"

"It's just kind of odd that your dad asked me to stop by there today—around three—to look at some acreage he wants me to clear for him."

"My dad called you and asked you to come on Sunday at three to look at trees?"

"Uh-huh."

"I don't believe it! They're out of control."

"Catch me up. Who's out of control?"

"My dad and my grandfather. They've been up to no good for a while now trying to get us all married off by interfering and butting into our lives."

"How do you mean?"

"Take Will and Cam, for example. They hired her to build the website hoping she'd fall for one of my brothers, and we all know how that worked out. They actually *messed* with Hannah's battery so Nolan would have to come to help her. Can you believe that? They sent poor Colton to a sex toy conference in New York so he'd be able to spend more time with Lucy. My grandpa bought the diner to keep Megan in town because Hunter was in love with her."

Gavin rocked with laughter. "They sent *Colton* to a *sex toy* conference? Seriously?"

"Yes! Totally serious! They're *crazy*!"

"Um, I hate to point out they're also crazy successful."

"And getting more brazen by the minute if they're inviting you to come to the house on 'business' at a time when they know I'll be there."

"So you think they know about us then? That something has been brewing?"

"Oh, they know. No doubt about it. They don't miss a thing. We had no idea how closely they pay attention until recently."

"What if we beat them at their own game?"

"How do you mean?"

"Invite me to dinner at your folks' house, Ella."

She studied him for a long moment before a smile stretched across her face. "Gavin, would you like to come to dinner at the Abbott asylum?"

"I'd love to. I thought you'd never ask."

CHAPTER 6

◆◆◆

Hope lies in dreams, in imagination,
and in the courage of those who dare
to make dreams into reality.

—Jonas Salk

Gavin went with her to the grocery store, where they picked out things they both liked for breakfast, lunch and dinner. More than once Ella wanted to fan her face just from having his extreme hotness close by, debating the merits of ham sandwiches versus turkey and wheat bread versus white. She let him win on the ham when she'd rather have turkey, but she refused to back down on the bread.

"You're thirty-four years old. There's no way you should still be eating white bread."

"Why not? I like it."

"It's bad for you. It's all flour and sugar and nothing much of anything else. You may as well be eating your sandwiches with cookies on either side of them."

"That actually sounds pretty good."

"Gavin," she said, laughing, "I'm serious!"

"Am I allowed to buy cookies? Because I do like my cookies."

"Only if you get some fruit, too."

"You're kinda mean, like my mom was when I lived at home."

Ella hip-checked him as they turned a corner, nearly sending him into the row of mac 'n' cheese.

Naturally, he zeroed right in on that. "Oh, I love orange cheese food. Can we get some of that?"

"Keep walking, Guthrie." Never had grocery shopping ever been this fun or romantic. Not once had she ever gotten giddy over bread or deli meat, but she had never bought enough for two either. This was happening. It was actually *happening*, and it was all Ella could do not to break out in song right there in the meat aisle, where Gavin was pondering the difference between two kinds of pork tenderloin.

"That one," Ella said, pointing.

"Are you going to cook this for me? Because you basically saw the outer limits of my culinary prowess this morning."

"I'll cook it for you." *I'd do anything for you*, she thought but didn't say. Dangerous thoughts. All the giddy hopefulness was messing with her better judgment where he was concerned. A tiger's stripes didn't suddenly change overnight, despite what the tiger would have you believe.

"What're we having with this tenderloin?" he asked, snapping her out of her grim thoughts.

"My grandmother used to make these baby potatoes that I love and her own applesauce."

"Am I drooling?" He pointed to his chin. "That's drool, right?"

"Attractive." They went back to the produce area to pick out the fruits and vegetables they needed.

Gavin got some bananas that met with her approval. "You're going to be a good mom someday, Ella."

She nearly buckled under the weight of that statement, coming from him of all people, the only man she could imagine fathering her imaginary children. On top of everything else that'd happened, it was almost too much to take in one twenty-four-hour period.

"El? Hello?"

"Um, oh, sorry. Those." She pointed to the apples she needed to make her grandmother's recipe.

"Was it something I said? About kids, perhaps?"

Ella shrugged, reluctant to let him see her emotional reaction to the subject of children. On their first official day together, he didn't need to know how she'd once dreamed of having a big family like her parents had. Now at thirty-one, she would be perfectly thrilled to have one baby.

"We need ice cream." She took off for the far end of the store without waiting for him. If they were going to talk about kids, she needed the kind of fortification only Ben and Jerry could provide.

Gavin caught up to her, reached around her and plucked a pint of Cherry Garcia from the cooler, dropping it into the basket. Then he went back and grabbed a container of Cake Batter for himself.

"You're like a twelve-year-old."

"Thank you."

"You would take that as a compliment," she said laughing.

"I was a cute twelve-year-old."

You're a cute thirty-four-year-old, too, she thought.

He trailed behind her as they headed for the checkout and nudged her aside when it came time to pay, sliding his card through the reader before she could reach for her wallet.

"I don't expect you to pay for my groceries."

"They're *our* groceries, and you can pay next week."

How could she argue with that? Even as her heart did a happy little leap at the mention of *next week*, his comment about kids and her future as a mother had popped Ella's giddy balloon, leaving her out of sorts and not at all sure what she had to be out of sorts about. It was a nice thing for him to say, and it wasn't his fault—entirely—that she didn't have kids yet when she'd always hoped to be a young mother.

But wasn't it his fault in a way? After all, she'd been waiting for him, whether actively or passively, for years. There'd been other guys. A few that might've been serious if the specter of Gavin Guthrie hadn't hung over everything, larger than life and exactly what her heart desired, even when he didn't seem to know she was alive.

No other man had a chance against the possibility of Gavin. How many times had she ended fledgling relationships with the words *It's not you, it's me*? And Gavin, she should've added, because he was always smack in the middle of her relationships even if he never met the guys she dated.

In the parking lot, Gavin loaded the bags into the back of his truck, which they'd retrieved from the biker bar, while Ella went around to the passenger side and got in. She watched him stow the cart in the corral before he got into the truck. For the longest time he sat there, looking straight ahead.

Ella was on the verge of saying something—she wasn't sure what—when he turned to her.

"Tell me what I did wrong in there."

She'd been unprepared for such a blunt question. "You . . . I . . ." *Jesus, Ella. Get it together.* "Nothing."

His eyes flashed with the starting of what might be anger. "Don't do that. Don't say it's nothing when it's clearly something. I told you I'd give this my all, Ella. You've got to do the same. You gotta meet me halfway."

He was right. She couldn't even try to deny that he was absolutely right. But how was she supposed to broach this particular subject on day one of the relationship she'd dreamed about having with him?

Reaching for her hand, he curled his fingers around hers. "Talk to me. I want to understand. I want to fix whatever I did."

"You didn't do anything. You struck a nerve that you didn't know was there."

"The kid thing is a nerve?"

She was on the verge of saying *sort of* or *kind of*, but that wasn't the truth. It wasn't what he deserved from her. "Yes."

"How come?"

In for a penny . . . "I used to think," she said with a sigh of resignation, "that I'd have a lot of kids, the way my mom and my aunt Hannah did."

To his credit, he didn't blanch or recoil or jump out of the truck in horror. Rather, he calmly said, "A lot, huh? Like ten?"

"Aunt Hannah only has eight."

"Not much difference between eight and ten."

"Most people only have two kids. They'd tell you that's a lot."

"Do you know that in all the years since Caleb died, neither of my parents has ever reminded me that I'm their only hope for grandchildren?"

"Oh," she said, caught off guard by the change in direction. "That's nice of them."

"My mom would be an awesome grandmother, don't you think?"

"They'd both be terrific, and you know Hannah's children will consider them grandparents."

"I do know that, and so do they. However, the continuation of the Guthrie name? It's all on me."

"That's a lot of pressure."

"They've never pressured me, but I'm aware of it. I don't want the Guthrie line to end with me."

"That's not a good enough reason to have kids."

"I know it isn't, and until recently, I've been too unsettled to even think about having a family. But now . . . Now, it doesn't seem so far off in the distant future."

"Now . . . What does that mean?"

"Now that there's an us and the possibility that you could be their mother—"

"Gavin, please. I have to stop you right there. It's way too soon for us to be having this conversation, and frankly, my fragile heart can't take it. I just can't allow myself to go there. Not yet."

"I'm sorry. I didn't mean to poke at a nerve or your fragile heart."

"You didn't do anything wrong, and I'm glad to know you aren't totally opposed to having kids someday, but I can't talk about that someday today."

"Fair enough." He started the truck and drove them back toward her place in town, where they'd dropped off her car on the way to the store.

They were quiet on the short ride, and Ella wished she could know what he was thinking. Her thoughts were all over the place, scattered and unorganized. He was saying—and doing—everything she could possibly want him to, but she was still wary. She wanted so badly to believe everything was possible for them, but until last night he'd not given her any reason to have one ounce of faith where he was concerned.

Hearing he could picture her as the mother of his children made her want to say to hell with caution and get busy making babies. More dangerous thoughts . . . She'd reined him in, but she needed to do the same to herself. Jumping ahead to someday wasn't wise when today required all her focus and attention.

Gavin followed her up the stairs to her apartment, each of them carrying grocery bags. This would be the first time he saw her home, and the thought of that made her oddly nervous.

She was so rattled she nearly dropped her keys. The door swung open and the scent of the sage candle she'd burned last night greeted them.

"Smells good in here," he said as he followed her into the kitchen in the back of the small apartment.

"My favorite sage candle." She loved being able to share even the simplest of things with him, such as her favorite scent and where she kept her cereal. Ella loved stashing his Cake Batter ice cream next to her Cherry Garcia. She loved knowing his favorite kind, and that he loved cookies, ham and white bread, as gross as that was.

Ella was reaching for the cabinet over the stove when his hands landed on her hips, making her forget what she'd been about to do.

He gathered her in close to him, his chin on her shoulder. "Sorry, but I couldn't stand to go another second without touching you."

She closed her eyes and focused on continuing to breathe as his nearness overwhelmed her.

"Did you need something up there?"

Gavin's question didn't compute until she realized he meant the cabinet. "I don't remember what I was doing."

His low rumble of laughter sent goose bumps down her arms and backbone. "How long do we have until we have to head to your parents' house?"

"About forty minutes."

He brushed aside her hair and began placing kisses on her neck that made her legs go weak under her. Fortunately, he had an arm locked around her waist to keep her from sliding to the floor. No man had ever had such an effect on her, and she was wise enough now to know that no other man ever would. He was it for her. He always had been, which was why the stakes were so high in this new game they were playing.

Then he was turning her and she couldn't spare the brain cells to think about the high stakes or the game. Not when Gavin Guthrie was apparently planning to kiss her. He moved slowly, cupping her face in big work-roughened hands and gazing into her eyes.

She wanted to kiss him—badly—but more than that she wanted to know his thoughts. "What're you thinking right now?"

"About how much I want to kiss you. I'm asking myself if this is real, if I really get to kiss Ella Abbott any time I want to. I'm wondering how I got lucky enough to have someone like you care so much about someone like me."

She curled her hands around his wrists and felt his pulse hammering under her fingers. "What does that mean? Someone like you? What's wrong with you?"

"Everything," he said softly. "Every freaking thing is wrong with me, but for the first time in a long-ass time, I want to make what's wrong about me right. For you."

Ella went up on tiptoes to join her lips to his. Like him, she couldn't believe she was now allowed to kiss him any time she wanted to. She was going to want to often. She hoped he was prepared for that. Judging by his enthusiastic response, he was more than prepared.

His hands slid down to cup her bottom, and then he was lifting her.

Ella curled her legs around his hips, bringing his hardness against her softness and drawing gasps of pleasure from both of them. Then he was lowering her to the sofa and coming down on top of her, all without losing a beat in the tongue-twisting kiss.

This kiss made the one they'd shared last summer at the beach in Burlington seem like child's play in comparison. She'd spent all the months since thinking she knew what it was like to kiss Gavin. She'd known nothing. The kiss on the beach had been just the start of what they were capable of together.

His hand slid under her sweater and came to rest on her ribs, making her skin burn under the heat of his palm. He broke the kiss, looking down at her as if to gauge her reaction. Then he pulled back, taking his nice warm hand with him.

"I'm sorry."

Ella covered her face with her hands.

He tugged on them until she gave way. "What did I do this time?"

"You stopped!"

"Because we have somewhere to be."

She glanced at the clock on her cable box. "In thirty minutes."

"That's not enough time for what was going to happen on this sofa if I hadn't stopped when I did."

Her heart beat erratically. "What was going to happen?"

"Clothes were going to start coming off." He leaned in to tug on her sweater. "Starting with yours." His lips were swollen from kissing her, his jaw was covered in stubble, and brown plaid flannel had never been so sexy. She could lie there staring at him until tomorrow morning, and it wouldn't be long enough to absorb the fact that Gavin was sitting on her sofa looking at her like he wanted to eat her up.

Not that she would say no to that . . .

"Quit looking at me like that," he said gruffly.

"How am I looking at you?"

"You know. I'm trying to be honorable by not jumping you the first chance I get, and you're lying there looking all sultry and sexy."

"Am I?"

"Ella! Stop it."

"I'm not doing anything."

"You're breathing. That's enough for me."

"I keep thinking I'm going to wake up, and it's going to be Saturday night and my Cherry Garcia would've melted during the time I had this amazing dream about sleeping with Gavin and grocery shopping with him and making out with him."

"You're not dreaming, and neither am I. For the first time in a very long time, I'm having a really good day, and it's all because of you."

"Thank you."

"Do not thank me. All the thanks goes to you, my little bulldog."

"Um, is that supposed to be a compliment?"

"Yep. You were tenacious like a bulldog, never letting me get away with anything and calling me out on my shit. You have no idea how much I needed someone to do that."

"I'm glad I helped, but let's retire the bulldog analogy."

Smiling, he tugged on her hand. "Let's get going to your parents' place so I can talk to your dad about the work he wants done before dinner."

Reluctantly, Ella let him help her up, but she wished they had nowhere to be so they could continue with the kissing. The kissing was good. Very, very good.

"Is it okay with your mom if I come to dinner?"

"Oh yeah. She makes enough to feed an army every week. I think my aunt Hannah and cousin Grayson will be there today, too. I heard he was in town visiting his mom this weekend."

"I haven't seen him in years. He's in Boston, right?"

"Uh-huh."

"Did he ever get married?"

Ella pushed her feet into the moccasins that had fallen off

when he carried her to the sofa. "Nope, but you can hardly blame him after what he went through with his parents."

"No kidding."

Ella's uncle Mike had walked away from his wife and eight children when the older kids were in high school and the youngest ones still in elementary school. "A lot fell to Gray as the oldest. He really stepped up for his mom and siblings. He probably has zero desire to have his own family after all that."

"Do they ever hear from their father?"

"Occasionally, but it's nothing regular."

"Can you imagine a man leaving his wife and children like that?"

"No man I know would do something like that, but then again, we never thought Uncle Mike would either. He loved family life and his kids and Hannah. They were a true love match, or so we thought."

Gavin held her coat for her before donning his own coat. "Did you ever find out what went wrong?"

"Not really. My mom suspects he had some sort of break-down or something happened with his job. But I've never heard the full story. I don't know if even my mom has heard the whole thing, and Hannah is her sister."

"And Hannah never remarried?"

"To be honest, I don't think they ever got divorced."

"Wow, and how many years ago was this?"

"Well, let's see, Gray is the same age as Hunter and Hannah, and they're going to be thirty-six in December, so almost twenty years ago, I'd say."

"Twenty years. How's it getting to be almost twenty years out of high school for us?"

"Don't say *us*. I'm quite a bit younger than you."

"Ha-ha," he retorted. "Only a few years."

"I've only been out of high school thirteen years, so speak for yourself."

"I'm at seventeen, so not a geezer quite yet."

"But getting closer every day."

Laughing, he said, "You're full of beans today, Ella. I like you that way."

"Got to keep you on your toes."

"That you do." He held the passenger door to his truck for her and then leaned in to kiss her as he belted her in. "Kissing you is becoming my favorite thing to do."

Ella ran her hand over the delicious stubble on his jaw. "Mine, too."

He kissed her again. "To be continued. Later."

"Can't wait."

"Mmm," he said, his lips vibrating against hers, "me either." He pulled away reluctantly, or so it seemed to her.

She watched him walk around the front of the truck and get into the driver's side. It was such a strange feeling to be free to look at him any way she wanted, to let him see the full extent of her desire for him, to not have to hide it anymore the way she had for so long.

He backed out of her driveway and headed in the direction of her parents' home. His hand found hers on the seat, and the brush of his skin against hers was all it took to set off a reaction that registered in all her most important places.

Good God . . . She had to get it together before she forgot her plans to be cautious, to take this slowly, to protect her heart. If all he had to do to make her forget about being careful was hold her hand, she was in bigger trouble than she'd thought.

After a quiet ride through Butler, they pulled into her parents' driveway and their yellow labs, George and Ringo, came bounding across the yard to greet them. Ella got out of the truck and bent to give each dog some love. She couldn't wait to have a home of her own someday so she could have dogs again. They'd always had dogs—all of them named John, Paul, George or Ringo—and Ella missed having pets, but that was the one thing her landlord didn't allow.

"Where's Mom and Dad?" she asked the dogs.

George barked and darted toward the house. The dogs rarely left her father's side, so she took George's word for it and followed her inside. Yes, George was a girl. It didn't matter to Ella's dad whether the dogs were male or female. They were all named after his favorite band of all time. He was a little over the top when it came to the Beatles, but his children indulged his obsession after being weaned on Beatles tunes growing up.

In the mudroom, Ella hung her coat and Gavin's on the hook with her name on it. Will's hook was to the left of hers and Charley's to the right. The symbolic act of hanging Gavin's coat on top of hers made Ella's belly quiver with excitement and joy before she remembered that she was trying not to get ahead of herself. Whatever. What was that old saying about once the genie gets outside the bottle there's no putting her back in? That about summed up her situation with Gavin. The genie was so far out of the bottle she'd never get back in at this rate.

Smiling, she glanced at Gavin and reached for his hand to lead him into the kitchen, where her mom was standing watch over something on the stove, and her dad was standing watch over her mom, hands on her hips, head tilted forward, saying something in her ear that was making Molly giggle madly.

I want that, Ella thought. *To be married nearly forty years and still be giggling with the man I love.* She cleared her throat. Loudly.

Lincoln Abbott turned, his face lighting up with pleasure at the sight of her and then zeroing right in on the fact that she was holding hands with Gavin Guthrie. "Hey, El, Gavin. Look, Molly, Ella's brought Gavin."

Molly turned down the heat under the pot on the stove and turned to hug and kiss both of them. "This is a nice surprise, Gavin."

"Hope you don't mind me crashing Sunday dinner."

"Of course not. You're always welcome here. You know that."

"Thanks, Molly."

Molly took a good long look at Ella before she enveloped her in a hug. "Keeping secrets, my love?" she whispered for Ella's ear only.

Ella pulled back and smiled at her mom.

"Do we have a few minutes before dinner, Mol?" Lincoln asked.

"About twenty."

"Let's go look at those trees then, Gavin."

"Sure thing." He squeezed Ella's shoulder and then followed her dad to the mudroom.

Ella watched them go, focusing in on the excellent fit of Gavin's faded Levi's jeans. Yum.

"Ahem," Molly said the moment the door closed behind the men and dogs. "Something you want to tell me?"

"There's been a bit of a development."

"So I see." Molly checked the pots on the stove and then returned her attention to Ella. "Care to share?"

"He . . . We . . . We're giving it a whirl."

"Well, that's a huge development. What brought this on?"

"It's been kinda happening for a while now."

"I'd noticed that, but I wondered if it was somewhat one-sided."

"It's not one-sided."

"Oh no?"

"No."

Molly wiped her hands on a dish towel that she had tossed over her shoulder. "May I speak freely?"

"When have you ever not spoken freely?"

"When what I have to say might hurt one of my precious children. I tend to be a little more circumspect in those situations."

"Whatever it is, just say it."

"You know I love Gavin. I love him as much as I loved Caleb, and as much as I love Bob and Amelia. The Guthries are family to us."

"I know."

"That said, I worry about whether Gavin is in the right place, emotionally, to be what you need."

"He's well aware of his issues, Mom. I'm well aware of them. We're working through them together."

"As of when?"

"Last night."

Molly folded her arms and leaned back against the counter. "What happened last night?"

Ella debated whether she should tell her mother the whole story. "He had a situation . . . And, apparently, I was listed in his phone as his 'in case of emergency' contact, so they called me. I went there—"

"Where is there?"

"A place called Red's."

"The biker bar on 114?"

"Yeah."

"Eleanor Abbott! Are you telling me you went, *alone*, to a biker bar on a Saturday night to bail him out of yet another scrape?"

"He was there." Ellie was determined not to squirm. "I wasn't alone."

"Honestly. And he condoned this?"

"He didn't know they were calling me."

"I don't like this. Not one bit. Is this how it's going to be? You bailing him out of 'scrapes' in bars?"

"No, that's not how it's going to be. He's determined to turn things around and to make a go of it with me."

"What if he can't turn things around? What if he only wishes he could and you get swept up in the mess he's been making of his life lately?"

"I don't know, Mom! I don't know what's going to happen or if he's going to be able to be what I want and need. What I do know is that I've wanted a real, legitimate chance with him for years, and now that I finally have one, I'm not going to squander it by worrying about what *might* happen."

"I don't want you to get hurt, Ella."

"I don't want that either, but I refuse to spend the rest of my life wondering what could've been because I was so afraid to get hurt that I didn't even try." She swiped at her face, angered by the tears that wet her cheeks. Why was she crying?

Molly drew her into a hug. "Sweetheart, listen to me. No one wants you to be happy more than I do. I know how much

you care for him. Anyone can see that. It's just that he . . .
Well, you may not be able to fix what's broken inside him,
sweet girl."

"I can at least try, can't I?"

"Of course you can. I just want you to be careful to protect yourself, and I don't want you going to biker bars alone.
You got me?"

"I'm thirty-one years old, Mom. If I want to go to a biker
bar, alone or otherwise, I will."

"I don't care if you're thirty-one or a hundred and one,
you're still my baby."

"You're planning to stick around until I'm a hundred and
one, aren't you?"

"You bet I am. This family would go to hell in a handbasket
without me."

"That's the truth." Eager to change the subject, Ella said,
"What's for dinner?"

"Roasted chicken and all the fixings."

"Sounds good. What can I do to help?"

With the dogs running ahead of them, Gavin walked with
Lincoln across the yard to the tree line.

"Couldn't help but notice you happened to be holding my
little girl's hand when you came into the house."

Whoa, Gavin thought, *we're going to dive right into it,
are we?* "Yes, I was. She's got very nice hands."

"Everything about her is nice."

"Yes, it is."

"She's far too good for you."

"I'm aware of that."

"Heard you got arrested a couple of months ago. Any
truth to that?"

"Yes, sir. I got into a fight with a guy in a bar who said we'd
wasted our time in Iraq."

"Huh. Well, I hope you punched his lights out."

"I did. Mr. Abbott—"

"Since when am I *Mr.* Abbott?"

"Since I started dating your daughter. Sir." Gavin stopped walking and turned to face Lincoln. "I want you to know that I care about her. I have for a long time, but it was never the right time."

"And now is the right time?"

"I don't know. What I do know is I can't fight what I feel for her anymore. I'm tired of fighting, in more ways than one. I can't go on the way I've been."

"So you're looking to my daughter to fix what's wrong in your life?"

"No. I'd never do that to her. What you said about her being too good for me. You're absolutely right. She's too good for most guys. But she makes me want to be good for her. She makes me want to be a better man so I'll deserve her."

"Not much I can say to that except ask you to take care of her."

"I will." Gavin was determined not to screw this up, which was actually a huge improvement over the months he'd spent not giving a shit about much of anything. He'd been going along, doing his thing, running his business, keeping his head down and soldiering on even though the pain of his loss was always with him. Then Caleb's dog died. Good old Homer. He'd been part of so many of their adventures that losing him had been like losing Caleb all over again.

"Let me show you the trees I want to get rid of," Lincoln said. "I'd like to turn them into firewood. I could use some of it here and send the rest up the mountain to Colton."

"We can do that for you."

They trudged deeper into the dense vegetation, where the height of the trees blocked the sunlight.

"I'm going to be keeping an eye on this situation with you and Ella. Just thought I should let you know that. You're a good man, Gavin, and I think you might even be worthy of my little girl. But you're going to have to prove that to me—and to others who'll be watching, too."

"I understand." If Ella had been his daughter, and she was getting involved with the likes of him, he'd be concerned, too. But now Gavin had one more reason to make sure he did right by her. He liked and respected Lincoln Abbott. Letting him down was the last thing he wanted to do.

Ella helped her mother finish the dinner preparations and was setting the table when Hannah and Nolan arrived. Hannah's baby bump was becoming more pronounced by the day, and her sister fairly glowed with happiness and excitement. It was nice to see after so many years of wondering if Hannah would ever bounce back from losing Caleb.

Nolan was perfect for her in every way and was obviously crazy in love with Hannah. Her sister deserved nothing less after all she'd been through.

"How's it going?" Hannah asked when she came into the dining room to help Ella.

"I'm good. How're you feeling?"

"Much better now that I'm not puking all day. Once in the morning, and that's that."

"I'm glad you're feeling better."

"Me, too. Now I can really enjoy being pregnant."

Ella was struck by a pang of envy that made her feel ridiculous, especially in light of her conversation with Gavin about kids. It had taken a lot for her to admit to him that she'd once hoped to have a big family. That didn't seem to be in the cards for her anymore, but that didn't give her the right to be envious of her sister.

"I happened to notice Gavin's truck in the yard."

"He's outside with Dad."

"I didn't see your car, and yet here you are. Which leads me to wonder if you came with Gavin."

"Maybe I did."

"Something you want to tell me?"

"Not if you're going to tell me all the reasons it's a bad idea."

"I won't do that."

"Promise?"

"Yes, Ella," Hannah said, smiling. "I promise."

"We're . . . giving it a try, I guess you might say."

"I'm happy for you. I know that's what you've wanted for a long time."

"Yes, it is."

"The only thing I'll say . . ."

"Ugh, I knew you'd have *something* to say."

"Just be careful, El. That's all. I don't want to see you hurt."

"Does anyone think *I* want that? Honestly?"

"No, but . . . Sometimes love is blind. This is no time to put blinders on."

"I know that. My eyes are wide open where he's concerned. I've seen him at his best—and his worst."

"I'm not sure that you have seen his worst."

Ella wanted to ask her sister what she meant by that, but more than anything she wanted out of this conversation before Gavin returned. "You've done your job as the big sister. You've warned me."

"Ella—"

"How's the new house? All moved in and settled?"

Hannah hesitated before she took the hint that Ella wasn't willing to talk about Gavin anymore. "Getting there. We're setting up the baby's room this week."

"Did you decide on your colors?"

"Since we're not finding out what we're having, we're going with yellow and beige."

"That'll be nice. Did you fill out the registry yet?"

"Last night. It's so hard to decide on everything."

"Make sure you send me the link so we have it when we throw your *surprise* baby shower."

Hannah laughed. "I'll do that." She finished placing cloth napkins at each place on the long dining room table. "Hey, El?"

"Yeah?"

"I only said what I did because I love you so much. I love him, too. I'll be pulling for you guys to make it work, and you know where to find me if I can help at all."

"Thank you," she said, genuinely touched by Hannah's love and concern.

The rest of the family began arriving a short time later, filling the house with noise and chaos that was reminiscent of when they'd all lived at home. Noise was the one thing Ella remembered most vividly from those days. It was happy chaos, but chaotic nonetheless.

She looked forward to seeing everyone at their weekly Sunday dinners but was always happy to go home alone to her quiet apartment. Gavin's hand on her shoulder was a reminder that this week she wouldn't be going home alone. She smiled up at him. "How was your walk with Dad?"

"Interesting." He leaned in closer to her. "I'll tell you about it later."

Ella wanted to purr from the satisfaction of knowing they'd have time alone together later to talk, among other things. Her sister Charley came into the kitchen, her eyes widening when she saw Gavin standing so close to Ella.

Charley and Hannah were the only two who knew how much Ella had suffered over Gavin, so Charley's wide smile was a welcome relief.

"Hey, guys," she said. "Gavin, nice to see you here."

"Nice to be here."

"Someone has been keeping secrets from her sister."

"It's a relatively new development," Ella said, leaning into Gavin because she could.

"I'll expect a full report at work tomorrow, if not before."

"I see how this is going to be," Gavin said, his tone inflected with amusement.

"You have no idea," Charley said before moving on to greet her parents.

"She scares me," Gavin whispered.

"She scares all of us."

That made him laugh, and Ella discovered that she quite liked the sound of laughter coming from him when he was usually so somber. He hadn't had a lot to laugh about lately. She would make sure he had plenty to laugh about going forward.

Elmer Stillman came in, his face red from the chill of the mid-November air, his smile stretching from ear to ear as usual. No one loved Sunday dinner more than Ella's grandfather did. The tradition had begun with him and his wife, Sarah, and their daughter Molly had carried it on after her mother died.

"I brought wine," Elmer said. "One of every kind."

Molly greeted her father with a kiss to his cheek. "Thanks, Dad."

"Hey, Gramps," Ella said, returning his hug and kiss. "How are you?"

"I'm wonderful, and you?" He eyed Gavin suspiciously, and that was when Ella knew for certain that he too was fully aware of her ongoing affection for Gavin.

"I'm fantastic."

"Gavin." Elmer extended his hand.

Gavin shook hands with him. "Mr. Stillman."

"Elmer. 'Mr. Stillman' makes me feel old."

"We can't have that," Gavin said.

"No, we can't. Nice to have you here."

"Nice to be here."

Ella's aunt Hannah and cousin Grayson Coleman came into the kitchen next. Hannah closely resembled Ella's mother, but Aunt Hannah wore an air of bitterness about her that anyone who knew her well could plainly see. According to Molly, Hannah had never gotten over the heartbreak of her husband leaving her alone to raise eight children. Who could blame her?

Grayson was as handsome and polished as ever. His dark blond hair was neatly trimmed, and he wore a white dress shirt under a navy V-neck sweater that looked like cashmere. He'd done well for himself as a lawyer in Boston, but Ella wondered if he was truly happy.

He hugged her and shook Gavin's hand. "Long time no see, Gavin."

"We missed you at Will's wedding," Ella said.

"I hated to miss it," Gray said. "I was in Europe for work, and there was no way I could get out of it. They didn't give us much of a heads-up before they got married."

"No, they didn't."

"Speak of the devils," Gavin said as the newlyweds came in wearing the big smiles that never seemed to dim now that they were officially married. They were so, so happy.

Ella adored her new sister-in-law, who fit right in with the Abbotts like they'd known her forever.

After they greeted Will and Cameron, Nolan came over to them and shook hands with Gavin. "What brings you to dinner?"

Gavin nodded his head toward Ella. "I was invited."

Nolan looked from Gavin to Ella and then back to Gavin again. "Oh. *Oh!* Wow, well, that's cool."

Ella laughed at her new brother-in-law's lightbulb moment.

"Hey, did you get the invite to Dylan's wedding in Turks later this month?" Nolan asked Gavin.

"Yeah, I got it. Are you going?"

"I don't think we should, but Hannah wants to go."

"She's not even six months pregnant, Nolan," Ella said. "She can still travel for a couple of months yet."

"But is it safe? What if something happens while we're there?"

Ella pinched her lips together to keep from laughing in his face.

Nolan scowled at her. "I can see you trying not to laugh."

"Take your wife to the Caribbean, Nolan. Have a second honeymoon. Your lives are about to get crazy. Take the time for yourselves while you can."

"What she said," Gavin said, pointing to Ella.

"Are you going?" Nolan asked Gavin.

"Probably not. Hard to get away from work." To Ella, he said, "I'm going to hit the bathroom. Be right back."

After he walked away, Nolan lowered his voice and said, "He never goes to Sultans things anymore unless they're here. Austin and Debra's wedding was the one exception, but that was because he had to go as the best man."

"Why do you suppose he doesn't go?"

"I think it's too hard for him without Caleb. He thinks of them as Caleb's friends, but they're his friends, too. Every bit as much his as they were Caleb's."

"I'll talk to him and see if I can convince him to go."

"That would be good. He always has fun when he's with them, but he's been weird about it since Caleb died. It would mean a lot to Dylan to have him there."

Ella's youngest brother, Max, came into the kitchen, looking tense and out of sorts.

"Hey." Molly smiled up at her son as he kissed her cheek. "What're you doing here? Thought you were spending the weekend in Burlington."

"Yeah, so did I. Don't ask." He grabbed a roll from a basket Molly was filling and continued through the kitchen to the dining room.

"What's up with him?" Ella asked her mom.

"Trouble in paradise with Chloe, apparently," Molly said, her brows knitting with concern. "I'm surprised he's here with the baby due any minute."

"He told me last week she doesn't want him around," Nolan said quietly.

Molly pounced on her son-in-law. "When did he tell you that?"

"When he brought his car into the garage for an oil change."

"Oh Lord," Molly said with a sigh. "The poor guy. This has to be eating him up inside."

Ella felt for her brother, who would soon become a father. He and his girlfriend, Chloe, hadn't been together long when she got pregnant. Max had tried to stand by her during the last few months, but Chloe hadn't made it easy.

Gavin returned to the kitchen and came over to her. "What's up with Max? He seems kinda wound up."

"Troubles with the baby mama, apparently."

"Oh damn. That's too bad."

Lucas and Landon came into the kitchen, pushing and shoving each other the way they had since the day they were born. They always brought the comedy with them, and Ella adored them, even if she wanted to knock their heads together half the time.

"Knock it off, you two," Molly said sternly.

"We haven't even done anything yet," Landon said.

"Preemptive strike," Molly replied. "It's only a matter of time before you do *something*."

"We are so misunderstood," Lucas said to his twin.

"Seriously."

"You are absolutely understood," Ella said, "which is why Mom feels the need for preemptive strikes."

"And here we thought you were on our side, El," Lucas said. "You're one of the nice ones. Usually."

Gavin laughed when her charming brothers planted kisses on their mother's cheeks.

"Hi, Mom," Lucas said with a shit-eating grin.

"Get out of here, the two of you, before I break out the rubber spatula," Molly said, smiling despite herself.

The threat sent the twins scurrying toward the dining room.

Ella's brother Wade came in, dropping a kiss on her forehead and then shaking hands with Gavin. "What brings you to dinner?" Wade asked.

"Ella did."

"Oh. Is that right?"

"Uh-huh." Ella gave Wade a little shove. "Now mind your own business and move along."

"I'm an Abbott. Since when do we mind only our own business?"

"Wade . . . I expect better from you than the rest of the clowns." He was the one brother who'd never pulled her hair or deliberately tried to rile her.

"All right. When you put it that way . . ."

Colton and Lucy arrived a few minutes later with Hunter and Megan in tow.

"Everyone's here," Molly said. "Let's eat!"

CHAPTER 7

——◆——

Time takes away the grief of men.

—Desiderius Erasmus

While everyone enjoyed the delicious roast chicken dinner, Landon stood and cleared his throat. "'Tis the season you look forward to all year long." He unfurled a scroll of paper. "Sign-ups to work at the Christmas tree farm!"

A chorus of groans and boos followed his announcement.

"Now, now. You can't fool me. I know you all love working at the farm every year, so don't be shy. Sign up now and sign up often. Boys, I need you cutting trees and dragging them to cars. Ladies, I need you selling cider, hot chocolate and donuts and collecting money. You know the drill."

"What if I want to cut the trees rather than dole out cider?" Charley asked.

"Whatever you want to do is fine with me, stud," Landon replied, "as long as you sign up for something. I need everyone to take at least three shifts over the next few weekends. Max, you're exempted this year due to the baby watch."

"Thanks. I'll fill in when I can."

"That's so not fair," Lucas said. "Why does he get to be exempt? I need to have a baby."

"Please for the love of God and the sake of the imaginary

child, do *not* do that," Lincoln said, making everyone laugh. Pointing to Landon, he said, "And don't you either."

Scowling at his father, Landon sent the sign-up sheet around the table with a pen.

Ella signed up to spend three Saturday afternoons working the hot chocolate stand, which was secretly one of her favorite things to do this time of year. She absolutely loved the Christmas season in the store and at the farm, so while the others grumbled, she happily put her name on the list.

"I'll take a few shifts," Gavin said. "I'm rather good at cutting down trees."

"That's the attitude I'm looking for," Landon said. "And he's not even *required* to work."

"Suck-up," Hunter grumbled.

"*Total* suck-up," Will said.

Gavin laughed at their good-natured teasing.

Ella smiled at Gavin and then watched him sign up for the same days she had picked. She had purposely avoided Thanksgiving weekend in the hope that she could talk him into going to his friend's wedding.

"I can't work any Saturdays in December," Charley said. "I'm in training."

"Oh thank God!" Colton said. "Someone is finally house-training her." The others howled with laughter.

"Very funny, but I'll have you know I'm in training to run a *marathon*."

"You are not," Ella said.

"Yes, I am."

"You haven't run since high school."

"I've been wanting to get back into it, so I joined a club and we do distance runs on Saturdays. We did six miles yesterday."

"I think that's wonderful, Charley," Elmer said. "Good for you."

"Thanks, Gramps."

"We've got plenty of Sundays you can take," Landon said to Charley.

"Let me see that sign-up sheet," Elmer said. "I can still cut trees with you whippersnappers."

"Gramps," Landon said, glancing at Molly. "You don't have to."

"Don't give me that nonsense," Elmer said. "I've been cutting Christmas trees since before you were a glimmer on the horizon."

"Still," Landon said, "we've got plenty of guys to do the heavy lifting. I could use someone to play Santa, if you're up for that."

"I'd rather cut trees. Let Linc play Santa. He loves that gig."

"Mom," Landon said. "Do something about him."

"What would you have me do? Tell my father he's too old to be cutting Christmas trees? I think I'll pass on that."

Her sister Hannah laughed. "Don't blame you, sis."

"I raised smart girls," Elmer said with a smile for his daughters. "They know not to cross their dear old dad."

"I'll take a couple of shifts," Grayson said, surprising them all.

"You don't have to, Gray," Landon said. "It's a pain for you, living in Boston and everything."

"I'm hoping to spend more time up here in the next few months, so I'm happy to help out."

"I won't say no to that," Landon said. "Give the man the form. It's the hap-happiest time of the year!"

"Speaking of the happiest time of the year," Ella said, "don't anyone forget the staff retreat next Friday night."

More grumbling followed her announcement.

"Why do you guys still complain when we do this every year before the holiday shopping season begins in earnest?" Ella asked.

"Because," Lucas said, "you make us give up a Friday night to hang out with the ladies from the store. Not that I don't like the ladies from the store, but they're not exactly my target audience."

"We have some new *young* ladies working the floor," Ella said. "You might be pleasantly surprised."

"New young ladies in Butler?" Landon asked, perking up. "How do we not know about this development?"

Max got up from the table, plate in hand. "I need to get back to Burlington." He leaned over to kiss his mother's cheek. "Thanks for dinner, Mom."

"Of course, sweetheart. Keep us posted?"

"I will. See you all later."

"Bye, Max," the others said.

After the storm door closed behind him, everyone looked to Molly.

"What's going on with him, Mom?" Colton asked. "He's gone completely silent on me at work on the mountain. I don't know what to do with him."

"I don't know for sure, but I think he and Chloe have broken up, and they're going to have to make some tough decisions after the baby arrives."

"Oh damn," Hunter said. "That's a tough one."

"I know I don't have to tell you all that he's going to need our support in the next few weeks. Will, I'd like you to try to talk to him if you would. He's always turned to you in times of trouble, and maybe he'd find it easier to talk to you."

"Sure, Mom. I'll do what I can."

"No matter what happens, we need to make sure he knows he's not alone in this."

"Of course he's not alone," Charley said. "When have any of us had the good fortune of being alone with a difficult situation?"

Her cheeky question made the others laugh.

Molly served two kinds of pie for dessert, and then everyone pitched in to help clean up. Well, the boys pretended to pitch in, ensuring they were more trouble than they were worth so that Molly would shoo them from the kitchen the way she did every week.

"We need to get their gig," Charley said when it was down to her, Molly, Ella, their sister Hannah and their aunt Hannah in the kitchen.

"Seriously," Ella said. "They've got it made."

"I don't know if I'd rather come back in my next life as a man or a well-kept dog," Molly said. "Not sure which has it better."

"A man," the women said in chorus.

After almost everyone had cleared out after dinner, leaving only Elmer, Molly's sister Hannah and her son Grayson, Lincoln invited Elmer and Gray to have a drink in his study so Molly could have some time with her sister.

"That's where he keeps the good stuff," Elmer said to his grandson.

"Well, let's go then."

"Bourbon?" Linc asked after he stoked the fire in the hearth.

"You know I won't say no to that," Elmer said.

"Me either," Gray said.

"Still feels funny to be pouring bourbon for kids we raised," Lincoln said to his father-in-law.

"That it does," Elmer replied. "Wait until you're pouring for the second generation of kids you raised."

"I'm still trying to get my head around becoming a grandfather any day now." Lincoln delivered drinks to both men and then went back for his before joining them in the seating area in front of the fire.

"Here's to becoming a grandfather," Elmer said, raising his glass to Grayson, his oldest grandchild. "One of the best days of my life."

"Thanks, Gramps." Grayson raised his glass to his grandfather. "I only beat Hunter and Hannah by a month."

"Got in right under the wire. That was such a happy time for Sarah and me—three grandbabies in one month. And now, I'm gonna be a great-grandfather thanks to my youngest grandchild. How's that for funny?"

"You never know what's going to happen," Grayson said, swirling the bourbon around in his glass.

Lincoln took note of the pensive expression on his nephew's

face. "Something on your mind, son?" He'd taken a special interest in Grayson and his siblings after their father left. Elmer had, too. They'd done what they could to fill a void that could never really be filled.

"I've been considering some life changes," Grayson said.

"What kind of changes?" Elmer asked.

"I worked for years to make partner in the firm," Grayson said.

"And you know how proud we are of that," Elmer said.

"He never misses a chance to tell people that you're a partner in a big Boston law firm," Lincoln added.

Grayson smiled at his grandfather. "Means a lot that you guys are proud. Thanks for that."

"You've earned everything the old-fashioned way," Elmer said. "Through hard work and determination. I admire that greatly."

"Which makes it that much harder to tell you I'm thinking about leaving the firm."

"How come?" Lincoln asked. "Thought you loved that place."

"I do. I did. It's just . . . Ever since I made partner, I seem to have lost my drive or something. I feel like I'm going through the motions. And one thing hasn't changed—all I do is work. Nonstop. Then I turned thirty-six last week, and one of my colleagues made a joke about how thirty-six is the 'this side of forty rather than that side of thirty' birthday. He was kidding, but it struck home. I'm going to be *forty* in four short years. I'm spending my entire adult life in an office, slaving away doing stuff I don't even care about most of the time."

"So what would you rather be doing?" Lincoln asked.

"That's just it. I'm not sure. I only know I don't want to be where I am anymore."

"Have you thought about coming home and hanging out a shingle?" Elmer asked.

"It's crossed my mind."

"You won't make bank like you do in Boston, but there's a genuine need here for a lawyer," Lincoln said. "Closest one is over in St. Johnsbury. Butler could use its own general counsel, if you ask me."

"I've been sort of toying with that idea. Mom also told me the town will soon be taking applications for town solicitor. I wouldn't mind doing that and working with Mom, too." Hannah Coleman had been the Butler town clerk for more than thirty years.

"That'd be a nice steady gig on top of the other work you'd be sure to get," Elmer said. "You'd bring the family business account home with you, of course."

"Yeah," Gray said. "I've always made it clear that account is mine whether I'm with the firm or not. They know that."

"We've got a lot going on with the acquisition of the new acreage up on the mountain and the new website about to go live, and now there's rumblings of a catalog and distribution center," Lincoln said. "We'll keep you busy."

"Who's rumbling about a catalog and distribution center?" Elmer asked.

"I'm going to be after the first of the year," Lincoln said with a cheeky grin.

Elmer chuckled. "Can't wait to see what the kids have to say to that."

"I got them to buy into the website, didn't I?"

"With a lot of help from your new daughter-in-law." For Grayson's benefit, Elmer added, "It's mighty hard to say no to Cameron when she's got a big idea."

"I'm hoping she'll be on my side with the catalog," Lincoln said. "If she's all for it, Will would be, too."

"You guys are a couple of old schemers," Grayson said, laughing at their back-and-forth.

"You have no idea," Lincoln said with a smile for his father-in-law.

"No idea at all," Elmer said. "But it sure will be nice to have you back in town, Gray."

"It'll be good to be home."

Hannah came to the door looking for her son. "What're you guys feeding my boy?"

"Bourbon and bullshit," Lincoln said, making the other men laugh.

"You ready to go, Mom?"

"Whenever you are."

"Some of us have to work tomorrow," Hannah said, "and you've got a long ride back to Boston."

"Yeah," Gray said, seeming depressed by the idea of that long ride. "I do."

Lincoln and Elmer stood to hug them both.

Elmer patted his grandson's face. "Keep us posted."

"I will. Thanks for this. It helped."

"We're always right here."

"Thanks, Gramps. I'll see you all soon."

"We'll be here," Lincoln said.

They kissed Hannah good night and then returned to their spots in front of the fire.

"That boy is in pain," Elmer said.

"I thought the same thing."

"There's more to this than unhappiness at work."

"Wasn't he seeing someone for a while there?" Elmer asked.

"I thought so. I'll see what Hunter knows. They're tight."

"We're going to want to keep an eye on our Grayson."

"You read my mind."

Driving back to Ella's place, Gavin thought about her family and how they were always fun to be around. The joking, the good-natured teasing, the obvious love they had for each other combined to give Gavin a sense of well-being that had been sorely lacking in his life of late. There was something about the Abbotts. You couldn't help but be sucked in by them, in the best possible way.

"Thanks for signing up to help at the tree farm," Ella said. "You didn't have to do that."

"I know I didn't. It sounds fun, though, and you'll be there, so it can't be all bad."

She smiled, but he couldn't help but notice she seemed troubled by something.

"Everything okay?"

"Sure," she said. "Why do you ask?"

"I don't know. You seem . . . off . . . since we left your parents' place."

She had no reply to that, which set his nerves on edge. What could've happened in the time they spent with her family? He supposed she'd tell him if she wanted to. It amazed him to realize how badly he wanted to be privy to her thoughts. Was she happy? Was she worried? Did she regret taking him to dinner? Had someone warned her away from him? That wouldn't surprise him. It wasn't like he didn't deserve to come with a warning label attached to him—*may be hazardous to your health and emotional well-being.*

As he pulled up to Ella's house and parked behind her car, it occurred to him that having his truck here all night would be equivalent to telling the town of Butler they were sleeping together. "I'm going to run home for a minute, but I'll be right back. If you still want me."

"Yes, I still want you. Hurry back."

He leaned over to kiss her. "I will." Gavin waited until she was inside before he pulled out of her driveway and headed home. Once there, he packed a bag with a change of clothes and his toothbrush and was heading for the door when the house phone rang. He took the call from his mother.

"Hey, Mom."

"Hi, honey. How are you?"

"I'm good. You?"

"Busy with the inn, but we're enjoying it."

Running the inn that Hannah had opened for war widows had given his parents a new purpose that they'd badly needed. "Glad to hear it's going well."

"Dad and I were saying tonight it's been weeks since the three of us had dinner. Want to come tomorrow night? I'll make ribs for you."

"Mmm, ribs." Even though he'd just eaten a huge meal, his mouth watered at the thought of his mother's ribs. "You know how to get my attention."

"Yes, I do."

"Could I bring a friend?"

His question was met with dead silence on the other end of the line.

"Mom?"

"A female friend?" The hope he heard in her voice was like a punch to the gut, making him realize how little reason he'd given her to be hopeful where he was concerned.

"Yes, a female friend."

"Of course you can bring her. Anyone we know?"

"You know her."

"That's it? That's all I'm getting?"

"Until tomorrow."

"Gavin, come on! You can't leave me hanging for twenty-four hours."

"It'll be here before you know it," he said, smiling. He'd smiled more today than he had in years.

"This is just mean."

That made him laugh. "Patience, Mother."

"Is this . . . Is it something serious?"

"Could be. It's new, so don't get too excited just yet."

"I'm already excited that you like her enough to bring her here."

"I like her a lot. I have for a long time."

"Gavin Michael Guthrie! You are *torturing* your mother!"

His dad chimed in from the extension. "Hey, Gav, why are you torturing your mother?"

"Because I asked to bring a friend to dinner tomorrow, and she needs to know right now who it is."

"So do I," his dad said, making Gavin laugh.

"See you guys tomorrow! Gotta run."

"Gavin!"

"Love you." He hung up laughing, which was another thing he'd done a lot of today. It felt good to have something to laugh and smile about again. It felt good to give his parents something to look forward to. It felt good to be around Ella, to be able to touch her and kiss her and not have to pretend any longer that he wasn't crazy about her.

In particular, it felt good to not be so twisted up in knots of grief and rage as he'd been so much of the time lately. The downward spiral had come on quickly following the one-two punch of Homer dying followed by Hannah's remarriage. He'd been doing fine. He would've said he'd gotten "over" his brother's death, if that were even possible. His life was orderly, if a bit boring. He worked long hours and made sure to see a lot of his parents. If every day was a lot like the day before, that was fine.

Then Homer died. Gavin could still remember the absolute devastation of hearing that his brother's beloved companion was gone. As ridiculous as it might seem to some, it had been like losing Caleb all over again. The three of them had been constant companions in college and whenever Caleb was home on leave from the army. His brother had been absolutely crazy about the mutt he'd found by the side of the road, and the mutt had been equally crazy about Caleb.

The funeral Hannah had held for Homer had been perfect and poignant and yet another reminder that his brother was gone forever. Saying good-bye to Homer had been like saying good-bye to Caleb again, and Gavin had found the entire day to be unbearable—except for the brief respite he'd found with Ella on the porch swing. Talking to her and sharing his pain with her had somehow made it easier than it would've been otherwise.

Around the time Homer died, Gavin had found out that Hannah and Nolan were dating. He'd reacted badly to that news and still regretted the way he'd treated two people he loved. After all they'd been through, Hannah was like a sister to him, and Nolan had been a close friend to him and Caleb since they first landed in Butler in middle school. Hannah and Nolan had deserved better than what they'd gotten from him, and he considered himself extremely fortunate that they'd both accepted his apologies.

Their wedding day, however, had been far more difficult than Gavin had expected it to be. Seeing Caleb's Hannah marry someone else, even a man he and his brother loved and respected, had been excruciating for him. He'd kissed Ella that day, and then totally screwed it up by pushing her away. The downward spiral that followed had come upon him fast and furious, erasing years of progress.

Yeah, he'd been batting a thousand lately. And now, despite all the reasons why she shouldn't, Ella had given him this amazing opportunity to spend time with her, to see if what had been simmering between them for years might now turn into something lasting.

He had the worst fear that if he screwed things up with her, any chance he had to be truly happy would be lost forever. Not to mention the toll it would take on her if their fledgling relationship turned into another disaster. He couldn't let that happen.

With his backpack on his shoulder, he locked up his house and headed across the yard to the big steel building where he kept the trucks and equipment for his logging company. He punched in the code that deactivated the alarm system and opened one of the big doors. Inside, he walked past the trucks with the Guthrie Logging name on the doors to the back corner of the big building.

Gavin pulled the tarp off his vintage Harley and wheeled it outside, closing the door behind him and resetting the alarm. Sitting astride the powerful bike, Gavin strapped on the helmet he wouldn't have bothered with before his brother was killed and his parents were left with only him. Now he didn't take chances with his safety the way he had before.

Before. And after. His life was divided neatly into two halves.

He fired up the bike and headed back to town, eager to be with Ella, to experience the sense of calm that came over him whenever she was close by. Navigating the winding roads between his home on the northern end of Butler and hers closer to town, Gavin knew a rare moment of excitement and anticipation.

He thought about what she'd told him earlier about

wanting a big family. In the last few years, he'd been so focused on building his business that he hadn't spent much time thinking about getting married or having a family. But now that he'd decided to take this chance with her, neither of those things seemed out of reach.

They were a long way from big decisions, but the fact that those things were even possible filled him with another emotion that had been in short supply recently—hope. He had something to look forward to. He had a reason to get up in the morning that didn't revolve around his work. He had someone who cared about him—probably more than she should, not that he was complaining. He had someone counting on him for more than a paycheck in the case of his employees and an occasional visit in the case of his parents.

He pulled into Ella's driveway and parked the bike in front of her car where it couldn't be easily seen from the street. Bringing his helmet with him, he went up the stairs to her apartment and knocked on the door.

When the door opened, his mind went blank and his mouth went dry at the sight of her in a slinky sexy robe, her long dark hair shining like always. Behind her, the apartment was aglow with light from candles and the fireplace.

She reached for his free hand. "Come in."

Struck dumb by the sight of her, he followed her inside, dropping his helmet and backpack inside the door.

"Are you okay?" she asked, gazing up at him with her heart in her eyes. She always looked at him that way, and he hoped she always would. He hoped he never gave her a reason to look at him any other way but with love and affection in her gaze.

"You look . . . God, Ella, you're beautiful."

"You should see yourself in that leather jacket with the bike helmet tucked under your arm. H-O-T. I didn't even know you had a motorcycle."

"I didn't want to leave the truck with the Guthrie Logging logo on the side in your driveway overnight. We don't need everyone talking about us until we're ready for them to talk."

She unzipped his coat and slid her arms around his waist inside the coat. "Thank you for thinking of that."

Gavin returned her embrace, the sense of relief at being back in her arms profound. He was further relieved that whatever seemed to be bothering her earlier had apparently passed. "No problem."

"Will you take me for a ride on the bike sometime?"

"Any time you want. It looks nice in here."

"I was afraid it was too much. I blew out all the candles, and then I relit them. I was about to blow them out again when I heard you coming up the stairs."

Unable to resist for another minute, he leaned in to kiss her. "It's not too much. It's just right."

Ella tugged on his jacket. "Take this off. Come get comfortable."

Gavin did as directed and then followed her to the sofa. "You build a good fire."

"We were trained at an early age."

"That was one of the first things we learned how to do when we moved here."

"You want a beer or some of your ice cream or anything?"

He shook his head. "There is one thing I want . . ."

"What's that?" Her cheeks were flushed with color, her lips parted and her eyes bright with happiness. At least he hoped it was that. He wanted to make her happy.

Leaning in again, he kissed her. "More of this."

Her arms came around him, drawing him closer to her.

Gavin went willingly, feeling like a starving man who'd finally found sustenance after a long, difficult journey. She was so soft and fragrant and responsive. He'd noticed that the first time he kissed her—the way she'd leaned into him, participating fully like now when her tongue rubbed up against his.

He flattened his hand over her belly and then tugged playfully on the tie to her robe. "What's under here?"

Breathless from the kiss, Ella said, "Why don't you untie it and find out?"

He glanced at her, seeming to gauge whether she was serious.

She was serious. Dead serious.

Gavin tugged at the silk tie, which gave easily. The robe fell open to reveal the matching silk nightgown she wore underneath. "Wow."

CHAPTER 8

—◆—

*Hope is like the sun, which, as we journey toward
it, casts the shadow of our burden behind us.*

—Samuel Smiles

Ella was on fire for Gavin. She'd never felt anything
remotely like what she did when he was holding her and
touching her this way. This, right here, was why no other man
had done it for her. It was why she'd waited for him. Mustering
her courage, she placed her hand on top of his and guided it
up to cup her breast.

She wanted to whimper from the sweet pleasure that
coursed through her, and then he caught her nipple between
his thumb and index finger, making her gasp. "Gavin . . ."

"What, honey? Talk to me. Tell me what you want."

Wrapping her hand around his nape, she guided his
mouth to her breast. He took the hint, suckling her nipple
through the silk of her gown until it was hard and tight.

Fisting his hair, she held him in place, hoping he would
never stop. She squirmed under him, trying to get closer,
and felt his erection press against her leg. Ella wanted to
touch him there. She wanted to touch him everywhere.

Then he was sliding the strap of her gown down her arm
to bare her breast to his lips and tongue. God, she'd never
felt anything better than the rasp of his whiskers against her

sensitive skin. The tug of his lips on her nipple made her want to forget all about propriety and taking it slow and guarding her heart. She was prepared, right in that moment, to give him everything.

Her breasts were on the smaller side, but incredibly sensitive, never more so than right now.

He shifted so he hovered above her, freeing her other breast from her gown and giving it the same attention.

She loved the sight of him bent over her, worshiping her, his soft dark hair and work-roughened hands touching her fevered skin as he licked and sucked and tugged on her nipples. The weight of his body kept her pinned to the sofa, unable to move, unable to address the thrum of desire between her legs. All she could do was clutch handfuls of his hair while he kept up the sensual torture.

"So beautiful," he whispered. "I've always thought so."

Hearing that, her overly involved heart soared with hope. "I've always thought you were, too. I wish you knew how often I've had to remind myself not to stare when you're around."

He looked up at her for a brief second before he kissed her.

As he kissed her, she began to unbutton his shirt, desperate for the feel of his skin against hers. When the last button sprang free, she pushed the shirt aside and pulled him down on top of her.

The contact of his chest hair against her breasts once again left them both stunned.

"God, that feels good," he whispered gruffly.

"So good."

"Ella . . . I'm trying to go slow and not pounce on you the first second I'm allowed to, but I . . . I really want to."

"I do, too. I want what you want."

"Are you sure?"

She couldn't help but laugh at that question and the earnest way in which he asked it. "Yes, Gavin, I'm sure. I've been sure forever, or so it seems. I don't remember not being sure where you're concerned." It was a ridiculously vulnerable statement, but she didn't regret speaking the truth. He was her truth.

"I'm sorry I made you wait so long."

"Are you going to make it worth the wait?"

"I really hope so." He pushed himself up and off her and then extended a hand.

Ella tugged her gown back up over her breasts and took the hand he offered.

"Which way to your room?"

She pointed.

"We're going to need some of these candles, I think."

Ella picked up two of the candles she'd lit earlier. Her heart beat so hard and so fast that she worried she might pass out or hyperventilate or do some other embarrassing thing like swoon. She was taking Gavin Guthrie to bed with her, and this time she knew exactly what would happen. But surely this couldn't really be happening. It had to be a figment of her overactive imagination.

But then his hands were on her hips and his lips on her neck as he followed her into the bedroom.

This was really happening. It was too soon, and yet nowhere near soon enough at the same time. How could it be too soon to do something she'd wanted forever? The official relationship was new. The attraction, the friendship, the spark, the love . . . None of that was new.

In fact, they'd been building to this inevitable moment since they'd kissed on the beach last summer and in every encounter since then, even if most of them hadn't ended the way she'd wanted them to. He was it for her. She'd had no doubt about that for a long, lonely time.

No way in hell would she do anything other than exactly what she'd wanted to for ages now.

She placed the candles on the bedside table and turned to him, her breath catching in her throat at how sexy he looked with his shirt unbuttoned and hanging open, his jaw covered in the stubble she loved so much, his lips swollen from their kisses and his hair mussed from her hands.

If a more perfectly beautiful man ever existed, Ella had never met him. She took a step closer to him, laying her hands on his chest inside the shirt and feeling his heart beat every bit as rapidly as hers.

His hands framed her face, and he looked at her. "I don't deserve you, Ella."

"Don't say that. You deserve to be happy."

"You can do better."

"I don't want anyone else. I've never wanted anyone else."

"It makes me feel lucky to hear you say that."

"I'm glad."

"I want you to feel lucky, too, that you took this chance on me. I don't want to disappoint you."

"Then don't."

"I'm going to try really hard not to."

"That's all I can ask for."

His hands dropped from her face to her shoulders to remove her robe. It billowed to the floor, a cloud of ivory silk.

The nightgown she wore under it ended at midthigh, and Gavin took a long, slow look at what he'd uncovered. He dragged his index fingers over her collarbone before hooking them under the straps of her gown.

Ella wondered if he could see the pounding pulse point in her throat. Her question was answered when he leaned forwarded to touch his tongue to the spot in her neck that throbbed for him. Her legs wobbled under her. She was never going to survive this if that was all it took for her to go weak in the knees.

His hands followed the fall of the straps down her arms, leaving a trail of goose bumps behind.

She reached for the button on his jeans, but he stopped her.

"Tonight is all about you, Ella."

"It should be about us."

"Next time."

Her hands fell to her sides in surrender, his tenderness her undoing. This man had owned her heart for so long. Now he wanted to own her body, too. Little did he know, she'd give him everything if only he'd let her.

The gown dropped to her waist and then to the floor, leaving her bared to him except for matching panties.

He took a step back, his hands on her shoulders, his gaze taking a perusing trip from her face to her breasts and below before coming back up. "Beautiful."

She'd never felt more beautiful than she did standing before him, waiting to see what he would do next. A hint of trepidation worked its way down her spine, acting as a reminder that if it all went bad after this, there'd be no bouncing back. She'd never get over him.

Gavin dropped to his knees before her, pressing his lips to her belly and making her body sing with pleasure and anticipation. His hands slid up the back of her legs to her bottom, where he squeezed and molded her cheeks before pulling her in closer to him.

She gripped handfuls of his hair to keep from falling over.

For the longest time, he was still, holding her tight against him, his breath warm against the sensitive skin of her abdomen. He held on to her as if she were a lifeline, keeping him anchored.

She wanted to be that for him. She wanted to be everything to him.

He picked her up, effortlessly, and settled her on the edge of the bed. "Lie back."

Since he'd knocked her breathless by lifting her the way he had, she focused on continuing to breathe as she did what he asked. Her legs were trembling madly and her entire body was on fire for him. All that, and he'd barely touched her. Then his hands were on her legs, sliding them apart as he dropped to his knees again and settled between them.

Good God . . .

With his hands cupping her bottom, he drew her to the edge of the mattress and buried his face in the V of her legs, breathing deeply, breathing her in. "You have no idea how often I've dreamed of being right here." His gruff whisper, the scratch of his whiskers, the heat of his breath . . . It was too much. It wasn't enough. "Even when I was pushing you away, I wanted to take you by the hand and drag you to the closest bed. You have no idea how badly I wanted that."

Hearing those words from him brought tears to Ella's eyes. Knowing he'd wanted her every bit as much . . . It made the difficult months leading up to this moment seem somehow more bearable.

He grasped her panties and dragged them down over her legs, tossing them aside before returning to his perch between her legs. His palms were flat against her thighs, his calluses rough against her skin. "So soft and so hot. You've had me wound up in knots for so long, Ella Abbott."

Moved by his words and the emotion she heard behind them, she arched her back, hoping he'd take the hint to move things along.

He did, and oh God, he was good. Thrusting his fingers deep inside her, he drew her clit into his mouth and sucked hard.

Ella detonated, her body seized by the most powerful orgasm she'd ever experienced. She might've screamed from the pleasure that ripped through her. And then he did it again, bringing her down and back up so quickly, she barely had time to recover from the first one before the second was upon her.

He stood and then came down over her, kissing her with lips and a tongue that tasted like her. It was all so earthy and erotic and everything she'd hoped it would be. She wanted to cry from the sweet relief, the pleasure and the hope that beat through her with every breath she took.

The scent of his cologne filled her senses, making her want to bury her nose in his neck and just breathe him in because she could.

But he had other ideas. Producing a condom, he dropped his pants and rolled it on, looking down at her all the while, seeming to gauge her readiness.

She was so ready. She'd been born ready for this man. Ella opened her arms to him, welcoming him into her body, her life, her heart, her soul. Everything she had was his to take.

Still watching her, he pressed into her. It had been a while since she last had sex, so the pinch of pain wasn't unexpected.

"Mmm, so tight and hot."

He went slowly, entering and withdrawing in small increments until her body began to yield to him. Bending over her, he drew her nipple into his mouth, sucking and licking it without losing a beat in the slow progression below.

She ran her fingers through his hair and wrapped her legs around his hips, still wanting to pinch herself that this was happening. She was making love with Gavin Guthrie. Best. Moment. Of. Her. Life. Someday maybe she'd tell him that making love to him had been the best moment of her life. For now, she wanted to relax and enjoy what had been such a long time coming.

His eyes opened, his gaze crashing into hers. That was when she knew he felt it, too—the enormity, the magnitude of what they were finally doing. He pushed into her, this time giving her everything he had, making her moan from the incredible feeling of being filled completely by the man she loved.

For the longest time, he didn't move as their bodies came together, throbbing and pulsing in time with each other.

She was on the verge of begging him to move, to do something, when he began to withdraw from her as slowly as he entered. Then he slammed back in, triggering another orgasm for her.

"Christ," he muttered, unleashed by her reaction. He pounded into her, one hand gripping her shoulder, the other cupping her bottom as he let loose. It was as if all the boiling frustration of the last few months had never happened. Frustration had been replaced by passion unlike anything she could've dreamed—and her dreams had been rather vivid where Gavin was concerned.

"Ella." Her name was like an oath, uttered in desperation. "Come with me. Come with me."

"Yes, Gavin . . ." She met him stroke for stroke, giving herself over to the moment, the love, the need, the craving desire. With every deep stroke he was ruining her for all other men. She knew it, and she didn't care. There'd never been anyone but him for her anyway. Now she had proof.

"El . . . Now. I can't . . ." He came hard, pressing deep

inside her, his fingers digging into her flesh as he let go, taking her with him into another epic release.

That had never happened before. She was lucky to come once during sex, let alone twice.

Gavin came down on top of her, warm and sweaty and breathing hard.

Ella wrapped her arms around him, wanting to stay right here in this perfect moment forever. For once, she wasn't yearning for something—or someone—she couldn't have. Everything she'd ever wanted was right here in her arms, and he seemed as happy to be there as she was to have him.

"Am I crushing you?" he asked.

"Not at all."

"You okay?"

"I'm great. You?"

He lifted his head to kiss her. "I'm fantastic."

Ella smiled up at him. It was great to hear him say that in light of his recent state of mind.

He kissed her again, nipping at her bottom lip.

She wrapped her hand around his nape to keep him there, opening her mouth to his tongue. After having a taste of him, she was hungry for more. She had a big week coming up at work with the staff retreat on Friday night and the subsequent kickoff of the holiday shopping season. They really ought to blow out the candles and go to sleep or she'd be a wreck tomorrow.

But with Gavin Guthrie naked in her bed and throbbing inside her, sleep was the very last thing on her mind.

CHAPTER 9

—•◆•—

The only cure for grief is action.

—George Henry Lewes

It had been a very long time since Gavin had felt as good as he did lying in Ella's arms after making love to her for the first time. The spinning had stopped, the sickening despair was gone and what remained was a tiny kernel of hope that wanted to bloom into something strong and lasting.

She was like an oasis, offering him things he hadn't known he needed. Her sweet softness was a welcome respite from the hell his life had become.

The stroke of her fingers through his hair soothed and calmed the restlessness he carried with him always.

"Gav?"

"Hmm?"

"Can I ask you something that's none of my business?"

"Sure."

"Why aren't you going to Dylan's wedding?"

The question took him by surprise, and he had no idea how to reply in a way that she would understand. "Work is so busy. It's hard for me to get away."

"Surely you have someone you could leave in charge for a few days."

"I suppose, but I'd be stressed out worrying about it the whole time I was gone, so why bother going?"

"Because your good friend is getting married, and he wants you there?"

Gavin already felt guilty enough about declining the invitation to Dylan's wedding. How could he explain that Dylan was really Caleb's friend, and the only reason he'd been invited was because he was Caleb's brother? "I'd love to be there." He said what she needed to hear, because the truth was too painful to discuss, especially when he was feeling so damned good for a change. "Dylan understands about the business and how hard it is for me to get away."

"Hmm."

"What does that mean?"

"Nothing, I'm just listening."

"Why do I feel like there's so much more you want to say?"

She didn't say anything for a long time. And then . . . "It's just, I wonder . . ."

"What do you wonder?"

"What's the point of being self-employed if you can't do what you want once in a while?"

"You're self-employed. Do you get to do whatever you want?"

"For the most part. We try to respect the fact that we have nice jobs and are fortunate to work for ourselves. We don't take advantage, but no one is hanging over our shoulders making sure we do our jobs. Hunter wants us there on time in the morning because it sets the right example for the sales force, and we agree with that. As much as we love the store and working for the family business, we have lives outside of work that we love just as much. It's called balance. You need to get some if you feel like you can't take a week off once in a while."

She made good points, and they were things he'd certainly thought of himself. However, work brought a rhythm to his days that he badly needed to stay on track. The thought of a week without work made him twitchy and nervous. If he hadn't had his business to focus on over the last seven years, he'd probably be institutionalized by now.

As much as he loved the way he felt when he was around her, especially now that they'd made love, she was the one mirror he couldn't avoid. She *saw* him so clearly. His bullshit didn't stand a chance against those insightful brown eyes that studied him so knowingly.

Grasping the base of the condom, he withdrew from her carefully.

"Bathroom's in there," she said, pointing to a closed door.

"Thanks." He went into the bathroom, disposed of the condom and washed up, avoiding the mirror over the sink. Her insightfulness unsettled him and made him aware of how tuned into him she really was. It was becoming painfully obvious to him that if they were going to do this, really give it an honest chance, he wasn't going to be able to get away with the old tricks. His artful dodger routine wasn't going to fly with Ella.

He wet a washcloth and brought it back to the bedroom. Sitting on the edge of the bed, he let his gaze take a perusing journey from her long legs to her flat abdomen to her small but perky breasts to her gorgeous face and the eyes that watched him so closely.

Gavin held up the washcloth. "May I?"

In a move so sexy, so innocent and so utterly captivating, she inched her feet apart, exposing herself to him. He forced himself to stay focused on the task at hand, even though he was already hard again for her. She was so damned gorgeous and sexy and the way she cared about him was a huge turn-on, even if it forced him to confront his deepest demons.

When he was done, he tossed the washcloth aside and climbed back into bed with her, wanting her close to him.

Apparently she wanted the same thing. Wrapped up in her, with her arms and legs around him, he felt himself falling into the soft, safe place she'd given him to land. "Ella . . ."

"Hmm . . ."

"You, this . . . It feels so good."

"Yes, it does. I want you to feel good, Gavin." She kissed him, and without breaking the kiss, he brought her with him when he moved to his back, loving the feel of her on top of him. The squeeze of her flat belly against his hard cock made him breathless with the need for more of her.

She broke the kiss and shifted ever so slightly on top of him, kissing his face, jaw, neck and throat, biting down on a tendon in his neck that made him want to howl from the jolt of pure pleasure that ripped through him. Then her tongue found his nipple, and he nearly levitated right out of bed when she brought her teeth into the act.

God, he was never going to survive her.

She continued a path downward, giving each muscle in his abdomen individual attention that had him clinging to his sanity. By the time she wrapped her hand around his cock he was prepared to beg her for relief. No begging was needed, however, when she dragged her tongue around the head, cleaning up the moisture that had formed during her slow, sexy seduction.

As she licked and sucked and stroked him exactly the right way, it occurred to Gavin that she'd obviously done this before—a thought that made him see red from the rage of imagining her touching another man the way she touched him. It was irrational, he knew, to think he was first, but God, the thought of her with any other guy was unbearable.

Then she took him deep into her throat, clearing his mind of every thought other than the most important one. This was going to be over—fast—if she kept that up. He grasped handfuls of her shiny dark hair. "El, honey . . . *Ella*."

She dragged her lips up his shaft, adding just enough suction and tongue action to nearly finish him off. His cock popped free, and she looked up at him with big brown eyes and lips swollen from taking him into her mouth. He had never, in all his life, seen anything sexier than the way she looked right in that moment.

"What's wrong?" she asked.

"Absolutely nothing. Come here." He held out his arms to her, and she crawled into his embrace.

"Why did you stop me?"

"I don't want to come in your mouth."

"Why not? I wouldn't have minded."

Gavin blew out a sharp, deep breath. No, he definitely did not deserve this woman, but for right now, for as long as she'd have him, she was his and he planned to fully enjoy every minute with her. "I'd much rather be inside you when that happens."

"Condom?"

"Back pocket of my jeans."

She kissed him again. "Let me up."

He let her go, reluctant to let her leave him even for the moment it would take to retrieve the condom. But he fully enjoyed watching her move around in the nude. He loved that she seemed comfortable in her body and didn't try to hide herself from him.

She turned to find him watching her, and a delightful flush colored her pale white skin. "What're you looking at?"

"You."

Holding up the other three condoms he'd brought, Ella came back to bed and returned to her roost on top of him. Using her teeth to tear open the wrapper, she held him in her thrall as she rolled the condom down over his hard cock. She came *this* close to finishing him off with the slow, seductive way she let the condom unfurl.

He gritted his teeth and tried to summon the control he needed for her. It had been a long time since he'd been with anyone, and he'd never been with any woman who mattered as much as this one did. He wanted to be what she needed in all ways—in the bedroom and outside it. Coming before she was ready was not what either of them needed.

Gavin reached for her.

She dodged him. "You had your turn. Now it's mine."

God, did she have any idea how incredibly sexy she looked sitting on top of him with her long hair nearly covering her breasts, her nipples hard and tight and almost begging him to sit up and suck on them, her legs spread, revealing the dark hair between them.

Unable to be entirely passive, he ran his hands over the soft, silky skin of her legs and up her waist to cup her breasts, temporarily distracting her from whatever she had planned and buying himself a little time to get himself under control.

"Mmm," she said. "I love when you touch me."

"That's good, because I love to touch you. You're so soft. Your skin is like silk."

She began to move on top of him, bringing the heat between her legs into direct contact with his cock.

"Ella . . ." He grasped her hips and tried to take over, but she wouldn't let him.

"Stop." .

Groaning, he dropped his hands to his sides.

"You don't always have to be in control of everything."

Funny statement when you consider he'd felt so out of control lately. But this, with her, was the best kind of out of control. He was more than happy to cede to her, especially since he was allowed to watch.

She continued to move on top of him, driving them both crazy if the hitches in her breathing were any indication.

He was on the verge of begging her, flat-out pleading, when she took him in hand and came down on him, enveloping him in her tight, wet heat.

Ella bit her lip, her face a study in concentration as she moved slowly to take him into her body.

Gavin hated the wince of pain he witnessed in her expression before pain became pleasure and she began to move her hips.

She was so fucking hot that there was no way he could keep his hands to himself, so he raised them to her breasts, rolling and teasing her nipples until she gasped from the pleasure and tightened around him. That nearly finished him off.

He sat up, wrapped an arm around her and drew one of those tight nipples into his mouth.

Gripping handfuls of his hair, she let out a sharp cry of pleasure that was followed by a flood of heat below. He sent his free hand down to where they were joined, teasing and coaxing until her orgasm crashed down over both of them, taking him right along with her.

Her nipple popped free of his mouth, wet and red from

the attention he had given it. He soothed it with soft strokes of his tongue that had her shuddering in his arms.

"You took over my show," she said, her voice hoarse and sexy.

"I helped it along. Am I forgiven?"

"I'll let it slide this time, but don't make a habit out of it."

"I could very easily make a habit out of this. Out of you."

Her arms encircled his neck, and she held on tight. "Me, too."

They used all four condoms and never did sleep. Ella was a wreck the next day. All the coffee in the world couldn't undo a sleepless night or the aches in her muscles from the workout she'd put them through. As tender as her muscles were, the sting of soreness between her legs had her full attention.

At eight o'clock, an hour after the time Gavin usually started work, they dragged themselves out of bed and into the shower, which became about much more than getting clean when he started kissing her under the hot water. He declined breakfast, telling her he'd grab something later as he pulled on his leather jacket.

Dazed and confused and zonked from not sleeping, Ella followed him to the door, wearing only the silk robe she'd greeted him in the night before.

"Don't let a tree fall on you or anything today," she said, suppressing another yawn. She was far, far too old to be up all night having sex. And she was far, *far* too old to have only just now experienced all-night sex.

"I won't," he said with a chuckle. "Don't worry about me." He hooked an arm around her waist and looked down at her, seeming to catalog her every feature. "What a great night."

"Best night ever."

"Mmm," he said, kissing her. "For me, too."

Because she couldn't resist touching him, she buried her fingers in his hair and kissed him like she hadn't spent all night kissing him, like his tongue hadn't spent nearly as much time in her mouth as his own. It wasn't enough. It would never be enough.

Groaning, he pulled back from her. "Witch, let me go to work before I get fired."

"You own the company. Call in sick."

"I can't," he said, groaning again. "And neither can you with your big event on Friday."

Ella would never admit to having forgotten all about one of the biggest events of the year for her at work. She was the lead on the staff retreat, and it needed her full attention this week.

"My parents invited us for dinner tonight," he said.

"Us?"

"I asked if I could bring a friend, but I didn't tell them who. My mom said I was torturing her. Do you want to come? Mom is making ribs. They're so good."

Ella smiled up at him, enjoying the lightness she saw in his eyes this morning. "I'd love to."

He kissed her again, lingering long enough that she wondered if he was considering calling in sick. "See you later?"

"Yes, you will."

"I'll miss you today."

Hearing those words from this man . . . "I'll miss you, too."

After one last tongue-twisting kiss, he tore himself free with another tortured groan, grabbed his helmet and backpack and was out the door before Ella knew what hit her.

For long moments after he left, after she heard the motorcycle start up and drive away, she stood by the door, stunned and exhausted and exhilarated and happy. God, she was so damned *happy*. More than once during the difficult months since that kiss on the beach, she'd contemplated the possibility that the reality of Gavin might not live up to the man she'd built him up to be.

But he'd more than lived up to her expectations. In fact, he'd surpassed them in every possible way. She could still feel his hands on her, the scratch of his whiskers, the stroke of his tongue, the almost painful stretch required to accept him into her body. She shivered, reliving the incredible pleasure.

And that they got to do it all again tonight . . . She'd never survive until then. How was she supposed to get through eight long hours in the office when she'd so much rather be with him?

Somehow she managed to dry her hair, get herself dressed and fed and filled with as much coffee as she could handle. Her eyes were gritty and her body buzzed from the need for sleep as well as the caffeine. Licking her lips, she discovered they, too, were sore. She'd put them through a hell of a work-out the night before. Thinking about the workout caused her nipples to tighten—painfully. They'd also been through a hell of an ordeal.

Ella giggled to herself as she pulled into the parking lot at the store and turned off the engine. She was close enough to walk to work, and she did most days, but today was not most days. Today was . . . Well, today was already the best day she'd ever had, and she was saving all her strength and energy for more of the same tonight.

CHAPTER 10

———— ◆ ————

There is no medicine like hope, no incentive
so great, and no tonic so powerful as
expectation of something tomorrow.

—Orison Swett Marden

E very muscle in Ella's body protested the journey up the
stairs and into the office, where she greeted Mary, their
administrative assistant, and her brothers Will and Hunter
before heading into her own office. Sitting behind her desk,
she winced at the bite of pain from between her legs but tried
to ignore the insistent throb as she powered up her computer.
Maybe if she was able to get through her long to-do list by
early afternoon she could take a half day and go home to nap
before dinner with Gavin's parents. She feared what she might
look like by dinnertime if she didn't get some sleep.

With her goal of a nap in mind, she finalized the plans for
Friday night with a company-wide e-mail that reminded everyone that the festivities began at five with presentations from
Ella and Lincoln, followed by dinner and dancing with a DJ
until midnight. She had a phone call with the management
of the Grange Hall to make sure everything was set for Friday,
and then she called the caterer to check in.

All her meticulous attention to detail was paying off. Everything was ready to ensure a good time for the employees and their families before the holiday shopping crush began.

Next up was a check of inventory to make sure everything Charley had ordered for the store was in place and ready to replenish supplies as needed. The holidays were their second most profitable time of year, following leaf-peeping season, during which people came from all over the world to view the spectacular Vermont foliage.

They no sooner completed that season than the holidays were upon them. By mid-December they'd be living for January. They got a small break during mud season before the new batch of maple syrup began to arrive in the store, bringing with it hordes of customers looking to stock up. It was the same thing every year, and Ella enjoyed the rhythms and cycles of the seasons outside and in the store. She loved the predictable nature of what they did, ensuring that customers received the same welcoming experience every time they set foot into the store.

She checked her watch. Almost eleven. Thank goodness she was busy and the time was going by quickly. She got up to stretch and was heading downstairs to work the floor for a while when Charley came into her office, shutting the door behind her.

"Good morning to you, too."

"You look like hell, and is that razor burn on your face?"

Ella's hand covered her cheek.

"Other side."

"Stop. Leave me alone."

"Not until you tell me everything."

"I'm not telling you anything."

"I was good enough to unload on when things had gone to shit with him. I think I deserve some of the dirty details."

Ella laughed, because how could she not? Charley was as outrageous as ever.

"Besides, it's obvious you've been thoroughly ravished, so don't try to deny it."

"It is?" She pulled a mirror out of her purse and studied

the patch of razor burn at her jawline, as well as her swollen lips and red eyes.

"Told you. Now spill the beans."

"You seem to already have all the beans figured out. Why do I need to spill them?"

"Was it good? Worth the long, agonizing wait?"

"Yes."

"To which?"

"Both."

Charley smiled. "Excellent. I was hoping it wouldn't be a giant letdown after all the buildup."

"Still could be. Who knows? We're taking it a day at a time, but he's trying. I'll give him that."

"Judging by the look of you today, he's putting forth one hell of an effort."

Ella couldn't help but laugh at that. "Indeed he is."

"I'm happy for you, Ella. You've been into him a long time, and you never gave up on him even when it would've been easier for you."

"I couldn't give up on him. I love him. I've always loved him."

"Sigh," Charley said, dropping into a chair. "What's that like? I've never met any guy that didn't drive me bonkers. I can't imagine falling in love with one of them."

"It'll happen someday. When it's meant to."

"I don't know about that. I might be too cynical for love."

"Somewhere out there is a guy who will love the challenge of defrosting your frigid, cynical heart."

Charley snorted with laughter. "If you say so. I pity the fool, whoever he is."

"We all do, Charley."

"Ha. Ha. Ha. Are you going to Hannah's to watch *The Bachelor* tonight?"

"I don't think so. We're having dinner with Gavin's parents, and I'm kinda tired. I'll be back next week."

"We'll give you a pass this one time."

"Gee, thanks. And you know, thanks for listening during the tough times. It really helped me to unload on you."

"I was happy to be there for you. I hated seeing you unhappy. Ravished and glowing is a big improvement."

Ella touched the rash on her cheek again. "You don't think Dad will be able to tell, will he?"

"Um, am I to say what you want to hear or the truth?"

"Oh God. I'll be avoiding him today then."

"Good luck with that."

"Maybe I'll also skip my daily walk through the store, too. I don't want people talking about us until we're ready for that."

"I'd say you let that cat out of the bag by bringing him to dinner yesterday."

"I don't care if the family knows."

"If the family knows, the town knows."

A niggle of unease settled in Ella's belly at the thought of people in town talking about her and Gavin. They weren't ready to be the subject of gossip. Not yet anyway. "I've got to get back to work. I'm trying to get out of here a little early today."

Charley dragged herself out of the chair where she'd made herself nice and comfortable. "I won't keep you."

"I meant to tell you—congrats on the training and everything. I think it's awesome—and amazing—that you're going to run a marathon."

"We'll see if it happens. The run on Saturday about killed me. My legs were on fire yesterday."

"It'll get better the more you do it."

"Hope so. The old gray mare ain't as young as she used to be."

"Oh please, you're thirty, not eighty."

"I felt eighty yesterday. Oh, and guess who's in the running group?" Charley asked with a scowl.

"Who?"

"Tyler Westcott."

"The one man under thirty-five in Butler that you haven't dated?" Ella asked.

Charley rolled her eyes. "I never dated Gavin Guthrie, and he's under thirty-five."

"You better not have dated Gavin. And P.S., I like Tyler. He's a nice guy, and he's totally into you."

"He is not. Why would you even say that? He's so boring I fall asleep the second he opens his mouth."

"He's not boring. He's quiet. There's a difference, and I know he's into you because he always watches you at the Grange dances."

"He does not. Don't make shit up."

"If that's what you have to tell yourself. Personally, I think he's super cute."

"Why don't you date him then?"

"Sorry, I'm very busy with the guy I have. I'll leave Tyler to you."

"Don't do me any favors. I'm out of here."

Watching her sister jet out of the room like her ass was on fire, Ella smiled. She couldn't wait to see Charley fall hard for her Mr. Right, even if Ella pitied the fool who took her on.

She got back to work, drafting some remarks for her father to share with the sales team, and then she sent them to him in an e-mail rather than walking them into his office the way she normally would. The last thing she needed today was Lincoln Abbott's shrewd eyes taking in her disheveled state. It was more than enough that Charley had seen right through her.

A knock on her door had her saying a silent prayer for anyone other than her dad. "Come in."

Hunter ducked his head in. "Can I have a minute?"

"Sure," she said, hoping he wouldn't notice the razor burn. Why hadn't she seen that and done something about it before she left the house? Because she'd been too sex-drunk to take the time to look in the mirror this morning. "What's up?" she asked when Hunter came in, closed the door behind him and took a seat.

"I wanted to talk to you."

"About?" Ella asked, though she suspected she already knew.

"Gavin."

"I've already been warned by Mom and Hannah, so you can save your breath."

"Could I just say one thing?"

"Can I stop you?" Ella asked with a sigh, crossing her arms and settling in to be big-brothered. That was something Hunter was exceptionally good at.

"I know you don't want to hear it, El. I didn't want to hear it when I first got together with Megan and people were telling me to watch out for her. Hell, she carried a torch for my *brother* for years before she went out with me. Nothing and no one could talk me out of being with her." He looked down at the floor before returning his gaze to her. "That said, I need you to know . . . I love Gavin. He's been my friend since I was a little kid, and he's a good guy. But—"

"Why did I know there was a *but* coming?"

"He's messed up on the inside, Ella. Messed up bad. He's not the same as he was before."

Hunter didn't need to tell her what he meant by "before."

"I know that," Ella said. "What you saw at Mom and Dad's didn't just start yesterday. It's been happening for a while now, and I've got my eyes wide open. Gavin told me himself that he's a 'fixer-upper.'"

"Are you sure you want to invest that kind of energy in something that might not be fixable?"

"If I recall correctly, you took on a bit of a fixer-upper yourself in Megan, and look at how that worked out."

"Fair enough. I hope you know . . . I only say this because I don't want you to get hurt."

"And I appreciate the concern. I really do. But there's no warning or concern or anything that anyone could say that will keep me from giving him an honest, legitimate chance."

"I'll hope it works out the way you want it to."

"Could I ask you something?"

"Sure."

"Are you going to Dylan's wedding?"

"Megan and I were just talking about that last night. She's trying to figure out whether the diner can get by for a few days without her, and if she can work something out, we're going. Why?"

"I want Gavin to go, but he's saying he can't leave work."

"He doesn't go to Sultan things anymore. Unless they're here. It's one of the many ways he's changed in recent years."

"I know. Nolan told me that." Ella chewed on the end of her pen. "What do you think he'd do if I bought tickets for us, made reservations and presented him with a done deal?"

Hunter tipped his head in thought. "I honestly don't know how that would go over. Back in the day, I would've said he'd love it. Now . . . I just don't know."

"Hmm, well, thanks for your opinion and everything else. I appreciate that you care."

"We all do, Ella."

"I know. I wish you all cared a little *less* than you do."

"That'll be the day." Smiling, he got up and headed for the door. "See you later."

Ella tried to return her attention to the computer, but her eyes were swimming and she couldn't stop yawning. She'd made it to three o'clock. That was a freaking miracle, all things considered. She turned off her computer and grabbed her purse and coat.

"I'm going home for the day, Mary. Not feeling too good today."

"Oh, too bad, Ella. I'll see you in the morning."

"See you then." She went down the stairs, praying for a clean getaway. The office had been unusually quiet today, for which she would be eternally grateful. As she pulled out of the parking lot and headed for home, she saw her dad and the dogs on the sidewalk in front of Lucas's woodworking barn. She tooted at them, returned their waves and continued on her way. Her bed was calling to her, and she was going to crash and burn if she didn't answer that call very soon.

Gavin's day had been a disaster until right this minute, as he took the stairs to Ella's place two at a time. His heartbeat was on overdrive because he was about to see her. During the course of the day, he'd relived their night together repeatedly, and he'd been a walking hard-on all day as he remembered every detail.

He knocked on her door and waited for her to answer. When nothing happened, he began to regret not calling to tell her he was on his way. He knocked again and waited and then tested the door to find it unlocked. He hoped she wouldn't care if he went in uninvited. Her purse was flung on a chair inside the door, along with her coat, which had one sleeve inside out.

Smiling, he had a feeling he knew where he'd find her and headed for her bedroom. Sure enough, she was fully dressed and out cold on top of her bed. He kicked off his shoes and crawled in next to her, putting his arm around her middle and drawing her in tight against him.

There, he thought, breathing in a deep Ella-scented breath. *There she is.* He took another deep breath and felt his heartbeat slip into a more normal rhythm.

She murmured in her sleep and then stirred, turning over to burrow into his embrace.

He couldn't fall asleep, not with his parents expecting them in thirty minutes, but his eyes were gritty from the night without sleep and it wouldn't take much to make him forget all about dinner.

"Where'd you come from?" she asked in a sleepy-sounding voice.

"You left your door unlocked. You're lucky I didn't find some other guy in here snuggling with you."

"I left it open for you."

"I don't like you sleeping with your door unlocked."

"I'll give you a key."

He kissed her forehead and then her lips because he couldn't wait another second to kiss her. "Missed you so bad today."

"It was the longest day ever, and I only made it until three."

"Sorry I kept you up all night."

"I'm not." She reached for him and drew him into a far more serious kiss, her mouth opening to admit his tongue.

Before he could think about what he was doing and where they needed to be, he was on top of her, devouring her. Now that he'd had a taste of her, he was ravenous for more. Apparently, he wasn't alone in that if the way she kissed him was any indication.

Her legs opened and wrapped around his hips, and he pressed against her, wishing he were deep inside her. He had to put a stop to this and get to his parents' house, but he needed another minute—or two—of Ella first.

Gavin eased his way out of the kiss, withdrawing in slow increments. "We have somewhere to be."

"Oh, God, your parents. I completely forgot. I'm a mess."

"You're gorgeous."

"My hair—"

"Is beautiful."

"I have razor burn."

Gavin studied her face and kissed the spot on her face he'd rubbed raw with his whiskers. "I need to shave for you before I touch you again."

"I love your scruff. Don't shave."

"I love your soft skin and don't want to mark it."

"You have to let me up so I can make myself presentable for your parents."

He pressed his hard cock against her one more time and kissed her. "There," he said. "Now I might be prepared to get through dinner." Rolling off her, he stared up at the ceiling as he throbbed with unspent desire. How there could be any more after what they'd done last night amazed him, but there seemed to be an endless supply where she was concerned.

She sat up and ran her fingers through her hair, attempting to restore some order. "You must be so tired."

"I'll sleep good tonight. We won't stay late at my parents'. Don't worry."

"I hope neither of us falls over at the table."

"It would give them something to talk about for days." He followed her with his gaze as she went into the bathroom. After spending this time with her, he wondered how he'd ever been able to resist her for as long as he had. He regretted that now. It felt so damned good to be with her that he wished he'd given in a long time ago. Maybe he could've avoided some of the recent disquiet if he'd let her in sooner.

No matter. She was here now, and he planned to do everything within his power to keep her.

A few minutes later, she emerged from the bathroom looking fresh-faced and put together.

He pulled himself up and out of her comfortable bed and then let her tug him along behind her as they headed for the door. "If I fall asleep in my mashed potatoes, will you rescue me?"

"Of course I will. I'm your ICE, after all."

Wrapping his arms around her from behind, he nuzzled her neck. "Yes, you are."

Ella turned and looked up at him. "Why did you make me your ICE anyway?"

"Because I knew you'd come no matter what. You're always there for me when I need you most, even when I was pushing you away."

She went up on tiptoes to kiss him. "Thank you for having such faith in me."

"I do have faith in you, and I want you to be able to have faith in me."

"I do, Gavin. Why do you think I never gave up on you, even when I probably should have?"

"Thanks for not giving up. I would've hated to miss out on this."

Her warm, sweet smile filled the darkness inside him with badly needed light. It also filled him with even more determination to be what she needed, to not let her down. If he ever hurt her . . . He couldn't even think about what it might feel like to have her look at him with disappointment rather than adoration. The fear of that sent a shudder through him as he followed her down the stairs.

CHAPTER 11

*A whole stack of memories never
equal one little hope.*

—Charles M. Schulz

As Gavin drove them to his parents' home in his truck, Ella thought about what he'd said about why he'd made her his emergency contact and how he'd known he could count on her. It was humbling to think that while she'd been nursing her broken heart, he'd been clinging to her like a life raft in a storm.

Ella wanted to be his safe harbor, to lead him from the darkness back into the light. She burned with love for him— the forever kind of love that wouldn't end until the heart inside her chest stopped beating. Even then, well into her next life, Ella would still love Gavin. It was just an irrefutable fact of her life.

They pulled into the driveway at his parents' well-kept home, and an attack of nerves assailed her. Of course she knew Bob and Amelia Guthrie well and had for years, but she was coming here tonight as Gavin's girlfriend or whatever she was now. It was different.

She hadn't been here since the awful weeks that followed Caleb's death when she and her mother and Charley had cooked for Bob and Amelia, delivering food weekly for a few months. It had seemed like a small thing to do in the face of such utter devastation.

Gavin's hand squeezing hers drew her out of her contemplation. Ella sent him a small smile.

"What's wrong?"

"I feel a little nervous, which is silly in light of how long I've known your parents."

"No need to be nervous. You know they love you, and they'll be thrilled to see us together."

"You really think so?"

"I know so."

His assurances went a long way toward allaying her nerves.

"Wait for me." He got out of the truck and came around to the passenger side, opening the door and extending his hand to her.

Ella took his hand, loving the smile on his face, the happiness that danced in his tired eyes and the excitement he seemed to feel at bringing her here.

He helped her out of the truck and kept his grip on her hand as they walked into the house and as his parents came out to greet them, only letting go so he could help her remove her coat.

"What a wonderful, wonderful surprise," Amelia Guthrie said, blinking rapidly as if trying not to cry. She hugged Ella. "This makes me so happy."

"Thank you," Ella said softly, relieved by the warm welcome and the obvious joy her presence had brought to Amelia.

Amelia released Ella and went on to hug her son. "You know how to keep some big secrets," she said.

Gavin's smile stretched from ear to ear when he looked at Ella. "It's something we've both wanted for a long time. We finally seem to have gotten the timing right."

"Nice to see you, Ella," Bob said when he hugged her. "And nice to see you smiling, son. It's been a while."

"Yes," Gavin said with a sigh, "it has."

Ella took hold of his hand and gave it a squeeze, hoping

to keep the bad from invading the good. The bad would probably always be right there, lurking below the surface trying to get out, but Ella would do everything in her power to keep the bad where it belonged. In the past.

They enjoyed a delicious dinner of barbecued ribs, mashed potatoes, homemade coleslaw and corn bread. Gavin ate like he hadn't seen food in a year, something his mother said happened every time she made ribs for him.

After dinner, Amelia suggested they take their dessert into the den to enjoy the fire.

"I need to bring in some more wood," Bob said. "Give me a hand, son?"

"Happy to." Gavin squeezed Ella's shoulder on his way out the door behind his father.

"I just have to say," Amelia whispered, the second they were alone, "this makes me so, so happy. I haven't seen him smiling like he has tonight since before . . ." She didn't have to finish that sentence. Ella knew what she meant. "You're perfect for him, Ella. You're just what he needs."

"I hope so. There've been a lot of stops and starts along the way, but we've agreed to give it a real try."

"I'll be keeping my fingers and toes crossed for both of you."

"Thanks, Amelia." Ella glanced over her shoulder to make sure Gavin was still outside with his father. "Could I ask your advice on something?"

"Of course. Anything."

Ella told her about Dylan's wedding, how Gavin planned to decline the invitation because of work and her idea about surprising him with the trip.

"Do it," Amelia said without hesitation. "It's exactly what he needs—time with his friends, time with you, time away from work. He pushes himself so hard and I know why, but he can't keep up that pace forever. No one can."

"You don't think he'll be mad that I'm forcing him to do something he said he doesn't want to do?"

"He wants to go, but it's easier for him not to. He needs to stop doing the easy thing and get back to living. This, with you, is an important first step."

"Thanks for the advice. I think I'm going to do it."

"Good. Bob and I are going, so maybe we'll see you there."

"I hope so."

Gavin and his dad returned, both carrying armloads of wood that they took directly to the cozy family room that included a wall devoted to Caleb's army service. The picture of him in his uniform, looking fierce and strong and so vitally alive put a lump in her throat. The same image now hung in the foyer of the inn that bore his name and was a stark reminder of what these three wonderful people had lost.

Ella noticed that Gavin sat with his back to Caleb's wall, as if it was too painful to face. She sat next to him on the love seat and reached for his hand.

He smiled at her, seeming relaxed and at ease even if he looked exhausted.

They spent another hour with his parents before Gavin began yawning his head off. "I had an early day today," he said, nearly making Ella laugh as he helped her up and then led her into the mudroom to get their coats. They'd had an early day all right. "Got to hit the hay before I fall over. Thanks for dinner, Mom."

"Yes, Amelia, thank you. It was delicious."

"You're so welcome." She hugged them. "I hope we'll see both of you again soon."

"You will," Gavin said, shaking hands with his dad, who hugged and kissed Ella. Gavin held the door for her and let her go out ahead of him. He helped her into the truck, and she could tell he was dying to kiss her but held off because his parents were standing in the doorway to wave them off.

He backed his big truck out of the driveway and beeped to his parents before turning off their street and pulling over to the side of the road.

"What's wrong?" Ella asked.

He reached across the center console for her, releasing the buckle on her seatbelt. "Kiss me."

She barely had time to protest or to remind him they'd be back to her place in minutes before his lips were devouring hers. He rendered her useless with the wet slide of his lips, the plunging thrusts of his tongue and the heat of his body drawing her in as close as she could get with the console in the way.

Groaning in frustration, he pulled away abruptly, threw the truck into drive and said, "Put your seatbelt back on."

Left reeling by his abrupt withdrawal, Ella fumbled with the seatbelt and managed to click it into place. Her lips were tingling from his fierce kiss, and she couldn't wait to be alone with him again.

This was crazy. They'd played cat-and-mouse games for months, and now that they'd agreed to be together, they couldn't keep their hands off each other. Not that Ella was complaining. She felt like she was seeing a whole new side of him, and she loved it.

He didn't say a single other word on the ten-minute ride to her place.

Ella didn't wait for him to come around to get her. When she met him at the front of the truck, he urged her forward with his hand on her lower back. On the way upstairs, he pulled at her coat from behind until she got the hint and unzipped it. He tugged it off her shoulders and went to work on her sweater next, easing it up and over her head while they were still in the hallway.

"Gavin," she whispered, shocked to be standing outside her door in only her bra. "I'm not the only one who lives here."

"Hurry up," he said in a low growl that left no doubt in her mind what he wanted.

Her nipples tightened in anticipation, setting off an insistent throb between her legs. She wanted him every bit as badly as he wanted her.

The door closed behind them and he dropped his coat on the floor. He pulled his button-down shirt right up and over his head and then pulled on the button to his jeans.

Ella was frozen in place, watching him reveal his muscular body to her.

"You're not hurrying," he said.

She removed her jeans, bra and panties and reached for him at the same second he reached for her. Before she knew what hit her, he had lifted her against the door and was entering her in one swift thrust that set off a shocking bolt of pain that made her grimace.

"Oh God, babe. I'm sorry. You're sore from last night."

"I'm okay. Just go slow."

He withdrew almost completely. "Shit. Condom."

Ella tightened her legs around him to keep him from getting away. "I'm on birth control. If you're safe, so am I."

"Oh my God, are you serious? Sex without a condom? What's that like?"

Despite the full-on assault on her senses, he made her laugh. "Want to find out?"

"You have no idea how badly. I'm safe, baby. I haven't had sex in a long time, and never without a condom." He pushed back into her, going slowly this time. "This is gonna be fast."

Her heart soared at hearing it had been a long time for him, too. She'd had far too much time to picture him with other women while she nursed her broken heart. "I'm good with fast."

"Does it hurt?"

"Not anymore." *This, this, this,* Ella thought as he drove into her over and over again, *is why I waited for him.* It had never been like this with anyone else. She'd never had a man tear her clothes off her body and take her against her door like a madman because he couldn't bear to wait the two minutes it would take to reach her bed.

In truth, she wouldn't have wanted that with the other guys she'd been with. She wouldn't have trusted them enough to let go so completely. With Gavin, she had no choice. He swept her up in a sea of sensation and pleasure that left her gasping and panting and coming harder than she'd ever thought possible.

And then someone was knocking on her door. "Ella? Are you all right in there? I heard something banging from the vestibule and didn't know what to make of it."

"Oh my God," she whispered. "It's Mrs. Abernathy."

Gavin snorted through his nose. They'd both had her for high school math.

"I-I'm fine, Mrs. Abernathy," Ella called through the door. "Sorry, just dropped something."

"If you're sure . . ."

"I'm sure."

"Did I see Gavin Guthrie's truck outside?"

"Yes, he's helping me with . . . We're hanging some pictures."

Gavin shook with silent laughter, his tears wetting her neck.

"All right then. Good night, dear."

"Good night."

While their bodies continued to throb from what they were doing before they were so rudely interrupted, Ella listened to the sound of Mrs. Abernathy's sensible shoes scuffing against the treads on the stairs.

Gavin laughed so hard, he made no sound. His laughter sparked hers, and before long, they were clinging to each other, tears rolling down their faces.

When he got himself under control, he grasped her bottom, lifted her off the door, and carried her to the bedroom, coming down on top of her. "I'll never be able to look Mrs. Abernathy in the eye again."

"How do you think I feel? I have to see her every day!"

"You need to stop banging in your apartment."

"It's that Guthrie boy. He's bad news."

He smiled at her, and she loved that look on him. "Yes, he is. I tried to tell you that."

"I'd like to finish banging now, please."

"Oh, so polite." Gavin kissed her and began moving inside her, starting slowly on the way to picking up where they'd left off. He had her so primed and ready from the session against the door, that it didn't take much to take her right back up again.

She clung to him, her arms wrapped around his neck, her knees snug against his hips, rocking into his every thrust.

"Ella, babe . . . Come with me. Come with me." He threw his head back as the orgasm overtook him. His release triggered hers, and she had to smother the urge to scream from the exquisite pleasure they generated together. "Feels so good, baby. So good."

She held him close as his body rocked with aftershocks.

"Holy shit," he muttered. "What a difference no condom makes."

"I take it you liked it?"

"If I loved it any more, I'd be dead."

"Don't joke about that, please."

He raised his head and kissed her softly, gently. "Sorry."

Ella brushed the sweaty hair off his forehead and took a moment to just look at him. She never, ever got tired of looking at him. He was so damned beautiful.

Kissing her again, he said, "I should probably go. We've been outed by Mrs. Abernathy."

"Don't go. I want to sleep with you."

"I'd hate to make you the subject of gossip, El."

"I don't care if people talk. I want them to know we're together. What do I care what people say?"

"I care," he said. "I don't want them talking about you."

"Then let's go to your place."

"Right now?"

"Right now." She pushed at his shoulder, and he withdrew from her, flopping onto his back to watch her as she got busy packing an overnight bag. "Get up before you fall asleep."

He groaned as he pulled himself out of bed and went into the bathroom to clean up and then to get his clothes in the other room. By the time he was dressed, Ella was ready. "Leave your car here," he said. "I'll bring you home in the morning."

"That's crazy. You don't need to make a special trip."

Cupping her face in his hands, he kissed her. "I want to make a special trip, and I'll bring you home."

"Okay." Her insides quaked when he looked at her that way, when he held her face in his hands and made her feel so cherished.

They packed up some of the groceries they'd bought for breakfast and rode to his house in contented silence, his hand wrapped around hers the entire way. He never once let go. Ella loved that. She loved every single thing about being with him this way—except for the nagging, gnawing fear that something would happen to mess it up.

After having even this small taste of what was possible between them, she wouldn't be able to handle something going wrong. And that made her feel madly vulnerable, like a live nerve ending walking around outside her body subject to severe pain at any given moment.

She'd gone into this with her eyes wide open, knowing what—and who—she was taking on. But that didn't make it any easier to picture a cataclysmic ending to their fairy tale.

That wouldn't happen. It couldn't. She'd make sure of it.

Gavin drove onto the grounds of Guthrie Logging after a short ride through town and into the foothills of Butler Mountain. He pulled up to his cabin and cut the motor. "Let me come around for you since the outside lights aren't on."

When he shut off the headlights, the darkness surrounded them, and Ella was glad he was coming to get her. The passenger door opened, and he held her hand to help her down from the truck. He kept a firm hold on her hand until they were inside the cozy cabin.

The door shut behind him and the lock clicked into place. Then he gave a gentle tug on her hand and once again had her pressed against a door before she could begin to gauge his intentions.

"No one to hear us hanging pictures here," he said with a sexy grin that lit up his gorgeous eyes.

"Good to know." She reached up to caress his face. "But you need sleep more than you need to hang more pictures."

"I hate to admit you might be right." He kissed her and then pulled himself off her, leading her into the bedroom. "You can have the bathroom first."

"I'll be quick." In the bathroom, Ella brushed her teeth and changed into lightweight pajama pants and a tank. When she returned to the bedroom, she found Gavin stripped down to boxers and was once again struck by the fact that she now got to look at him—all of him—any time she wanted to. "Your turn."

"Get the bed warm for me."

"You got it." Snuggled under the warm down comforter and soft flannel sheets, she listened to the water running in the bathroom and waited for him with breathless anticipation. She was in big trouble where he was concerned, and the trouble got bigger with every minute she spent with him.

CHAPTER 12

——◆——

*All human wisdom is summed up
in two words; wait and hope.*

—Alexandre Dumas

Gavin crawled into bed and immediately reached for her. She curled up to him, her hand on his abdomen, her legs tangled up in his.

"You're wearing far too many clothes," he said. "If we'd stayed at your place, we would've slept naked. I feel penalized for protecting your reputation."

Ella laughed. "You're very cute when you're petulant."

"You're very cute when you use big words. Now take all this crap off, will you? I want to feel your skin against mine."

Gavin Guthrie wanted to sleep naked with her. He wanted to feel her skin against his. His gruffly spoken words had her on the verge of overheating as she pulled the tank over her head and then removed her pajama pants and panties.

The second she tossed her clothes onto the floor, his arms came around her, drawing her into his warm embrace. When she felt the press of his hard cock against her bottom, she realized he'd removed his underwear, too. Good God. How was she supposed to sleep when he was hot and hard and ready behind her?

Though she was as tired as she'd ever recalled being, her body was wide awake and yearning for more of him.

"You feel so good, Ella. So, so good."

"You do, too." Even the rough scrape of his hairy leg against hers was an instant turn-on.

His hand slid from her belly up to cup her breast, his fingers tweaking her nipple until it was hard and tight.

"We have to sleep, Gavin."

"We will."

"When?"

"After."

She was about to ask more questions, but he began to enter her from behind while continuing to keep her tight against him with one arm while his other hand toyed with her nipple. Ella couldn't seem to breathe as she waited to see what he would do next. He kept up the slow, shallow strokes until she was ready to plead for more. She wanted all of him. She wanted to be possessed by him. She was already addicted to the feel of him deep inside her, the way he stretched her nearly to the point of pain before the pleasure kicked in.

Grasping his comforter, she pressed back against him, trying to get more, but his tight hold on her made it impossible to do anything other than turn over control to him.

"Easy, baby," he whispered, his warm breath against her neck setting off a chain reaction that touched every sensitive part of her. "I've got you. Relax and let me love you."

Hearing that word from his lips while his body was joined intimately with hers brought tears to her eyes. She blinked furiously, trying to contain that which could not be contained. Her heart was about to burst from the surge of emotion. She hadn't known it was possible to feel so much.

He kept up the small, maddening movements until she was prepared to beg if need be to move things along. Before she could do that, however, he grasped her hips and turned them so she was under him, thrusting into her fully in one deep stroke that triggered her orgasm.

She cried out from the powerful release.

"Yes, baby, let me hear you." Gavin rode her release until her body stopped quaking and then held still inside her, still hard. He peppered her back with kisses and began to move again, slowly at first and then faster until he, too, was coming in a last deep surge. "Now I can sleep." Kissing her back again, he withdrew and got up to use the bathroom. He returned with a washcloth that he used to clean her up.

Her face was still wet from her tears, which he couldn't see. It was just as well. He didn't need to know what an emotional wreck she was.

He again gathered her in close to him, his hand caressing her arm. "Hey, El?"

"Hmm?"

"I just want you to know . . . I've laughed more, smiled more, felt more in the last two days than I have in the last seven years. I thought you should know that."

She couldn't contain the sob that escaped from her tightly clenched jaw.

Gavin moved quickly, arranging her under him so he could kiss the tears from her face. "What's this? What's wrong?"

"Nothing is wrong. Everything is perfect."

"Then why the tears?" he asked as he brushed them away.

"Emotional overload."

"It feels good, though, doesn't it?"

"It feels so good. So incredibly good."

He bent his head to kiss her, giving her gentle strokes of his tongue before withdrawing slowly. "Don't cry, Ella. I can't bear to see tears on your gorgeous face."

"Can't help it. They're happy tears."

"I suppose I can live with happy tears." He moved to his side and brought her with him, settling her into the crook of his arm and neck where she could breathe in the appealing scent of his cologne.

Ella wanted to stay awake and enjoy every second of being close to him this way, but she could no longer fight the exhaustion that dragged her under.

*   *   *

She awoke to darkness, an empty bed and uncertainty about where she was until the events of last night swept through her mind to remind her that she was in Gavin's bed. But where was he?

The scent of coffee wafted into the bedroom along with the low hum of the TV.

What the hell time was it? A glance at the bedside table clock indicated it was just after six. An ungodly hour to be awake.

She dragged herself out of bed and into the bathroom to brush her teeth and use the facilities. Then she stumbled back into the bedroom in search of the clothes he'd made her remove the night before. Thinking about that and what had followed made Ella's body tingle as she got dressed.

He was an amazing lover, but then she'd always known he would be. Before now, before him, sex had never been particularly enthralling for her. But with him, she could easily become addicted to the way he made her feel every time he touched her.

Still, hovering beneath the surface of her happiness, was that tingle of fear. By going all in, by giving him everything, she was fully exposed. If it didn't work out, if something happened . . . No. She couldn't go there. She wouldn't. Not when she was determined to enjoy this time with him after wanting him for so long.

With her resolve back in place, she stepped out of the bedroom to find him standing in the kitchen, mug of coffee in hand, dressed in another pair of well-worn jeans and a blue flannel shirt, rolled up to reveal the long-sleeved thermal he wore under it. He looked at her with satisfaction and possessiveness in his gaze. "Morning. Did I wake you?"

"No." She went to him and wrapped an arm around his waist, noticing his hair was still damp from a shower she'd slept through. "Did you sleep?"

"Yeah, I slept great. You?"

"Same."

He put down the mug and wrapped his arms around her. "Good. I want you well rested for tonight."

"What's tonight?"

"More of the same." Kissing her, he let his hands wander down to cup her ass, drawing her in tight against his instant erection. "You've got me completely addicted to being inside you."

It was a good thing he was holding her so tightly or she might've dissolved into a puddle on the floor. "I'm feeling rather addicted myself."

"Good problem to have."

"A very good problem."

"Coffee?"

"Please."

He poured her a mug and dished up some eggs and toast for her.

"And here I thought I'd already seen the outer limits of your culinary talents," she said, taking a seat at the bar to enjoy her breakfast.

"I like to surprise you."

"You do surprise me."

He leaned on the counter, closing the space between them. "How so?"

"You tried to warn me away. You tried so hard to scare me off. And since you failed so miserably, I keep wondering what you were so afraid of."

After a long look down at his coffee, he shifted his gaze to meet hers. "I'm in a good place right now, largely thanks to you. But the dark moods come on me when I least expect them, and sometimes they last awhile."

"Maybe they won't come back if you're happy."

"We can hope not, but they always seem to come back, no matter what I do."

Ella put down her fork and pushed her half-finished breakfast aside. "I'm not afraid of the dark, Gavin."

"You haven't seen the dark. How can you know that?"

She reached across the counter for his hand. "Last night, you said you've been happier in the last few days than you've ever been. I have been, too. I'm not going to run away the second things get difficult or challenging."

"I don't expect you to put up with me when I'm dealing with that."

"I want to put up with you all the time—good, bad, ugly. I'm here, and I'm not going anywhere. Unless you want me to."

He bent his head over their joined hands, bringing hers to his lips. "I want you right here with me, which still makes me feel selfish at times."

"Why would you feel selfish when I'm exactly where I've always wanted to be?"

"You're so open and honest. Does it ever scare you to have so much on the line?"

After he'd just complimented her honesty, she couldn't very well lie to him. "Yeah, it does. Sometimes. But then you hold me and kiss me and make love to me, and the fear becomes so secondary to how I feel when I'm close to you."

"How do you feel?"

"Overwhelmed in the best possible way. Thrilled to finally have a chance to see what this could be. Hopeful for both of us. Madly, completely and utterly turned on, like I've never been before."

"Those are all good things."

"Yes, they are, and they make the fear easier to handle."

"I don't want you to be afraid."

"Goes with the territory. Any time we put our hearts on the line for something so important, a little fear is to be expected."

"For the second day in a row I have no desire to go to work and every desire to spend this day with you."

"That's what weekends are for."

He kissed her hand again before releasing it. "How many more days until the weekend?"

"Four."

"That's a lifetime."

"You'll survive."

"I'm not sure I will." With a deep sigh he turned away

from her, rinsed out his mug and left it to dry on a dish towel. "Can you be ready to head into town in a few minutes?"

"Yep." While he went into the bedroom, she finished her coffee and took her plate to the sink to wash it. She was drying it when the invitation to Dylan's wedding caught her eye on the counter. Glancing over her shoulder to make sure Gavin was still in the bedroom, Ella picked up the RSVP card and saw that he had checked the "Sending Regrets" box but obviously hadn't mailed it yet.

It was none of her business. She knew that. But she wanted to do this for him anyway. She wanted to give him back some of what he'd lost when Caleb died, and his friends were a great place to start. She tucked the card into the built-in bra in her tank and then went into the bedroom to get ready to go.

"What's up tonight?" he asked.

"I'm making that pork tenderloin you made me buy."

"With the applesauce and potatoes?"

"Yep."

"I'll never survive until dinner."

"I'll make you a ham sandwich for lunch when we get back to my place."

"Mmm, with lots of mayo?"

"Ewww. If you insist."

"I do. I insist."

If yesterday had been a great day for Ella, today was even better because she'd caught up on her sleep. She floated through her daily routine on a cloud of happiness, trying to work while sensual memories assailed her. The way he'd entered her from behind and driven her slowly mad before giving her what she wanted and needed.

The heated kiss he'd left her with this morning after bringing her home. The promise of more of the same tonight.

A knock on her office door reminded her that she was at work and expected to function, not daydream. "Come in."

Her brother Wade ducked his head in. "Busy?" Wade

most closely resembled Will with his honey-colored hair, but his face was leaner, more angular, and his hair was much longer than Will's.

"Never too busy for you."

Smiling, he came in and shut the door, which had Ella wondering what was on his mind.

"What's up?"

As he always did when he came into her office, he grabbed the stress ball on her desk and took a seat to play with it. "I was about to ask you the same thing. You've been hiding out all week, when you're not walking around with a goofy grin on your face."

"My grin is not goofy."

"It's extremely goofy. Everyone is talking about it, in fact."

"Whatever. It's high time I gave them something to talk about, wouldn't you say?"

"High time for sure." He moved the ball from hand to hand. "You're being careful, right?"

"No," Ella said with a sigh. "I'm not being careful at all. I'm in this so deep, Wade."

"You've been in it so deep with him for a long time now."

"Yes, I have. And now that I have him, so to speak, it's made all the years of wanting him so worth it."

His face set in an oddly contemplative expression. "That must be nice."

"It is nice. It's . . . It's amazing. I always sort of knew it would be this way, but now I know it for sure."

"I'm happy for you, Ella. You know that, right?"

"Sure." Why did she hear yet another *but* coming?

"I just hope he doesn't disappoint you."

"You and everyone else I'm related to." She leaned her elbows on the desktop. "Everyone is saying the same thing. Even he is saying it."

"And yet . . ."

"And yet, even though I know it's a slippery slope, I've never been this happy, Wade. Ever."

"Do you know why you're my favorite sister and my favorite sibling?"

"Why?" she asked, touched by words he'd never said out loud before.

"Because you're the least judgmental person I know and the nicest. No matter what's going on, you're always up, always positive, always optimistic. Those are such admirable qualities. I think we all wish we were more like you."

"Stop," she said, feeling leaky around the eyes. Her normally reserved brother was rather effusive today. "That's not true."

"It is true. You're everyone's go-to person when they need a pick-me-up. Good old Ella is there for everyone. I honestly think there are those among us who would kill anyone who hurt you, even someone we love as much as we do Gavin."

Incredibly touched by his sweet words, Ella said, "I love you for caring so much and for all the nice things you said about me, even if I don't feel I deserve such high praise."

"You deserve it, Ella. You deserve the best of everything. Don't settle for less, you hear me?"

"I won't. I promise."

"Good." He returned the stress ball to the desk. "Then my work here is finished."

"Are you ever going to tell me who it is that has *you* tied up in knots?"

CHAPTER 13

Wade seemed momentarily stunned. "What?"

"You think I don't know, but I do. I've known for a long time there was someone."

"Doesn't matter," he said bitterly. "She's not available to me."

"I knew it! Who is she? Tell me everything."

Wade sagged back into the chair. "Nothing much to tell. We're friends. She's married. Not happily, but she won't talk about it. I worry he's knocking her around, but I can't prove it. Now I don't even really talk to her anymore." He shrugged. "It's not going to happen, so what's the point of thinking about it?"

"I know that feeling, when it all seems so hopeless."

"In this case, it is hopeless. She's married to someone else."

"What's her name?"

He hesitated before he said, "Mia."

"How did you meet her?"

"At a yoga retreat."

"When?"

"A year and a half ago."

"Oh God, Wade . . . And all that time . . ."

His shrug was confirmation.

Filled with sadness for his dilemma, Ella got up and went around the desk, sitting in the chair next to his. "Why didn't you tell me?"

"Nothing to tell. It was over before it began."

"Why do you think he's knocking her around?"

"She's always got bruises on her arms that she says are because she's clumsy, but they look like fingerprints to me. Like someone grabbed her hard. She denies that he's hurting her."

Ella took a deep breath and blew it out. "You're worried, though."

"Hell, yes, I'm worried! I keep telling myself it's not my deal. She's not mine. She's married to him, not me. And every night I lie awake wondering how she is, if she's hurting, if she's scared, why she doesn't call me anymore. It fucking sucks."

Ella picked up the stress ball and put it back in his hands, covering them with hers. "I can't imagine what that must be like."

"Every day I say this is the day I'm not going to think about her anymore, and every night I'm right back in hell, left to wonder where she is, if she's okay, whether she ever thinks of me the way I think of her."

"Why haven't you told me about her before?"

"I don't know." He squeezed the ball and then glanced at her. "I told Hannah once in a weak moment. I needed to tell someone, and she was willing to listen."

"I'm glad you told someone. You shouldn't have to go through this alone."

"You're not mad I told Hannah and not you?"

"No, Wade," she said, smiling at his reference to the special bond the two of them had always shared. "I'm not mad. I hope Hannah was able to give you some good advice."

"She did."

"If there's anything I can do, anything at all . . ."

"I know. Thank you. Don't tell anyone, okay?"

"I never would."

"I gotta get back to work figuring out how to incorporate sex toys and marital aids into our health and wellness line. Never thought I'd say that sentence out loud."

Ella snorted with laughter. "Good old Dad strikes again."

"Thank goodness it's going to be your problem getting the sales force onboard. No way I can imagine having that conversation with all the lovely grandmothers who work for us."

"You're so cute that they'd be filled with warm thoughts of Wade Abbott on cold winter nights."

"Eww."

Ella lost it laughing at the face he made.

"On that note, I'm outta here." He tossed the stress ball to her and made a hasty exit.

After he left, Ella couldn't stop thinking about what he'd told her and how awful it had to be caring about Mia the way he did but not knowing if she was okay.

Since she was apparently taking a break from work, Ella stood and stretched and then left her office to cross the hall to Hunter's. "Knock, knock."

"Hey, what's up?"

Ella stepped into Hunter's office and closed the door. "I need a favor."

"Okay . . ."

"It's a weird favor and you may not approve, but I need the favor anyway."

"That was a hell of an intro. Lay it on me."

"I want to take Gavin to Dylan's wedding, and I need you to help me with the logistics. I don't know Dylan as well as you do."

He tapped his mechanical pencil against his lip as he contemplated her request. "I thought Gavin said he wasn't going to the wedding."

"That's what he said. Yes."

"So, um . . ."

"Nolan told me he never goes to Sultan things anymore, except for when they're here."

"That's true."

"It's because he thinks of them as Caleb's friends, not his. But they're his friends, too. Everyone has said that."

"You might be wading into shark-infested waters here, Ella. Gavin is weird when it comes to stuff that involved Caleb. I suspect it's been part of his coping mechanism to distance himself from things he associates with Caleb."

"By doing that, he's also distancing himself from people who care about him. I hate that for him. I hate that he's been living half a life for all these years. I want to remind him of things he used to enjoy. If he can't do those things with Caleb anymore, he can still do them with me and you and all his other friends."

"It might be too hard for him," Hunter said softly.

"The first time. Maybe the second and third time. But eventually he'll start to associate new memories with old friends."

"Are you prepared for him to be unhappy that you've done such a thing?"

Her stomach knotted at the thought of making Gavin unhappy. That was the last thing she wanted to do. "I hope he'll be pleasantly surprised."

"You're playing with emotional dynamite."

"Maybe so, but you know what he told me last night?"

Hunter cringed. "Is it PG-13?"

"Yes," she said with a laugh. "He said it's been years since he laughed or smiled as much as he has with me in the last few days. I want to give him more to smile about. That's all this is."

"And if you get a few days in the tropics with the guy you love . . ."

"Bonus."

Hunter shook his head, his disapproval still obvious, but he clicked away on his computer and then looked up at her. "I sent you an e-mail with Dylan's address."

"Thank you."

"Your heart's in the right place with this, Ella. Don't think I can't see that. But just be prepared for it to not be as easy as you think it's going to be."

"Nothing with Gavin has been easy, except for the way I feel about him. Loving him is the easiest thing I've ever done."

"I know that feeling, but I also know Gavin, and he's different since Caleb died."

"Of course he is. We all are."

"No one more so than Gavin. The grief runs deep. All the way to his bone marrow."

"Grief isn't the only emotion he's capable of feeling. I'm determined to prove that to him."

"Just make sure it's not at your own expense."

"I'm getting tired of everyone warning me off the man I love."

"I know that feeling, too. Everyone thought I was crazy for getting involved with Megan, especially when she'd been so crazy about Will for so long. Didn't matter. I get it. But none of us wants to see you sucked into the rabbit hole Gavin's been in for years now. In fact, I can almost promise you that I'll throw myself in front of that if I see it happening."

"I don't want you throwing yourself in front of anything, Hunter. I'm asking you and everyone to respect my judgment and my privacy. I know we're up in each other's business all the time, but I won't welcome interference in this case."

"Ella—"

"Gavin has a right to be happy, especially after everything he's been through. I'm going to make him happy."

"Okay."

"Okay? That's it? You're actually going to stand down?"

"If that's what you want."

"It is. Don't worry about me. I'm a lot tougher than I look."

"I will worry about you because that's my job as your big brother."

Ella rolled her eyes at him. "Focus your big-brother bullshit on Charley and leave me alone."

"It's easier to focus on you. You're not as mean as she is."

"Wimp."

"Damn straight."

Ella walked out laughing and encountered her dad returning from somewhere with Ringo and George in hot pursuit.

"Just the girl I wanted to see," Lincoln said. "Step into my office."

She didn't bother to remind him that she was no longer a girl. Nor did she take the time to tell him she didn't want to hear Gavin warnings from him, too. Resigned to losing control of her day, she followed her father into his office.

"Close the door, will you?"

Ella wanted to tell him there was no need to close the door because they weren't going to talk about the thing he wanted to talk about. But arguing with him would take time she didn't want to waste when she had a special meal to cook for the man she adored. She'd taken advantage of Gavin's ungodly wake-up time to come into work more than an hour earlier than normal with plans to also leave early.

She took a seat in front of her dad's desk. "What's up?"

"I wanted to go over the remarks for Friday night. You've given me a great start, as always, but I need your opinion on a few things."

"Oh," Ella said, pleasantly surprised to realize they were going to discuss business rather than her love life. However, this was Lincoln Abbott, and his interest in his children's love lives had been at an all-time high recently. So she remained wary.

They went over the remarks Ella had drafted for him, thanking the sales team for their dedication to the family and the store, gearing them up for the holiday rush and reminding them of several new product lines that were expected to get a lot of attention this year.

"I'd like to mention the toys," Lincoln said.

"You've got that covered in the part about special gifts for the young people."

"Not those toys."

"Oh . . ." Ella did not want to sit in a room with her father and discuss sex toys. Uh-uh. No way. "It's probably too soon. We're not ready to roll that out yet."

"We're ready to tell them it's coming in the New Year."

"But that has nothing to do with the upcoming holiday season."

"It's a great time to start the conversation with everyone there. The next company meeting doesn't happen until the picnic in July."

"We can call another company-wide meeting before then, if need be."

"That's just more work. I want to tell them about it. Will you write me a paragraph or two about what we're doing and why?"

"I still don't know what we're doing or *why*."

"Yes, you do. You sat in Colton's presentation and heard the numbers and why it makes sense to add the line to our store."

"Fine. I'll write something for you. Anything else?"

Eyeing her shrewdly, Lincoln sat back in his big leather chair and scratched Ringo behind the ears. "How are things?"

"Things are good. How are things with you?"

"Just fine."

"Great. Glad we had this conversation." She began to get up to leave.

"Ella."

"Dad, please. I know exactly what you're going to say and I've already heard it from Mom, Hunter, Hannah, Wade, Charley . . . It's beginning to feel a bit like piling on. I know you all care, and I appreciate that. But if you really care, please just stay out of it."

"All I was going to say is that I like Gavin. I like him for you."

Ella was so flabbergasted that her mind went totally blank. She had not expected him to say that. "Oh. Well. Thanks. I like him for me, too."

He smiled. "He's a good guy."

"Yes, he is. So . . . That's it? That's all you're going to say?"

"That's it."

"Okay, um, I . . . I'll get you that paragraph."

"Thank you, sweetheart."

Baffled and confused and more than a little relieved, Ella left her father's office and returned to her own. For the next hour she labored over the paragraph her father wanted, trying to set the right tone so the sales force wouldn't be alarmed by the new product line. She made sure to assure them that there would be lots of on-site training before the line went live and anyone who had concerns was welcome to bring them to the management at any time.

She sent it off to her dad via e-mail, hoping to avoid another sex toy conversation with her father. No one ever said there wasn't a downside to working for the family business. She couldn't wait to share this story with Gavin when she saw him later.

Ella thought of him while she ate the ham sandwich he'd made for her while she made his for him. She pictured him eating his sandwich and thinking of her. She'd made it with lots of mayo, just the way he wanted it, while he spread a thin layer of mustard on hers.

It was such a small silly thing, but she'd absolutely loved making lunches with him. Inside her brown bag, she saw a piece of paper and pulled it out. *Hope you're having a good day,* he'd written. *You're standing right next to me, and I can't wait to see you later.*

Ella sighed with pleasure at the sweet words and the sweeter sentiment. It felt so damned good to let loose all the feelings she'd kept contained for so long, to let the whole world know how she felt about him.

With her heart full to overflowing with love for him, she sent off an e-mail to Dylan, telling him what she wanted to do and asking if he'd be willing to help put her plan into action.

She moved on to other things, trying to forget about the message she'd sent to Dylan. Until her e-mail chimed with a new message and she immediately clicked right over to read it.

Hey Ella, Dylan had written, *so nice to hear from you, and I love your idea of surprising Gavin with a trip to the wedding. It would mean so much to me to have him there. I can easily add you to the reservation at the resort. They're*

*holding a couple of extra rooms for us until the week before,
so good timing. Am I holding one room for you guys or two?*

He included some other details about the wedding and a
link to the resort where it would take place.

Ella clicked on the link and began to drool at the sight of
the crystal-clear blue water, white sand, palm trees, sunsets
and breathtakingly romantic rooms. Imagining herself in paradise with Gavin was further impetus to make this happen.

She wrote back to Dylan. *Thanks for all your help. The
resort looks AMAZING! One room will do. Thanks again
and congratulations!*

He replied right away. *Sounds like my buddy Gavin has
been keeping secrets . . . Happy for you guys and especially
happy for him. It's high time he got back to the land of the
living. See you soon, Ella.*

Bolstered by Dylan's kind reply, she logged on to a travel
website to discover there were still plenty of seats available on
flights. They'd leave from Boston the day after Thanksgiving—
Black Friday, she thought with a gulp—and return the following Friday. Before she could purchase the tickets, she had to
see about putting Charley in charge of the floor during one of
the busiest weeks of the year in the store.

Ella checked the time on her computer. Just after three.
She had an hour before she wanted to head home to start
cooking and needed to make it count.

CHAPTER 14

————◆————

*They say a person needs just three things to be
truly happy in this world: someone to love,
something to do, and something to hope for.*

—Tom Bodett

Gavin's workday had been a study in crisis management,
beginning with the equipment failure in the mountains
that had forced them to halt all operations for the day. He'd
sent his mechanics to figure out what was going on, but in the
meantime, the men who worked the north woods were at a
standstill.

Standstills cost him money.

He'd no sooner dealt with that when two of the men working
at a local job returned to the yard, one of them cradling his
bloody hand while the other went in search of a first-aid kit.
With one quick look, Gavin could see that the wound needed
stitches.

"Get him to the ER," Gavin said to the man who'd brought
him back to the yard.

"What's in the water today?" asked Clinton, his second
in command, when the other two had left for the hospital.

"Who the fuck knows? And why would they come here
instead of the hospital when he's bleeding like a stuck pig?"

"Um, well, sometimes they aren't the sharpest tools in the shed?"

Most of the time, the guys who worked for him were reliable and bright. But sometimes they weren't. "Did they say what happened?" Gavin asked, dreading the reams of paperwork that resulted from an on-the-job injury.

"Something about a strip of bark and a fall." Clinton checked his watch. "I gotta jet. We have Trish's ultrasound appointment at four. She'll skin me alive if I'm late."

"I remember. Go ahead, and good luck with that."

"Thanks. Call me if you need anything."

"Surely we've exceeded the day's quota for catastrophes."

"Knock on wood," Clinton said with a smirk.

"Very funny."

Clinton went spinning out of the parking lot a few minutes later, waving to Gavin as he left. He was happy for his long-time employee and his wife, who'd been trying to have a baby for a while now and were finally getting their wish.

He went into the office, hoping to hear from the mechanics with an update about the repairs being made to the equipment up north. While he waited, he paid some bills, caught up the accounting software and used the office line to return customer phone calls. His employees would know to call his cell phone.

His corner of Butler was one of two areas, Colton's mountain being the other, that had reliable cell service. And he was damned thankful for that. It would be much more difficult to run his business without a cell phone.

It was starting to get dark by the time the cell rang with a call from one of his men—not the one he'd been hoping to hear from.

"Yeah, hey boss, so a funny thing happened on the way back to town."

Gavin's gut clenched. "What happened?"

"The truck jackknifed and we've got a load of wood blocking I-89."

"Were people hurt?" Gavin asked, paralyzed by the

image of massive logs rolling off one of his trucks onto cars sharing the road. It was one of his recurring nightmares as the owner of a logging company.

"No, man, I got super lucky. No one was near me at the time."

Thank God for small favors.

"We got a real fucking mess up here. Can you come help me out?"

"Where are you?"

"Just south of St. Albans."

Fuck, that was two hours away. "Yeah," Gavin said with a sigh, "I'm on my way." He should've actually knocked on wood earlier when Clinton suggested it. Before he left the office, he called the Green Mountain Country Store, asked for Ella and was put through to her voice mail. "Hi, this is Ella Abbott. I can't take your call right now, but please leave a message, and I'll get right back to you. Thanks."

The sound of her voice made him smile for the first time since he parted with her that morning. "Hey, babe, it's me. Total cluster of a day here, and I have to go rescue one of my guys over in St. Albans, so I'll be late tonight. I'll be over as soon as I get back to town. Call my cell if you need to reach me." He rattled off the number. "I've been thinking about applesauce all day. Among other things. See you soon."

Gavin pulled out of the yard a few minutes later and pressed the pedal to the floor. He had a four-hour round-trip and God only knew what kind of a mess waiting for him when he got there.

Ella arrived home right at four and flipped on some music to keep her company while she peeled a dozen apples, mixed them with apple juice, lemon juice, brown sugar, cinnamon, ground cloves and her grandmother's secret ingredient—maple syrup from the family's sugaring facility on the mountain.

"Thank you, Colton," Ella said, as she did every time she used the syrup her brother produced each year. He and Lucy had spent much of the autumn in New York but were back now for Thanksgiving and the birth of their first niece or nephew.

With the apples simmering in a pot on the stove, she prepared the pork tenderloin for baking and thought about the situation with Max and Chloe. She couldn't imagine how difficult it would be to break up with her partner when they were about to bring a baby into the world. Max had been forced to grow up practically overnight when Chloe got pregnant, and he'd held up admirably. But this new development had Ella worried about her baby brother.

Next she set her sights on the small white potatoes that she would fry with onions and garlic and oil. They were one of Ella's favorite things to eat, and she couldn't wait to share them with Gavin.

Another hour and a half or so and he would arrive. She couldn't wait to see him. Eight hours apart felt like a lifetime, which she knew was ridiculous. But after waiting so long to be with him, every minute she spent apart from him was painful.

With all her prep work finished, Ella decided to indulge in a nice hot bath in the old claw-foot tub that was one of her favorite things about her apartment.

She spent more than an hour reading and lounging in the tub before getting out to dry off. In the cabinet she contemplated the array of scented lotions that her sisters were always giving her for one occasion or another. Charley and Hannah both loved the smelly stuff, and tonight she was thankful for their good taste as well as Bath & Body Works.

Was she in a Warm Vanilla Sugar mood or Japanese Cherry Blossom? Perhaps in honor of their upcoming vacation, it was an Oahu Coconut Sunset kind of night. No, she'd save that for the trip. In the end, she chose Carried Away because the title matched her mood.

She was most definitely carried away by Gavin Guthrie, and she hoped he would carry her away again as soon as possible. With that in mind, she chose a slinky black nightgown with a matching thong and covered it with a red silk robe. The other thing her sisters loved beyond all reason was lingerie. She'd never cared enough about any man to wear for them the things they bought her. She was glad now that she'd saved them for Gavin. Her body tingled in anticipation.

After lighting her favorite sage candle, she went into the kitchen to check on dinner. The apples were soft and ready to be mashed. In her family there were two schools of thought when it came to applesauce. Some preferred the puréed version. Ella was a fan of the chunkier version. So rather than putting the apples in the food processor, she smashed them with a potato masher and put them in the refrigerator to cool.

The potatoes were nicely browned and smelled so good she nearly drooled in anticipation. A peek into the oven revealed that the meat was almost done, too. She turned the temperature down to keep it warm.

Ella poured a glass of chardonnay and took it into the living room. She lit the fire and sat on the sofa staring into the flames, wondering how much longer she had to wait until he'd arrive.

By seven, she was beginning to worry. She called his home number from memory—yes, she'd memorized it and wasn't proud of that—but he didn't answer, so she looked up the number to his office in the phone book. No answer there either.

Ella bit her thumbnail as a nagging worry began to assail her. What if one of the dark moods had come on him today and he was off doing something self-destructive? Was he in a bar somewhere? Was he spoiling for a fight? She poured another glass of wine and tried to force herself to relax, to not think the worst. But his recent track record made that a difficult challenge.

At eight o'clock she was seriously considering calling his parents to get his cell number when she remembered the ICE call. She ran for the portable phone and scrolled through the incoming numbers. When she saw the one from the other night, she pressed the call button.

Gavin answered on the third ring. "Ella?" The connection was crackling and fading in and out. ". . . my message?"

"What? You're cutting out."

". . . fucking mountains."

Mountains? What was he doing in the mountains? And what message had he left for her? There were no messages on her machine.

". . . call you back." The line went dead, and Ella stood with the phone in hand ready to scream from frustration. She'd never been a particularly impatient person until right now. Twenty long minutes passed before the phone rang again.

"Gavin."

"Yeah, babe. So sorry. I had no reception in the mountains."

"What are you doing in the mountains?"

"Didn't you get the message I left on your voice mail at work?"

She winced. "No, I left early to come home to make dinner."

"Shit, I'm sorry. I'll be there in about an hour. Am I still welcome?"

"Yes, of course you are."

"I'm really sorry, Ella. Today was a disaster at work in more ways than one."

"I'll see you when you get here."

"I can't wait." He lowered his voice, which told her he wasn't alone. "I've been looking forward to applesauce all day."

The double meaning in his statement couldn't be denied. "Me, too."

"Wait for me, El. I'm coming."

"Okay." She didn't want to hang up, but she pressed the button to end the call and then held the phone to her chest. Returning to the sofa and her wine, she curled her legs under her and tried to force herself to relax. Then she called in to her voice mail at work and listened to his sweet message, smiling at his applesauce comment.

She felt so bad for doubting him, for thinking the worst when he'd been off taking care of his business the way he should be.

Just over an hour later, she heard the roar of his motorcycle arriving in her driveway. She ran to the door and threw it open as he came running up the stairs.

"I'm so sorry, babe." He wrapped an arm around her waist and lifted her into his arms, kissing her. "I'm sorry." Stepping into her apartment, he kicked the door closed behind him.

She held his face in her hands and kissed him. "Don't apologize. You were working."

"Were you worried?"

She bit her lip and nodded.

"Did you think the worst?"

She hesitated for only a second before she nodded again. "I'm sorry."

"It's okay. I understand. I haven't given you much reason to have faith."

"Yes, you have. You're trying. That matters."

He let her slide down the aroused front of him. "You look amazing and you smell like a dream. What is that?"

"It's called Carried Away. It suited the mood I've been in lately."

"That suits my mood, too."

"Are you hungry?"

"Famished."

She took him by the hand and towed him behind her into her cozy kitchen, where she'd set the small table for two. Gesturing to one of the chairs, she said, "Have a seat."

He slid into the chair she'd indicated. "This looks so nice. I'm sorry I messed it up."

"You didn't." She retrieved a beer she'd bought with him in mind from the fridge, popped it open and put it in front of him. "Relax. Your hell day is over."

"Thank God for that."

"What happened?"

While she put dinner on the table, he told her about the three-crisis day he'd endured at work.

"Does that happen a lot?"

"None of it ever happens—not on that scale anyway. It

was like the universe was conspiring to keep me away from you."

"Your man who went to the ER," she asked, slicing the pork and putting it on a plate. "Is he okay?"

"Twenty stitches later, he's fine but out of work for a week. And the paperwork I'll have to file on the incident will take me that long to complete."

Ella winced. "That doesn't sound like fun."

"It sucks, but I'm glad he's okay. I've been really lucky with no major injuries for my employees despite the dangerous work they do every day."

"What's up with the equipment in the mountains?"

"Still waiting to hear, but I've got my fingers crossed that it's an easy fix. Until they get it up and running again, I've got six guys twiddling their thumbs and still being paid."

"So they work up there all the time?"

"During the week. We rent a house up there and they stay up there Sunday through Thursday and come home for the weekends."

She brought the food to the table and took a seat across from him.

"Come over here."

"Over where?"

He pushed out his chair and gestured to his lap.

A rush of heat overtook her at his blatant invitation, making her face—and other areas—feel hot. She got up and went around the table to sit on his lap. He wrapped his arm around her and then used his free hand to fill his plate. Then he proceeded to feed them both from one plate. It was the single most intimate moment of her life, sharing a chair, a plate, a fork with him. He fed her bites of applesauce and then kissed the sweetness off her lips.

Everything tasted better than it ever had before, and the solid press of his erection against her bottom kept her in a constant state of arousal as they ate and he raved over the food she'd prepared.

Gavin put down the fork and ran his hand up her inner thigh.

Ella shuddered from the powerful charge of desire that simple touch created. The drag of his calluses over her skin set off a chain reaction that traveled from her lips to her nipples to her clit. She quite simply burned for him.

"Gavin."

"What, babe?"

"I . . ."

He swept her hair out of his way and began kissing her neck.

She leaned in to get closer to him.

"What were you going to say?"

"Can we go to bed? Right now? Please?"

"The bed is so far away." Before she could protest that it was only in the next room, he had arranged her so she faced him, straddling his lap. He pulled open the button to his jeans, unzipped slowly and carefully and freed his incredibly hard cock from the confines of his pants.

She could barely keep up as he pushed aside her thong and surged into her, filling and stretching her nearly to the point of pain before her body relented and let him in.

"Who needs a bed when we have a perfectly good chair?" he asked, his hands cupping her bottom under the nightgown and squeezing as he drove into her again.

Ella had never had sex on a kitchen chair before, and quickly discovered she'd been missing out.

He was relentless, manipulating her body as if she were weightless, lifting her up and down and then up, only to release her again, fully impaling her.

With her arms around his neck, Ella cried out from the thrill of his possession, for that was the only word that came to mind. She felt possessed by him in the best possible way.

Gavin pushed the robe off her shoulders, letting it drop to the floor. The straps of her gown slid down her arms until her breasts were bared to him. He took full advantage, drawing her right nipple into his mouth as he rolled his hips, touching off wave after wave of sensation that had her on the verge of release.

"Gavin," she gasped.

He heeded her unspoken plea and pressed his fingers against her clit, stroking her to completion.

Her head fell back, and she might've slipped off his lap without the strong hold he had on her as he found his release, too.

"Mmm," he said on a low growl, "I love having dinner with you."

Ella couldn't believe it was possible to laugh while her body continued to vibrate with wave after wave of incredible pleasure. But he made her laugh, he made her happy, he made her want more of what they'd had together. So much more. She was beginning to realize that whatever time they were able to spend together would never be enough. She'd always want more. "I love having dinner with you, too. We should do it again tomorrow. And the day after."

"The day after that, too."

"Absolutely."

"This is so good, Ella," he whispered fiercely, his lips brushing against her jaw. "It's so damned good."

She blinked back the tears that suddenly filled her eyes. "I always knew it would be."

"You had so much faith in me, even when I didn't deserve it."

"You always deserved it. None of what happened was your fault."

"Some of it was my fault," he said with a sigh. "I let the rage get the better of me at times, and I'm not proud of that." Keeping his arms around her, he stood, kicked off his jeans, walked them into the bedroom and came down on top of her, all without losing their intimate connection.

"That was very impressive," she said, running her fingers through the silk of his hair, because she could. Because she'd wanted to every time she'd laid eyes on him for years.

"What was?"

"The caveman carry into the bedroom."

"You're light as a feather."

"Sure, I am."

He kissed her. "You fit perfectly in my arms."

"I'm glad you think so."

"Dinner was amazing. Thank you. The applesauce more than lived up to the hype."

"You're welcome, and I'll make it for you any time you want it."

"I'm going to want a *lot* of applesauce." As he said the words, he began to move above her.

That's when she realized he was hard again and apparently fully recovered. She was never going to survive insatiable Gavin. In past relationships, it was a busy night if they had sex once. With Gavin, once was never enough. Would that change over time or would they always want each other this way?

"Stop thinking and just feel," he whispered. "Just feel." He withdrew from her slowly, leaving her bereft without him hard and strong inside her. Beginning at her throat, he kissed her everywhere—along her collarbone and down to her breasts, teasing them with soft kisses everywhere but where she wanted them most.

With her hand on the back of his head, Ella tried to direct him.

"Be patient."

"I have no patience."

He took mercy on her and ran his tongue over her nipple, back and forth until she was about to start begging.

"Gavin!"

Laughing, he drew the hard tip into his mouth, sucking and biting down nearly to the point of pain.

Ella jolted and almost climaxed from the live current that traveled from her nipple to her clit. Good God . . .

He kept up the slow, sexy seduction until she was reduced to a quivering mess of sensation.

She was right on the brink when he pushed into her again and sent her flying over the edge, screaming from the power of her release. Nothing had ever been like this. Ever. Wrapping her arms around him, she drew him into a kiss that ended when he threw his head back and came with a low growl. He was so fierce and beautiful, his strong jaw clenching, his eyes closed and his lips parted.

Ella took a mental picture of what he looked like as he lost himself in her. It was something she wanted to remember always. She held on tight to him, locked in the bliss they found together. It was everything she'd ever hoped it would be and so much more that she'd never dreamed possible.

If they could have this, just this, for the rest of their lives, Ella would never want for anything else.

CHAPTER 15

There is no grief like the grief that does not speak.

—Henry Wadsworth Longfellow

On Thursday night, Gavin's parents invited them to a cocktail reception at the Guthrie Inn.

"We don't have to go if you don't want to," Ella said, tuning in to his reluctance.

"I want to support my parents. The inn has been so good for them."

"But?"

"No buts," he said, forcing a smile for her. He honestly didn't want to go. He didn't want to be around women who'd lost their husbands to war. Though he supported the wonderful work his parents and Hannah were doing at the inn, he didn't want anything to do with it.

But he couldn't very well tell his parents that, not when the inn had given them new focus and energy as they worked in Caleb's name to help others. It would be petty of him to undermine their newfound purpose by appearing less than supportive. He couldn't do that to them.

So they went.

His mother greeted them with the big, bright smile that

used to be so much a part of who she was until her son's death dimmed the light inside her.

It was a relief to see her eyes dancing with excitement and joy again. Gavin hadn't realized how much he'd missed that until now.

"Come in, have a drink, and Hannah made some delicious appetizers."

"Sounds great," Ella said. She was stunning in a black sweater, sexy gray pants that showed off her spectacular ass and even sexier black boots.

Gavin was so damned proud to have her at his side. This last week with her had been right out of a dream. He'd forgotten what it felt like to be happy—truly, deeply *happy*. Everything, even the supremely crappy days at work, had been easier to deal with knowing he got to go home to her each night.

His gaze shifted from Ella's sexy body to the picture of his brother that adorned the foyer now that the Guthrie family home was the Capt. Caleb M. Guthrie Memorial Retreat. Caleb's fierce expression in his official Army Ranger photo got to Gavin every time he allowed himself to look at it. Almost eight years later, it was still a vicious punch to the gut to remember he would never see that face again.

Gavin forced himself to look away lest he be dragged down into the rabbit hole of despair once again. He refused to let that happen when he had so many good things happening in his life. Resisting the rabbit hole had become a part-time job, but it was easier now with Ella by his side.

With her hand curled around his, he followed Ella into the kitchen, where her sister was arranging bruschetta on a platter. Hannah was beginning to show in the subtle rounding of her abdomen. Her cheeks were fuller, too, but her eyes told the true story. She'd rediscovered her joy, and it was a lovely thing to see indeed.

For so long after Caleb died, the two of them and his parents had been like the walking wounded, none of them quite sure how to go forward without the man who'd been at the center of all their lives. The other three were showing signs of recovery. Perhaps it was time for him to let it happen to him, too.

Caleb wasn't coming back, as much as he wished otherwise. None of the raging, fighting or drinking had done a damned thing to assuage his bitter loss. If possible, he'd only succeeded in making everything worse.

Gavin took a deep breath, forcing his wandering mind to stay in the present rather than drifting to the past where trouble lay.

As she talked and laughed with her sister, Ella kept a firm grip on his hand, as if she knew he needed the connection.

He gave her hand a gentle squeeze that she returned, making him feel as connected to her as he did when they made love.

Nolan came into the kitchen, carrying an empty tray. "You're a hit, babe. Everyone is clamoring for more."

"Here you are," Hannah said, smiling widely at her husband as she handed him the platter of bruschetta.

"You've been thoroughly domesticated, Nolan," Gavin said in a teasing tone.

"Watch out," Nolan said, nodding to his and Ella's joined hands. "It could happen to you, too, my friend."

Ella grinned at him, and suddenly the thought of being domesticated didn't seem so bad if she were the one doing the training. He could get on board with her brand of domestication.

Hannah filled more trays, and they helped her carry them into the room that used to be her sitting room and was now a gathering place for inn guests. A roaring fire added to the cozy atmosphere as groups of women enjoyed drinks and the food Hannah had lovingly provided.

Gavin's parents circulated, filling glasses and checking on their guests. On a table laden with food, Gavin retrieved a bottle of beer out of a bowl of ice and cracked it open. Ella's parents joined the party as did her brother Will and his wife, Cameron, who'd designed the inn's website.

A lot of work had gone into creating this oasis for women struggling to put their lives back together after unimaginable loss. Sadly, even with the wars in Iraq and Afghanistan over or winding down, the need for the services they provided here was still acute. The inn was sold out through next summer.

Amelia used the handle of a fork against her crystal glass to get everyone's attention.

The din in the room quieted and all eyes turned to Gavin's mother.

"I want to thank you all for being here tonight," Amelia said. "We hope to make these parties part of our overall effort to include our lovely guests in the community of Butler so they will always feel like they have a second home here. In the months since our opening, we've had more than fifty guests from twenty different states come to spend some time with us. All have left with new friends, an enhanced support network and yet another place to call home. I want to say a special thank you to Cameron Abbott, who is here tonight, for her amazing work on our website."

A polite round of applause had Cameron smiling and blushing from the attention. "My pleasure."

"And to my daughter-in-law for life, Hannah Roberts . . . This was all your doing, and Bob and I couldn't be more proud of all you've done to ensure that Caleb's legacy lives on forever."

As Hannah blinked back tears and kissed his mother's cheek, Ella looked up at Gavin, seeming to check on him. He smiled down at her, hoping he was reassuring her.

"I've asked Cindy, one of our current guests, to say a few words," Amelia said, "so I'll turn it over to her. Cindy?"

A petite blonde walked to the front of the room, her cheeks flushed with what might've been nerves. Gavin noticed she still wore her engagement and wedding rings on her left hand, and the sight of those rings made him unreasonably sad for someone he'd never met.

"Thank you so much, Amelia, Bob and Hannah for this lovely gathering tonight as well as the warm welcome I've received this week. It's been such a treat to get away from it all, to spend some time in this beautiful corner of the country and to be with you all." Her gesture encompassed the other guests. "I feel like I've made lifetime friends here, and I'll always be grateful for the respite." She took a deep breath before she continued. "Like many of you, my life has been split in half—before and after. On a regular Tuesday morning, I was getting my kids ready for the day when my doorbell rang. I expected my neighbor who came two mornings a week to take my daughter to preschool. Because my son was an infant, she saved me the trouble of packing up both kids to deliver Brianna to her. I had my son on my hip when I swung open the door to men in uniform. I don't remember much of that day. Apparently, I passed out at the sight of those men, but my maternal instincts were still intact because I somehow managed to shield my baby with my own body so he wasn't injured. I can't even think about what my poor daughter had to endure with her mom out cold on the floor, her brother screaming and men she didn't recognize at the door. She was four then. I hope she won't remember it, but she also won't remember much about her father, and that breaks my heart."

Listening to Cindy's story, Gavin broke out in a cold sweat as the memories from his own darkest day came back to him like a horror movie he could never escape.

"It wasn't supposed to happen to us," Cindy continued. "Lance's unit was one of the last to deploy to Iraq before the final troops left. They were on a humanitarian mission, bringing badly needed aid to the Iraqi people, who'd endured a decade of war. He was hit and killed by a stray bullet fired in one of the villages where they were working. The bullet had nothing to do with the war, apparently. Sometimes, when I allow myself to think about that—how his death had nothing at all to do with the war . . . Well, it's better if I don't think about that."

Gavin couldn't do this. He couldn't stay in this hot, suffocating room and listen to Cindy's tragedy unfold before him. Releasing Ella's hand, he slipped out of the room, hoping no one would notice him leaving. He didn't want to be rude, but he also didn't want to pass out from overheating either.

He cut through the kitchen and went out into the backyard, where he could finally breathe again in the cold November air. Bending at the waist, he propped his hands on his knees and focused on drawing deep breaths of cold air into his lungs.

Not surprisingly, Ella came out right behind him. "Gav? Are you okay?"

"Yeah, sorry. It was so hot in there I felt like I was going to pass out."

She laid her hand flat against his back. "Is that all it was?"

"Yeah, sure."

"Gavin."

Here was the one person he couldn't bullshit with his assurances that he was fine when he wasn't. She saw right through him. The mirror he couldn't escape.

"Rabbit hole alert."

"Ah, I see. Come here."

Resigned to accepting her comfort, he stood to his full height and turned to her.

She put her arms around him and held on tight, letting him know with one simple gesture that he wasn't alone.

"Sorry."

"Please don't apologize."

"My parents and Hannah have probably heard a lot of those stories since the inn opened, but I haven't. Brought it all back. That day . . ."

Ella ran her hand over his back in small, soothing circles. "Do you want to tell me about it?"

He never wanted to think about it again, let alone say the words out loud.

"Maybe if you tell me, then I'll know and you won't be alone with it anymore. It'll be our burden to share, and I can help you avoid the triggers."

"I don't want you to share my burden, Ella. That's not what we're doing here."

"It's not? So you're only signing on for the good stuff? No hard stuff, no bad stuff, no ugly?"

"I don't want you mired in my ugly."

"Even if I want to be?"

He looked down at her beautiful face. Even in the dark

he could see her affection for him shining through. "You're crazy, you know that?"

"Crazy about you, Gavin Guthrie."

"The feeling is entirely mutual." He kissed her softly. "I'll tell you about it, but not here. Let's go home."

"Whatever you want to do."

They went back inside, where the party was carrying on with happy voices and conversation. He hoped his parents hadn't noticed him backing out of the room while Cindy was talking.

"Oh, there you two are," Bob said when they entered the kitchen.

"We were just getting some air," Ella said, "but we're going to head out now. We've both got early days tomorrow."

"We're glad you could come," Bob said. He hugged Ella and shook hands with Gavin, his shrewd gaze giving him a close once-over. Despite Ella's efforts to cover for him, he knew his dad was clued in to his distress. "We'll talk tomorrow, yes?"

Though asked as a question, Gavin knew it wasn't a request. "Yeah."

They said their good-byes to the others and were on the way to his place a few minutes later. Around the fringes of his mind, the darkness hovered, threatening to swoop in and drag him down. It had happened too many times before for Gavin not to recognize the signs of impending trouble.

He was thankful for Ella's presence and regretful, too. He'd meant it when he said he didn't want her to see his darkness, but the thought of sharing the burden, of not having to go it alone any longer . . . Her offer was too tantalizing to resist, and that made him feel like a world-class bastard.

Ella had felt it happen. Standing beside Gavin while Cindy shared her heartbreaking memories, Ella had been immediately aware of the tension that invaded him, the stiffness to his body, the change in his breathing. She'd been about to get him out of there when he released her hand and made the move on his own.

She wasn't entirely sure she was doing the right thing by encouraging him to talk about the event that had triggered his reaction tonight. Too bad she couldn't consult with Hannah, but her sister was still at the party and Gavin . . . He was pouring himself a fortifying drink of amber-colored liquor.

Raising the bottle in her direction, he silently asked if she wanted a drink.

Ella nodded. She needed the fortification as much as he did.

Bringing two glasses, Gavin joined her on the sofa. He'd stoked up the fire in his woodstove, and the room was warm and cozy.

"We don't have to do this, you know," Ella said.

Swirling the liquid around in his glass, he watched it closely. "I've never talked about it with anyone."

His confession took her breath away. "Ever?"

He shook his head. "Of course my parents and Hannah and I have talked about funny memories and we've paid tribute on anniversaries, the annual road race and now the inn. But I've never talked to anyone about what losing him did to me." He finally looked at her. "Except for you. That day at Homer's funeral, when we were on the porch swing . . . That was a first for me. I thought you should know that."

Ella couldn't have spoken if she had to. She reached for his free hand and cradled it between her hands.

"I suppose it's obvious to everyone that it wrecked me because of the way I've acted at times. I'm not proud of that, but I've learned there's no rhyme or reason when something like this happens. Grief affects everyone differently." After a long pause, Gavin said, "I've been thinking over the last few days that if we're going to do this, really do it the right way, you should know what you're getting. And what happened tonight . . . I guess that just proved that I'm not as far along in this process as I ought to be by now."

"I want to know, Gavin. If we share the load it won't be so heavy for you to carry alone. And there's no timetable. No one is holding up a stopwatch and timing how long it takes you to get over your brother's death. I'm certainly not doing that. I fully expect that you'll never completely get over it."

"You're so sweet." He put down his glass and ran his thumb over her jaw. "So strong and capable. I'm afraid of using your strength as a crutch."

"It's not a crutch if it's freely given."

After a long pause, he sighed deeply and began to speak. "I didn't want him to go into the army. I had a bad feeling about it from the beginning. Hannah did, too. She and I talked about it a lot the year they were seniors and I was a junior at UVM. He had this great opportunity to play professional hockey, and he was going to turn that down to go into the army? Neither of us got how it was even a decision. I've since come to know that the desire to serve at that level is either in you like it was in him or it isn't. It's not in me. It never was, even after being brought up by a career army officer. I've felt guilty about that for a long time—that he gave so much and I had no desire at all to give anything to the military."

Ella had to resist the urge to speak, to offer comfort. That he was talking about these things to her was a huge gift that she didn't receive lightly. It might be the most important conversation they'd ever have. She was already surprised to hear that Gavin hadn't wanted Caleb to go into the army.

"The last time he was home, before that final deployment, we went camping for a few days, just the two of us and Homer, of course. We never went anywhere without good old Homie. It was the first time we'd been able to get away by ourselves in a couple of years, and we had a lot of laughs as always. But the whole time we were gone and in the days before he left, I had this low buzz of foreboding. I didn't recognize it then for what it was, but I had a knot in my stomach the size of a fist that would not go away. I thought maybe I was getting sick from Caleb's camp cooking or something. I didn't know then that it was fear. Raw, gritty fear. I never told anyone that when I said good-bye to him on the day he left for Iraq, I had the worst feeling I'd never see him again."

"Gavin . . ." Ella brushed the tears off her cheeks,

wishing she could be stronger for him, but her heart was breaking.

"At the time, I chalked it up to my overactive imagination. He was going to a part of Iraq where the fighting was mostly over. They were there to help train the Iraqi army and to provide aid. It wasn't about active combat. Not this time. Even knowing that, I couldn't shake the aching, gnawing fear. I'd wake up in the middle of the night in a cold sweat, thinking the worst. I was a fucking mess for weeks."

"And you didn't tell anyone?"

"Who could I tell? My parents? Hannah? They didn't need to hear that, not when they were contending with their own worries." He shook his head. "At times, I seriously wondered if I was going insane. My brother was a grown man, the toughest dude I'd ever known. He was a highly trained army officer who could kick the shit out of anyone who dared to cross him. And here I was, a quivering, fearful wreck of a man in comparison. I hated myself for feeling the way I did."

"It wasn't your fault, Gavin. You can't help the way you feel. None of us can." It killed her to hear that he had suffered so profoundly in utter silence.

"I know, but still . . . It felt ridiculous to be so worried about a man who was more than capable of taking care of himself, especially when he'd been in far more dangerous situations than the one he was in then." His shoulders hunched, he looked down at the floor, desolation coming off him in waves. "I was working outside of town, clearing land for a new development when my dad called. He asked if I could come to the house right away. I asked him why, and he just said . . . 'Please come, Gav.' I knew. I just *knew*. I didn't want to go there. I actually thought about getting in my truck and driving north to Canada. I almost did it, too. Even all these years later, I'm still ashamed to admit how close I came to just driving away."

"No one would've blamed you."

"Wouldn't have changed anything," he said with a shrug. "And besides, I'd like to think I'm a better son than that. My parents needed me, so I went. I'll never forget the sight of that blue four-door sedan with U.S. government plates sitting outside the house when I arrived. If I'd been looking for confirmation, there it was. I found out later that they'd already been to Hannah's house."

Ella couldn't bear to remain separate from him any longer. She crawled into his lap and put her arms around him.

He was slow to respond, as if he didn't think he deserved the comfort. But then his arms came around her, and he buried his face in her hair.

She was relieved that he was allowing her to comfort him. He'd been in bad need of some comfort for far too long.

"I finally went in there, and my parents . . . They were just wrecked. My mom was out of her mind. My dad had gone silent. He was blaming himself, I'm sure. He'd been so proud when Caleb went into the army. The chaplain told me what'd happened, and I remember thinking it was the most ridiculous thing I'd ever heard. He'd been blown up while playing a game of *soccer*? For real? It made absolutely no sense to me, and it still doesn't. It never will."

Ella drew in a shaky deep breath and ran her fingers through his hair, wishing there was something she could do or say that would help him. But all she could do was listen and offer what comfort she could.

"I don't remember much about the rest of that day or the weeks that followed. It's all a bit of a blur to me. The one thing I do remember, painfully and sickeningly, was that I never told Caleb how afraid I was for him. It was on my mind constantly, that maybe if I'd told him he would've been more careful."

"Oh God, Gavin," she whispered. "You haven't been carrying *that* around with you all this time, have you?"

"I don't think about it every day anymore, but I'll always wish I'd told him."

"He would've laughed it off. He would've said you were being ridiculous, that he was fine. You know how he was."

"Yeah, I do, and I also never wanted to put something in his head that didn't need to be there. Not when he had so many other things to think about."

"It wouldn't have made any difference. You know that, don't you?"

He shrugged, not entirely convinced.

Ella took him by the face and forced him to look at her. "It was his time to go. Nothing you or any of the rest of us who loved him could've done or said would've changed that irrefutable fact. This was how his life was meant to play out, even if we don't like it."

"I don't like it. I hate it."

"I hate it, too. I hate it for you and your parents and Hannah and all his friends and extended family. I hate it for all of us. But you know what I'm certain of?"

He shook his head.

"Caleb would hate, absolutely *hate*, that you feel any guilt whatsoever about what happened to him. He made his choices, and he owned them, Gavin. Nothing you could've said or done would've changed the outcome for him, as much as you'd like to think otherwise."

"I don't really believe I could've changed the outcome. I just like to think I could have," he added with a ghost of a smile.

"He knew you loved him. He died with no doubt whatsoever that he was well and truly loved by so many people. I have to believe he was at peace with himself and his life in that last moment."

"I hope so. I like to think he never knew what hit him."

"He didn't."

They sat quietly, wrapped up in each other's arms, and after a while, Ella felt him begin to relax ever so slightly. She wanted to know what he was thinking, if it had helped to talk about it, whether he was tired or sad. But she didn't ask. She remained stoically silent, hoping he was getting whatever he needed from her.

After a long period of silence, she ventured a glance at him and saw that he was gazing into the fire, lost in thought. She reached up to caress his face, running her thumb over the stubble on his jaw.

He looked down at her. "Thanks."

"Any time." She swallowed the hot ball of fear that

wanted to lodge in her throat. Had they done more harm than good by talking about this stuff that caused him so much pain? "Are you okay?"

"Yeah, I think I am." He took a deep breath. "What happened tonight . . . Cindy's story . . . I wasn't expecting that. Things like that . . . some people can just hear them and commiserate and go on. For me, it tends to tear the scab off the wound, which starts the spinning. I might've gone off and done something stupid, but I didn't do that this time. Because of you. Because you were here when I needed you."

"I always want to be here when you need me."

"Will you let me do the same for you?" he asked. "Will you lean on me the way you've allowed me to lean on you?"

"There's no one I'd rather lean on than you."

His smile lit up his face, and the eyes that had been so desolate a short time ago came alive again.

"I love that smile of yours," she said, tracing it with her finger.

"I love having a reason to smile again. Thanks for that, too."

"My pleasure."

"Speaking of your pleasure, it's been hours and hours since I kissed you."

"I was wondering when you were going to notice that."

Still smiling, he brought his lips down on hers for a kiss that went from soft and sweet to hot and sultry in about ten seconds.

Ella held him close to her, loving the feel of his lips on hers, the roughness of his whiskers, the passionate thrust of his tongue. She loved everything about kissing him and being with him this way, whether they were talking about the worst day of his life or kissing passionately, she loved it all. When he tightened his hold on her and stood to carry her into the bedroom, she squeaked in surprise that quickly turned to desire. Sleeping next to him every night had quickly become her favorite thing in the world, and she couldn't wait to snuggle into his warm embrace once again.

He put her down next to the bed and helped her out of her clothes while she did the same for him.

She wanted to brush her teeth and wash off her makeup, but he gathered her up into his warm embrace, his head leaning against her shoulder.

Ella wrapped her arms around his waist, loving the feel of his skin against hers, the roughness of his chest hair and the scent of his cologne. She loved everything about him, even more so after their conversation about the worst day of his life. His love for his brother ran deep, even after all these years.

"Will you do something for me?" Ella asked.

"Anything you want."

"Sit on the edge of the bed."

He did as she requested.

"Now lean back and get comfortable." She reached for a pillow and dropped it to the floor before kneeling in front of him.

"Ella . . . What're you doing?"

"Exactly what I want to do. Nothing more, nothing less."

He blew out a deep breath. "I so don't deserve you."

"Yes, you do, Gavin." She ran her hands from his calves to his knees and inner thighs, settling between his legs. "You deserve me, and I deserve you."

His fingers slid through her hair as she bent her head to run her tongue up the length of his erection, making him tremble. She loved his reaction so much she did it again.

"Ella," he whispered. "You're killing me."

"Relax and enjoy it."

"Right," he said with a tense laugh. "Relax when you're doing that?"

Equal parts amused and aroused, she wrapped her hand around the thick base and began to stroke him while continuing to tease the tip with her tongue. Never before had she wanted so badly to rock a man's world with her mouth and tongue and hand.

She wanted to give Gavin cause to think about this moment for days. Drawing him into her mouth, she sucked lightly while lashing him with her tongue and stroking him faster with her hand.

His fingers tangled in her hair, which made her scalp tingle. "Ella . . . Baby, if you keep that up . . . Oh *fuck* . . ."

She'd never before allowed a man to come in her mouth, but she'd never loved any of them the way she loved Gavin. So when his fingers tightened around her hair, when his breathing became shallow and rapid, when his thighs tightened, she didn't stop. Rather she kept it up until he raised his hips and came with a groan.

Then he released her hair and fell backward onto the mattress, his chest and abdomen heaving like a bellows.

Ella licked him clean, absorbing each tremor and aftershock before moving up to rest on top of him.

His arms encircled her.

She closed her eyes, basking in the incredible sweetness of the moment with the man she loved beyond reason. At some point in the last few days of incredible bliss with him she'd forgotten all about her plans to be careful, to guard her heart, to be wary. She was all in and getting in deeper by the minute.

CHAPTER 16

Hope will never be silent.

—Harvey Milk

G avin drove her home in the morning, so early it was still dark when they pulled up to her place. "I'm so not ready for how cold it is today," he said.

"Happens every year around this time."

"Always catches me by surprise."

"I have something that'll keep you warm today," she said as he followed her inside to have breakfast before they went their separate ways for the day.

"I can't wait to see this."

They stepped into the front hall and Ella nearly jumped a foot when Mrs. Abernathy appeared out of the gloaming.

"You're off to an early start this morning, Ella," the older woman said. She wore a bathrobe and held a mug of coffee.

"As are you, Mrs. Abernathy."

"Good morning, Gavin."

"Morning," he muttered as he followed Ella up the stairs. "God, she scared the shit out of me."

"Me, too."

Inside the apartment, they took off their coats and Ella headed directly to the coffeemaker.

He was right behind her, molding his body to hers and making her forget about what she'd been doing. "It's going to be all over town by noon that we're sleeping together. Are you okay with that?"

Ella tipped her head to give him better access to her neck. "I don't care if you don't."

"I don't. But your parents . . . Your dad . . . What will he say?"

"I'm thirty-one, Gavin. What can he say?"

"Um, a lot?"

"He and my gramps have been on a campaign to get us all settled down and happy. This is exactly what he wants."

"He wants me making mad, crazy love to his beautiful daughter every chance I get?"

She laughed. "He might not want that, but he wants me happy."

"Are you happy, Ella?"

"How can you ask me that? I've never been so happy in my whole life." She turned to him, resting her hands on his chest. "I've finally got what I've always wanted. How could I be anything less than elated?"

"I like that word. Elated. It looks good on you."

She reached up to caress his face. "Happy looks good on you, too."

"It feels good." He leaned in to press his lips to hers. "It feels so good."

With his lips sliding over hers and the hard press of his erection against her belly, Ella was tempted to forget all about the big day she had ahead of her at work. She wanted nothing more than to drag him back to bed for more of what they'd shared during the night. She ought to be completely exhausted, but rather she was buzzing from the incredible high they'd found together.

"You want pancakes?" he asked, tearing himself away from the kiss reluctantly.

Ella let him go just as reluctantly. They had a long day ahead before they could be together again later. Thinking about that would give her something to look forward to today. "That sounds good." She got out the ingredients and left him to start their breakfast while she went into her bedroom. In the closet, she found the sweater she had knitted for him during the long months she'd spent wishing for what she had now.

She held up the gray fisherman's sweater that she'd poured her heart and soul into making for the man she'd loved from afar. It had seemed like such a silly thing to do at the time, but throwing herself into the project had given her an outlet for the yearning that had taken her over.

What would he think when she told him she'd made it for him? She'd planned to save it for Christmas, but that was too far away. She wanted him to have it now. She wanted it to keep him warm today. So she summoned her courage and returned to the kitchen, sweater in hand.

He looked up from the griddle he was watching over. "What's that?"

"It's for you."

Gavin turned down the heat on the burner so the pancakes wouldn't burn. He took it from her and held it up. "Wow, that's nice."

"I made it for you."

"You *made* this? Seriously?"

"Uh-huh."

"When?"

"Um, well, over the last couple of months when I was busy being frustrated with you and our, um, situation. I could either knit you a sweater or stab you with the needles. I chose the former."

His low chuckle made her smile. "It's beautiful. Truly. A work of art. I had no idea you could knit, let alone make something like this."

"My grandmother taught me to knit when I was eight. I've been doing it ever since. It's my stress reliever."

"I'm very impressed."

"Try it on."

He flipped the pancakes and then pulled the sweater over his head. It was a perfect fit, as Ella had known it would be.

She'd spent years studying his sexy body and had felt like an expert on all things Gavin Guthrie long before this week's master class.

She adjusted the collar of his denim shirt and patted his chest. "Looks great. Very sexy."

Hooking an arm around her neck, he drew her in for a kiss. "I'll never take it off."

"Yes, you will," she said meaningfully.

"Well, I suppose I could be convinced for the right incentives." He kissed her again and then released her to deal with the pancakes.

They sat together at the table to eat, sharing the butter knife and the syrup. It was all so domesticated and comfortable, and Ella would be perfectly content to start every day this way for the rest of their lives.

"Hey, El," he said, putting down his fork.

"Yeah?"

"I want to you know . . . It means so much to me that you thought of me this way." He rested his hand flat against the sweater. "When we weren't together and I'd given you every reason to believe we never would be. That you had faith in me and us . . ."

"I didn't always have faith, not after our last go-round. I'd started to accept that it wasn't going to happen." She offered a wry smile over the top of her coffee mug. "But I finished the sweater anyway. I told myself I was done with you after that."

He reached for her hand and linked their fingers. "And yet you still came when they called you that night."

"Old habits die hard."

"Thank God for that. I'm so glad you came when they called, that we decided to give this a try."

"Me, too."

"I hate to say I have to go, but I have to go."

Ella stuck out her bottom lip.

"We're staying in bed this entire weekend, you got me? Don't make any other plans."

"Christmas tree farm Saturday afternoon, and family dinner on Sunday."

"I might let you out for those things, but otherwise, you're all mine after your deal tonight."

"Okay then. Will you do me a favor and not make any plans for next weekend?"

"Why? What's up next weekend?"

"If I tell you, then it won't be a surprise."

"I suppose I can be persuaded to go along with a surprise from you. So about tonight . . . Is it okay if I come by after work or is it only for employees?"

"Oh, you can definitely come. We do the meeting part between five and six and then we have dinner and dancing with a DJ at the Grange. I'd love for you to come by. I should've asked you before now, but I didn't think you'd want to."

Holding both their plates, he stood and bent to kiss her. "I want to."

Suddenly, Ella couldn't wait for tonight.

Though her day was frantically busy seeing to the final details for that night, she took the time to call Gavin's mother. She couldn't delay this call any longer if she was going to pull off the big surprise next weekend.

"Ella," Amelia said, "this is a nice surprise, and I'm so glad you called. I was worried about Gavin last night."

"He had a couple of rough moments, but we got through it. I think."

Amelia's deep sigh came through the line. "I didn't know Cindy was going to talk about the day she found out. I feel like I owe Gav an apology for that."

"You don't. Not at all. He understands that's what the inn is for and he wants to be supportive of what you all are doing there."

"I keep hoping that one of these days it'll get easier for him. They were so close. So, *so* close. As their mother, I was always proud of their tight bond. But after Caleb died . . . Gavin was never the same."

"I know. It's been hard to watch for everyone who cares about him."

"I'm glad he has you now, Ella. I said to Bob last night . . . What a lovely couple you make and how happy he seems when you're around. It's so nice to see that spark of life in his eyes again. It's been gone so long I wondered if we'd ever see it again."

"You're going to make me cry, Amelia."

She laughed. "I'm sorry. You didn't call me to cry, did you?"

"No," Ella said, laughing. "I was hoping you might be able to help me pull off the wedding surprise. I talked to Dylan and we're all set to stay at the resort. I'm going to get plane tickets today, but my one worry is about Gavin's work. He said the reason he wasn't going to the wedding was because of work—"

"That's bull," Amelia said forcefully. "He's hiding behind work to get out of doing things and being around people that remind him of his brother. Don't let him pull that crap."

Ella laughed. "All righty then!"

"I don't mean to be cranky about it, but I'm tired of him hiding out and avoiding the life he used to enjoy. I think it's great that you're surprising him with this trip and forcing him out of his bubble. So what can I do to help?"

Fortified by Amelia's support, Ella said, "He's mentioned his number two man at work is Clinton, but I don't know him so I wondered if you or Bob might be willing to get in touch to put him on notice that Gavin is going to be gone for a week."

"Bob would be happy to do that. They know each other from a poker game they're both in."

"That would be great. His work was the only thing about this plan of mine I was worried about."

"We'll take care of that. Don't you worry."

"Okay, then I guess I'll buy the plane tickets. Fingers crossed he's happy about this."

"Oh, he will be. It'll be great. Thank you again, Ella. It's really such a sweet thing for you to do."

"It's my pleasure." They said their good-byes, and Ella fired up her computer to buy the plane tickets. Since she hadn't been anywhere fun in a couple of years, she splurged on first-class seats. As she was punching in her credit card number, she hoped she was doing the right thing. Despite Amelia's assurances, Ella still wasn't entirely confident that Gavin would love her surprise.

But the thought of a week in paradise with him had her pressing the purchase button.

Ella was onstage with Charley, going through the PowerPoint presentation they'd put together to brief the sales team on the new holiday merchandise when she saw Gavin sneak in the main door to the Grange. She faltered briefly before picking up her train of thought and carrying it to the finish line.

They took questions for a few minutes before turning over the stage to their father.

Lincoln's job was to thank the employees for their dedication over the next few busy weeks. He always did a great job of talking about the store his father-in-law's parents had founded and the historical significance of the Stillman and Abbott family business within the town of Butler.

"I call your attention to my father-in-law, Elmer Stillman, second-generation proprietor of the Green Mountain Country Store."

Elmer stood and waved to the gathering while the employees clapped and hooted and hollered for Elmer. He loved every second of the attention they gave him every time the company came together this way.

"My children," Lincoln continued when the applause died down, "are the fourth-generation proprietors of the store, and I know I speak for Elmer when I say we are thrilled to have them actively involved in the running of the family business. Where are my kids?"

The ten Abbott siblings stood and waved to the group, as they had for years now, since they first began to wander into the family business one by one, until they were all playing a role in some way or another. It had never been expected or demanded of them, but each of them had come home to Butler after college, eager to continue their family's legacy.

Ella had been no different. She'd studied business and marketing at the University of Vermont, always with the idea of coming home to the family business at the end of school. Now nearly ten years later, she couldn't imagine any other life or career than the one she had working side by side with her father and siblings every day. The family business suited her, and she'd never had any desire to be anywhere else.

"Not only has the Green Mountain Country Store been a four-generation business for our family," Lincoln said, "it has been for many of your families, too. Please stand if you are one of our fourth-generation employees."

A group of young adults stood to applause from the others.

"How about our third-generation employees?" Lincoln said. "Including my lovely wife, Molly, who sits on our board of directors. And now our second-generation folks?"

This group, led by Elmer, was older, many of them with white or gray hair and big smiles filled with pride for their long careers with the Stillman-Abbott family business.

"And now, a round of applause for our last remaining first-generation employee, Mildred Olsen, who at the age of ninety-one continues to work as an accounts payable clerk."

As the whole room burst into applause, Hunter helped Mrs. Olsen to her feet and stood with his arm around the woman who reported to him as the company's chief financial officer. According to Hunter, Mildred was still sharp as a tack and had no plans to retire.

She waved to the other employees as they stood as one to cheer for her.

Ella approached Mildred with a bouquet of the older woman's favorite pink tea roses and bent to kiss her lined cheek.

"Thank you, sweetheart," Mildred said.

Ella reached for the microphone her father handed to her and walked it over to Mildred.

"I just want to say thank you to the Abbott family, and Hunter in particular, for continuing to allow me to do the job I love," Mildred said softly into the microphone. "I started working for Elmer's parents when I was eight, old enough to sweep the floors and take out the trash for a dollar a week.

That dollar made a huge difference for my family during some difficult years, and I've been here ever since. Thank you again for making me a part of your family. I love you all."

Ella blinked back tears at the sweet old lady's heartfelt words. She hugged Mildred and returned the microphone to her dad while Hunter guided Mildred back to her seat.

Lincoln cleared his throat. "Thank you, Mildred, for your service and dedication. It's employees like you—all of you—who have allowed us to serve the community of Butler for all these years, and we look forward to many more years to come. As your chief executive officer, I embrace my role in preserving the legacy instilled by Elmer, his parents and faithful employees like Mildred and all of you. I believe any business that stands still runs the risk of being left behind. With that in mind, I'm always seeking new ideas and products that will keep customers returning to us time and again to see what's new and exciting in our store. I'm very pleased to announce tonight that we will soon add a new line of intimate accessories to our health and beauty department. These items are designed to keep the spark alive for customers of all ages. As we get closer to the launch of this new product line, we'll bring in special consultants to train our sales team to assist customers and answer questions. We hope we can count on your support of this new endeavor as well as others that will be coming as we grow and expand. It is my goal, always, to keep one foot in the past where our company traditions are celebrated and honored while also keeping an eye on the future and adapting to the times.

"I'm going to leave you with a short video that debuts the store's wonderful new website designed by my daughter-in-law, Cameron Abbott. The website is set to go live on January first, and we expect a new influx of customers coming to Butler to check out our store. I want to thank Cameron and my future daughter-in-law Lucy Mulvaney for putting together the video. We hope you enjoy it. Thank you again for being here tonight, for your hard work throughout the year and for your contributions to the success of the store."

The lights went dim and the big screen at the front of the

IT'S ONLY LOVE 167

room lit up with the video Cameron and Lucy had been working on for weeks to show off the new website to the employees. They'd done a fantastic job of capturing the spirit and
essence of the Stillman-Abbott family businesses, from the
store to the sugaring facility to the Christmas tree farm
Landon ran to Lucas's woodworking barn to Hannah's jewelry studio. Interwoven were screenshots from the new website that so perfectly captured the store and life in Vermont.

Though Ella had seen the video several times already,
she was sucked in once again, which was how she missed
Gavin's approach until his arm slid around her waist and he
brought her in close to him. The scent of Gucci Black filled
her senses with the essence of her man, her love.

CHAPTER 17

———◆◆◆———

*Only people who are capable of loving
strongly can also suffer great sorrow, but
this same necessity of loving serves to
counteract their grief and heals them.*

—Leo Tolstoy

"You looked so hot up there," Gavin whispered, his lips brushing against her ear and setting off a reaction she felt in all her most important places. "I loved seeing you in your professional mode."

It was all Ella could do to remain standing, to remember she had a room full of employees to consider, that it would be hours yet before she could be alone with him. She covered the hand he had flattened over her abdomen and realized he was still wearing the sweater she'd given him.

Any second now the video would end, the lights would come back on and their employees would see her standing in Gavin's arms as if she belonged there. Did she belong there? She sure hoped so. Did she care if people saw them? Not really. As the video came to an end and the audience burst into applause for Cameron and Lucy, Ella took a deep breath and tried to relax before the lights came back on.

Just as they did, Gavin's arm dropped from around her,

and he took a step back, making the decision for her. She appreciated his respect of her professional space, but part of her wanted him to make a big public declaration. She wanted there to be no doubt in anyone's mind that they were together, that he was hers and she was his.

But were they ready for that after only a week together? Hell, she'd been ready for years now, but it was probably too soon for public declarations. They'd get there when the time was right, and the thought of that, of the whole town knowing she and Gavin were a couple, was just another thing to look forward to.

With the formal part of the program over, everyone lined up for the buffet dinner of barbecued ribs and chicken, potatoes, salad, coleslaw and corn bread. The menu was as much a part of the tradition as the meeting itself. When Ella first started working in the office, she'd suggested changing up the menu, an idea that had been greeted with shocked silence from her family members.

At dinner, Ella asked Gavin to join her at a table full of employees and their spouses. The family always spread out among the employees at these events, but tonight they wanted to take the pulse on the new line. The ladies at her table were all abuzz over the new products, a thought that made Ella chuckle.

"What's so funny?" Gavin asked, leaning in close to her.

"They're 'abuzz' over the product news my dad shared with them. I crack myself up."

He smiled. "That's funny. So when do we get to try out this new product line? Don't you need focus groups? How do I volunteer?"

She drove her elbow gently into his ribs. "Knock it off. We're in public."

"I'm not doing anything."

She gave him a meaningful look. "Yes, you are."

"Oh, do tell."

"Not now. Not here."

"How much longer do we have to stay?"

"Until it's over."

Groaning, he took a drink from his beer bottle. "I'm never going to make it until then."

After dinner, a DJ got everyone up and dancing. Ella stood off to the side with her sisters, Wade, Colton, Lucy and Cameron. "So what's the buzz on the new product line?" Ella asked with a smile. It would be a while before that joke got old.

"Lots of questions, a few raised eyebrows, but otherwise no real outrage," Hannah said.

"Same at my table," Cameron said. "Mildred asked if she could test them out for us."

That sent the rest of them into fits of laughter.

"I'll never get that image out of my head," Colton said.

Lucy ran a soothing hand over his back. "It's okay, honey. She was probably just kidding."

"God, I hope so."

Hunter and Megan joined them. "What's so funny?" Hunter asked.

"Mildred wants to try out the new product line," Ella said.

Hunter's face went totally blank.

"He's in shock," Megan said bluntly, setting off another wave of laughter as she fanned his face.

"We need to be more mature about this if we expect the others to buy in," Wade said.

"Maturity is so totally overrated," Charley said. "Take him, for example." She nodded to their brother Max, who was sitting alone at a table, an untouched beer in front of him while he stared off into space.

"I was surprised to see him here tonight," Hannah said. "I thought he was staying in Burlington until the baby arrives."

"Chloe told him she'll let him know when she's in labor," Colton said. "Otherwise, there's no reason for him to be there."

"Wow," Hunter said. "What the hell?"

"Will tried to talk to him this week," Cameron said softly. "He's not talking about it. Not even to Will."

Ella's heart ached for her brother, who'd always been happy and lighthearted and fun to be around until recently.

Seeing him so down and despondent broke her heart. Hopefully after the baby arrived he'd rebound and be able to put his focus on the baby rather than on the relationship that wasn't working.

After several fast songs, the DJ slowed the tempo with "A Thousand Years."

Gavin approached her, took her hand and led her from the group without a word to anyone. His sexy, possessive gesture did funny things to her insides, which only continued when he wrapped his arms around her and left no room for doubt that they were together with the way he held her close to him.

Ella felt every eye in the room on her and them as they moved together to the song that summed up the depth of her love for him.

"Relax, babe," he whispered in her ear. "I've been dying to hold you all day."

What else could she do when he put it that way but relax into his embrace?

The dance floor filled with other couples, including her parents, Will and Cameron, Hunter and Megan, Colton and Lucy, Hannah and Nolan as well as employees and their spouses. Surrounded by family and friends, Ella felt less on display but no less overwhelmed to be dancing in public with Gavin for the first time as his girlfriend or significant other or whatever they were to each other now.

Because the DJ knew exactly who he was working for tonight, the next song was one by the Beatles, "The Long and Winding Road."

"Another song that suits us," Gavin whispered, setting her on fire with his husky words, the scrape of his whiskers against her neck, the scent of his cologne and the tight squeeze of his arms around her. Between them, his arousal pulsed against her belly, reminding her of what to expect when they got home. She couldn't wait.

Lost in the song, the moment, the magic of being in his arms, she was instantly aware when his body filled with tension.

Ella raised her head off his shoulder. "What's wrong?"

"What's he doing here?" Gavin asked in a much harsher tone than she'd heard from him before.

"Who?"

"Ed Sheehan."

"He works at the tree farm. Why?"

"Since when?"

"I'm not sure exactly when he started," Ella said. "A couple of years maybe?"

"He's the guy I fought with that night at the bar. He said—"

"I remember," Ella said, sparing him from having to repeat the hateful words and filled with fury over what Ed had said to Gavin.

Gavin released her so suddenly she nearly stumbled.

"I . . . I can't be in the same room with that guy. I'm sorry."

He stunned her when he turned and walked away, leaving her standing in the middle of the dance floor surrounded by her employees, parents, siblings and their partners, all of whom looked on in surprise and dismay.

Ella started to go after him, but something stopped her. First of all, she couldn't leave. This event was her responsibility, and it wasn't over yet. Second of all . . . She'd gone after him for the last time. He'd chosen to leave, to walk away from her. It would have to be his choice to come back. She couldn't continue to make that choice for him.

"Um, what just happened?" Charley asked after Ella walked off the dance floor.

"He saw Ed Sheehan here."

"So?"

"Apparently, Ed told him we wasted our time in Iraq, which led to the bar fight last summer."

"Oh damn. I didn't know the fight was with him."

"I didn't either."

"Tell Landon to fire him," Charley said emphatically.

"Is it wrong that I want to do that?"

"Hell no, it's not wrong. We lost our brother-in-law over there. How anyone in this town could say such a thing to Gavin, of all people, is beyond me."

"What's wrong?" Colton asked when he joined them.

Charley filled him in.

"Are you fucking kidding me? Where's Landon?"

Their younger brother was across the room, surrounded by some of the store's youngest female employees.

Colton rolled his eyes. "Look at him."

"Why are you rolling your eyes?" Charley asked. "A year ago you would've been right there with him."

"I don't know what you're talking about," Colton said as he went to retrieve Landon.

Ella watched Ed, talking and laughing with some other guys from the farm, blissfully unaware of what was going on around him. He was a big, burly guy with muscles on top of muscles, and though Gavin was no slouch in the muscle department, he was lucky to have walked away relatively uninjured from a fistfight with Ed.

Colton returned with Landon, who was pissed about being pulled away from his female admirers.

"Tell him," Colton said, giving Landon a final push that landed him in front of Ella and Charley.

"Tell me what?" Landon asked, one eye over his shoulder at the women as if to make sure they didn't get away.

"Ed Sheehan," Charley said.

"What about him?"

"Remember the fight Gavin was in last summer?" Ella asked.

"In the bar on 114?" Landon asked.

Colton and Charley looked to her to fill in Landon.

"That's the one," Ella said. "He fought with Ed after Ed told him we'd wasted our time in Iraq."

Landon's amiable expression hardened. "He said *what*?"

"That we'd wasted our time in Iraq," Ella said again, each word causing her the same pain it had to have caused Gavin at the time. No matter what your thoughts were on the war, saying that to someone who'd lost his only sibling there was so far outside the boundaries of propriety it wasn't even funny.

Landon turned away from them and crossed the room to

the table of employees from the Christmas tree farm. He pointed to Ed and indicated he should follow Landon.

With a shrug for the other guys, Ed got up to follow Landon through the main doors to the parking lot outside.

Colton crossed the room to the doors to keep an eye on what was happening outside through the window to the right of the entrance.

Filled with anxiety, Ella watched Colton, knowing he'd be through the doors in an instant if Landon needed backup. Hopefully, Ed would go quietly without causing more trouble.

She breathed a sigh of relief when Landon came back inside, his face flushed from the cold and the confrontation. He nodded to Colton and then crossed to where Ella and Charley still stood together.

"He's history," Landon said bluntly.

"Did you tell him why?" Charley asked.

"Yeah, and I reminded him that my brother-in-law was killed over there, and no one in this family or the Guthrie family wants to hear his opinions or employ someone who'd say what he did to Gavin."

"What did he say?" Ella asked.

"That we're all a bunch of warmongers, yada yada. I didn't listen. I told him to get lost and stay away from us and our property."

"Thank you, Landon," Ella said. "I know it's a tough time of year to be down a worker."

"We don't need his kind on our payroll."

"No, we don't." She gave her brother a kiss on the cheek. "I appreciate you handling that."

"No problem." He smiled, and she could see he'd already shaken off the unpleasantness with Ed. "Can I get back to my ladies now?"

"By all means," Ella said.

"There may be hope for him," Charley said as they watched him return to the women who'd waited patiently for him.

"Our baby brother is growing up," Colton said.

"If you did, there's hope for him, too," Charley said, drawing a snort of laughter from Ella.

Colton bent at the waist and picked up Charley, swinging her in circles, making everyone around them laugh at the way she pounded on his back.

"Put me down, you immature idiot!"

Ella stood back to keep from getting knocked over by their foolishness.

Colton put Charley down right in front of Tyler Westcott.

Charley sputtered at Colton and pushed her hair back from her face, looking up to see Tyler standing there watching her, an amused expression on his handsome face. He really was adorable, Ella thought, wishing Charley would give the poor guy a chance.

"Hi, Charley," he said, nodding to Ella and Colton.

"Tyler. What're you doing here?"

"I brought my mom." He nodded to Vivienne Westcott, who waved at them from across the crowded room. She worked in the bakery at the store. "She doesn't like to drive at night."

"Oh," Charley said. "That's nice of you."

"Would you like to dance?" Tyler asked.

"I, um, well, ah . . ."

Ella nudged her sister to remind her that Vivienne was watching.

"Sure," Charley mumbled, nudging Ella back.

"Great," Tyler said, beaming. He was tall with really nice wavy dark hair and blue eyes that stood out even behind a set of black-framed glasses that made him look smart and sexy at the same time.

They walked away together, Charley turning to glare at her siblings over her shoulder. Had she been expecting them to bail her out?

"I like him," Colton said.

"I like him, too," Ella replied.

"If he likes her, I also feel sorry for him."

"Stop it. She's awesome, and when the right guy comes along, she'll lose her claws."

"We can only hope so. I'm going to find Lucy. Are you okay?"

"Sure."

"I don't blame Gavin for being upset to see that guy here."

"I don't either." She did blame him, however, for leaving the way he had, but she'd take that up with him when she got the chance. *If* she got the chance. No, *when* . . . Definitely *when*.

CHAPTER 18

——◆◇◆——

*Hope is tomorrow's veneer over
today's disappointment.*

—Evan Esar

Charley wished she could click her heels together three times and be anywhere but in Tyler's arms on the dance floor of the Grange with her entire family looking on—or so it seemed to her.

She hadn't wanted to dance with him, but what were her options with his mother watching so hopefully when he came over to her? *Ugh.* Vivienne was a nice lady and a great employee, and Charley would never want to offend her. Which was how she ended up dancing with Tyler to "Stay with Me," of all things.

Shoot me now. Please.

"Are you ready for tomorrow?" Tyler asked.

For a second her brain froze before she realized he meant the group run. "I hope so."

"Did you get to run at all this week?"

She shook her head. "We were too busy getting ready for tonight."

"Were you sore after last weekend?"

"For a day or two." In truth, she'd been hobbling around all week, not that she'd ever tell him that. It had been years since she'd done a distance run, and she'd been foolish to jump right in with six miles the first time out.

"You're really going to need to run during the week, too, if you're going to be ready by May."

"I know that." Charley didn't mean for that to come out so sharply, but she hardly needed him telling her how to train. He always did this to her. He made her feel stupid and inadequate and . . . on edge. His presence put her on edge, and she didn't like the edge. She didn't like it one bit. She particularly didn't care for dancing with him. She didn't like that she could smell his cologne or that she could feel the well-toned muscles of his shoulder under her hand.

She didn't want to know what Tyler Westcott smelled like or felt like under the pressed dress shirts he favored. He reminded her of her brother Hunter, which wasn't a bad thing, per se. It just wasn't *her* thing.

"Will you have dinner with me tomorrow night?" he asked in a low, soft tone for her ears only.

"What? No, I will *not* have dinner with you."

He laughed. "Tell me how you really feel."

"I just did. I have before. Why can't you take no for an answer?"

"Because I don't believe you mean it."

She drew back from him, looking up, trying to gauge whether he was for real. Apparently, he was. "How can I convince you?"

"By saying no another two dozen times, at the very least."

"Are you some sort of masochist?"

"I must be if I want to go out with you."

The song, blessedly, came to an end, but he didn't let go of her.

"Um, the song is over."

"So?"

"So let go. Stop being a creep."

He smiled down at her.

That arrogant little smirk made her want to smack him. She couldn't stand how he always looked at her as if he knew her better than she knew herself. When she'd joined the running club, she'd nearly quit when she discovered he was a member, too. Now she was wishing she had quit—so she wouldn't have to see him every week for six months and so she could sleep in tomorrow.

Running a marathon had been a stupid idea after all. If putting up with Tyler's knowing smirk every week for the next six months was part of the deal, she might have to reconsider her new life goal.

Long after the song ended, long after he should've let go, he finally released her but managed to snag her hand before she could get away. "I'm not giving up on you, Charlotte. And P.S., I don't buy all your abrasive bullshit. Underneath all that bluster, there's an interesting woman lurking. I'd like to get to know that woman."

He released her hand and walked away, leaving her standing in the middle of the crowded dance floor, her mouth hanging open in shock.

What. The. Hell.

Gavin felt like a dick for leaving the way he had. The image of Ella's astonished expression as he turned away from her on the dance floor refused to leave his mind. He shouldn't have left like that, as if he couldn't control himself for a couple of hours to support her when she'd been so damned supportive of him.

"You're a fucking loser," he said as he drove home through the darkness that had descended over Butler and its outskirts. With no moon to guide the way, the roads were darker than usual tonight.

He'd never told her that Ed had been the guy he'd fought with, so how was she supposed to know? It had been a shock to see him sitting among the Abbotts' employees like he belonged there after what he'd said about the war. Surely they wouldn't want a guy like that in their midst. Would they?

"Shit," he muttered to the darkness. Every time he took a step forward something smacked him backward. Every goddamned time.

This was exactly why he'd told Ella he was a bad bet. He never knew when the shit would rear its ugly head to set him back.

He approached the one-lane covered bridge and slowed to a crawl as he drove across the bridge, slamming on the brakes when he saw something big and black blocking his way. Flipping on the high beams, he saw Fred the moose standing across the road and groaned. At least he hadn't run into Fred the way Cameron had.

Gavin laid on the horn, trying to get Fred to move along, to no avail. He remained stubbornly still. Gavin opened the window. "Fred, come on, give me a break, will you?"

"Moo."

"Seriously? Can this day get any more fucked up?" He sat there for twenty minutes, but Fred never budged. When it became clear that Fred wasn't going to move, Gavin put the truck in reverse, backed up over the one-lane bridge, turned around and headed back into town. He'd have to take the long way home.

As he drove through the quiet town, he began to wonder if Fred hadn't actually done him a favor, for he was now driving toward Ella's house rather than away.

For the first time in an hour, Gavin had reason to smile. "Freaking Fred. He's better at this shit than I am."

A glance at the clock on the dash indicated it was after ten. He probably had an hour or more to kill before Ella would be home, which gave him just enough time to run a quick errand. He had some groveling to do, and he needed all the reinforcements he could get.

Thirty minutes after the DJ played the last song of the evening and everyone had left, Ella was almost finished stacking chairs and breaking down tables. Colton and Hunter were sweeping the floor and her sisters were in the kitchen with her mother, Cameron, Lucy and Megan wrapping up leftover food. They'd sent Hannah home to bed, and Lucas and Landon had left with the young women from the store.

"Another great time," Lincoln said when he stacked the last of the chairs on top of the cart that held them. "Well done, honey."

"Thanks, Dad."

"What were they saying about the new product line?"

"Everyone's abuzz over it," she said with a smile. "That joke isn't going to get old for a while."

"I suppose I deserve that."

"It's what you get for being so progressive."

"I couldn't help but notice that Gavin left somewhat abruptly, and there was some sort of scuffle between Landon and Ed Sheehan."

Ella nodded, not surprised that her dad had tuned into the drama. "Ed was the one who told Gavin we wasted our time in Iraq, which led to the bar fight last summer."

Lincoln's face tightened with outrage. "I hope Landon fired him."

"He did."

"Good. People have a right to their opinions about war and politics and religion, but to say that to someone who lost their brother . . ."

"It's obscene."

"On that we agree, my dear." He put his arms around her. "You've gotten involved with a complicated man. A good man. A man I respect. I ache for what he's lost, but I love you far too much to watch you be hurt by that good, complicated man. I just hope you're being careful to protect your heart."

Ella laughed even as she blinked back tears. "I'm not being careful at all. I'm crazy in love with him, and I have been for longer than I can remember." She wiped away the tears that spilled down her cheeks. The emotional reaction irritated and embarrassed her.

Her dad smiled down at her, his love shining through the way it always did. "You're our practical child, the one who always thinks before she acts, who plans everything with meticulous attention to detail. Those qualities make you exceptionally reliable and good at what you do for a living, but they aren't necessarily the skills you need in this situation with Gavin." He pressed his lips to her forehead.

Comforted by his love and words of wisdom, Ella said, "What skills do I need?"

"Besides patience and fortitude?"

Ella laughed again. "Yes, other than that."

"I don't know, honey, but I do know that you're more than up to whatever challenge he presents. If anyone can lead that boy out of the darkness and back into the light, you can."

Touched and bolstered by his confidence in her, Ella looked up at him. "You really think so?"

"I know so. Just don't let him be less than what you deserve. You hear me?"

Ella nodded. "I won't."

"Good." He hugged her again. "Now go on home and get some sleep. I'll lock up here. You did great tonight, but then you always do."

"Love you, Dad."

"Love you, too."

On the short ride home, Ella thought about what her dad had said about the complicated man she'd fallen in love with. It helped to know he respected Gavin and liked him. That made it easier to tolerate the hurdles they were sure to encounter.

She wanted so badly to go to him, to seek him out. But she couldn't do that. She'd done that too many times already. Ella had no doubt at all that he cared deeply for her, as deeply as he'd ever cared for any woman. However, she couldn't keep this relationship going on her own. He had to meet her halfway.

Though it pained her greatly, she drove to her home rather than his. She would drown her sorrows with Ben and Jerry and get back to work on the blanket she was knitting for her new niece or nephew. It wasn't like she didn't have a life separate from him.

Ella trudged up the stairs, mentally and physically exhausted from the week at work and the emotional ups and downs of her time with Gavin. She made a beeline for the freezer, where her pint of Cherry Garcia sitting next to his pint of Cake Batter made her miss him fiercely.

She pulled the lid off her pint and dug a spoon into the creamy goodness. Taking the ice cream with her, she went into her bedroom, kicked off the heels she'd worn to work and changed into flannel pajama pants, a long-sleeve T-shirt and her favorite moccasin slippers. Tonight was all about comfort anywhere she could find it.

Settled on the sofa with her ice cream and a down comforter over her lap, Ella pulled out her knitting bag and got to work on the blanket, determined to focus on the project rather than wondering where Gavin was, what he was doing and whether he regretted taking off the way he had earlier.

Anger and frustration fueled her work as the multicolored yarn came together in rich pattern of pinks, blues and yellows. She couldn't wait for the baby to arrive, to have someone new to love, to watch him or her grow up and be part of his or her life from the first day. Though she'd hoped to be a mother many times over by now, being an aunt would have to do, and she planned to be the best aunt ever to Max's baby as well as Hannah's.

A sob escaped from Ella's tightly clenched jaw. She dropped a stitch and tossed aside the blanket in aggravation. It was a bad night when Ben and Jerry were unable to work their usual magic and when she started dropping stitches. That hadn't happened since she was first learning. Her grandma Sarah, who'd said she was a knitting prodigy, would be appalled, a thought that had Ella actively sobbing.

A soft knock on the door startled her out of the pity party. She swiped at the tears that refused to stop coming, even when she tried to mop them up with the comforter.

A second knock brought her to her feet. "Who is it?"

"Me."

She contained the powerful urge to run to the door, to throw it open, to jump into his arms. "What do you want?"

"I want to talk to you."

"I'm not really in the mood to talk. It's been a long day."

"Ella, please open the door. Give me the chance to apologize. Please?"

Sighing, she went to the door, leaned her head against it for a long moment before she turned the knob. The first thing she saw and smelled were roses—lots of roses in every imaginable color—pink, red, white, yellow, coral.

"I didn't know what color represented 'I'm sorry for being a dick' so I got one of each color hoping the right one is in there somewhere. And oh fuck, you've been crying. God, Ella, I'm so sorry."

"I'm not crying because of you. It's because I dropped a stitch, and I never drop stitches, even when I was angry-knitting that sweater for you."

He leaned against the doorframe, a small smile occupying his exquisitely handsome face. "Angry knitting. Is that a thing?"

"It is when you're involved." She turned away from him and returned to her post on the sofa, tugging the comforter over her lap. "Come in and shut the door before Mrs. Abernathy comes up here to see what's going on."

He closed the door and went to the kitchen. "Where do you keep vases?"

"Under the sink."

While he saw to putting the flowers in water, she scooped up another mouthful of ice cream, needing all the fortification she could get to deal with him. The roses had been a nice touch. She had to give him that. And they probably hadn't been easy to find this time of night in their remote corner of Vermont.

He joined her on the couch, curling one leg under him so he could face her. "I'm sorry I left the way I did. I shouldn't have done that, and about two seconds after I did it, I regretted it."

Ella repeatedly dug her spoon into the pint, refusing to look at him or to acknowledge his sincere apology. That was when she realized she was well and truly angry with him for the first time. In the past, she'd been frustrated and despondent. Now she was just pissed.

"Ella."

She continued to take out her anger on the ice cream. Poor Cherry Garcia. Then Gavin was taking the pint from her and putting it on the table. With his fingers on her chin, he compelled her to look at him. "I'm sorry I left."

"Why did you?"

He looked away for a second before bringing his gaze back to her. "I saw that guy, and I saw red. I was afraid I'd make a scene if I stayed, that I'd embarrass you and your family by getting into it with him again."

"So you embarrassed me by walking away from me while we were dancing, leaving me there alone with everyone looking at me?"

Wincing, he said, "Not my finest moment. I'm so sorry, Ella. I just had to get out of there before I did something stupid."

She turned her face away from him, forcing him to remove his hand, and then gathered the comforter in closer, fortifying herself against the powerful attraction she felt for him, even when she was angry. "Landon fired him."

"What?"

"Landon fired Ed. He doesn't work for us anymore."

"Simple as that?"

"Yes, Gavin, as simple as that. None of us like what he said to you, and we don't want someone like that working for our company."

"Wow," he said, sagging into the back of the sofa. "That's pretty awesome."

"It took about five minutes after you left to get rid of him. If maybe you'd given me the chance to address it, I could've saved you the trouble of leaving."

"It didn't occur to me that you all would do that."

"*Why* did it not occur to you, Gavin? Caleb was an Abbott as much as he was a Guthrie. Didn't you think we'd be as outraged as you were by what Ed said? This fight is not yours alone. It belongs to everyone who loved Caleb and everyone who lost someone in Iraq. *We* are as offended by him as you are."

"I . . ." He blinked several times in rapid succession. "Thank you." He took a deep breath, seeming to fight with his emotions. "For being outraged, for getting rid of him, for letting me in here tonight when I hardly deserve to be here. For everything, Ella."

"You don't have to thank me for doing the right thing."

He reached for her hand and brought it to his lips, running them back and forth over her knuckles. "Yes, I really do. Even though Hannah and my parents have been on this journey with me from the beginning, I've felt alone with it for so long. To know I'm not anymore is . . . Well, it's amazing. You're amazing."

As always, his touch rendered her powerless to resist him. "You're not alone anymore. Unless you want to be."

"I don't want to be. I want you. I want us. I want it all."

"You have no idea what you do to me when you say those things."

"What do I do? Tell me. I want to know."

"You make me feel hopeful and giddy and excited and . . ."

He leaned in closer, so close his lips were only a few inches from hers. "And what?"

"You know."

"Tell me anyway."

Ella's body heated from the inside, making all her most important parts tingle with awareness of him. "Turned on."

"Yeah?"

She nodded.

He tugged on the comforter and tossed it aside. "Have I ever told you how hot you are in flannel?"

Ella laughed, her heart beating in rapid time as he looked at her in a way that left no room for interpretation as to what he wanted from her. "Sure I am."

"You're the hottest babe in flannel I've ever laid eyes on."

"You should get out more."

"I've gotten out plenty. I know what I'm talking about." He ran his hands over her legs, exploring every part of her that was covered in the flannel he liked so much. "And you were smoking hot in that skirt and those heels tonight. When

I walked into the Grange and saw you on that stage, I almost started to drool."

"You had me with the roses. Just so you know."

His hands landed on her ass and tugged her toward him, arranging them so he was above her, between her legs, looking down at her. "So the drool wasn't necessary?"

"It was a nice touch but not critical to your recovery."

"I love you, Ella."

She gasped, feeling as if she'd been punched in the gut by three little words that packed a huge wallop. "You . . . you . . ."

"Love you." He kissed her, softly, sweetly, devastatingly.

CHAPTER 19

———◆◆◆———

Once you choose hope, anything's possible.

—Christopher Reeve

"Please don't say that because you think I'm mad—"
She never got to finish that thought because he was too busy kissing her with deep, penetrating strokes of his tongue.

He kissed her until she was weak beneath him, until all the fight had gone out of her, until she couldn't resist him, as if she ever could. "I would never say something I've never said to any other woman only to get out of trouble."

"You've never said that to *anyone*?"

"Nope."

"What about Dalia?"

With his eyes open and fixed on hers, he shook his head and then kissed her again. "I was saving it for you."

"Gavin," she said with a sigh. "Please don't walk away from me again."

"I won't. I promise."

"I love you, too. I've loved you for so long I don't remember a time when I didn't love you." Ella would never forget the way he looked at her as he kissed her again and again and again.

They began to pull at clothes, equally frantic in their efforts to bare each other.

The flannel pajama pants he'd admired ended up tangled around her ankles. His jeans were pushed down only far enough to free his cock, her T-shirt up only high enough to reveal her breasts.

This was madness, she thought. Utter madness. And love. Gavin Guthrie loved her. In light of that amazing revelation, all the pain and agony of the last few months fell away into the nothingness of the past. What did it matter now that they had this, now that they had each other? He plunged into her, his fingers digging into her shoulder and hip as he held her in place for his fierce possession.

"God, Ella . . . You feel so good. So hot and tight." He swooped down on her mouth, his tongue mimicking the strokes of his cock as his chest hair abraded her nipples.

It was too much. It was not enough. It was everything she'd always known it would be but so much more, too. He'd never been like this before, unleashed and unrestrained, and she loved it. She loved him. How freeing it was to be able to admit that to herself and him, too.

He broke the kiss and shifted his focus to her nipple, sucking and tugging and licking while she held on tight to his hair, as if she could control the uncontrollable.

"Ahh, Ella. Ella, Ella, Ella . . . I love you so much."

His words triggered the release that had been building from the moment he brushed his lips over her knuckles. She came so hard she saw stars.

"Oh Christ . . . Ella . . ." Groaning loudly, he rode her orgasm into his own, surging into her repeatedly until he dropped, spent, on top of her. "Wow."

"Mmm, wow indeed." She ran her fingers through the damp strands of his hair, loving everything about him, even when he was sweaty. That thought made her giggle.

"What's so funny?"

"I was just thinking that I even love your sweat."

"That's sexy, babe."

"It is. I love that I made you sweaty."

"You make me very sweaty, among other things." He ran his hand over her hip, up to her ribs, stopping to cup her breast. "Are we going to be okay, Ella? Are we going to be able to make this work?"

"As long as you stay with me rather than running away when things get hard."

"I will. I'm here to stay."

"Then we're going to be just fine."

They slept in the next morning and stopped at Megan's diner for breakfast before heading to their afternoon shift at the Christmas tree farm. As they got out of Gavin's truck, Landon walked over to greet them. He wore his usual seasonal uniform of heavy coveralls, a skullcap and leather gloves. His face was red and ruddy from the hours spent outside in the cold. He shook hands with Gavin.

"Thanks a lot for coming to help," Landon said.

"My pleasure."

"I'm not sure we can afford a professional tree cutter of your caliber," Landon said with a teasing smile.

"I'll give you the friends and family rate." Gavin paused before he added, "Thanks for what you did last night, Landon. I didn't mean to cause any trouble."

"You didn't," Landon said, his amiable expression hardening. "He did, and we don't want his kind around here. Personally, I can't believe anyone in this town would say such a thing to you, knowing who you lost over there."

"Means a lot to me. Thanks again."

Ella rested her hand on Gavin's back, offering her support.

He smiled at her and put his arm around her. "Is this where we go our separate ways?"

"Yep," she said. "I'll be over there." Ella pointed to the shack where her mother and Aunt Hannah were doling out hot chocolate, cider and donuts to families who'd come to tag their Christmas trees. By next weekend, they'd be returning to cut them down and take them home.

"Come on, Gavin," Landon said. "I've got a whole bunch of cutting for you to do." In addition to the tag-and-cut program, the Stillman Family Christmas Tree Farm supplied trees to retailers all over the state and the rest of New England.

"I *love* to cut," Gavin said. Before he let Landon lead him away, he kissed Ella square on the lips in front of her brother, her mother, her aunt and anyone else who might've been looking. "Save some hot chocolate for me."

"Oh, um, I will."

He smiled at her before he walked away, whistling as he went.

Ella watched him go, her lips tingling from the kiss. In four hours, they could make their escape and return to his place until family dinnertime tomorrow. She couldn't wait to be alone with him again. Turning to head for the shack that housed the concessions and cash register, Ella found her mother and aunt watching her.

"What?" she asked them.

"You," Hannah said. "Kissing Gavin Guthrie in public all of a sudden."

"It's certainly not all of a sudden." Ella stepped into the small wooden structure, where the scent of chocolate and cider mixed with the pervasive fragrance of Christmas coming from the thousands of trees on the property. Ella loved it here. She always had.

"Is that right?" Hannah asked.

"Uh-huh," Ella said.

"You approve of this?" Hannah asked her sister.

"Hardly matters if I do," Molly said. "Ella is a grown woman who knows her own heart. But for what it's worth, I think the world of Gavin, just like I thought the world of his brother."

"He sure is easy on the eyes," Hannah said, making them all laugh.

"You don't know the half of it," Ella said with a dirty wink.

"Oh my ears!" Hannah said, covering them while Ella laughed again. "On that note, I'm outta here since my relief has arrived." She kissed Ella's cheek. "I'm happy for you, Ella. I hope it works out for you two."

"Thank you, Auntie."

"I'll talk to you this week," Hannah said to Molly.

"Yes, you will."

After Hannah left, Ella rang up a young family that had tagged a tree and bought a wreath, hot chocolate and donuts. The kids, who were maybe five and seven, were bundled up and bursting with Christmas excitement. Thanks to her work at the store and full immersion in the season, Ella had never lost that feeling. Christmas was still her favorite time of year.

It would be even more so this year, with Hunter and Megan's wedding the weekend before the holiday.

Watching the kids consume their donuts with barely restrained glee filled Ella with yearning for the family she'd nearly given up on having. Last night, Gavin had told her he loved her. In the bright light of day, everything seemed possible now that she knew for sure he felt that way about her. That changed everything.

"You're fairly glowing today, my dear," Molly said as she doled out cider to another young couple who were heading off to find their tree.

"I'm happy."

"It makes *me* happy to see *you* happy. You're in love then?"

"Madly." What a relief—an overwhelmingly powerful relief—to be able to admit how she felt about Gavin. Finally.

"How does he feel?"

"The same."

"Oh, El," Molly said, tearing up. "That's so wonderful."

"Yes, it is." Ella gazed out at the distant fields, where she could see Gavin working beside her brother as they loaded trees onto a flatbed. "It might seem like it happened fast to everyone else, but it didn't. There was nothing fast about it."

"I know that, sweetheart. We all do."

"I guess I wasn't as circumspect as I thought I was when it came to him."

"You were in a tough spot, wanting a man who was emotionally unavailable."

"It was tough. But what we have now . . . It was well worth the wait."

"So that's it? All sewn up and together forever?"

"I can't imagine anything could tear us apart after what we've shared this week."

"Ella—"

Ella held up her hand to stop whatever her mother was about to say. "Please, Mom. Please don't say it. I've been warned every which way to Tuesday by just about everyone who loves me—and that's a lot of people. I love him. He loves me. I finally have what I've always wanted. You know how much I love you, but frankly, I just don't want to hear any more warnings."

"Fair enough."

"Are you mad?"

"No, sweetheart, of course I'm not mad. I actually understand better than you think."

"What do you mean?"

"When I was dating Dad, I had more than one person warn me about taking on a flatlander, how he'd never be happy here, how someone with his education would want bigger things than a country store in Butler, Vermont. People who barely knew me warned me."

Ella was riveted by this information. "Did that worry you? That other people couldn't see him being happy here?"

"A little. Part of me thought they were right. Here he had a Yale education. How was he ever going to be happy running our little store in this little town?"

"And yet . . . Who's happier than he is?"

"That's my point. I knew in my heart that he'd be fine here. He knew it, too. We both had the one thing we wanted more than anything, so everything else was just details."

"I love that you still feel that way about each other even after all this time," Ella said with a sigh. "When we came in the other day, and he was making you giggle . . . It just . . . It gave me hope."

"He makes me giggle every day."

"Please spare me the gory details."

Molly's face lit up with a big, dirty smile. "The details are *extra* gory now that we've rid our barn of all the rug rats."

"Oh my God." Ella covered her ears and gave a pretend shriek. "Make it stop."

Molly peeled Ella's hands off her ears. "I hope you understand that what I'm telling you is that if you're with the right one, everything else falls into place the way it's meant to."

"I can't imagine anyone ever being more right for me than Gavin, even with all his imperfections."

"Everyone has imperfections. Some are just more pronounced than others. Gavin's world was tipped upside down by something outside his control, and he's spent years trying to right it again. Don't think I haven't noticed how relaxed and happy he looks with you by his side. It's been a long time since he's been that way."

"His mother said the same thing."

"I know. She told me."

"When did you talk to Amelia?"

"When she called me to have a little squeal over the fact that our kids are dating. Again."

"Hannah and Caleb happened such a long time ago that it's easy to forget sometimes that you and Amelia have already been down this road once before."

"Yes, we have, and we're no less thrilled this time than we were then."

"Really?"

"Really."

"I've always thought of Hannah and Caleb as this sort of epic romance that the rest of us mere mortals could only aspire to."

"They were beautiful together, but you and Gavin are every bit as epic and every bit as beautiful, especially when you consider the long road you traveled to get where you are now. You never gave up on him."

"I sort of did. For a while there."

"No, you didn't. If you had, you wouldn't have gone the other night when they called you to come for him."

"I didn't know I was going for him when they called."

"Didn't you, Ella? Didn't you sort of suspect it was him?"

"I guess I did."

"And still you went. You never gave up on him. Not for one minute. There'll come a time when you'll be tested again. It'll be a decision not to give up then either."

"You say *will* like you're certain it'll happen."

"It will, Ella. I'm certain it'll happen, because it always does. Even the most epic of romances have their bumps. Just ask your sister about what it was like to be married to his brother. She'll tell you that for all of Caleb's wonderful qualities, he could try her patience like no one else ever has before or since. And that's saying something when you consider she had eight younger siblings."

"So it's a Guthrie thing. Is that what you're saying?"

"No, sweetheart, it's a *man* thing. It's a man-woman thing. There're always going to be challenges, no matter who you're with. The important thing is to be sure you're with the right one. Then the challenges don't seem so insurmountable."

"I'm with the right one. I'm three thousand percent sure of that."

"Then it'll work out the way it's meant to."

Ella clung to her mother's assurances. The thought of it not working out with Gavin after everything they'd been through wasn't something she cared to think about. Especially not when she was so busy being happy with him.

They were awakened out of a sound sleep by the phone ringing at Gavin's house before dawn on Wednesday.

"What the hell?" he muttered as he grabbed for it on the bedside table and checked the caller ID. "For you." He handed the phone to Ella.

"Hello?" she asked, suddenly nervous at the thought of someone calling her at his place.

"It's me," her mom said. "I thought you'd want to know

Chloe's in labor. We're packing up and heading for Burlington and taking Thanksgiving with us. Dad has shut down the office for the day if you want to head over."

Ella was still processing the fact that her mother had called her at Gavin's house at five in the morning.

"Ella?"

"I'm here. Thanks for calling, Mom. Did Max say anything about how she's doing?"

"I don't think he knows anything more than that. See you there?"

"Yeah, I'll be there at some point today. I have to go in to work for a short time before I leave." Her head began to swim with details about her new niece or nephew, her brother and what he was going through, the start of the holiday shopping season in the store, the relocation of Thanksgiving to the lake house in Burlington, and the trip with Gavin that she planned to tell him about on Thanksgiving.

"See you when you get there. Love you."

"You, too, Granny."

Molly groaned as she hung up.

"Did your mom really call you here at five in the morning?" Gavin asked.

"She really did."

"How am I ever going to look either of them in the eye again?"

"I'm sure it's no surprise to them that we're sleeping together."

"Still, I liked it better when they weren't entirely sure."

"I bet you did," she said, laughing at the dismay she heard in his voice.

He took her hand and kissed her knuckles. "Morning, Auntie Ella."

"Oh, I like the sound of that. I can't wait to hold that baby."

"So you're going to Burlington today," he said.

"I guess I am. That wasn't in my plans."

"You'll be there for Thanksgiving?"

"Mom said they are packing up the turkey and bringing everything to the lake house, so that's the plan."

Gavin turned on his side, put his arm around her and snuggled her in close to him. "What am I supposed to do without you for all that time?"

"You could come over to Burlington."

"I can't leave my folks for Thanksgiving."

"I know," she said with a sigh, loving that he was so faithfully devoted to his parents but sad to know they'd be spending the holiday apart. "But I'll be back tomorrow night to give you your surprise." Her stomach knotted with excitement and a lingering bit of fear that he wouldn't be as happy about her surprise as she was.

"I can't wait for this surprise of yours."

"I hope you like it."

"I'm sure I will."

Ella wished she could be so sure herself.

"So thirty-six hours with no Ella. That's cruel and unusual punishment after you've gone and gotten me addicted to you."

"Addicted? That sounds serious."

"It's super serious. Life-threatening even."

Ella ran her fingertips over the stubble on his face. "I love you like this."

"Like what?"

"Happy, playful, funny."

"I'd forgotten I had those things in me until you showed me they're still there." He turned them so he was on top looking down at her. Then he began kissing her neck, making her want him yet again. It never ceased to amaze her that she wanted him all the time.

"Do you think it'll always be like this?" she asked.

"Like what?"

"Crazy."

He glanced up at her, grinning. "It is kinda crazy, isn't it?"

"I've never been like this with anyone."

"Like what?"

"Insatiable."

"That's such a good word, and by the way, I don't want to think about you doing this with anyone else."

"I never did *this* with anyone else. Everything is different with you."

Cupping her breasts, he ran his tongue over one sensitive tip and then the other. "Are you sore from last night?"

"Tender more than sore."

"Mmm," he said, his lips vibrating against her nipple. "I need to be more careful with you."

"No, you don't. I like you just the way you are."

"Unrestrained and unrefined?"

"Exactly like that."

"Let me give you gentle and tender before I have to let you go for thirty-six endless hours." His lips were soft and persuasive as he set her on fire with desire for more of him, all of him. By the time he entered her, slowly and carefully, Ella was clinging to what remained of her sanity.

"God, you're so perfect," he whispered. "I could live inside you and never want for anything."

Ella clung to him, her fingertips digging into the dense muscles of his back as he moved above her, destroying her one deep stroke at a time. Her body seized in a contraction of endless pleasure that went on for what felt like forever. She had never felt anything quite like it.

"Ella," he whispered. "I love you so much. Love you."

She couldn't speak over the huge lump in her throat, so she held on tight to him as he lost himself in her.

The slide of his lips over the dampness on her face was the only indication she had that tears were rolling down her cheeks.

"Sweet Ella. How did I survive before you made me fall in love with you?"

Ella burrowed her nose into the nook between his neck and shoulder, breathing him in. She needed to get up, to get moving, to get to the office for a couple of hours before she headed to Burlington to hopefully meet her new niece or nephew. But she couldn't bring herself to move.

"Are you okay?" he asked, gazing down at her with sweet concern in his eyes.

"I'm way better than okay."

"Why the tears?"

"I can't help them when you say the things you do while you make love to me like that."

"I've never said those things to anyone before you."

"I still feel like I have to be dreaming that you're saying them to me."

"You're not dreaming." He kissed her lips, her cheeks, the tip of her nose and then her lips again.

"I have to go."

"I know."

"You have to let me go."

"I know." He said the words but made no move to withdraw from her.

"Gavin . . ."

"I don't want to let you go. I don't want to have to live without you for two days."

"I'll be back before you have time to miss me."

"No, you won't."

"Will you be okay tomorrow? I know how hard the holidays have to be for you and your parents."

"We'll get through it. We always do."

"I wish I could be there with you. I'll come home early to have dinner with you guys."

"You should have dinner with your family. I'll be waiting when you get here."

"I'll leave as soon as I can. I promise."

"Call me tonight?"

"Yes, yes, I'll call you." She would have to borrow a cell phone from Lucy or Cameron. "It might be a New York number, so make sure you take the call."

"I'll take the call because it might be you. I feel like a lovesick fool because I don't want to let you go for even a couple of days."

"I'm okay with that."

He smiled, kissed her and finally withdrew, leaving her feeling bereft without the heavy feel of him inside her. "How about a shower?"

"A platonic shower?"

"Completely," he said with a wicked grin that let her know there'd be nothing platonic about it.

What did it say about her that even after having him three times overnight and with a thousand other things she needed to be doing, she followed him willingly into the shower?

She had it bad, and bad had never felt so good.

CHAPTER 20

———◆———

Hope begins in the dark, the stubborn
hope that if you just show up and try to
do the right thing, the dawn will come.

—Anne Lamott

Though she was sleep-deprived and eager to get to Burlington, Ella put in a couple of hours at the store, making sure everything was in place for the official day-after-Thanksgiving start to the holiday shopping season. She hadn't missed a Black Friday in the store since she graduated from college. Only for Gavin would she consider missing this one.

Charley popped her head in Ella's office just after nine thirty. "Heard anything more from Burlington?"

"Not yet. You?"

"Nothing. What time are you heading over there?"

"I'm shooting for noon."

"Could I hitch a ride with you? My car needs oil, and I haven't gotten around to getting it into Nolan's."

"Sure. Then we can go over all these notes I've made for you so you can cover for me next week."

"You are going to owe me so big for that it's not even funny."

"So you've said, at least a dozen times now."

"Just making sure you heard me," Charley said with a grin. "When are you telling him about the trip?"

"Tomorrow night."

"That doesn't give him much time to get his shit together."

"It also doesn't give him much time to come up with a thousand reasons why he shouldn't go." She'd given careful thought to the timing and decided the less time he had to think about it, the better off he'd be. Or so she hoped.

"You really think he'll do that?"

"I'm not sure what to expect, to be honest. He's got some sort of issue where the Sultans are concerned. I'm not sure if it's a big issue or a small one. I guess I'll find out tomorrow night."

"What'll you do—and I'm just playing devil's advocate here, so don't shoot me—if he says he won't go?"

"I don't know. I'm trying not to think about that possibility."

"For the record, I think he'd be crazy not to go after you went to so much trouble to arrange the trip and everything."

"Thanks. I'm hoping for the best."

"Me, too, Ella. It's a really nice thing for you to do. I hope he sees that."

"I hope so, too."

"I'll be ready to go at noon," Charley said. "Maybe we can grab lunch at the diner before we leave?"

"I'd be up for that."

"Okay, see you then."

Alone in her office, Ella printed out a brochure for the resort, their plane tickets and some pictures of the romantic settings in Turks and Caicos. She couldn't wait to see those sites with Gavin by her side, and the thought of it not happening . . . Well, she couldn't entertain that possibility. She just couldn't.

At noon, she and Charley crossed Elm Street to the newly renamed Green Mountain Diner, run by their future sister-in-law Megan. They ducked into a booth and Megan came over to them.

"Hi there," she said with a friendly smile. "Do you guys need menus?"

"I don't," Charley said.

"Turkey club and a Diet Coke?" Megan asked.

"You got it."

"Ella? You want your usual?"

Normally, she went for a salad, but she was absolutely famished today. "I'll have the same as Charley."

"Coming right up. Any news from Burlington?"

"Nothing," Charley said. "I'm dying to know what's going on. We're heading over there from here."

"Hunter should be there any time now. I'm so bummed that I can't get away with the big Thanksgiving dinner here tomorrow."

"What's Hunter going to do about Thanksgiving?" Ella asked.

"He's coming back tonight to give me a hand here," Megan said, her cheeks flushing ever so slightly. "I told him he doesn't have to, but he insisted."

"He wants to be where you are," Ella said with a smile for the woman who'd made her oldest brother so happy.

"That's what he said, too. I'll get your order in and grab your drinks."

"Thanks, Megan," Charley said. When they were alone, she added in a whisper, "I never expected to like her as much as I do."

"She's really great when you take the time to get to know her."

"I can't believe Hunter is getting *married* next month!"

"When it's right, it's right," Ella said with a sigh.

"Why the sigh?"

"I guess I'm envious of him and Will and Hannah and Colton. They've got it all figured out, and I want that, too. I want to know that Gavin and I are together forever and nothing will ever come between us." The thought of something coming between them filled her with fear, which was slightly irrational in light of what had transpired between them only that morning.

"Earth to Ella. Where'd you go off to?"

"I was just thinking."

"About what?"

"If I tell you, you won't tell anyone else, will you?"

"Jeez, I didn't earn any points by keeping the big Gavin secret for as long as I did?"

"True." Though she'd prefer not to tell anyone her private business, she was dying to tell someone, and Charley had proven herself trustworthy in recent months. "This morning, when we were . . . together . . . It was just . . . I don't know how to describe it."

"We're talking about sex, right?"

Ella gave her a withering look.

"What? I'm just making sure we're on the same wavelength. Are we?"

"*Yes*," Ella said, exasperated.

"I bet it's really good with him. He's got the whole studly, brawny, sexy thing going on like Caleb did, too."

"It is *amazing* with him, but this morning it was . . . I don't have the words."

Charley fanned her face. "Wow. I've never seen you speechless before."

"I was after that. I was speechless. There's like this connection between us that defies description."

"You're lucky. That's hard to find."

"You're going to find it, Charley. I know you are."

"I'm not holding my breath, and I'm perfectly happy just the way I am."

Megan returned with their drinks. "Hunter called from the hospital. They're saying it could be another couple of hours until your new niece or nephew arrives."

"Oh, good for us but bad for Chloe," Ella said. "I hope she's doing okay."

"I hope she's not a dick to Max after the baby's born," Charley said bluntly.

"That, too," Ella said.

"She'll have the Abbott army to contend with if she is," Megan said.

"Indeed she will," Charley said. She perked up and waved

someone over to their table, sliding in to make room for Elmer. "Hey, Gramps."

"This is a nice surprise," Elmer said. "Three of my favorite ladies all in one place."

"Coffee?" Megan asked him with a warm smile that was full of affection. Elmer had that effect on people.

"Would love some, honey. Thank you."

"Are you going to Burlington, Gramps?" Ella asked.

"I'm leaving shortly with Wade. He offered to give me a lift."

"You can come with us if you'd rather get there alive," Charley said.

"Your brother is a very good driver, and I already said I'd go with him, but thanks for the invite."

"Ready to be a great-grandpa?" Ella asked.

"I can't wait. Have you heard any more?"

They told him what Hunter had reported through Megan.

"This is so exciting," Elmer said. "It's been a while since we had a baby in the family."

"It's funny that Max was the last baby, and now he's having one of his own," Ella said. "I vividly remember the day he was born."

"I do, too," Charley said with a smile for her sister. They were eight and nine years older than Max. "And here he is beating us to parenthood."

"He always was an overachiever," Elmer said. "And he's going to be a great dad to that little one."

"Yes," Ella said, "he is." A fierce pang of yearning overtook her. She wanted to be a mom. For so long, when it seemed like it wasn't going to happen with Gavin, she'd managed to contain the yearning. But now . . . Now the yearning was like a live wire burning inside her.

After a delightful lunch full of laughs with their grandfather, Ella and Charley set out for Burlington to meet their new niece or nephew. They arrived at the hospital shortly after three to hear that Chloe and Max were in the delivery room, and the baby was coming soon.

The waiting room was full of Abbotts, eager to meet their new family member.

"Where's her family?" Charley asked Ella.

"I don't know that she has much family. Does she?"

"No idea."

Molly, who'd been pacing from one end of the small room to the other, dropped into the chair on the other side of Ella's. "I hope he's holding up all right in there."

"I'm sure he's doing great, Mom," Ella said. "Charley was just wondering where Chloe's family is."

"I've had no success whatsoever in getting your brother to tell me what the deal is with her family. Apparently, they were less than thrilled to hear about the baby and haven't had much to do with her since she got pregnant."

"Can you imagine being that shitty to your own kid?" Charley asked. "It's a *baby*, not a drug bust, for crying out loud."

"That's how Dad and I feel, too. Would we have chosen this for him at this point in his life? Probably not, but it's his life, not ours. It wouldn't occur to us not to support him."

"That's because you're great parents," Ella said.

"Don't make me cry, sweetheart. I'm already a hot mess waiting to meet my grandbaby."

Ella put her arm around her mother, who laid her head on Ella's shoulder. "That's going to be one lucky grandbaby."

"You're making me cry."

Hannah and Nolan arrived a short time later, followed by Wade and Elmer. And with their arrival, the entire family was there when Max came bursting through the double doors an hour later wearing light blue scrubs, a cap on his head and a smile that stretched from ear to ear.

"It's a boy," he said with tears streaming down his face. "I have a *son*!"

Molly and Lincoln rushed to hug him while everyone else waited their turn to congratulate him.

"How's Chloe?" Molly asked.

"She's kind of out of it, but she did great. He's a big boy. Almost nine pounds."

Ella winced at that news. Ouch!

"What's his name?" Colton asked.

"Caden," Max said. "Caden Lincoln Abbott."

"Oh hell," Lincoln said, swiping at his tears. "Thank you, son."

"Thank *you*. All of you. I can't believe you're all here."

"Where else would we be?" Hannah asked, wrapping her arms around Max when he broke down again.

"I don't know what's going to happen now," Max said between sobs. "It's all so screwed up."

"You'll go back in there and be with your son," Lincoln said, rubbing Max's back. "Just be there and you'll figure out the rest."

"Dad's right," Molly said. "Your place right now, today, is with him. You'll work things out with Chloe as you go."

Max nodded and rubbed his eyes with the sleeve of the gown he'd worn in the delivery room. "I'll bring him out as soon as I can."

"We'll be right here waiting to meet him." Molly went up on tiptoes to kiss his cheek. "We'll be right here for as long as you need us."

"Okay." He smiled weakly at the gathered group before returning to his son.

"Lord," Molly said when he was gone. "The poor guy. He's so excited and so terrified at the same time."

"Like any new parent," Lincoln said, his arm around his wife.

What her father said was true, Ella thought, but they all knew this situation wasn't typical, and she had a bad feeling it could get a whole lot worse before it got better for Max.

His heart pumping with adrenaline and joy and a healthy dose of anxiety over what lay ahead, Max returned to Chloe's room. As usual, he had no idea whether he'd be welcome there, but bolstered by the support of his family, he didn't really care if she wanted him around. The baby was his son, too, and he planned to be there for him in every way possible.

He took a fortifying deep breath and pushed open the

door, surprised to find Chloe asleep and Caden crying piti-
fully. Rushing to the bassinet next to Chloe's bed, Max bent
over his son, trying to decide what he should do. He'd taken
the class offered by the hospital on his own when Chloe had
refused to go with him, so he knew the baby wanted one of
three things—food, a diaper change or someone to hold him.

Since he could help with two of those three things, he
first checked the baby's diaper and found it was dry, so he
carefully picked him up, making sure he was tightly swad-
dled. Patting his little back, Max moved around the room with
him, putting a bounce in his step as he went, which seemed to
settle the little guy.

"Yeah," he whispered, "that's it. I'm your dad. I've got
you." The tsunami of emotions that came with seeing his
son born were upon him once again as the tears flowed
freely down his face. Watching him enter the world had been
the most amazing moment of his entire life, and Max would
never forget it.

Chloe let out a groan before her eyes opened. Her blond
hair was matted, and her face was still bright red from the
strain of pushing out the baby. She'd spent most of the hours
in labor begging for something more for the pain. "What's
wrong with him?"

"Nothing. He's fine. Are you okay?"

"I'm great," she said sarcastically. "I've got a hundred
stitches between my legs, but other than that . . ."

"You want me to get the nurse?"

"They said no more pain meds for an hour. I just want to
sleep."

"I'm going to take him to see my parents, if that's okay."

"I don't care."

There was so much Max could say to that, but today
wasn't the day. Today was Caden's day, and it would be for
the rest of his life. Max held the baby close to his chest as
he left the room and walked to the waiting area, eager to
show off his son to his family.

When Max stepped through the double doors with the
baby in his arms, his entire family rushed them.

"Oh my God, he's so cute!"

"And so tiny!"

"That face, look at that little face!"

"He looks like you, Max."

"Can we hold him?"

Reluctant to be parted with him for even a minute, Max eased the baby into his mother's arms.

"Well hello there, little man," she whispered through her tears. "Oh, Max, he's beautiful."

His dad stood behind his mom, looking down at his new grandson with tears in his eyes, too. "You done good, son. He's a fine-looking boy."

Ella put her arms around him.

Max leaned into his sister's embrace, grateful for the unwavering support of his family.

"How ya holding up?" Ella asked.

"I'm great. Best day of my life."

"How's Chloe?"

"In pain and grumpy, but I suppose I would be, too, if I were her."

"Where's her family?" Ella asked softly.

"Not here. Not coming."

"That's just so wrong."

"I know. I agree. I feel bad for her. It's just another thing she blames me for."

"Max . . ."

He made an effort to shake off his worries about Chloe. "Not today. Today is Caden's day."

"Yes, it is. Congratulations again, Max."

"Thanks."

CHAPTER 21

❧━◆━❧

Hope is faith holding out its hand in the dark.

—George Iles

With most of the family staying in Burlington through Thanksgiving, Ella and Charley left after seeing the baby to stake out a room at the lake house.

"Max seems good," Charley said after they'd put their stuff in the room they usually shared.

"I hate that he's so worried about what's going to happen with Chloe now that the baby is here."

"I wish she didn't have to act like he got her pregnant all on his own. I mean look at him . . . She was probably a more than willing participant."

"I'm sure she was. No one ever thinks it's going to happen to them."

"I just hope it doesn't get ugly."

"I hope so, too." Ella put her long hair up in a ponytail. "Mom said she brought everything she'd bought for Thanksgiving. Want to make the pies with me?"

"Sure."

They were rolling out piecrust when the others began to arrive. Will built up the fire in the huge stone fireplace while Colton carried in more wood. Lucy and Cameron joined

Ella and Charley in the kitchen while Nolan insisted Hannah take a nap.

"Only if you come with me," she said to her husband, who followed behind her with a dopey smile on his face.

"I want a nap," Charley said.

"Keep rolling," Ella retorted.

By the time their parents got to the house a couple of hours later, they had four pies cooling on the counter, twenty pounds of potatoes had been peeled by Will and Colton, who'd protested the entire time, stuffing had been made and the turkey prepared for baking.

"Oh my goodness, girls," Molly said. "You did everything!"

"Will and I peeled the potatoes," Colton said. "Don't let them tell you otherwise."

"Thank you, Colton."

"And Will," Will called from the living room, where he had found a football game to watch on TV.

"And Will."

"How's the baby?" Charley asked.

"He's beautiful," Molly said. "I got to give him a bottle before I left."

"She's not breastfeeding?" Hannah asked.

"She said the baby wasn't interested in breastfeeding, so the nurses set him up with a bottle."

"How hard did she try?" Hannah asked.

"I wasn't in the room, so I don't know. She's been crying a lot. I think she's in a lot of pain."

"Poor thing," Hannah said. "She's so young."

"And all alone," Molly said. "How any mother can stay away when her child is in labor is beyond me."

"And me," Hannah said. "I want my mommy right there with me when my time comes."

Molly patted her daughter's shoulder. "And she'll be there."

They made deli sandwiches for dinner, popped corn in the fireplace and even found the makings for s'mores left over from when Colton and Lucy had been there last summer. It was a great night with most of the family there.

"Who wants to go out drinking?" Landon asked around ten.

"Ohhh, college girls," Lucas said, scrambling to his feet. "Count me in."

"I'll go, too," Wade said.

"Take a cab, boys," Molly said.

"Yes, Mother," they said in unison.

"Feels like old times," Molly said, leaning her head against Lincoln's shoulder. They were sharing a sofa with Elmer while the others were scattered about the room, some on the floor. Cameron was using Will's belly as a pillow.

Ella leaned over to quietly ask if she could borrow Cam's phone.

"Sure." She wiggled it out of her back pocket.

"Hey," Will said. "Watch the merchandise, woman."

Cameron giggled at him. "Sorry, I've got plans for your merchandise later. We can't have it getting injured."

"Ewww," Landon said. "Mom, tell them that's not allowed."

"I'll do no such thing. They're married and can do whatever they want."

"So can we," Colton said to Lucy, "'cuz we're engaged."

"No comment," Molly replied, making the others laugh.

"Too bad Hunter and Megan can't be here," Elmer said.

"They're off running your diner and making Thanksgiving for the masses," Molly reminded her father.

"And they're doing a fine job of it."

With Cameron's phone in hand, Ella slipped out of the room undetected, or so she hoped. She couldn't wait another minute to talk to Gavin. It felt like a year rather than hours since she'd last seen him.

He answered on the first ring. "There you are."

"Hi there," she said, filled with relief at the sound of his voice.

"Well, what's the good word? Boy or girl?"

"A boy named Caden Lincoln Abbott. Eight pounds, twelve ounces, twenty-one inches long."

"Oh wow, that's great, Ella. How's Max doing?"

"He's elated and emotional and thrilled. The baby is so cute."

"How about his girlfriend?"

"Sore and grumpy from all accounts, but I suppose that's to be expected."

"You wouldn't be. Grumpy, I mean."

"How do you know that? I've never pushed a nine-pound baby out of my body. I might be a raging bitch afterward for all we know."

"You wouldn't be. I know you wouldn't. You'd be all glowy and sparkly and happy. Am I allowed to say that?"

"Yeah," she said gruffly, overwhelmed by the picture he painted. "You're allowed."

"I want to see that someday. I want to see you holding our baby after giving birth."

"Gavin . . ."

"Too much?"

"No."

"What's wrong?"

"Nothing, you just make me want things when you talk like that."

"I want the same things."

"I'm fanning myself right now. It's getting warm in here." His low chuckle made her smile. "How was your day?" she asked, steering the conversation into safer terrain.

"It was actually not bad. We finally got the repairs completed up north in time for everyone to come home for the holiday weekend. We'll get them back up there Monday to hit it hard. We've got some lost time to make up for."

Ella swallowed hard, hoping he wasn't about to say that he needed to be up there with his men next week. She couldn't wait to tell him about the trip so she could stop worrying about all the many ways it could go wrong. "I'm glad you got it fixed."

"Me, too. Huge relief."

"Now you can relax and enjoy the holiday."

"Yeah." That one word was so tinged with sadness that Ella heard it through the phone.

"You can try to enjoy it? Lots to be thankful for this year."

"You're right about that. The holidays are tough . . . It's

hard to pretend everything is okay when someone is missing."

"I know. Do you want me to come home early? I could have dinner with you and your parents. That would be fine with me."

"You need to be with your family. You don't have to do that."

"What time are you eating?"

"My mom said around four or so. How about you?"

"Two. I'll head home right after dinner. I'll meet you at your mom's."

"Are you sure?"

"Gavin," she said, laughing, "don't you know by now that I'm very, *very* sure?"

"Yeah, baby, I know, and that makes me feel so lucky. I wish you were here right now."

Ella settled into bed, under the covers where it was warm and cozy. "What would we be doing if I were there?" She tucked the phone between her ear and the pillow.

"More of what we did this morning and last night."

"This morning was amazing. I thought about it all day."

"So did I."

"It was different, wasn't it? Than the other times?"

"It was incredible," he said in that gruff, sexy voice she loved so much. "It always is, but that was something extra special."

"We need to stop talking about what we can't have."

"I vote for talking more about it."

Charley knocked on the door and came in. "Is it safe in here? You're not having phone sex, are you?"

"No, Charley, I'm not having phone sex."

"Yet," Gavin said, laughing.

Charley grabbed a sweatshirt out of her bag and scurried toward the door. "I'm outta here."

"She's gone," Ella said.

"Now about that phone sex . . ."

"Stop."

"I don't want to. I want to talk about how soft you are, how responsive. Your sweet nipples—"

"Gavin! Stop! I can't have phone sex with you on Cameron's phone."

"It's not like she'll know."

"*I'll* know."

"Such a good girl."

"That's right, and don't forget it."

"You're not always a good girl. Sometimes you're very, very bad."

"I have no idea what you're talking about."

"Oh, and that prim, prissy tone . . . Do you have any idea how hard that makes me?"

"I have to go."

"You do not."

"I'm having a sleepover with most of my family. You're like the devil at the pajama party."

"You love me."

"Yes, I do."

"I'm going to hate sleeping without you tonight."

"Me, too. I'm addicted. But we can get through one night, right?"

"As long as it's only one."

"What're you doing tonight?"

"Sitting around watching football and wishing you were here."

"So you're staying in?"

"Yes, Ella, I'm staying in and behaving myself while you're out of town."

"I didn't mean it that way."

"It hasn't even been two weeks since you picked me up at a bar, so it doesn't offend me that you'd be worried about that."

"Haven't things changed since then?"

"*Everything* has changed since then."

His assurances warmed her all the way through.

"Don't worry, El. I'm on my best behavior. I have promises to keep. Important promises."

"I love you, Gavin. And I love being able to tell you I love you."

"I love you, too. I'll see you tomorrow."

"See you then." She waited for him to end the call. "You're supposed to hang up now."

"Not until you do."

"I don't want to."

"Neither do I."

Ella smiled widely. "Let's hang up together. One, two, three . . ."

"You first."

"I'm going now."

"So am I."

"Night, Gavin."

"Night, Ella."

Their phones clicked off at the same time, and Ella lay there for a long time afterward thinking about him, wishing she were with him and counting the minutes until she could see him again.

Everything about this Thanksgiving felt different to Ella from every other one that came before it. For one thing, it was the first one they'd spent in the lake house. For another, the family football game happened on the beach rather than in the field next to the barn. It was strange not to have Hunter and Max with them, which was also a first. It was the first Thanksgiving in which they'd taken turns going to the hospital to visit Max and Caden, who'd had a good first night.

It was the first Thanksgiving that Ella had somewhere else she'd rather be—or rather the first time she wished she could be in two places at once. It wasn't unusual to see Lucas and Landon nursing hangovers, but it was unusual to see Wade in the same condition.

Ella plopped down next to him on a blanket on the beach. A chilly wind blew in off the lake, but the bright sunshine kept the day from being too cold to be outside. "You're looking rough."

"Gee, thanks," Wade said with a wan smile. "Remind me not to try to keep up with those two buffoons." He gestured to Landon, who was showing off his backflip skills. "If I did that right now, I'd puke all over the place."

"Not like you to get loaded."

"Maybe it's more like me than you think."

"Wade . . . That's not going to make anything better."

"Actually, for a short time last night, it did make things better. I was with the chick magnets and had just enough booze in my belly to forget about why I wanted to get drunk in the first place."

"Did you meet someone?"

"Nah. Nothing like that. It was fun, though."

"I'm glad you had fun."

"Not so fun today, though. Can't remember the last time I was this hungover."

"Thanksgiving dinner will soak up the booze and make you all better."

"I'm counting on that."

They were sitting down to dinner an hour later when Max came in, seeming upset. "Am I too late for dinner?"

"Right on time." Molly jumped up to get another place setting while the others made room for him at the table. "How's the baby?"

"He's great."

"And Chloe?"

"Miserable as usual lately. Motherhood hasn't changed that." He loaded his plate with turkey, mashed potatoes, gravy, stuffing, green bean casserole and the other sides. "I've got to be back in an hour. I don't want to talk about her. But I've got lots of new pictures." He passed his phone around so everyone could see the pictures.

"He's a beauty," Elmer said proudly.

Max put down his fork, bent his head and seemed to be trying to control his emotions.

"Max, honey," Molly said. "What is it?"

"Chloe's being impossible. She doesn't want to take care of him, but she doesn't want me doing it either."

"What do you mean she doesn't want to take care of him?" Hannah asked.

"She doesn't show any interest. She says she's in pain and she's tired." He ran his fingers through his hair. "But everything I do for him is wrong. I had to get out of there for a minute. Now I'm thinking I shouldn't have left. What if she ignores him the whole time I'm gone? And how will I leave them to go to work not knowing if she's going to take care of him or not?"

"Don't worry about work," Colton said. "Not now. That's the last thing you need to think about."

Charley, who was sitting next to Max, put her arm around him. "She's probably freaking out, but she'll get it together. What choice does she have?"

Max drew in a long deep breath, seeming to summon the fortitude he needed for the situation. "I should get back to the hospital. They're letting her stay for one more night because she's in such bad pain."

"Do you want to take dinner back to her?" Molly asked. "I could have it ready in a minute."

"Sure, thanks, Mom."

"We'll be here in Burlington for as long as you need us, son," Lincoln said. "You're not alone in this."

"Thanks," Max said, his jaw tight with emotion. "I appreciate you guys moving the holiday over here on my account. Sorry I can't stay longer." He looked over to Will and Hannah. "Hope you have fun on the trip and at the wedding."

"We will," Hannah said, "but we'll be checking on you, too."

Max nodded, then accepted the bag that Molly handed him and a hug from her. "It's all going to work out fine. I promise."

"I sure hope so."

"We'll be over to check on you in the morning, and I'll borrow a phone to check in with you later."

"Okay."

After he left, the gathering was considerably more subdued.

"I hate that he's so torn up when this should be the happiest time in his life," Will said.

"You speak for all of us," Colton said. "It sucks. What is

it she wants from him anyway? He's been right by her side through it all."

"She probably doesn't know what she wants," Molly said. "In addition to the fact that she's twenty-one, she's full of hormones and her family has turned its back on her. I can't imagine what she must be going through. What's important is that Max is doing the right thing by her, even if she can't see it at the moment."

"Mom's right," Lincoln said. "As long as he's doing all he can to support her and the baby, his conscience can be clear. And we'll be here for at least a week to make sure they have everything they need."

Ella helped clear the table and pack up the leftovers before she went into her room to grab her stuff. To Charley, she said, "I'm going to head back to Butler now. Do you want to come or hang here for a while?"

"I'll go back later with Will and Cam. Good luck with everything tonight. I hope the surprise is a huge hit and that you have a great trip."

Ella hugged her sister. "Thanks for the support and for covering for me at work." After saying her good-byes to everyone else, Ella headed off to Butler, pressing a little harder than usual on the accelerator because she was so eager to be with Gavin.

CHAPTER 22

———◆◆———

*God puts rainbows in the clouds so that each
of us—in the dreariest and most dreaded
moments—can see a possibility of hope.*

—Maya Angelou

I t had been an odd Thanksgiving for Gavin. He'd spent
most of the day wishing Ella were there to make everything better, but his parents were also different today. Sure,
his mom was scurrying around making the traditional turkey
dinner, but they were also packing for their trip to Turks and
Caicos in the morning. Apparently, they were on the same
flight from Boston with Hannah, Nolan, Will, Cameron,
Hunter and Megan. They'd even hired a limo to transport
them all from Vermont to Logan Airport.

His parents were excited about the trip, excited for the wedding, excited about everything lately, or so it seemed to him.

"Too bad you couldn't get away to come with us, Gav,"
his dad said while they watched football before dinner.

"Things are nuts at the yard," he said, as he always did.

"You know . . . No man lies on his deathbed wishing he'd
spent more time at work."

"What's that supposed to mean?"

"You know what it means."

"You ever run your own business, Dad? No, I didn't think so."

"Point taken. However, you have excellent employees who are more than capable of covering for you for a few days so you can get away. Everyone needs a break once in a while. That's all I'm saying."

It was nothing Gavin hadn't told himself, repeatedly, especially after the invitation had come for Dylan's wedding and everyone began making plans to go. He'd never had any intention of going for reasons that were his and his alone.

By three thirty he was standing in front of the window that looked out over the driveway watching for Ella. He and his parents sat down to eat at four, and as it did every year, Caleb's glaring absence left an empty space across the table and in Gavin's heart. He missed him so much—every day, but more so on days like this that were set aside for family, and he was forced to confront how small his family had become.

Over dinner, his mom said she wanted to talk about what they were thankful for. "I'll start," she said with a warm, happy smile. "This year I'm thankful for my husband and son and what we've managed to weather together. I'm thankful to have been Caleb's mother, to have the incredible blessing of his life to cherish for the rest of mine." She took a deep breath, dabbed at her eyes and continued. "I'm thankful for the inn that Hannah started, which has given Dad and me all new purpose this year and for the grandbaby she will soon bring into our lives. I'm thankful for your beautiful smile, Gavin. I've missed it, and it's nice to see it back again. And for that, I'm most thankful to Ella, who has given you reason to smile again. That's my list."

"Ditto," his dad said.

"That's a cop-out," Amelia said, smiling at her husband.

"How so? I'm thankful for all those same things."

"All right, fine. Be that way. What about you, Gav?"

Gavin felt surprisingly emotional after hearing his mother's heartfelt list, and her inclusion of Ella touched him deeply. "I'm thankful for all those things, too. Mostly for you guys. I'm glad we always have each other even if we don't see each other every day. You know I'm right there for you, or at least I hope you do."

"Of course we do," Amelia said, laying her hand over his. "You've been a wonderful son to us your entire life, but never more so than since we lost your brother."

Gavin forced a smile for his mom as he contended with the lump in his throat. For as long as he'd lived, he'd done so in the shadow of his much more accomplished older brother. He'd never minded the shadow and had missed it after it was gone, but the irony that Caleb had been the one to die young wasn't lost on him. It should've been him. Caleb had had a wife he'd adored, an incredible career, so many talents and a future filled with promise.

Whereas Gavin had none of those things. He would always wish it had been him instead of Caleb. It would've been easier for everyone if it had been him. But as he waited to see Ella again, for the first time in a long time, he was glad it hadn't been him. He finally had something worthwhile to live for again, and he couldn't wait to see her.

They had finished dinner and were cleaning up when a knock on the mudroom door had him bolting across the kitchen. Gavin threw open the door, and there she was looking fresh-faced and beautiful and as happy to see him as he was to see her. He pulled her into his arms and held her tight against him, breathing her in and filled with relief to have her back where she belonged.

Two weeks ago, he would've shied away from that thought, but now he couldn't deny that she belonged to him, and he belonged to her. And he liked it that way.

"There you are," he said after a long moment of silence.

"Here I am."

"Missed you."

"Missed you, too."

He drew back from her and gazed down at her lovely face before stealing a quick kiss. It took all he had to remember where he was and that he couldn't lose himself in the kiss or her. Not now anyway. But the minute he could spirit her away from his parents' house all bets were off.

He helped her out of her coat and took her by the hand to lead her into the kitchen where his mother was preparing to serve up the one pie she'd made—apple because it was his favorite. She normally made a lot more food, but because they were leaving town for a week, she'd dialed it back this year.

"Ella!" Amelia rushed over to hug and kiss her. "Happy Thanksgiving and congratulations on the new nephew."

"Thank you. He's beautiful."

"I'm sure he is, and I love his name."

"I do, too." She hugged and kissed his dad and gratefully accepted the pie his mother offered.

Gavin fixed her a cup of coffee the way she liked it and brought it to the table, which now seemed less empty with that fourth seat filled by someone he loved. He couldn't take his eyes off her. She looked so good, but then again she always did. From her shiny hair to the rosy glow of her cheeks to her gorgeous brown eyes and delicious pink lips, she was the most beautiful woman he'd ever known—inside and out.

He couldn't remember a time when he hadn't been drawn to her. She was so kind and sweet and always thinking of others before herself. He'd recognized those qualities in her long before the time they'd recently spent together and had probably been in love with her for years, if he were being honest with himself.

Every time he'd laid eyes on her, he'd wanted her. Never more so than right now when she chatted happily with his parents about their upcoming trip while enjoying her pie and coffee. She seemed to be in no particular rush to get out of there while he was on the verge of spontaneously combusting from the desire that coursed through him.

Running her fork through a dollop of whipped cream, she brought it to her mouth, her eyes catching his across the table.

He covered his moan with a cough that didn't fool Ella. Standing so fast he nearly knocked over his chair, Gavin took his plate to the sink, rinsed it and put it in the dishwasher. "We've got to get going."

"So soon?" his mom said. "Ella just got here."

"Yes, Gavin," Ella said. "I just got here."

The glare he sent her was met with a grin that told him she knew what he wanted and was enjoying making him wait. Well, two could play at that game. As soon as he had that thought, he had to squelch it or risk walking around with an embarrassing bulge in his pants.

Rather than indulge in thoughts about his plans for later, he continued to load the dishwasher, making as much noise as he could to vent his frustration.

"Go easy on my plates, Gavin," his mother said sternly, making Ella laugh.

It was nice to hear laughter in this house again, even if it was at his expense. He'd happily take the lumps to bring some light back into his life and that of his parents. Ella was all light and joy and peace. He was drawn to her like a magnet to steel, the pull impossible to deny or resist, not that he wanted to do either of those things. Not anymore.

Right in that moment, standing at his mother's kitchen sink, he became acutely aware of the fact that he needed to marry her to ensure she'd never be anywhere other than with him, where she belonged. If one night away from her had left him reeling, the thought of the whole rest of his life without her was like imagining a return to the barren waste-land of nothingness where he'd been stranded for far too long. After the taste of heaven he'd had with her, he had no desire whatsoever to return to that life.

Filled with irrational fear of all the many ways he could still screw this up, he resolved to act sooner rather than later to make this relationship permanent. Once she had his ring on her finger, she wouldn't be able to get away. She'd be stuck with him, for better or worse. And he'd be gloriously, blissfully stuck with her.

He couldn't wait for that.

Ella decided an hour with Amelia and Bob was enough to be polite, enough to make Gavin suffer a little and enough to get her nerves under control before the reveal of the big surprise. He'd had nothing to add to the conversation about his parents' trip other than to wish them safe travels and a good time and to give Dylan his best.

He'd never once said he wished he were going, too.

But she refused to let that omission derail her. Of course he wouldn't say that because he had himself convinced he *couldn't* go. She was about to prove otherwise.

"You ready?" he asked from his spot next to her on the sofa.

"If you are."

He glared at her, letting her know how ready he was to leave—how ready he'd been for some time now.

"It was so nice of you to cut short your holiday with your own family to spend some time with us," Amelia said when she walked them to the door.

"It was well worth it for that pie of yours," Ella said. "I need your recipe."

"I'll write it down for you. It's Gavin's favorite."

"Thanks for a fabulous day, Mom," Gavin said, kissing her cheek. "Have a great trip and be safe."

"We'll call you while we're away."

"Don't worry about me. Just have a good time."

"I will worry about you, and I *will* call you."

"Thanks for the warning," he grumbled with a good-natured grin for his mother.

"He's all yours for the next week," Amelia said when she hugged Ella.

"I'll keep a close eye on him."

"That sounds good to me," he said. With his hand on Ella's back, Gavin led her out of the house. "Your place or mine?"

"Mine."

She could tell he was surprised to hear her say that, because they'd been spending most nights at his place thanks to her nosy landlady.

"It's closer," she said meaningfully.

"Hurry." He patted her ass and sent her along to her car, which was parked behind his truck.

As Ella followed the speed limit to the letter, she could

almost feel him boiling behind her. She'd felt him on slow simmer the whole time she'd been at his parents' home, trying to be polite while she visited with Bob and Amelia when all he wanted to do was get her out of there.

It was heady stuff to be wanted that way by the man she loved. But it was also fun to play with him a little, to make him wait, to build the tension.

She pulled into her driveway with him right behind her. Before she could gather her purse and the backpack she'd taken to Burlington, he was upon her, opening her door and reaching for her seatbelt. "Gavin! Wait."

"I've already waited long enough."

"Five more minutes won't kill you."

"It just might. Move it." He "helped" her out of the car and propelled her along with the force of his own desire. Her feet barely touched the ground on the way inside or as they went up the stairs as one being, his arm around her waist moving her along. Once again, she felt swept away by him, overtaken in the best possible way. The potent excitement of being back in his arms was overshadowed only by the lingering fear of how her surprise would be received.

Inside her apartment, he took the backpack from her and dropped it with a thud inside the door. Then he removed her coat, her sweater and was working on her jeans by the time she caught up to him.

"Gavin, wait, I want to talk to you—"

"After. We'll talk after." His coat, sweater, boots and jeans ended up in the same pile with her clothes. When they were both down to underwear, he took her hand and led her to her bedroom. "Come here, baby." He drew her into his arms and breathed a heavy sigh. "Don't go away anymore without me, okay?"

"Okay," she said, heartened by the comment. Perhaps her surprise would be a big hit after all.

His hands were everywhere—on her back, her shoulders, her ribs, cupping her breasts and squeezing her ass—as if he were taking inventory to ensure she'd returned to him whole and intact. Kneeling before her, he helped her out of her panties and then removed her bra before standing.

She helped with his boxers and drew him into bed with her.

"I thought I was going to *die* watching you eat whipped cream at my mother's," he whispered against her neck. "I wanted to dive across the table and have you right there."

"You don't think that would've shocked your parents?"

"You'll notice I managed to control myself. Just barely."

"No need to control yourself now."

His low growl was his only warning before he took her mouth in a series of savage kisses.

Ella was breathless as she tried to keep up with him. She'd never seen him so undone by desire, and she loved it. Though she couldn't wait to tell him about the trip, she would wait until after they'd slaked the ravenous need that she felt every bit as acutely as he did. She gave herself over to him, surrendering entirely.

"God, Ella, you're so sexy. I wanted you the second you walked in the door with your cheeks all flushed from the cold. How do you do that to me? How do you make me so crazy?"

"You do the same to me. I thought about you all the way from Burlington when I was driving way faster than I should've been because I couldn't wait to see you."

He stopped kissing her and raised his head so he could see her face. "Don't do that again."

"Do what?"

"Drive too fast when you're on your way to me. Don't take chances with your safety."

"I didn't—"

"Promise me you won't do that again."

Because it seemed to matter so much to him, she said, "Okay, I won't."

"Promise."

"I promise."

"Good," he said, kissing her softly and with less urgency than he'd shown a few minutes ago. "If anything ever happened to you . . ."

"Nothing is going to happen. I'm right here and I love you."

"I want to touch you everywhere and make you pay for making me suffer at my parents' house, but more than anything I need to be inside you right now."

"Yes, Gavin . . . Please." She raised her hips and offered herself to him. Everything she had to give was his. It always had been and always would be.

He drove into her and dropped his head to her chest.

While her body stretched and burned from his entry, Ella ran her fingers through the hair she loved so much and tried to relax, to accommodate him.

"Nothing is like this," he whispered. "Nothing."

She smoothed her hands over his back and down to grip his ass, holding him inside her until she felt ready for more. "Make love to me, Gavin."

"Gonna be fast."

"That's okay. We've got all night."

Her words seemed to unleash something in him. He pounded into her repeatedly, taking them both on a wild ride that ended in one perfect moment of utter unity as they came together, groaning and clinging to each other as the tremors took them over.

He sagged into her arms, his big body vibrating from the powerful release. "Love you, Ella. Love you so much."

"I love you, too."

"Thanks for not giving up on me."

"I'll never give up on you."

CHAPTER 23

— ◂ ◦ ▸ —

No one ever told me that grief felt so like fear.

—C. S. Lewis

They stayed there like that for a long time, the room growing darker before he finally withdrew from her and moved onto his back, bringing her with him. She wanted to curl up to him, to wallow in the heat and comfort of him next to her, but it was time to tell him about the trip. Preparations had to be made by both of them to be ready to leave at six in the morning. She couldn't wait any longer.

Kissing his chest, she said, "Let me up for a minute."

"As long as you come right back."

"I'll come right back."

He kissed her lips before letting her go. "Hurry up."

"Always in such a hurry."

"Only when you're around."

Her heart pounding with excitement, she used the bathroom and then went to find the packet she'd printed at work the day before. "Here goes nothing," she whispered as she returned to the bedroom. Before getting back into bed, she turned on the bedside lamp.

Gavin winced from the sudden onset of light. He blinked her into focus. "What've you got there?"

"Your surprise."

"Oh, I'd almost forgot about that." He raised himself up on one elbow. "What is it?"

"Before I tell you, I want you to know that I did this for you because I think you'll enjoy it and I want you to be happy. I hope you'll like it."

"I'm beyond curious."

Her mouth was suddenly dry as she handed over the packet of papers that included plane tickets, pictures from the resort and information about their reservation.

He opened it, looked it over and then glanced at her, his jaw tight with tension. "What is this, El?"

"It's a trip to Dylan's wedding, all paid for and arranged. We leave in the morning."

"You . . . You set this all up?"

"I did," she said, swallowing hard. "And don't worry about work. Your dad talked to Clinton, and he's more than happy to cover for you next week so you can get away."

"My parents know about this, too?"

She nodded. "So does Dylan. He was very excited about it and said to tell you how much it'll mean to him to have you there for his wedding." As she spoke, she couldn't help but notice that he didn't seem happy about the surprise. He seemed . . . less than pleased.

"I can't believe you did this."

"I thought it would be fun to get away from it all for a week, to go to your friend's wedding—"

"I can't go, Ella. There's no way I can go."

"What do you mean? I just told you, work is covered—"

"It's *not* covered." He got up out of bed and pulled on his underwear and then rested his hands on his hips. "Clinton is great, but he's never been left in charge before. I can't just walk away from my responsibilities for a week because you think it would be fun."

"Gavin, let's talk about it—"

"I'm really sorry. It was nice of you to do this and to think of me this way, but I can't do it."

"You're closed down for the weekend. You could come for a few days. Surely your business wouldn't fall apart if you missed a couple of days. I'm missing one of the biggest weeks of the year in the store, and it'll be fine."

"Because you have people to cover for you. I don't have that."

"Yes, you do!"

"So two weeks together and suddenly you know my business better than I do? Wow. That's one hell of an accomplishment." He turned away from her and went into the other room.

Frantic to salvage this disaster, Ella scrambled out of bed and pulled on a robe before following him into the living room, where he was getting dressed. She was shocked to see him getting ready to leave. "What're you doing? Where're you going?"

"I'm going home. I'm sorry to disappoint you, but we both knew I would eventually, so it's better that it happen sooner rather than later. You deserve someone who could receive an amazing gift like this with grace and appreciation. I'm not that guy."

"Would you please stop and just talk to me? Tell me what's really going on here."

"I did tell you, but you don't believe me when I say I can't be away from work."

"Okay, so we won't go."

"You should go. You spent all that money. You shouldn't let it go to waste."

"Go without you? To your friend's wedding?"

"He's your friend, too. You and your brothers and Hannah have known him for years."

"Gavin, you're being crazy. Why would I go to Dylan's wedding without you?"

"Because you'll be out all that money if you don't go."

"Please stay and talk to me."

"What's there to talk about? You've always wanted more from me than I'm able to give. This is the proof."

"So that's it? It's over? Just like that? Because I tried to do something nice for you?"

"No, because you're too good for me. You deserve better."

"Gavin, I swear to God, if you walk out that door, don't come back. You won't be welcome."

"I'm sorry, Ella. You'll never know how sorry I am that I couldn't make this work."

With those words, he walked out the door, closing it behind him. As the lock clicked into place, Ella stared at the door, riveted by the memory of making love with him there. Her eyes filled with tears that she barely registered.

"What the hell just happened here?" It defied explanation. It defied belief. Never in her worst nightmares had she expected the reaction she'd gotten from him. She'd expected that he might be a little tense about work, but she'd thought that perhaps he'd call Clinton and go over everything with him and at least *try* to make it work.

But he hadn't done that. He'd just said thanks but no thanks and then left. She couldn't believe he'd actually *left*. There had to be more to this than work. But what was it and why wouldn't he tell her rather than end a relationship that was making them both happy over a trip no one was going to force him to take?

It didn't make sense. It didn't add up.

Ella stared at the door for a long, long time before she turned and went into the kitchen to call his mother.

Gavin's hands were shaking so badly he could barely drive. God, what had he done? It would be a very long time, if ever, before he forgot the shattered expression on her lovely face. He was a heartless bastard for letting this happen in the first place. That was where he'd made his first mistake.

The time with her had been amazing—the best days of his life—but all along he'd been waiting to fuck it up. He'd known he would. He couldn't tell her why he didn't want to go to the wedding. He'd never told anyone why he'd taken a step back from his brother's friends after Caleb died.

How could anyone understand what he barely understood himself?

No, he'd done the right thing. He kept telling himself that over and over again on the lonely, dark ride home. For a brief moment he thought about driving out of town to a place where no one knew him so he could get drunk in peace.

But he rejected that idea and headed home, where he had plenty of whiskey and could tie one on in the privacy of his own space.

He pulled up to the cabin and went inside where it was cold and dark. If only his fucking hands would stop shaking, he thought as he built up a fire in the woodstove. When his legs would no longer support him in a squat in front of the fireplace, he fell back to the floor, coming to rest against the sofa.

"What the fuck did I do?" Her face . . . that incredibly beautiful face and the way she'd stared at him as if he'd lost his mind . . . The memory of that would haunt him forever. How could he have done that to her? He couldn't bear to think of the time, effort and expense she'd gone to in order to surprise him, only to have it spit back in her face because he was a pathetic loser who couldn't find his way out of the swamp of grief and regret his life had become.

Leaving had been the right thing to do.

No, his heart cried out from its painful post inside his chest. It had *not* been the right thing to do. He'd barely survived one day and one night without her, and now he'd sentenced himself to the rest of his life without her all because he was too much of a coward to confront the truth?

"God, what did I do?" He sat on the floor and ran his fingers through his hair over and over again, wishing he had the courage to go back and face her, to try to explain, to make her see. But she'd told him he wouldn't be welcome back if he left, and she'd meant it.

He'd finally pushed her too far. He'd finally managed to push her right out of his life.

A knock on the door brought him to his feet, his heart leaping in the hope that it might be her, that maybe she'd come after him one more time. But it wasn't Ella. It was his dad, and he didn't look happy.

"Let me in, Gavin."

"This isn't a good time, Dad."

"I'm not leaving until I talk to you, so step aside and let me in."

Gavin recognized that steely tone in the colonel's voice and knew he was staring defeat in the face. He stepped aside. His dad walked into the house and went straight to the fridge, where he retrieved a beer. He held it up to ask Gavin if he wanted one.

Gavin shook his head. He wasn't at all sure he could keep it down. "What're you doing here anyway?"

"Ella called Mom."

Gavin sighed, imagining that conversation.

His dad took a drink from his beer. "What the hell is wrong with you?"

"You want the whole list or just the top ten?"

Bob put the beer down on the counter and ran his hand over his mouth. Gavin couldn't recall the last time he'd seen his dad so agitated. Well, yes he could . . . He'd looked just like this on the worst day of their lives. Gavin felt a tinge of shame at having driven him to that state again.

"I've let this go on far longer than I should have," Bob said in the tone he used to save for his sons when they tried to step out of line, which was usually every day.

"You've let what go on?"

"You and your bullshit. Do you know what it did to your mother to hear you'd gotten arrested in a bar fight at thirty-four years old?"

"Do you even *know* why I got arrested in a bar fight?" Gavin had never spoken about the incident with either of his parents. In fact, he'd harbored a tiny hope that they hadn't heard about it.

"Does it matter?"

"It fucking *mattered to me* or it wouldn't have happened. The guy I fought with said we wasted our time in Iraq."

Bob blew out a deep breath, his shoulders sagging under the weight of his own grief. "I'm sorry. I would've hit him, too."

"Despite what you think, I'm not out there looking for trouble."

"And yet it keeps finding you anyway. How could you turn down Ella's gift of the trip to the wedding? How could you do that to her, son? That girl *loves* you. Anyone can see that. Hell, even you have to see that."

His heart ached so badly. It had only ever hurt that badly once before. Gavin rubbed his hand over his chest, wishing that were all it took to ease the ache. "I see it," he said.

"Then *why*? *Why* would you do this to her?"

"I told her I couldn't go to the wedding, and she did this anyway. I don't know what she was hoping to accomplish."

"She was hoping to blast your head out of your ass and get you back into the land of the living where you belong! Dylan is one of your *best friends!* He has been since you were in elementary school. He's getting *married*. He wants you there. That's where you ought to be. If I can see that and your mother can see it and Ella can see it, why in the name of God can't *you* see it?"

"He's not my friend. He was Caleb's friend."

"Oh, for fuck's sake, Gavin. Is that what this is about?"

Gavin had never, in all his life, heard Bob Guthrie drop the F word. That was enough to shock him so profoundly he could hardly recall the question his father had asked him. But then he remembered. "No, it's not just that."

"Those guys love you as much as they loved Caleb. Everyone can see that but you. Why is that?"

"He was the heart and soul. I was just along for the ride. I was always along for his ride."

"That is so not true. You have no idea how important you were to him if you can say something so stupid. Without Gavin, there's no Caleb. You gave him his swagger and made him into the badass he became by challenging him on every bit of bullshit that came out of his mouth from the second you could first talk. Your mother and I used to call you the ballast. You kept the ship from rolling over under the weight of his personality and his ego. You were the yin to his yang."

Gavin had never heard these things before, and each revelation left him reeling.

"Nothing in my life has ever made me prouder than the deep friendship you two shared. You were more like twins than any twins I ever met. My very first thought upon hearing he'd been killed wasn't for me or your mother or Hannah. It was for *you*. I simply couldn't imagine one of you without the other."

"Dad . . ." Gavin needed this to stop before he completely lost his shit. This was the last thing he could bear to face tonight after he'd already royally fucked things up with Ella.

"I've watched you wither away over these last few years, becoming a man who bears no resemblance whatsoever to who he was before that day. I've watched you bury yourself in your work to the exclusion of your friends and even your family at times. I've stood by and let you do your thing because who am I to say how you're supposed to grieve your only sibling and closest friend? But I will *not* stand idly by and watch you sabotage your relationship with that lovely woman because you can't get out of your own goddamned way. I won't let you do it."

"Too late," Gavin said glumly. "I've already done it."

"It's never too late."

"This time it might be."

"You need to go over there and fix this, Gavin. If you think you've suffered over Caleb, you haven't seen suffering until you lose the woman you love forever. How's it going to feel to know she's out there somewhere, married to someone else, having his babies and living her life with him while you're still here mired in your own shit, wishing for something that's never going to happen?"

The picture his father painted of Ella happily married to someone else scared the living hell out of him. It had been his greatest fear in all the months before they got together— that she would finally meet someone she liked better than him. "You think that's what I'm doing? Sitting here wishing Caleb would come strolling in the door like he owns the place just like he used to?"

"Something like that."

"Well, I'm not. I know he's dead. I know he's not coming back. I know Homer's dead and Hannah's remarried and you and Mom are up to your eyeballs in the inn and everything is going along swimmingly for everyone. I get it."

"So you're pissed off that everyone has moved on except for you? You honestly think your mom or me or Hannah will ever truly move on and get over what happened to him? If that's what you think, you ought to spend a few nights at home so you can see how little sleep I get since my son died because he was stupid enough to follow in my footsteps."

"Dad . . . That's not true. He was doing exactly what he wanted to do."

"Yes, he was, and I know that. I know it all the way down to my bone marrow. But guess what? It still hurts like a son of a bitch anyway. I miss him every damned day. I wake up every morning wondering how I'm supposed to get through another day without him out there somewhere, living his life. Sometimes I like to imagine what he'd be doing now. I always picture him with a bunch of kids trailing behind him, caught up in whatever magic he'd be creating that day."

When Gavin raised his hand to his face, he realized it was wet with tears.

"And don't think I can't remember what an ornery son of a gun he could be, too. Most contrary person I ever knew. Half the time I wanted to knock his block off for being so mouthy and opinionated. The rest of the time I wanted to bow down in awe to him and you, the two amazing human beings your mother and I somehow managed to raise. The two of you together were the most perfect thing in my life, son. Watching you try to carry on without him has been the toughest part of this for me—and your mom."

Gavin wiped his face, mortified to have broken down in front of his father but riveted by the things he'd said.

"Seeing you with Ella, seeing you happy again, your eyes sparkling with delight the way they used to when he was alive . . . I said to your mother after dinner the night you brought her over the first time that maybe here was someone who could fill at least part of the void, if not all of it."

She had filled the void, and he was only just now realizing that.

"You can't let her get away, Gavin," Bob said, his tone considerably softer now. "You can't. I honestly fear that if you do, you'll never get over it."

His father's words landed like an arrow full of panic in the vicinity of his battered heart.

"I don't want to go to that wedding."

"Why not? And do *not* say because Dylan's not your friend."

"He is my friend."

"Then *why*, Gavin? Why, why, *why*? I talked to Clinton. He was thrilled to be in on the surprise and promised he'd do everything he could to keep things running smoothly here while you're gone. You have no good reason not to go."

"I have a very good reason not to go."

"But you're not going to tell me what it is?"

"No." If he told anyone, he would tell Ella. For some strange reason, he thought she might be the only one who would actually understand.

"That lovely young woman went to a lot of trouble and expense to do something nice for you. If you let that go to waste, if you walk away from her, you're a fool."

"I guess I'm a fool then."

"I'm disappointed, Gavin, and I don't toss that word around lightly."

"I'm sorry to have disappointed you."

"Just remember one thing . . . Nothing can't be fixed. Nothing."

Gavin didn't argue with his father, who squeezed his shoulder on the way past him. Some things couldn't be fixed, no matter how badly you might want to.

"I might be disappointed about this, but I always love you. I'd never want you to think otherwise."

"Love you, too, Dad."

After his father left, Gavin thought about what he'd said and realized that he had to try to make things right with Ella. He couldn't leave it like this. Even if she never forgave him for not going on the trip, he had to at least try to explain why he couldn't go. He grabbed his jacket and was out the door a minute later.

CHAPTER 24

❧

To weep is to make less the depth of grief.

—William Shakespeare

More than an hour after Gavin left, Ella emerged from the shock to discover she was angrier than she could ever recall being with anyone. More than anything, she was confused. She couldn't sit still, couldn't stop pacing the length of her small apartment, like a pent-up animal looking for a way to escape its confines.

Except there was no escape from this untenable situation. There was nowhere she could go to hide from her own feelings. But she didn't have to face them alone. She needed someone who understood Gavin. She needed Hannah. Without a thought to the time, she picked up the phone and called her sister.

Hannah answered on the third ring, sounding sleepy.

"Hannah."

"Ella?" Now wide awake, Hannah said, "What's wrong?"

"I know it's late and you're tired and pregnant and . . . But could I come over?"

"Of course. Come over. I'll put on the light."

"Thanks. I'll be right there."

"Are you okay to drive, Ella?"

"Yeah, I'm okay to drive."

"All right. I'll see you in a few."

Ella hung up the phone and ran for her bedroom to pull on yoga pants and an old UVM sweatshirt that dated back to her college days. Jamming her feet into moccasins, she grabbed her purse and keys and was out the door two minutes later. The night was foggy and murky, so she took her time driving to Hannah's, aware of her own disquiet and not looking to bring any further disaster upon herself by ramming into a tree or a moose.

At some point in the last few months, she'd begun to think of Nolan's house in the woods as Hannah's place, too. It had been oddly strange and emotional to help her sister move out of the home she'd shared with Caleb and into her new home with Nolan. She could only imagine what that had been like for Gavin, who'd pitched in with the guys to help move some of the bigger items.

"You're not thinking about him anymore," she reminded herself, laughing out loud at the preposterous thought. She'd have to be dead to not think about him anymore.

She pulled up to Hannah and Nolan's home and cut the engine, taking a second to gather herself before she went inside.

Hannah waited at the door, wrapped up in a plush robe that was tied over her protruding midsection. The first thing Hannah did was hug her. "What's wrong?"

"He's an ass."

"I assume we're talking about my lovely brother-in-law?"

"Who else?"

"Tell me what happened."

"Where's Nolan?"

"Asleep. I wore him out."

"I'm so sorry to barge in on you guys. I know I got you out of bed—"

"Ella." Hannah led her to the sofa where they sat together. "Tell me."

Ella replayed the disastrous presentation of her gift trip to the wedding and told her sister what he'd said and done.

By the time she was finished, she had new tears on her cheeks and fresh anger in her heart. "I knew it was a gamble, that he would be worried about work, but for him to end things with me over it. That I just don't get."

"He's running scared, Ella. You caught him off guard, and he's running."

"He said he wouldn't do that. He promised to give us a real, honest chance, and it was going so well. Why would he do this?"

"I don't know, honey. I honestly don't know. He's got all these dark corners inside him that he doesn't let anyone see. It's hard to know what goes on in that brain of his."

"What do I do, Hannah? How do I fix this? I told him we don't have to go on the trip if he really didn't want to, but he left saying I deserve better and how he was bound to disappoint me sooner or later, and it was better it happen now. Did he go into this expecting it to end?"

Hannah mulled that over. "It's possible he went into it expecting to eventually disappoint you, and this felt like a self-fulfilling prophecy or something."

"It was only intended as a surprise to get him away from it all for a few days, so we could spend time together and he could go to his friend's wedding. That's all it was to me."

"It was obviously something much more complicated for him."

"I should've listened to him when he said he didn't want to go, but Amelia was all for the surprise and Bob . . ." Ella shook her head, still trying to process how it had gone so terribly wrong.

"You did a really nice thing for him, Ella. No matter how he took it, the gesture was a lovely one."

"For all the good it did me. Now we've apparently broken up and any chance I had with him is lost. No good deed goes unpunished."

"You want to know what I think you ought to do?"

"That's why I'm here."

"Go on the trip. Take a break from him, from work, from everything and have a nice, relaxing vacation. We'll be there, Will and Cam, Hunter and Megan, Bob and Amelia. We'll all make sure you have a great time."

"Gee, that sounds fun. A romantic getaway with my siblings and their partners as well as the couple I'd hoped might one day be my in-laws. Woo-hoo, sign me up."

"You've already made the arrangements, and it's too late to back out now without losing the money. Why let it go to waste? Maybe some time apart will help Gavin get his head on straight when he realizes how much he misses you."

With her elbows on her knees, Ella let her hair cover her face. "I don't think I can go back to him after this. I told him if he left it was over, and I think I mean that."

Hannah put her arm around Ella's shoulders. "Nothing has to be decided tonight or even tomorrow. Come with us on the trip, and we'll figure it out when we get back. Let him miss you."

Ella leaned into her sister's comforting embrace. "Okay. I'll go."

"Are you packed?"

Nodding, Ella said, "I packed two days ago because I was so excited."

"Then stay here tonight. We'll run by your place in the morning to pick up your bag before we go. How were you planning to get to Boston?"

"We were going to drive."

"Then you can come in the car with us. It can take ten and we're at eight."

Ella wiped away more tears that kept coming at the thought of going on the trip without him. "Everyone will know that he shot me down."

"That's on him, not you."

"I played this all wrong, Hannah."

"You played it just right. What you did was done out of love for him. No one could ever blame you for caring too much." She kissed Ella's cheek. "Let me get you a pillow and blanket. I'll be right back."

"Are you sure you don't mind me bombing in on you guys?"

"Don't be silly. I already rocked Nolan's world. He's out cold until the morning, and we won't have time for anything then. Our pickup is at six."

"In that case," Ella said with a weak laugh for her sister. "I'd love to stay."

"Great. I'll fix you up with something to sleep in and a toothbrush. I'm glad you called, Ella. There's no need to go through this by yourself. I just wish I had more insight into why he would've done such a thing."

"So do I." While Hannah was off gathering what Ella needed for a sleepover, it occurred to Ella that she might never understand why he'd reacted the way he did. And wouldn't that be awesome? To have the rest of her life to try to figure out what had gone so terribly wrong with the man she loved beyond all reason. That thought was the most profoundly depressing of the many thoughts she'd had since it all went bad earlier.

Hannah returned with clothes, a toothbrush, a pillow and a blanket. "Make yourself at home. Anything you need."

"What if Nolan wakes up, and I scare the hell out of him?"

"He was awake just now, and I told him you're staying."

"Thanks again, Hannah."

"Any time. This is what big sisters are for."

When she was settled on Hannah's comfy sofa, Ella stared up at the dark ceiling for what seemed like hours. She had no way of knowing for sure how much time went by, but sleep remained elusive. She must've drifted off at some point because the sound of someone pounding at the door woke her up.

For a moment, she couldn't figure out where she was. But then she remembered coming to Hannah's and spending the night on her sofa. She also remembered the disaster with Gavin and began to ache all over again.

She heard movement in Hannah's room and heavy footsteps leading to the door. It opened, and she heard Nolan's tense voice along with that of another man.

"What're you doing here?" Nolan asked.

"Came to see my boy for the holiday. Ain't that allowed?"

"It's the middle of the night. Have you been drinking again?"

"You ever get tired of being so high and mighty, boy?"

Feeling as if she were intruding in her brother-in-law's business, Ella wanted to shrivel up and disappear.

"Are you awake?" Hannah whispered.

"Yeah."

"Sorry about the disturbance."

"What's going on?"

"Nolan's father. He comes to visit every now and then."

"In the middle of the night?"

"Always in the middle of the night."

Listening to Hannah, Ella realized everyone had their own burdens to carry. Some were just heavier and more obvious than others.

"Messes him up for days afterward."

"Should I go? I could sneak out the back door. If you guys need some time alone . . ."

"No, it's fine. We have to get up soon anyway."

Nolan came back in a few minutes later, wearing only a pair of sweats that showed off his muscular shoulders, chest and abdomen. He went directly to Hannah. "Why are you up?"

"Just checking on you. Is he gone?"

"For now."

"What did he want this time?"

"What does he always want?" Nolan asked with a weary sigh. "Sorry about that, Ella."

"Please don't apologize. I'm grateful for the loan of your sofa."

"Our sofa is your sofa." His arm around Hannah, he said, "Come on, honey. Let's get you back to sleep. You promised you'd take it easy if I agreed to the trip. I'm going to hold you to that."

"Yes, dear," Hannah said. "We'll see you in a couple of hours, El."

"I'll be here."

They went into their room and closed the door, but Ella

could hear them whispering. She wanted what Hannah had—
a man who cared so much about her that there was nothing
he wouldn't do for her or let her do for him. She wanted the
love, the commitment, the promise of forever. Unfortunately,
the only man she wanted all that with was eternally unavailable to her.

She'd meant what she said earlier to Hannah. After what
happened tonight, she wasn't sure she could allow him back
in again. It hurt too much—more than ever this time after
what they'd shared over the last couple of weeks. Here she
thought they'd made so much progress. But they'd never gotten past the starting line if it had come undone so easily.

Hannah was right about the trip. It would do her good to
get away for a week, to give them both some space to think
about what'd happened and what, if anything, they were
going to do about it. Right now, in this moment, she didn't
believe anything could be done. Maybe she'd feel differently
a week from now. Only time would tell for sure.

CHAPTER 25

—◄◆►—

Grief can't be shared. Everyone carries it
alone. His own burden in his own way.

—Anne Morrow Lindbergh

G avin sat outside Ella's house all night, but she never
came home. He thought about driving around to her
siblings' homes to find her but decided that tracking her
down when she didn't want to be found would do nothing
to help his case. And what case did he plan to make? He
wasn't sure exactly. All he knew was he had to try to explain
himself to her and beg for yet another chance.

How many chances did one man deserve from a woman
before she decided he wasn't worth the bother? He had to be
getting close to wearing out his welcome with Ella. Except
he kept hearing her tell him she loved him. She'd loved him
as recently as yesterday. Hopefully he hadn't killed all that
love with his ham-handed reaction to her gift.

Gavin was still sitting in his truck in Ella's driveway
when a stretch limo pulled up to the curb. Ella got out and
then got right back into the car when she saw his truck.

He jumped out of the truck. "Ella, wait. We need to talk."

Hannah got out and came over to him. Nolan was right
behind her. "Leave her alone, Gavin," Hannah said. "She
doesn't want to talk to you. Not now. We've got a plane to

catch, and we're going to get her suitcase. You need to leave."

"Not until I talk to her."

"That's not going to happen," Hunter said, emerging from the limo with Will in tow.

"Come on, you guys. Are you being serious right now? This is *me*." He'd been friends with Hunter and Will Abbott for most of his life. Were they really going to pull this shit on him now of all times?

"She doesn't want to talk to you, Gavin, so it's not going to happen," Will said.

Gavin took a step toward the limo.

Will and Hunter took a step toward him.

"Don't do this, Gav," Hunter said softly. "If you want to talk to her in the next week, you know where to find her."

"So that's the plan? Blackmail me into doing something I don't want to do?"

"There's no plan," Will said. "Or at least there isn't anymore. You saw to that, didn't you?"

"Please ask her to give me five minutes."

"We don't have five minutes." Hannah returned with Nolan, who carried Ella's bag. "We're due at your parents' house right now. We've got a plane to catch and a friend's wedding to get to. We'll miss you, Gavin, but then we always do at Sultan stuff." Hannah went up on tiptoes to kiss his cheek and patted his shoulder on her way by.

The show of affection didn't go unnoticed or unappreciated. Even after he'd broken her sister's heart, Hannah still loved him. Thank God for small favors. He stood there and watched them put the suitcase in the trunk. The driver held the door for them as they got back in the car. It took off a minute later in the direction of his parents' home.

Left alone in the cold early-morning darkness, Gavin knew a moment of pure, unadulterated panic. Ella had reached her limit. She had nothing left to say to him. It was a miracle it hadn't happened before now. As he got back into his truck and threw it into reverse, he decided it didn't matter if she had nothing left to say to him. He had stuff to say to her, and somehow he was going to find a way to make her listen.

The subdued group of travelers picked up Gavin's parents and headed out of town, only to be stopped just outside downtown Butler by an obstruction in the road.

"Seriously?" Hannah said, reaching for the door handle.

"Don't even think about it," Nolan said sternly.

"We're going to miss our flight!"

"We've got hours until our flight," Nolan said. "Stay put." He got out of the car and went around to the front, where the driver was trying to move Fred along.

"He's not going to budge until he gets what he came for," Hannah the moose whisperer said. "Get on out there and talk to him, Cam."

"No way," Will said. "Enough already with his crush on Cam."

"He just wants to say good-bye before she leaves town for a week," Hannah said.

"And how do you know that?" Hunter asked his twin.

"I thought we'd concluded a while ago that I speak Fred."

Bent at the waist, Cameron climbed over the others to get to the door.

"Cam, wait for me," Will said, following her.

"What the devil is the deal with that moose?" Amelia asked.

"He's got a thing for Cameron," Hunter said. "A bit of a crush, if you will."

"But wasn't she the one who hit him that time?" Amelia asked.

"He's decided not to hold it against her," Megan replied.

Though her heart was broken into a million pieces by the confrontation with Gavin at her house, Ella watched the goings-on with a detached sense of amusement. How could you not be amused by a moose that had a crush on your sister-in-law? With the doors and windows open, they could hear Cameron and Hannah speaking with Fred, asking him to move along and let them by.

Ella kept thinking about Gavin and his desperate pleas to talk to her. Her heart had nearly leaped from her chest when she saw him in her driveway waiting for her and looking as if he'd been there all night. She'd sent her brothers out to tell him she wasn't interested in what he had to say, but that wasn't exactly true. She was very interested, but after her siblings had been good enough to offer her a ride to Boston, she wasn't about to make them all late.

What she and Gavin had to say to each other couldn't be said in a minute or two. And it was going to have to wait until she got home. With Fred blocking their path out of town, Ella wondered if the moose was trying to help her—and Gavin—by keeping her from leaving with things unsettled between them.

That's giving a moose an awful lot of credit, Ella thought.

After a loud "moo" that made Amelia jolt in her seat, Fred ambled off into the woods. Will, Cameron, Nolan and Hannah got back into the car.

"Can we please go now?" Nolan said.

"Yes, dear," Hannah said. "We're all set. Fred knows when Cameron will be back, and he's promised to keep an eye on things around here while we're gone."

"You're all tapped," Nolan said. "Seriously tapped in the head."

Megan laughed. "I think so, too. For the record."

"Thank you," Nolan said to her. "I feel like I'm surrounded by lunatics who actually think a *moose*, a *wild animal*, cares what they have to say."

"You can't really argue with our success, though, can you?" Hannah asked him.

"Spoken by the chief lunatic."

"Awww, he loves me so much."

Ella loved the banter between her sister and her husband, who had the patience of a saint when it came to his wife and the moose she seemed to understand so well. But seeing them so happy together, expecting their first baby and overcoming the obstacles life—and moose—put in their way made her doubly sad for the way things had ended up with Gavin. All she'd ever wanted was what Hannah and Nolan had, what her other siblings had found with their life partners.

And she wanted it with him. Was it too much to ask to spend forever with the man she loved? It was beginning to seem that way.

"How'd you manage to get free of the diner for a week?" Hannah asked Megan.

"Butch of all people. He heard us talking about the trip and how I couldn't possibly make it work, and he told me to shut up and go, that he was more than capable of keeping the place from burning down while I'm gone. We'll see if that's true."

"And Gramps is going to check in every day," Hunter added. "As the proprietor, of course."

"He'll be more trouble than he's worth," Will said with a chuckle.

"I think that's his goal. He's afraid Butch might put him to work."

"We'll see who causes the greatest disaster," Nolan said. "Butch or Skeeter, who's in charge of the garage against my better judgment."

Ella remained silent as the conversation swirled around her. Gavin's parents had hugged her when they got in the car, but they hadn't said anything more. She figured they'd find a chance to talk later. Right now, she was grateful for the others, whose presence made it impossible for them to talk about it while she was still feeling so raw.

How long would it take this time before she could take a deep breath without excruciating pain? How long would it take to get over him after sharing such extraordinary closeness with him over the last couple of weeks? Every minute they spent together was imprinted on her heart in permanent ink. She would never forget a second of it.

When her eyes filled, she looked down, desperately

trying to control her emotions. The last thing she wanted to do was break down in front of his parents or her siblings.

A warm hand curled around hers with a gentle squeeze.

Ella looked over at Megan, who was sitting next to her. Megan continued her conversation with Hunter, Will and Cameron without missing a beat. The show of quiet support from the woman who would soon be her sister-in-law touched Ella deeply.

Despite the agony of what had transpired with Gavin, Megan's thoughtful gesture reminded her that she was not alone. In her family, she would never be alone, and for that, Ella was especially thankful today.

Ella's flight landed in Providenciales an hour after the others. She'd told them not to wait on her, but she wasn't surprised to find Hannah and Nolan in the terminal when she cleared customs. He scooped up her bag and carried it to the car from the resort that awaited them.

She hugged Hannah. "I told you not to wait."

"You're not the boss of me. I'm the big sister—and getting bigger by the day. How was the flight?"

"I don't really know. I slept for most of it." The empty seat next to her had been occupied by someone from coach, who'd been thrilled to get the upgrade to first class. Ella tried not to think about the thousand dollars she'd spent on a seat for Gavin that had gone to waste. She ought to send him a bill.

"That might be a blessing in disguise."

"Everything hurts, Hannah. Every part of me hurts."

"I know, honey." Hannah linked her arm with Ella's as they followed Nolan to the car. "And it will for a while, but we'll get you through this. We're going to have a wonderful time here. A week in the tropics is just what the doctor ordered for all of us."

"I'm glad you're here."

"I'm glad *you're* here."

On the short ride to the resort, Ella tried to appreciate

the brilliant blue sky, the palm trees, the gorgeous views of the water and scenery, but the dull ache inside had her full attention. It only intensified when she was shown to her romantic, seaside room with the huge king-size bed that reminded her of just how alone she really was, even with Hunter and Megan on one side of her and Hannah and Nolan on the other.

A knock on the adjoining door had her opening her side to Hunter.

"Hey," he said. "How's your room?"

"Spectacular. How's yours?"

"Same." He eyed her carefully. "You okay?"

"I've been better, but I'm determined not to be a total drag this week. We've all earned this break, and I won't spoil it for everyone."

"No one is worried about that, Ella. We're far more worried about you."

She shrugged off his concern. "You all tried to warn me. It's my own fault."

"It's not your fault. It's his fault. He's a fool, and he knows it."

"Regardless of whose fault it is, it's over, and I've got to accept that."

"It may not be over. You never know what's going to happen."

"I think it has to be over. I can't keep doing this to myself. What's the definition of stupid? Doing the same thing over and over and hoping for different results. That's me."

"You're anything but stupid, Ella."

"I'd be completely stupid to stay on this merry-go-round any longer."

"Do yourself a favor, and try to put it aside this week so you can enjoy your vacation. Some time and space away might help to give you some perspective."

"Perhaps," she said, saying what he wanted to hear mostly because she'd already made up her mind. No amount of time in the sun would change the irrefutable fact that she and Gavin were just not meant to be as much as she might wish otherwise.

When a knock sounded on the other adjoining door, Ella went to admit Hannah and Nolan.

"Ready to check this place out?" Hunter asked the others.

"Whenever you are," Hannah said, glancing at Ella, who nodded. If the alternative was sitting alone in the romantic room she'd expected to share with Gavin, then yes, a walk around the resort was preferable. "What about Will and Cam?"

"They're 'napping,'" Hannah said, making air quotes around the word *napping*.

The ache inside Ella intensified at that news. She wanted to be "napping" with Gavin, but that would never happen again. "Let's go," she said before she could break down into a sobbing mess like she wanted to.

With the sun shining warm upon them, they walked on winding paths through lush, fragrant vegetation, past a crystal-clear pool with a swim-up bar that Hunter said he couldn't wait to put to use. Beyond the pool area, they stepped onto sugar-white sand that was warm under their feet and walked to the water's edge. Ella had never seen water so blue in her life.

It was the most beautiful place she'd ever been, and the thought of spending a week here surrounded by happy couples who were madly in love suddenly seemed like the worst idea she'd ever had.

She wished she were home on her sofa with Ben and Jerry, nursing her wounds in private the way she had in the past. Staring out at the endless blue Caribbean, she decided she'd stay for the wedding and then get the hell out of there on Sunday. It was a big week in the store. She'd be better off there than here wishing for things that would never be.

Ella was having a late lunch with her siblings and their mates when Dylan and his fiancée, Sophia, found them. His eyes danced with joy as he hugged each of them. He was tall, blond, muscular and handsome. Sophia was tiny next to him, and she, too, glowed with happiness and excitement. Ella felt small for being envious of a woman she hardly knew. What must it be like to be about to marry the man you love, to have all your decisions made and the future laid out before you with as much certainty as anyone could ever hope to have?

"Thank you for coming so far, you guys," Dylan said. "Means so much to have you here."

"It's certainly no hardship," Hunter said, gesturing to the beautiful view of the Caribbean from their table.

"I appreciate it more than you'll ever know."

Ella kept waiting for him to ask about Gavin, but when he hugged her, he only said, "I wondered if he would come. I didn't tell anyone he might. Just in case . . ."

She gave him a wan smile as she fought through her emotions. What did it say that even his close friend had expected him to bail, but she'd never seen it coming? "We tried."

"No matter. I'm thrilled you're here, and we'll make sure you have a great time."

"Thank you, Dylan. Sorry to crash your party."

"You're not crashing. Not at all."

"You're very sweet to say so."

He squeezed her shoulder. "Where's Will? He's here, right?"

"The newest of the newlyweds are *napping*," Hannah said disdainfully.

"Lose the attitude, Mrs. Roberts," Nolan said. "You're going to be napping soon, too."

"Good napping or the kind where you actually make me sleep?"

"Both if you're very lucky."

Ella stood somewhat abruptly. "I, um, I'm going back to the room for a little while. I'll catch up with you all later."

"Ella—"

"I'm fine, Hannah." Before she broke down in front of all of them, she walked away, certain she—and Gavin— would be the topic of conversation after she was gone. What did it matter? Let them talk. Hopefully, in a few months, everyone would forget they'd ever been together. Especially her. If only there were a pill she could take to wipe her memory clear of the incredibly special moments she'd shared with him. Right about now, she'd give everything she had for that pill.

On the way back to her room, she ran into Gavin's parents, who looked to be on their way to the pool or beach. She hadn't really gotten the chance to talk to them earlier with the others all around them.

Amelia hugged her. "I'm so sorry it worked out this way."

"So am I."

"I tried to talk to him," Bob said.

Ella squeezed his arm. "Thanks for trying."

"We want you to know," Amelia said, glancing up at her husband before returning her gaze to Ella. "We think you're perfect for him, and I know it's asking a lot, but if you could just be patient with him for a little while longer. He's been different lately. We've both seen it, and it's because of you."

"I've been patient a long time where he's concerned. This didn't just happen between us recently. It's been stopping and starting for a while now. Since the summer."

"Oh, well . . ." Amelia seemed surprised to hear that. "Underneath it all, he's such a great guy."

"I know he is, Amelia. He's . . . Well, you don't have to sell me on him. The thing is . . . I'm just not sure I can compete with his demons."

Bob put his arm around his wife. "We need to let the kids work this out on their own, hon. If it's meant to be, it'll be."

"We're pulling for you, Ella," Amelia said. "He was so happy with you. I have to believe he regrets not coming."

"Maybe so. I'll see you later, okay?" She hugged and kissed them both before continuing on her way, feeling even more shredded than she had earlier.

CHAPTER 26

━━◆◆◆━━

*What we have once enjoyed deeply we can never
lose. All that we love deeply becomes a part of us.*

—Helen Keller

Inside her room, Ella curled up on her bed, resting on her side so she could look out at the beautiful scenery. She couldn't help but wonder what Gavin was doing, if he wished he'd handled things differently last night, what he'd wanted to say to her this morning. There was a phone next to her bed, and she could probably call him without too much bother and get answers to all her burning questions.

She entertained that thought for a fleeting second before dismissing it. She was all done chasing him. No one could ever accuse her of not going after what she wanted or not trying to make it work. The thing was, she couldn't make it work by herself. He had to want it, too, and despite his assurances, he apparently didn't want it as badly as she did.

With those unsettled thoughts swirling in her mind, she drifted off to sleep, dreaming about him and the magic they'd found during their two short weeks together. When she awoke hours later, the sky had grown dark, and her heart was heavy with the knowledge that she would remember every precious detail of those weeks for as long as she lived.

A soft knock on the door between her room and Hannah's

got her up from the bed. Her sister was gorgeous in a floral dress that hugged her considerable curves. She looked lush and happy and well rested. "You look beautiful, Hannah."

With her hand on her rounded belly, she said, "I had to call in the tentmaker for this trip."

"The tentmaker does good work."

"Are you coming to the rehearsal dinner?"

Ella leaned against the doorframe, exhausted despite her nap. "Would it be awful if I skipped it? I just don't have it in me tonight."

"It wouldn't be awful, but it might be better to be with us than here alone."

"I'd rather be alone tonight, Han."

"Are you sure?"

"I'm positive. I don't have a game face today. Hopefully, it'll be back in time for the wedding."

"What about dinner?"

"I'll order some room service."

"But you will eat. Promise?"

"Yes, Mom, I'll eat."

"Sorry to hover, but I'm worried about you. We all are."

"Please don't worry. I'll be fine. I just need a little time to myself to process it all."

"I understand. Is it okay to check on you when we get back?"

"I wish you would."

Hannah hugged her. "Hang in there."

"I'm hanging."

"I'm going to kill him when I get home."

"Don't do that. Amelia would never get over it—and neither would I."

"Those Guthrie boys always were a handful. Some things never change. I wonder all the time if Caleb ever would've settled down into regular life after the army."

"Life after the army? Like twenty years from now?"

Hannah bit her lip and shook her head. "He was going to get out after that last deployment. We made the decision before he left. He'd had enough of the deployments, and we were thinking about having kids." She rested her hand on her belly. "He didn't want them to grow up the way he did, moving all the time and always missing their dad."

"God, Hannah . . ."

She smiled softly and shrugged. "Life's a bitch."

"It certainly can be. I'm so sorry."

"Don't be sorry. I miss him every day, but I'm really happy with Nolan. And I know you're going to find your happily ever after, too. I *know* it."

"I wish I were so sure. I don't think it's going to be with Gavin."

"Maybe not, but there's someone out there who's going to appreciate the amazing, thoughtful, loving woman you are. You just can't give up on love because of this, El. That would be the worst thing you could do."

Nolan came up behind his wife and rested his hands on her shoulders. "Is she hovering, Ella?"

"Just a little, but it's okay."

"How're you doing?" he asked.

"I've had better days, but I'll be all right. I'll see you guys later. Have fun at the dinner."

Hannah hugged her. "Love you," she whispered.

"Love you, too."

Nolan surprised Ella when he kissed her forehead and hugged her. "Sorry you're going through this. There're a whole lot of guys who love you who want to put a hurt on him right now."

Touched to realize Nolan was one of them, she blinked back tears as she drew back from him. "Thanks, but that's not going to fix what's wrong here."

"Maybe not, but it sure would make us happy."

Ella laughed and brushed away tears. "Go on and have fun. I'll see you later."

After they left, Ella picked up the room service menu and looked it over. Though she'd promised Hannah she would eat, the thought of food turned her stomach, so she put down the menu. Maybe later. She went out to the deck that overlooked the beach and the vast Caribbean. As she leaned against the rail, the warm, soft air made her hair flutter in the light breeze. The sun dipped toward the horizon in a blaze of color that promised a spectacular sunset.

In the courtyard below, a group of children chased a soccer ball around, all of them dressed for dinner with their hair combed into submission. Their laughter and excitement caused the ache inside her to intensify into a sharp pain of regret.

Twenty-four hours after he turned down the chance to come with her, she was still trying to figure out how it had all gone so very wrong. Maybe she would never understand.

The phone in her room rang, setting her heart to racing. Was it him? What if it was? Did she want to talk to him? Not really. Not yet. Only the thought of her parents trying to reach them had her dashing inside to grab the extension by the bed. "Hello?"

"Is it true?" Charley asked without preamble. "Did he refuse to go?"

Ella sat on the edge of the bed. "Yes," she said, her shoulders sagging. "It's true."

"I'm going to find him and beat the living shit out of him."

"No, you're not."

"I really might."

"As much as I appreciate the sentiment, it won't fix anything. In fact, it'll make everything worse because then I'll have to bail you out of jail."

"It's worth going to jail. Are you okay?"

"I've been better."

"I'm glad you went without him."

"I'm not. I should've stayed home. The last place I need to be is smack in the middle of someone else's happily-ever-after. Not to mention our happily coupled siblings surrounding me. After the wedding tomorrow, I'm coming home. I'd rather be at work than here."

"Said no sane person ever."

"I'm not feeling so sane tonight."

"What happened? What did he say?"

"It's not even worth repeating. It's over. That's the bottom line."

"I don't get it."

"That makes two of us. Tell me some good news. How's the baby?"

"He's so cute. I saw him again before we left Burlington last night. They were going home from the hospital this afternoon."

"How's Chloe?"

"Sore and cranky. She didn't have much to say to us when we were there."

"And how's Max?"

"In love with his son and dealing with her the best he can. I don't envy him this situation. And I don't envy your situation."

"I have no situation. Not anymore."

"Ella, you can't give up—"

"Yes, I really can, Charley. At some point, enough becomes enough. I'd be a masochist to let this continue after what's already happened."

Charley's deep sigh said it all.

"How was the store today?"

"Crazy busy. Just how we like it."

"Good. Anything you couldn't handle?"

"Nope. I got it covered. Don't rush home on my account."

"Thanks for covering for me. I'll be in on Monday."

"Call me if you need me. You know where I am."

"Yes, I do, and thanks for checking on me. Don't beat up Gavin."

"I'll try to resist the urge."

"Bye, Charley." Ella put down the phone and stretched out on the bed, which seemed to be the only place she wanted to be. Her limbs felt weighted, and her head was aching almost as badly as her heart. She didn't really want to be home, where every corner of her life would remind her of him. But she didn't want to be here either. How sad was it that she didn't want to be anywhere because no matter where she went, he came with her. He was so deeply embedded in her heart that it would be a long time, if ever, before she left him behind.

Ella surprised herself by sleeping amazingly well. She woke with a new determination to get through the day so she could head home in the morning. After the wedding, she was meeting with the concierge, who'd agreed to help change her flight.

She had breakfast with her siblings and Gavin's parents, during which they talked about everything other than the elephant sitting in the middle of the table. Ella was thankful that they'd tuned into the fact that she didn't want to talk about it anymore. What was there to talk about? They'd had a thing. It was over now. End of story.

Except . . .

No, Ella, end of story.

While the others headed off to take a tour in a glass-bottom boat, Ella took her e-reader to the pool, determined to salvage at least one day of this disaster to work on her tan. She stayed until four and even had an umbrella drink of rum punch that warmed her up on the inside.

With the wedding at six, she headed back to her room to shower and get ready. On the way, she ran into Cameron and Will, who were returning from the beach, holding hands as always. They were so damned cute, and seeing their happy, smiling faces reminded her once again of what she'd almost had with Gavin.

"Hey, guys." She forced a smile for their benefit. "How was the beach?"

"Heavenly," Cameron said. "Will had to drag me away so we'll have time to get ready."

"How are you?" Will asked, his insightful gaze taking a perusing look at her.

"I'm fine. I enjoyed the pool."

"Ella—"

"I'm really fine." She patted her brother's chest. "I'll see you at the wedding, okay?"

"Yeah. See you then."

As she climbed the stairs to her room, Ella realized it was going to be even worse when she got home and had to answer questions about what'd become of her and Gavin. Tears flooded her eyes when she thought about Mrs. Abernathy coming to the door when they were making love against it.

It had been the funniest, sexiest, most embarrassing, unforgettable moment of her life. How was she supposed to live without him now that she'd tasted paradise in his arms?

That question weighed heavily on her as she showered, dried and straightened her hair and dressed in the yellow dress she'd brought for the wedding. When she'd packed the dress, she'd done so with Gavin in mind, hoping he'd like how it looked on her. Hell, she'd done everything with him in mind for so long now that it would be nearly impossible to break the habit.

But break it she would. He hadn't given her much choice in the matter.

She walked to the beachfront wedding with her siblings and their partners, all of them in a festive mood. Ella absolutely refused to be a drag, so she participated in their good-natured banter and tried to pretend like she wasn't shattered on the inside.

When they arrived at the beach, the other Sultans, who had come from all over for Dylan's wedding, greeted them with hugs. Thankfully, Dylan hadn't told anyone that Gavin was supposed to be with her, so she didn't have to answer any questions. They were a boisterous group in the best of circumstances, but never more so than when they got together for a happy occasion.

Caleb's death had been hard on all of them, but they'd made an effort over the years to keep in touch, to keep up the traditions he'd started and to honor his memory in any way they possibly could. As always, though, the man who'd been at the center of their shenanigans was blatantly missing.

Ella could only imagine how difficult it must be for Hannah to continue to be a part of the group that was such a big aspect of Caleb's life. But with Nolan by her side, she glowed with happiness and excitement for Dylan and Sophia. Somehow she had found the strength to move on. If only Gavin could do the same.

You're not thinking about him. Not now.

Dylan and Jack, his best man, joined them, greeting the group with hugs and slaps on the back. Smiling from ear to ear, Dylan was tanned and wearing a pink dress shirt and khaki pants. Not every guy could pull off the pink shirt, but it suited him.

Ella stood back to watch as Hannah pinned a pink rose to his shirt and then patted his chest. He looked down at her, a thousand emotions seeming to pass between the two of them in the matter of an instant.

Hannah smiled up at him and he put his arms around her and held her tight until Nolan tapped him on the shoulder to end the emotionally charged encounter with a laugh.

Watching Hannah share a special moment with one of her late husband's best friends left a huge lump in Ella's throat.

They gathered in a half circle around the arbor that had been erected on the beach. It was surrounded by a stunning array of tropical flowers in bright oranges, pinks, yellows and reds. As the sun began to dip toward the horizon, a local man began to play the ukulele to the tune of "Somewhere Over the Rainbow."

Preceded by three bridesmaids dressed in periwinkle gowns, Sophia's dad escorted her onto the beach and into the arms of her future husband. The joy on the faces of Dylan and Sophia was like a knife in Ella's broken heart. It was all she could do to remain standing, to watch them exchange vows and not run away like she wanted to.

And then an arm slipped around her waist from behind, and the scent of Gucci Black stole the breath from her lungs. *Oh God . . .* Her body recognized his as he drew her in tight against him. He never said a word as they stood together and watched Dylan and Sophia exchange rings.

Since she was standing behind her siblings and Gavin's parents, no one noticed he was there. But Ella noticed. Every nerve ending in her body was on full alert, and her heart beat so fast she had to remind herself to breathe. With his big hand flat against her belly, a thousand thoughts went through her mind in the time it took for Dylan and Sophia to be declared husband and wife. What was he doing here? What did it mean? Why had he come? What would she say to him? What did he have to say? How would it change things?

Despite her iron-clad resolve to be done with him, his appearance here filled her with a tiny kernel of hope that couldn't be easily snuffed out.

The applause of the wedding guests roused her from her frantic thoughts.

Gavin released her to join in the applause.

Ella turned to him. "What're you doing here?"

"You really have to ask?"

CHAPTER 27

✦✦✦

We must accept finite disappointment,
but never lose infinite hope.

—Martin Luther King, Jr.

The sight of her beautiful face, wary and uncertain as she looked up at him, settled the storm that had been raging inside Gavin since he last saw her. It had been the right thing to come after her, to try to fix what had gone so horribly wrong. But before he could do that, they had a wedding to get through.

His mother let out a happy little squeal when she saw him standing beside Ella. He hugged her and then his father.

"Good to see you here, son," his dad said gruffly.

"Good to be here."

One by one, the Sultans approached him, hugged him, welcomed him and said how happy they were to have him there. Dylan, who'd been receiving congratulations from his family and Sophia's, drew him into a bear hug.

"I'm so fucking glad you're here, man," Dylan said for Gavin's ears only.

"Me, too. Sorry I was late. I caught the end."

"Better late than never."

"Glad you think so. Thanks for having me."

"I guess we'll see," Gavin said, glancing at her.

She caught his eye and then looked away.

"One thing I'll tell you for certain," Hunter said, his tone leaving no room for interpretation. "If you hurt her again, you're going to have seven very unhappy Abbott brothers to answer to. Am I clear on that?"

"Yeah," Gavin said. "Crystal clear."

"Good," Hunter said. "Don't fuck it up."

"I'm going to try really hard not to."

"You do that," Will said.

Cameron came over to her husband and looped her arm through his, and his expression immediately softened. "Everything okay over here, boys?"

"It's all good," Will said with a glare for Gavin. "Or at least it had better be."

"What do I do?" Ella asked Hannah as quietly as she possibly could, waiting until Gavin was engaged in conversation with Jack and their other friend, Austin, to consult with her sister.

"What do you want to do?" Hannah asked.

"I don't know. Part of me wants to tell him to get lost, that it's too little, too late. But the other part of me—"

"Will never have any peace until you hear whatever he's come to say."

"Yes," Ella said with a sigh. "I hate myself for wanting to hear what he's come to say."

"Don't hate yourself. You're only human, and for some strange reason, you love the guy."

"Yeah, I do, even if I've tried to convince myself otherwise in the last two days." One touch from him, one breath of his arresting scent, and she'd been drawn right back into love with him. That was all it had taken.

"You can't talk yourself out of loving him, even if you think that's what's best for you."

"I can't let him do this to me anymore, though, Hannah. The yo-yo effect is making me crazy. He said he was all in until he wasn't, and I can't do that again. I just can't."

"Then you have a decision to make. Give him another chance or don't. Which would be harder to live with?"

"I honestly don't know."

"You need to decide—ASAP. He looks rather . . . determined."

Ella couldn't deny that she'd noticed a different sort of air about him since he'd arrived out of the mist at the wedding. Like he'd resolved something important in the time they'd spent apart. "Since he came all this way, I suppose I'll hear him out. And then I can decide what I want to do."

"For what it's worth, that's what I would do, too."

"It's worth a lot. Thanks, Hannah, for everything the last few days."

Hannah curled her arms around Ella's arm and rested her head on Ella's shoulder. "That's what big sisters are for."

They enjoyed a delicious dinner of jerk shrimp, chicken and beef, rice, salad, vegetables and succulent fruit. The courses kept on coming, along with wine and champagne and rum punch.

Though he sat next to her at dinner, Gavin made no attempt to get her to talk to him. But she was acutely aware of his presence nonetheless. Every so often his leg would brush against hers under the table or his arm would land on the back of her chair, the possessive gesture setting off a primal need in her.

She wanted to hate him for what he'd put her through, but she didn't hate him. No, she loved him as much as she ever had, and as she fixated on his muscular forearm and the sprinkling of dark hair, she was forced to acknowledge that she would always love him. No matter what happened next.

After dinner, everyone got up to dance, leaving Ella alone at the table with Gavin. Every nerve ending in her body was on full alert, waiting to see what he would do.

"Take a walk with me?" he asked in a low intimate tone.

She looked at him for a long moment, taking in the rugged, handsome features that had held her captive for so long, and then nodded, powerless to deny him, even though she knew she ought to.

He helped her up and out of her chair and guided her from the pavilion with his hand on her lower back.

Ella felt the eyes of everyone she knew on them as they walked out and was deeply grateful for the protective presence of her siblings, who would be there for her no matter what transpired between her and Gavin. She took comfort in the certainty of their unwavering support.

They stepped onto the beach, and Ella kicked off her shoes, leaving them by the stairs.

Gavin did the same, removing his flip-flops and putting them next to her sandals. Then he took hold of her hand and led her to the water's edge. He wore a white linen shirt that showed off the wide expanse of his shoulders, along with khaki pants that hugged him in all the right places. As always, the sight of him made her want to drool with lust. No matter what had transpired between them, her desire and deep, abiding love for him were the two things she could never deny.

"It's beautiful here," he said, gazing out at the moon-beams on the flat calm water.

"It sure is."

He turned to face her, taking hold of her other hand and bringing their joined hands to his chest. "I'm so sorry, Ella. Before I say anything else, I need you to know that. I screwed this up so bad, and I'm very, very sorry. I have been since the other night when it first happened."

"Will you tell me what exactly happened? Because I'm not really sure."

He took a deep breath and released it slowly. "What you did, arranging the trip and everything, it was a really nice thing for you to do. I'll always be sorry that I reacted the way I did."

Ella had so many questions that she didn't ask. She needed him to tell her what this was about. She needed him to *want* to tell her.

"Ever since Caleb died," he began haltingly, "I've struggled with where I fit among the friends we shared. It's really hard for me to be around them. More than anything, the time I spend with them reminds me so profoundly of what's been lost. They're great guys, the best guys I've ever known. I love every one of them. They're our very best friends, and yes, they were and are *our* friends, not just his. Despite how it might seem sometimes, I really do know that."

He released her hands and turned to face the water. "As much as I love them, and as much as I loved Caleb . . . They're a bunch of crazy bastards. Some of the shit we've done would give you gray hairs if you knew about it. They're always pushing the envelope, coming up with new ways to challenge themselves and each other. A lot of that came right from Caleb, the craziest of the crazy. There was nothing he wouldn't do, especially if someone dared him. I once saw him jump from the top of a waterfall, having no idea what was on the bottom."

Ella crossed her arms against a sudden chill, which was odd because the night air was warm and humid.

"Scared the fucking shit out of me when he did stuff like that. The rest of them, they just went along with whatever he cooked up. You name it, we've done it. We've outrun avalanches on mountains and zip-lined in the jungle, jumped out of perfectly good airplanes. They've been talking lately about climbing a mountain somewhere. The e-mails and texts from that crew would make for a good reality TV show."

As Ella listened to him, she began to get an idea of where this was headed—and then he confirmed it for her.

"I can't do that shit anymore," he said softly. "I just can't take those kinds of chances. I can't do it to my parents."

Drawn to him the way she always was, Ella laid her hand on his back and leaned her head against his shoulder. "Why didn't you just say so?"

"Because I've never said it to anyone before. I've never come right out and acknowledged that I'm unwilling to go along with their crazy shit anymore because my parents have already lost one son senselessly. I'll be damned if they'll lose another."

"Gavin . . . *Anyone* would understand that."

"I don't think the guys would understand. They'd call me

a pussy and say I'm a chickenshit, which would piss me off and make me forget why I can't do whatever it is they want me to do. It's just easier for me to keep my distance than to resist their crazy ideas."

"So you cut yourself off from people you love rather than just tell them what you told me? That doesn't make sense."

"Maybe not, but it's how I've coped. When you told me about the wedding, that's what I was thinking about. It wasn't about you or coming here with you, despite how it might've seemed. My coping mechanism was threatened, and I lashed out at you, which was the wrong thing to do. It was the worst thing I could've done, and I'm sorry. I hope you can forgive me."

"I already have," Ella said. How could she not when he spelled it out so plainly?

"You have?" He turned back to face her, stepping closer. "Really?"

"Yes, really."

"Thank God, Ella. Thank you for understanding. I promise this will never happen again. I was such an ass. I'm so sorry."

"It will happen again."

"But wait, you just said . . . You understand."

"I understand what happened the other night, and I appreciate you coming here and clueing me in as to what went so wrong. That answers a lot of questions for me."

"But?"

"But . . . I don't think I can do this anymore, Gavin. As much as I wish I could, I just don't think I can put myself through it."

His arms came around her like bands of strength, binding her to him. "Please don't say that. I fucked up. I told you I would. But I'm determined to not let it happen again. I need you so much. More than you'll ever know. I feel like my entire life has come down to you and how much I need you. I'll do whatever you want me to do, just please don't tell me it's over. Please, Ella."

As tears poured down her cheeks, she pressed her face to his shirt.

"Baby, don't cry. I'm so sorry I hurt you. I'd give anything to go back to Thursday night when we were still in bed and everything was perfect."

"Before I ruined it by trying to surprise you."

"You didn't ruin it. I did. I take full responsibility for that. I love you so much, El. I'll always love you. Please give me another chance to be what you need. I won't let you down this time."

She cried softly in his arms, wrapped up in his strength and that irresistible scent.

"Ella, say something. Tell me what you're thinking."

"The part that hurt the most wasn't that you didn't want to go on the trip. It was that you walked away from me over it. What you said that night . . . That's the part I can't stop thinking about. I didn't care about the trip. I always knew it was possible you might not want to go or be able to . . . But that you ended it with me five minutes after we made love. I can't get past that, Gavin, as much as I wish I could."

"That was a huge mistake. I overreacted. I was scared. I said things I shouldn't have said."

"How do I know that's not going to happen again?"

"I'm promising you, right here and right now, that will never happen again."

"How can you promise that? If you'd asked me Thursday if it would happen, I would've said no way. I don't know if I can live with the fear of something I say or do setting you off and making you walk away. It's like walking through a minefield."

His body went rigid and he winced.

"Oh God, Gavin, I'm sorry. I shouldn't have said that."

"It's okay. It's an apt description."

"I should've thought of another way to say it."

He drew back from her, and framed her face with his hands, brushing away her tears with his thumbs. "I love you, and I'm standing here promising I will never walk away from you again, no matter what. All I have to give you is my word, Ella. I give you my word. What happened the other night will never happen again."

She wanted to believe him. She wanted so badly to believe him, to hang on to his assurances with everything she had. But the pain was still so fresh, so present. The ache in her chest had dissipated somewhat since he arrived, but it hadn't gone away entirely.

"Ella?"

"I want to believe you. I really do."

"You can believe me. I've had two incredibly long days without you to figure out that there's nothing I wouldn't do to fix this, to have you back in my arms where you belong. Tell me you still love me, that I haven't ruined us completely."

"I do still love you—"

His lips came down on hers, hard and swift, his tongue persuading her to open her mouth to him, to welcome him back in. His arms came around her, holding her in place for his fierce possession.

This was insanity. One minute she was thinking about how she could convince him to let her go. The next minute she was so wrapped up in him again that the thought of letting him go seemed the most preposterous thing she'd ever considered.

Because she had no choice where he was concerned, she wrapped her arms around his neck and lost herself to his kiss. Many minutes later, he broke the kiss and turned his attention to her neck, setting off a shiver that traveled all the way through her. "Take me back to your room, Ella. I need you. I need to show you how much I love you."

Though she was still confused and not at all convinced that taking him back was in her best interest, she joined her hand with his and walked with him to where they'd left their shoes. Without another word passing between them, they picked up their shoes and carried them as they walked barefoot through the winding path that led to her room.

She proceeded up the stairs ahead of him, acutely aware of his eyes on her as she went. Outside her room, she used the keycard she'd tucked into her dress to open the door.

"Tell me what you're thinking," he said as the door clicked shut behind them. "What you're feeling."

"I feel powerless."

"Ella, honey, you have *all* the power here."

"No, I don't. You have the power to ruin me."

"I don't want to ruin you. I just want to love you. That's all I want."

"I'm scared of how much I love you. It hurts me when you can't be what I need."

His eyes filled and he closed them, his jaw tightening as he wrestled with his emotions. When he opened his eyes, he showed her his heart. "I'm going to be everything you need, and then some. I'll never let you down again, Ella. I promise you with everything that I am, you can trust me."

God, she wanted so badly to believe him. She'd never wanted anything more than she wanted to take his assurances to the bank and invest them in her future. As he kissed her neck and unzipped her dress, Ella closed her eyes and tried to give in to the desire he always stirred in her.

But in the back of her mind was the scene from Thursday night, when he'd made love to her and then walked away from her because he'd let his demons come between them. What would she do if that happened again?

She told herself to let go of the past, to start fresh from this minute forward and hope for the best. Except . . . She couldn't do that. She couldn't pretend like the other night hadn't happened, as much as she wanted to.

"Stop, Gavin. Stop."

"What's wrong?"

"I can't do this. I can't just pick up where we left off like nothing happened. You hurt me. Deeply."

"Ella—"

She turned away from his outstretched hand. "And you embarrassed me in front of my family and your parents and friends. Everyone knew you were supposed to be with me. What am I even doing here without you? Dylan is a wonderful guy, but he's not my friend. He's yours."

"I wish there was something I could say that would convince you how sincerely sorry I am."

"I believe you. I know you're sorry. I know you wish it

didn't happen. But it did happen, and I can't act like it didn't."

"So I've ruined everything? Is that what you're saying?"

"I don't know. I need some time to process it. I'm not sure how I feel about it, and until I figure that out, I can't do this."

"What can't you do?"

"This! I can't have sex with you and be with you this way. I'm confused and conflicted."

He sat on the bed, leaning on his knees, his head down and his eyes hidden from her. "Conflicted how?"

"My better judgment is telling me to get out while I still can, that this relationship isn't healthy for me. But my heart . . . My heart cries out for you, it beats for you, it loves you and only you." She swiped furiously at the tears that cascaded down her face.

After running his fingers through his hair repeatedly, he finally looked up at her. "I'm rooting for your heart to prevail."

Though the tears continued to come, she laughed.

Gavin stood and came over to her. "What do you want to do?"

"I—I was going to go home tomorrow."

Placing his hands on her shoulders, he said, "Please don't. Stay here with me this week. Let's have this time together to see if we can put this back together."

Ella thought about it for a minute before she nodded. "Okay."

"I'll see about getting my own room."

"You don't have to do that."

"You said you wanted some time—and I assume some space. I don't want to crowd you."

"It's okay. You can stay here. With me."

"You're sure?"

Ella nodded again.

He caressed her face, and Ella leaned into his touch. "What can I do, Ella? Tell me what to do."

"I don't know. I just know I'm not ready to jump back in

with both feet. That doesn't mean I don't want to be with you. I do. Very much so."

"That's a good place to start."

The phone rang, and Ella moved away from him to answer the call from the concierge, who was checking on the meeting she'd requested for after the wedding. She looked at Gavin, who was watching her closely, when she said, "I've decided to stay for the week."

CHAPTER 28

If it were not for hopes, the heart would break.

—Thomas Fuller

Sleeping next to Ella but not being able to touch her and love her the way he wanted to was absolute torture for Gavin. She was so close yet so far away. He couldn't say he blamed her for wanting to proceed with caution. Until he'd proven that he intended to be what she needed, she'd be crazy to go all in again, and she was anything but crazy.

But lying beside her, knowing what they were capable of together and not being able to have it? Torture. And he had only himself to blame for their current predicament.

Turning on his side, he could make out the faint outline of her profile in the darkness that was offset only by the nightlight in the bathroom. She was so pretty all the time, but never more so than she'd been standing slightly removed from the rest of the wedding guests as she watched Dylan and Sophia exchange vows.

He'd planned his arrival to coincide with the vows so he could sneak in and take her by surprise at a time when she couldn't object. He wouldn't soon forget the way she'd stiffened when she realized who had put his arm around her. Right in that instant he'd known he faced a huge battle to win her back.

The battle for her love and trust was one he intended to win. He considered it a small victory that she'd allowed him to stay in her room, to sleep in her bed, to spend this week together.

"Are you awake?" she whispered.

"Yeah. I thought you were asleep."

"Can't sleep."

"How come?"

"Gee, I wonder."

Her saucy retort drew a low chuckle from him. "Come here."

"I'm here."

"Closer."

She turned to face him.

"Not close enough." He held out his arm to her, and waited, his heart beating faster all of a sudden, to see if she'd take him up on the invitation.

After a long pause, she slid across the mattress, closing the gap between them.

Gavin gathered her in close to him, wrapping his arms around her. "That's so much better." He ran his fingers through her long hair, combing the silky strands. "After I saw you on Friday," he said, speaking softly to her, "at your place . . . I already knew then I'd made a huge mistake the night before. When I saw you get out of the car, and the look on your face when you saw me there . . ."

"I couldn't talk to you then. I couldn't make everyone else wait when they had a plane to catch."

"I know that now, but at the time . . . I wanted to die because I'd put that wary, uncertain expression on your gorgeous face. I never want you to look at me that way again, Ella. I never want to give you cause to look at me that way again."

She surprised him when she brought her hand to cup his face, her touch electrifying as always.

He turned his face into her hand, kissing and nuzzling her palm and feeling the tremble that went through her body. So responsive . . . So in tune with him. So perfect for him in every possible way.

"Will you . . ."

"What, baby? What do you want?"

"Will you kiss me? Just that and nothing more?"

"I'd love to kiss you. It's my favorite thing to do."

He felt her smile as his lips came down on hers, finding her in the dark.

Her arms curled around his neck to hold him in place as her mouth opened to his tongue.

Gavin poured all his love and devotion and regret and need into that kiss, hoping it conveyed everything he felt for her.

She kissed him back with enthusiasm that matched his own, and he had to remind himself that she'd asked for a kiss. Only a kiss. Hands that wanted to wander were restrained, held in check flat against her back, burning through the silk nightgown that clung to her alluring curves. Those curves were off limits to him tonight, so he threw himself into the kiss.

He explored every corner of her warm sweetness, sucking on her tongue until she moaned into his mouth. Her body arched into his, seeking relief he wasn't allowed to provide. He respected her boundaries, even as he pulsated with need and desire.

Ella's fingers were buried in his hair, her nails scraping against his scalp.

God, he couldn't get close enough.

By the time she broke the kiss, he was fully on top of her, his arms wrapped tightly around her while her legs intertwined with his.

"That was some kiss," he said, sliding his lips over hers. He couldn't get enough of her. He would never get enough.

"Mmm, good kiss."

"Do you think you can sleep now?"

Her reply came in the form of a deep yawn.

"I'll take that as my cue to leave you alone." Though he continued to ache with unspent desire, he settled next to her, his arm looped around her waist, thankful to have her there beside him.

"Gavin?"

"Hmm?"

"I'm really glad you came here, even if you didn't want to."

"I want to be wherever you are."

She turned over and snuggled up to him, her head on his chest, her hand flat against his abdomen, a mere inch above the part of him that throbbed for her.

This was going to be a long, long night.

Ella woke to Gavin, fully dressed and holding a tray that included a bright orange flower in a vase. "What's this?" she asked, pushing hair back from her face.

"Breakfast in bed for my love."

"Oh, wow. Thanks."

"No problem." He waited until she sat up to place the tray on her lap. "I got us a beach cabana, too, with one of those shade things. Can't have that pretty skin of yours burning."

"Thank you." She took a sip of coffee and a careful look at him. He seemed tired, restless, unsettled. "What's wrong?"

His eyebrows lifted. "Wrong? Absolutely nothing is wrong. For once."

"Why do you seem tired?"

"Because I didn't sleep that great. Jet lag or something."

"We're in the same time zone as home."

He shrugged it off. "I don't know. I just couldn't sleep."

The phone rang, and Gavin handed the extension to Ella. "Hello?"

"Hi, Ella, it's Jack. Hope I didn't wake you."

"No, we're up."

"I'm looking for Gavin, and I heard he might be with you."

"Sure, hang on." She held out the phone to him. "For you. It's Jack."

Gavin took the phone from her. "Hey, what's up?" After listening to whatever Jack had to say, Gavin replied, "Nah, I can't today. I'm hanging with Ella. But you guys have fun." He paused again, listened and glanced at her. "I gotta be honest—I can't do that stuff anymore. I'm an actual adult these days and have too many people counting on me to take crazy chances." He listened again, chuckled. "Say what you will, my friend, but I'm not changing my mind." Another pause. "Sure, I'd love to meet for drinks when you get back. I'll see you then."

"What're they up to?" Ella asked when he'd returned the portable phone to the cradle.

"Some sort of shark diving thing without the cage."

"That sounds fun."

"You think so?"

"Not really," she said with a laugh.

"I'd much rather spend the day with you than with a bunch of sharks."

"I'm strangely complimented by that."

He leaned over to kiss her forehead. "As well you should be."

"Hey, Gav?"

"Yeah?"

"I'm proud of you for telling him the truth. I know that wasn't easy for you."

"It was easier than it would've been before I talked to you about it yesterday. And for what it's worth, apparently your brothers and brother-in-law are pussies these days, too."

Ella laughed. "It'll happen to the rest of them someday."

"I can only hope it happens soon. I'll leave you to eat in peace."

"Don't go. Help me out here. There's enough to feed an army."

"Are you sure?"

"Yes, I'm sure." She lifted a forkful of omelet and held it out to him. Holding her gaze, he took the bite.

After breakfast, they changed into swimsuits and headed for the beach, where he continued tending to her every need, beginning with applying her sunscreen and then by producing a Bloody Mary that left her feeling pleasantly buzzed and peaceful. Her siblings joined them in nearby cabanas, everyone enjoying the sun and sand and clear blue water. They were friendly to Gavin if not overly talkative. She could live with that. It was the most relaxing day Ella could remember having in a long time.

As relaxed as she was, however, Gavin seemed wound up, agitated, unable to sit still. "What's wrong?" she asked as they returned to their room late that afternoon to shower for dinner with his parents.

"Nothing's wrong."

"You're tense. You have been all day."

"Did you have a nice day?"

"I had a great day."

"That's all that matters. I want you happy."

"That's not all that matters."

"It is for now."

He used the keycard to open the door, gesturing for her to go in ahead of him. The moment the door clicked shut behind them, she turned to him, resting her hand on his chest. "Tell me what's wrong."

"Nothing is wrong, Ella. Nothing a cold shower won't take care of."

"Oh." She let her gaze travel down the front of him, stopping just below his waist where the evidence of his arousal left no room for interpretation as to what had him so wound up.

"It's your fault," he said in a teasing tone. "You and that itty-bitty bikini you pranced around in all day."

"My bikini is neither itty nor bitty," she said. "And I don't *prance*."

"It's both itty *and* bitty, and I'm only human, babe. And P.S., you most certainly do *prance*."

She raised her hands to his shoulders and went up on tiptoes to kiss him.

He reacted instantly, cupping her bottom and lifting her into his arms as he devoured her with his lips, teeth and tongue. With his erection pressed against her, Ella wanted to forget all about the many reasons she'd planned to keep him at arm's length.

Then she was falling, landing on the bed with him on top of her as the kiss took a turn toward the wild and frantic. The only thing standing between what they both wanted were her bikini bottoms and his bathing suit. He kept his hands on her bottom, squeezing as his tongue thrust into her mouth.

Ella arched into him, needing the relief only he could provide.

He broke the kiss, panting and staring down at her, seeming as dazed as she felt. "We have to stop or we won't be able to."

"Don't stop yet."

"Ella . . ."

"Please don't stop yet."

A muscle in his cheek pulsed from the tension that gripped them both. "Untie your top."

With trembling hands, Ella did as he asked, baring her breasts to him.

He groaned as he dipped his head to run his tongue over the hard point of her nipple, drawing it into the heat of his mouth and running his tongue back and forth. The whole time he continued to press against her sex, letting her know what he really wanted with every thrust of his hard cock against her tingling clit.

God, she was actually going to come from the combination of what he was doing to her nipples while he pressed against her.

"Gavin . . . Don't stop."

"I'll never stop loving you, Ella. Never." He sucked hard on her nipple and thrust against her until she came with a sharp cry of pleasure. "Yes, baby, yes. Let me hear you."

Mindful of their neighbors and who they were, she didn't fully give in to the urge to scream, but she wanted to.

"Mmm," he said against her nipple as he continued to stroke his tongue over her sensitive skin. "You're so hot when you come. I could watch that all day and never get tired of seeing you let go."

She ran a hand down the front of him, cupping his hardness. "What about you?"

"That was more than enough for me."

"It wasn't enough for me. Turn over."

"No, El, really . . . We don't have to."

"Turn over."

Sighing, he flopped onto his back. "If you touch me, I'll explode."

"That's kind of the idea, isn't it?" She kissed her way down the front of him, paying homage to his rippling abs before freeing him from the board shorts he'd worn to the beach.

"Ella . . . Christ . . ." As she stroked him, he raised his hips, and true to his word, he came within seconds of her first touch. "Told ya."

"Feel better?"

"A little." He tucked a strand of her hair behind her ear. "I won't feel completely better until I can do that inside you again, until you stop waiting for me to fuck up again, until I'm sure that *you're* sure you can trust me to be what you need. Then I'll feel better."

She rested her head on his shoulder. "Today was a good day."

"Tomorrow will be, too. So will the day after and the day after that. You're stuck with me."

CHAPTER 29

*And now these three remain: faith, hope
and love. But the greatest of these is love.*

—1 Corinthians 13:13

Over the next few days, Gavin went out of his way to make sure his actions matched his words, choosing Ella's company over that of his friends, arranging a candle-light dinner for two on the beach one night and leaving her only once—to play golf with the guys on Thursday afternoon ahead of the dinner Dylan was hosting the night before everyone was due to head home.

While the guys were golfing, Ella spent the afternoon at the spa with Hannah, Cameron and Megan. After a massage and facial, she returned to the room to dress for dinner. Gavin was in the shower when she got back. He emerged a few minutes later with a towel wrapped around his waist and came to find her on the deck.

"Hey, baby," he said, kissing her temple as he wrapped an arm around her waist. "How was the spa?"

"Heavenly. How was the golf?"

"An exercise in frustration."

She smiled up at him. "Seems to be the word of the week, huh?" Though they'd continued to make out every chance they got, among other things, they'd yet to actually make love.

"It's been a great week. I'm sorry it's already time to go home. Maybe we can come back here sometime."

"Maybe."

"Can we take a walk on the beach before dinner?"

"Sure. I need to grab a quick shower, and then I'm all yours."

"I like the sound of that. All mine." He leaned in to kiss her. "Don't keep me waiting too long. I've already had to be without you for hours today."

He was wearing her down. There was no way to deny the heady feeling that overtook her whenever he said things like that or looked at her in that particular possessive way. Tonight, before they returned to their real lives and whatever awaited them there, she would make love with him. She couldn't wait to be close to him like that again.

Ella rushed through her shower and dried her hair until it hung in waves down her back. The tropical humidity would undo the work of the straightener, so she didn't bother, leaving it to curl naturally. She dressed in a floral halter dress and slipped her feet into a pair of wedges. A coat of lip gloss finished off her outfit. She emerged from the bathroom to find Gavin dressed in a yellow polo and plaid shorts. He was so handsome, and despite the ups and downs they'd encountered, he still took her breath away.

"Wow," he said on a low whistle. "You look amazing."

"So do you."

He held out a hand to her. "Shall we?"

Ella took his hand and followed him from the room. The sun was still an hour or more from setting, but the beach was largely deserted except for a few late-day sun worshipers. They walked a long way down the beach, almost to the end of the resort's property.

"Come check this out," he said, nodding to a cabana that had been erected on the beach. Gauzy curtains fluttered in the breeze, ready to seal off the occupants from the outside world.

"What is it?"

"You'll see."

Inside the cabana, a member of the resort staff awaited

them. "Mr. Guthrie, Ms. Abbott, welcome." Beside a double lounge chair, a bottle of champagne chilled in an ice bucket and a tray of fruit, cheese and crackers was on a table. "I trust everything is to your liking, sir?"

"It is," Gavin replied. "Thank you so much."

"My pleasure. Enjoy."

"You did this?" she asked when they were alone.

"Yep."

"When?"

"Today when I was supposedly golfing."

"You didn't play golf?"

"Nope. I did this, among other things."

"What other things?"

He gestured to the lounge. "Have a seat, make yourself comfortable and I'll tell you."

Burning with curiosity, Ella did as he asked, kicking off her shoes and sitting on the lounge.

Gavin popped the cork on the champagne and poured glasses for both of them before joining her. "Snack?"

"Sure."

He placed the tray on the canvas cushion between them.

Ella ate a strawberry and a piece of pineapple. "This is nice. Thank you."

"You're welcome."

"Are you going to tell me what else you did today when you were supposed to be golfing?"

"I went shopping."

"You . . . you did what?"

"I went shopping," he said again, amusement dancing in his eyes.

"For what?"

He slid a hand under one of the pillows and produced a small velvet box that he handed to her. "For this."

Ella's heart kicked into overdrive as she studied the box he'd put in her hand. "W-what is it?"

"Open it and see."

"Gavin . . . I don't know . . ."

He placed his much larger hand over hers. "Open it, Ella."

Though her hands trembled madly, she managed to flip open the box to discover a stunning diamond ring nestled in black velvet. "Oh . . . Oh my God. Gavin . . ."

He put the fruit tray back on the table and turned to her. "I realized this week that there was only one thing I could do to make you absolutely certain that I'm in this to stay. That I needed to go big or go home, as Caleb used to say." He cupped her cheek, compelling her to look at him. "I love you more than I can ever tell you. I've loved you for as long as I can remember. Every time you came to my rescue, I fell deeper in love with you. And when I thought I'd lost you forever, I experienced the kind of grief I've only known one other time in my life. I don't want to feel like that ever again. I don't want to spend another day without you. I don't want to sleep another night without you tucked in next to me. I don't want to live without the special joy that only you bring to my life. I was a dead man walking until you set your sights on me, Ella, and you single-handedly brought me back to life. I know I'm a bad bet, but I'm determined to be what you need. Will you please marry me and be mine forever, even on the days I don't deserve you?"

Here he was, the Gavin she'd always known lived inside the shell of a man who'd been so lost after his brother's death. And this Gavin, the Gavin she had loved so much for so long, was saying everything she'd ever wanted to hear—and a few things she hadn't dared to hope for.

"Ella, baby, you're making me sweat here."

"I love you so much. You'll never know how deeply my love for you runs through me. When I thought we were over, I couldn't imagine how I'd find the wherewithal to go on without you. And then when you came here and you put your arm around me during the wedding and surrounded me with your familiar scent, I was able to breathe again for the first time since you left."

"I'll never leave you again. I promise, even if you turn me down cold today, you're stuck with me."

"I'm not turning you down cold."

"You're not?"

She shook her head. "I'm saying yes, Gavin. Yes, to everything—the good, the bad and the ugly. I want it all with you. I'm all yours. I always have been."

"Thank God," he whispered before he kissed her. Resting his forehead against hers, he stared into her eyes. "You're really going to marry me?"

"I'm really going to marry you, but only if you let me have a lot of babies."

"Whatever you want. There's nothing you could ask me for that I wouldn't give you if I could." He picked up the box from her lap, withdrew the ring and slid it onto her left hand. "There. Now it's official."

"Not quite yet."

"What did I forget?"

"Take me back to the room and I'll show you." She started to get up from the lounge, but he stopped her.

"Hang on a second." He got up and pulled the curtains closed, sealing them off from the outside world. "I can't wait that long."

"Are you sure no one will see us?"

"I'm pretty sure I can't wait even five more minutes to make love to my gorgeous fiancée."

"Who am I to argue with a man in love?"

He smiled then, and the tense uncertainty she'd seen in him all week disappeared. "This dress is crazy sexy, but it's got to go."

Ella drew the dress up and over her head, enjoying his sharp gasp of surprise when he saw that she'd worn nothing under it.

"Seems like I'm not the only one who made plans for this evening."

"You're overdressed for this party, Mr. Guthrie. Let me help you."

Working together, they got rid of his clothes.

"This is very risky and decadent," she said as he came down on top of her, naked, muscular and gloriously aroused. She was still trying to believe that he'd really proposed, that she had forever to spend with him, that her nights of eating

Cherry Garcia alone were over. The sparkling diamond on her finger was a dazzling reminder that it had really happened.

"Are you happy, Ella?"

"I've never been happier."

"Neither have I, and that never could've happened for me without you."

"Same goes. No one else would've done it for me like you do. It was always you."

"Tell me you love me. I need to hear it again."

"I love you, Gavin. I'll love you forever."

He slid into her in one deep thrust that had both of them gasping from the sheer magic they created together. "I love you, too, Ella. I'll give you everything I've got for the rest of my life. You can count on that."

"That's all I've ever wanted."

EPILOGUE

——◆——

With George and Ringo in tow, Lincoln headed out to the trees to check on the work Gavin's men had completed while he and Molly had been in Burlington welcoming their first grandchild. And what a fine, strapping little fellow Caden Lincoln Abbott was. His son had surprised and delighted him with the baby's middle name. You never knew for sure if you were having an impact on your kids, but at times like that, you felt like maybe you'd done something right.

The older kids were back home now, after a fun trip to the Caribbean to marry off their friend Dylan. He and Molly would've liked to have been there, too, but had declined Dylan's invitation because of the baby's pending arrival. They'd been where they needed to be to help Max through the first few uncertain days that came with new parenthood.

He was doing a fine job so far. If only the same could be said for Chloe, who had no interest—or so it seemed to them—in their son or their grandson. Max had some difficult days ahead of him. His youngest child had grown up awfully fast this last year, and Linc worried about what was ahead for Max and baby Caden.

"Hey, you're back!"

Lincoln spun around to see his father-in-law crossing the lawn to him. "About a half hour ago."

"How're things in Burlington?" Elmer asked.

"Tense."

"Ah, damn. How's our Max holding up?"

"Admirably, all things considered."

"What's up with that girl? She's got the best guy in the world and an adorable son."

"Max thinks she's depressed. He's taking her to the doctor on Monday. In the meantime, he's taking care of the baby pretty much on his own and doing a fine job of it."

"You must've had to drag Molly out of there."

"She didn't want to leave him yet, but I needed to get back to work, and they've got to figure out what's next. They can't do that with us underfoot."

"I guess not." Elmer shaded his eyes for a closer look at the recently thinned thicket. "Gonna be nice to have a forestry specialist in the family. He does good work."

"I was just thinking the same thing. Our friend Gavin has stepped up to the plate and hit one right out of the park."

"I gotta be honest. I didn't see that coming."

"Neither did we, but we're thrilled about it because we know it's what she wants. *He's* what she wants. We could hear the joy in her voice when they called us last night."

"I could hear it, too. It was so good of them to call me. I must confess, however, I'm a little disappointed that our services weren't needed in this instance."

"Right? We're going to have to call this one a draw."

"Agreed," Elmer said with a sigh. "We were no match for Ella after she set her sights on Gavin. Charley, on the other hand, is going to need all the help she can get."

"How so?"

"Did you see her dancing at the Grange with Tyler Westcott?"

"Yeah, so?"

"That boy has his eye on her."

"Really? He's such a nice young man. What does he see in Charley?"

Elmer threw his head back and laughed. "It's not very nice to say that about your own daughter."

"Even if it's true? She'd tell you herself she's a piece of work. We tease her all the time about pitying the fool who takes her on. She eats it up."

"If you ask me, Tyler's the fool who's going to take her on, and knowing what we do about the challenge he faces where she's concerned, I think it's the least we can do to help him along a little."

"What do you have in mind?"

"Let's take a walk, and I'll lay out my plan."

Lincoln whistled to the dogs and followed Elmer into the woods.

ACKNOWLEDGMENTS

Thank you for reading *It's Only Love*! I hope you enjoyed Gavin and Ella's story. To chat about the book with other readers, please join the It's Only Love Reader Group at facebook.com/groups/ItsOnlyLove5/. Spoilers are allowed and encouraged in the group. To keep up with the latest news about the Green Mountain Series (and Fred the Moose), join the Green Mountain Reader Group at facebook.com/groups /GreenMountainSeries/. Make sure you join my newsletter mailing list at marieforce.com for regular updates about books, appearances and other news, and subscribe to my blog at blog. marieforce.com to keep in touch between newsletters.

Special thanks to Team HTJB for all you do to keep things running smoothly while I'm writing: Julie Cupp, CMP; Lisa Cafferty, CPA; Holly Sullivan; Isabel Sullivan; Nikki Colquhoun and Cheryl Serra. To my Berkley editor, Kate Seaver, as well as everyone at Berkley and Penguin Random House, and my agent, Kevan Lyon, thanks for your support of the Green Mountain Series.

As always, thank you to my husband, Dan, and our kids, Emily and Jake, who support my career every day. Love you guys!

My appreciation goes to Jon Wright at Taylor Farm in Londonderry, Vermont, for a great conversation about the logging industry in Vermont. Obviously, the business and the politics of forestry and logging are far more complex than presented here, but hopefully I was able to give you a glimpse of what Gavin's professional life might be like. Holly and I also LOVED the sleigh ride!

Special thanks to my sister-in-law Kris Swank, fragrance counter expert, for consulting on the perfect scent for Gavin, and for making sure my son always smells so good.

And thank you most of all to the readers, who make this the best "job" anyone could ever hope to have. You all are the best, and I appreciate every one of you more than you'll ever know.

xoxo
Marie

If you missed Will and Cameron's wedding story,
turn the page for a preview of the novella

YOU'LL BE MINE

Available now as an e-novella
and in the anthology Ask Me Why

❦

Along with their parents,
Patrick Murphy & Lincoln and Molly Abbott,

Cameron Murphy and Will Abbott

invite you to attend their wedding
on Saturday, October 24, at 2 P.M.
at their home in Butler, Vermont.

Reception to follow immediately.

Two days before her wedding to Will Abbott, Cameron Murphy shut off her laptop at exactly one forty-five in the afternoon and left it in the office she shared with her fiancé. She wouldn't need the computer for two weeks. The next time she returned to the office, he'd be her husband and they'd be back from their honeymoon.

Filled with giddy excitement, Cameron turned off the office light and closed the door behind her. Will was already gone for the day, running last-minute wedding errands while she finished up at work.

Their office manager, Mary, stood up and came around her desk to give Cameron a hug. "Enjoy every minute of this special time," she said, nearly reducing Cameron to tears.

"Thank you so much, Mary. I'll see you tomorrow night, right?" She was one of a few special friends invited to join the family for the rehearsal dinner Will's parents were throwing at the big red barn where Will and his siblings had been raised.

"Wouldn't miss it for the world."

"I'll see you then."

Cameron skipped down the stairs and into the store where she was greeted with more hugs and good wishes from the employees. While no one would mistake her little old nuptials for the royal wedding, it sort of had that feel to it. In Butler, Vermont, the Abbotts were royalty. With a family of ten children and businesses that employed numerous members of the local community, an Abbott wedding was big news.

She accepted a hug, a kiss, best wishes and a cider doughnut from Dottie, who ran the doughnut counter. After talking wedding plans with Dottie and the other ladies for a couple of minutes, Cameron took her doughnut to the store's front porch to enjoy it in relative peace. With only two days to go, she was no longer worried about fitting into her dress, so she took a seat on one of the rockers and ate her treat in guilt-free heaven.

She'd no sooner begun to relax than who should appear on a leisurely stroll down Elm Street but her very own stalker, Fred the Moose. Cameron sank deeper into the rocker, hoping Fred wouldn't notice her. In all her years of living in New York City and after scores of first dates, she'd never had an actual stalker—until she came to Vermont and slammed her MINI Cooper into Fred, the Butler town moose. Since then he'd taken such a keen interest in her that Will's dad, Lincoln, had recently concluded that Fred had a crush on her.

Fantastic. A moose with a crush. With her dad due at two, and Patrick Murphy always on time, the last thing she needed was yet another mooseastrophy. Fortunately, Fred didn't see her sitting on the porch and continued on his merry way, leaving Cameron to breathe easier about Fred but not about her dad's impending arrival.

The thought of her billionaire businessman father in tiny Butler had provoked more nerves than anything else about the upcoming weekend. Marrying Will? No worries at all. Getting through the wedding? Who cared if it all went wrong? At the end of the day, she'd be married to Will. That was all that mattered. But bringing Patrick here to this place she now called home?

Cameron drew in a deep breath and blew it out. She hoped he wouldn't do or say something to make her feel less at home here, because she loved everything about Butler and her life with Will in Vermont. She'd experienced mud season—along with a late-season blast of snow—spring, summer and now the glorious autumn, which was, without a doubt, her favorite season so far.

How could she adequately describe the russet glow of the trees, the vivid blue skies, the bright sunny days and the chilly autumn nights spent snuggled up with Will in front of the woodstove? The apples, pumpkins, chrysanthemums, corn husks tied to porch rails, hay bales and cider. She loved it all, but she especially loved the scent of woodsmoke in the air.

Cameron couldn't have asked for a better time of year to pitch a tent in their enormous yard and throw a great big party. All her favorite autumn touches would be incorporated into the wedding, and she couldn't wait to see it all come together on Saturday. At Will's suggestion, they'd hired a wedding planner to see to the myriad details because they were both so busy at work.

At first, Cameron had balked at the idea of hiring a stranger to plan the most important day of her life, but Regan had won her over at their first meeting and had quickly become essential to her. No way could Cameron have focused on the website she was building for the store and planned a wedding at the same time.

She glanced at her watch. Three minutes until two. Patrick would be here any second, probably in the town car he used to get around the city. Under no circumstances could she picture her dad driving himself six hours north to Vermont. Not when there were deals to be struck and money to be made. Time, he always said, was money.

He'd shocked the hell out of her when he told her he wanted to come up on Thursday so he could spend some time with her and Will before the madness began in earnest. Her dad would be sleeping in their loft tonight, and Will had already put her on notice that he would *not* have sex with her while her dad was in the house. She couldn't wait to break his resolve.

The thought of how she planned to accomplish that had

her in giggles that died on her lips at the familiar *thump, thump, thump* sound that suddenly invaded the peaceful afternoon.

No way. No freaking way. He did not!

If this was what she thought it was, she'd have no choice but to kill him. Warily, she got up from her chair and ventured down the stairs to look up at the sky just as her father's big, black Sikorsky helicopter came swooping in on tiny Butler, bringing cars and people to a halt on Elm Street.

One woman let out an ear-piercing scream and dove for some nearby bushes.

Equal parts amused and aggravated, Cameron took off jogging toward the town common, the one space nearby where the bird could land unencumbered. As she went, she realized she should've expected him to make an entrance. Didn't he always?

Nolan and Skeeter were outside the garage looking up when she went by.

"What the hell was that?" asked Nolan, who would be her brother-in-law after the wedding. He was married to Will's sister Hannah, who'd become Cameron's close friend since she had moved to Butler.

"Just my dad coming to town."

"Jumping Jehoshaphat!" Skeeter said. "Thought it was the end of the world."

"Nope, just Patrick Murphy coming to what he considers the end of the earth. Gotta run. See you later."

"Bye, Cam," Nolan said.

"I assume that's with you," Lucas Abbott said, gesturing toward the town common with his thumb, as Cameron trotted past his woodworking barn.

"You'd be correct."

"That thing is righteous. Does he give rides?"

"I'll be sure to ask him."

"Nice."

Cameron sort of hated that everyone in town would know her pedigree after her father's auspicious arrival. Maybe they already knew. In fact, they probably did. The Butler gossip grapevine was nothing short of astonishing. If the people in town knew who she was, or who her father was, no one made a thing of it. After this, they probably would, which saddened her. She loved her low-key, under-the-radar life in Butler and wouldn't change a thing about it.

But she also loved her dad, and after thirty years as his daughter, she should certainly be accustomed to the grandiose way he did things. She got to the field just as he was emerging from the gigantic black bird with the gold PME lettering on the side: Patrick Murphy Enterprises. Those initials were as familiar to Cameron as her own because they'd always been part of her life.

Hoping to regain her breath and her composure, she came to a stop about twenty yards from the landing site and waited for him to come to her—by himself. That was interesting, as she'd expected his girlfriend-slash-housekeeper Lena to be with him.

With her hands on her hips, Cameron watched him exchange a few words with the pilot before shaking his hand, grabbing a suitcase and garment bag as well as his ever-present messenger bag, which he slung over his shoulder. Wait until he experienced Butler Wi-Fi, or the lack thereof.

He was tall with dark blond hair, piercing blue eyes and a smile on his handsome face, and as he walked to Cameron, her heart softened toward him, as it always did, no matter how outrageous he might be.

She took the garment bag from him and lifted her cheek to receive his kiss. "Always gotta make an entrance, don't you?"

"What's that supposed to mean?"

"The *bird*, Dad. You scared the hell out of everyone. They thought we were being attacked."

He looked completely baffled. "I told you I'd be here at two."

"I was watching for a car, not a chopper."

Recoiling from the very idea, he said, "I didn't have six hours to sit in traffic on the Taconic. As it is, my ass is numb after ninety minutes in the chopper."

"We do have airports in Vermont, you know."

"We checked on that. Closest one that could take the Lear

is in Burlington, which is more than two hours from here. Time—"

"Is money," she said with a sigh. "I know."

"Besides, you're taking the Lear to Fiji, and for the record, I'd like to point out it wasn't my idea to move you out to the bumfuck of nowhere."

Cameron laughed at his colorful wording. "This is *not* the bumfuck of nowhere. This," she said, with a dramatic sweep of her arm, "is the lovely, magnificent town of Butler, Vermont."

"It's as charming as I recall from the last time I was here for Linc's wedding."

"Are you being sarcastic?"

"Me? Sarcastic?"

"I thought Lena was coming with you."

"Yeah, about that . . . We've kind of cooled it."

"Is she still working for you?" Cameron had spoken to her recently and hadn't heard that she was no longer in Patrick's employ.

"Oh, yeah. It's all good."

Cameron was certainly used to the way women came and went in her father's life. She'd learned not to get attached to any of them. They didn't stick around long enough to make it worth her while. "Well, it's great to see you and to have you here. I know it's not what you're used to, but I think you'll enjoy it."

He stopped walking and turned to her. "You're here. That's all I need to enjoy myself, honey."

Cameron let the garment bag flop over her arm so she could hug him. "Thank you so much for coming, Dad."

He wrapped his arms around her. "Happy to be anywhere you are."

They stashed Patrick's bags in Cameron's black SUV. "Where'd you get this beast?"

"Will insisted I trade the MINI for something built for Vermont winters. I don't love it, but as I haven't survived a winter here yet, I'll take his word for it."

"So this is the store, huh?"

"Yep."

"Show me around."

"You really want to see it?"

"I really do."

She took Patrick's hand, eager to introduce him to all her new friends. "Right this way."

He followed her up the stairs to the porch and into the Green Mountain Country Store in all its glory.

"Wow." Patrick took a look around and glanced up at the vintage bicycle fastened to one of the wooden beams above the store. "I feel like I just stepped into an episode of *Little House on the Prairie.*"

"Isn't it amazing? I'll never forget the first time I came in here. It was like I'd been transported or something." She looked up at him as he took in the barrels full of peanuts and iced bottles of Coke and products from a bygone era, a simpler time, hoping he'd see the magic she saw every time she came through the doors to the store. "That's dumb, right?"

"Not at all. It's quite something. I'm wondering, though, how in the name of hell you built a website for a place like this."

Cameron laughed. "Slowly and painstakingly."

"I can't wait to see how you've captured it."

She tugged on his hand. "Come meet Dottie and have a cider doughnut."

"Oh, I don't think—"

"You have to! Your visit won't be complete without one." She led him back to the doughnut counter where Dottie was pulling a fresh batch from the oven. "Perfect timing. Dottie, this is my dad, Patrick, and he's in bad need of a doughnut."

Dottie wiped her hands on a towel before reaching across the counter to shake Patrick's hand. "So nice to meet you, Patrick. We're all very big fans of your daughter."

"As am I."

"Can I get one of those for him?"

"Of course! Another for you, sweetie?"

"Absolutely not! I've got a dress to fit into on Saturday,

so don't tempt me." To Patrick, Cameron added, "Dottie is the devil when it comes to these doughnuts."

"Why, thank you," Dottie said with a proud smile as she handed over a piping-hot doughnut to Patrick.

Both women watched expectantly as he took a bite.

His blue eyes lit up. "Holy Moses, that's good."

"*Right?*" Cameron said, pleased by his obvious pleasure. "I limit myself to two a week, or I wouldn't fit through the doors around here. Come on upstairs and check out the office. See you later, Dottie."

"Bye, Cam. Nice to meet you, Patrick."

"You, too."

He followed her through the store, stopping to look at various items as they went.

"That's Hannah's jewelry," Cameron said of the pieces that had stopped him for a closer look. "She's Will's older sister, twin to Hunter, who's the company CFO."

"She does beautiful work."

"I know! I'm a huge fan. I have a couple of her bracelets. Helps to have friends in high places."

"I'm glad you're making friends here."

They proceeded up the stairs to the offices on the second floor. "So many friends. And now Lucy's here a lot, too, which makes it even better."

"Back so soon?" Mary asked when they arrived in the reception area. "I didn't think I'd see you here again for at least two weeks."

"I wanted you to meet my dad, Patrick."

Mary came around her desk to shake his hand. "So nice to meet Cameron's dad. We adore her here."

"So I'm hearing. Nice to meet you, too."

"This is our office." Cameron opened the door and turned on the lights so her dad could see her workspace.

"*Our* office?"

"Mine and Will's."

"You two *share* an office? They didn't give you one of your own?"

"We tried," Mary said. "Those kids are inseparable."

Cameron blushed and shrugged. "What she said. Besides, if I'm in another office, how am I supposed to play footsie with him during the day?"

"Ugh," Patrick said with a grunt of laughter. "TMI. I'd go crazy sharing office space with anyone, especially such a small one."

"Not everyone can have an acre in the sky to call their own," Cameron said disdainfully.

He tweaked her nose. "It's not a full acre, and I do need my elbow room."

"You're a spoiled, pampered brat, and we all know it."

Mary laughed at their sparring.

"Don't listen to her, Mary," Patrick said with a wink, which had Mary blushing to the roots of her brown hair. "We all know who the spoiled brat is here."

"Yeah, and it's not me."

"I'm afraid I have to side with your daughter, Patrick. There's nothing spoiled about her. She works harder than all of us put together."

"Thank you, Mary. I'll make sure Hunter hears about your fifty percent raise."

They left Mary laughing as they went back downstairs.

"What's her story?" Patrick asked.

"Who, Mary?"

"Yeah. She's adorable."

"Dad . . . Don't. She's a really nice person. Leave her alone. She wouldn't stand a chance against your brand of charm."

"Why can't I have a little fun while I'm in town?"

Cameron stopped on the landing and turned to him. "She's off-limits. I mean that."

"Don't be so touchy, Cam." He kissed her cheek and proceeded ahead of her into the store.

She watched him go with a growing sense of unease. She'd be watching him this weekend and keeping him far, far away from Mary—and all the other single women in Butler.